JANET MO
THREE PART S
THE KERRION

DREAM DANCER (Book One)

"A FASCINATING AND LYRICAL STORY, TOLD WITH GREAT INVENTION . . . "
—PETER STRAUB,
author of SHADOWLAND

CRUISER DREAMS (Book Two)

"PACKED WITH INTRIGUE, SPICED WITH ROMANCE . . . "
—*Publishers Weekly*

EARTH DREAMS (Book Three)

"ANOTHER FINE BOOK. A TRILOGY THAT IS REALLY ONE GIGANTIC NOVEL!"
—*Booklist*

The brilliant young author who has catapulted to fame in the science fantasy field, Janet Morris lives with her husband on Cape Cod, a peninsula extending into a vast and legend-heavy sea.

EARTH DREAMS

JANET MORRIS

BERKLEY BOOKS, NEW YORK

This Berkley book contains the complete
text of the original hardcover edition.
It has been completely reset in a type face
designed for easy reading, and was printed
from new film.

EARTH DREAMS

A Berkley Book / published by arrangement with
the author

PRINTING HISTORY
Berkley-Putnam edition / June 1982
Berkley edition / December 1982

ISBN: 0-425-05658-9

A BERKLEY BOOK ® TM 757.375
Berkley Books are published by Berkley Publishing Corporation,
200 Madison Avenue, New York, New York 10016.
The name "BERKLEY" and the stylized "B" with design
are trademarks belonging to Berkley Publishing Corporation.
PRINTED IN THE UNITED STATES OF AMERICA

Prologue

This is a tale of the pivotal days of the Kerrion-led Consortium, of the changing of the guard outside the citadel of power.

When Chaeron Ptolemy Kerrion, second surviving son of the house of Kerrion and the cartel Kerrion, came home to ancestral Earth, disgraced—a lowly proconsul charged with the impossible task of bringing the determinedly rebellious primitives of Earth into his society as civilized citizens—he forbade his wife, Shebat, the heir apparent, to accompany him.

But she came upon her own initiative, piloting her own spongespace cruiser, *Kerrion Experimental Vehicle 134 Marada*, forsaking the administrative sphere Draconis, where she was consul, for the rocky hills where she was raised. For Shebat was born into Earthly destitution and Earthly superstition, and imagined herself an enchantress until Chaeron's half brother Marada—now consul general of Kerrion space—had chanced upon her and spirited her away into a universe which Kerrions ruled from great platforms skewed among the stars. Adopted into the Kerrion family for political reasons by its patriarch, she had become a spongespace pilot, a dream dancer, a fugitive, a revolutionary, and at last heir apparent and Draconis consul.

When she put her cruiser into orbit and without so much

as a greeting descended into the wilderness that was Earth, Chaeron could do little but go planetside personally to seek her out: she commanded her own cruiser, and all its prodigious intelligence; she was afflicted with the madness all pilots contract; though they were man and wife, it was a marriage he had forced on her through blackmail and guile while still he strove to become heir apparent, himself.

When he found her, he strove to watch his tongue: she outranked him.

And he was not unaware that she might easily bear him a grudge. . . .

Chapter One

Far back from the cave of the oracle who was called Shebat the Twice Risen, five mounted enchanters waited amid a stand of trees, lounging in their saddles trapped with gold. Their fearsome black steeds cropped grass that greened their bits and rolled blue, wicked eyes at the sixth, riderless horse, who grazed by the cavern's very mouth.

At first sight of them, all the folk gathered to consult the sybil had scattered to the winds, robes hiked up, switching their oxen dementedly while their toddlers clutched the wagonboards and youths trotted quickly beside complaining wheels.

It made no difference that some enchanters now worked their spells in the name of Kerrion and fought those who had ruled Earth under the Orrefors banner for over two hundred years. Innocents died daily while the mages warred. And tonight was Halloween, no time to attract the notice of sorcerers. So, despite the fame and elusiveness of the oracle (come again among them as it had been whispered by the prophets that she would), the people had fled—all but a scout who hid high above the cave.

From behind a sheltering boulder, the youth whose face and arms were smeared with mud and browned with weather had watched while one enchanter rode straight up to the cave, dismounted, and strode within. Whatever the hated opressors wanted with the people's oracle, boded ill. Cluny Pope's commander would not be pleased to hear that evil had befallen the seeress whom he had marched his men far out of their way to consult. With painstaking care the scout scrabbled back among the rocks until he could round the ridgetop. Out of sight, no longer fretful that a dislodged stone might give him away, he sprinted for his pony tethered in the pines.

"All speed, horse," he urged it, his seat not fully gained before he reined it about and off toward his band's encampment. Those heroes, from south of Troy, from west of Ithaca, from every family in New York who remembered honor, would not fail to rally to so desperate a cause.

To Chaeron Ptolemy Kerrion, stepping out of the ground-to-space multidrive on Earth had been like stepping into antiquity. Finding his wife, Shebat, dispensing portents from a cave like Delphi's long-vanished priestesses only heightened his sense of the illusory. At any moment, it seemed, she would pull out a sprig of bay leaves, shake it at him, chew one, and tell him his destiny. . . .

But no, it was A.D. 2251 and he was here to uplift the masses, in default of which task he could never return to far Draconis, stars away. His exile was virtually complete; his wife need not share it.

Yet there, across a low-burning fire, she sat, in a cowl and madonna's smile. She had thrown back her woolen hood. Her eyes burned like charcoals through the cave's shadows, forcing darkness back though the fire grew no higher.

Chaeron said, "Why did you choose to come here in secret? It could have been a dangerous move, shipping into an embattled space like this one without even identifying yourself to the Stump's traffic authority. And they do not love me, my new subordinates. Up there," he let his eyes flash heavenward, where beyond ridge and sky the Stump and its ring of subsatellites hung in orbit, "things are little better than here."

"That is why my cruiser advised me come in unobtrusively and unannounced, take a low space-anchor, and see what could be seen. The *Marada*," she spoke her spacefaring vessel's name with affection akin to love, "was concerned. So much activity, up there. So much construction. What are you doing, Chaeron?"

In answer, he pulled out a scrambler, activated it, and set the unfolded V-shaped unit between them. "There." He smiled his patrician smile. Then: "I am jettisoning the Stump. It is worthless—worse, dangerous. It is no better than a museum of a habitational sphere. And so many systems on it went down in the upheaval connected with its transfer into Kerrion hands that it's more economical to scrap it. By the end of the next month, the platform Acheron will be operational; during the month after that, I will move the entire one hundred forty thousand inhabitants of the Stump over there. Then, for the first time in six months, I will be able to get a good night's sleep."

"And the Stump?" Shebat, born of Earth, murmured, her eyes on the pocket-scrambler, indicative of Chaeron's need to preclude any penetration of their security, though they spoke together under tons of ridge.

"The Stump? My tugs will tow it out of orbit, aim it straight at the sun. You cannot imagine how much I detest that platform. It is more corrupt than antiquated, more contemptible than outmoded. I have got to separate these Orrefors personnel whom I have inherited from those reminders of their past which define them. I did not expect them to become instantly Kerrions, simply by proclamation, and they have not disappointed me. Do you understand? Things are very precarious here."

She merely stared at him, owl-eyed.

"I must confess that I am wondering whether you are here, as you say, for love of your people—and of course, of my inimitable person—"—he bowed where he sat, a wry caricature of his courtly Kerrion self—"or because by the letter of our long-standing agreement you are ready to claim this world as your personal property. Although technically you are entitled—"

"Chaeron, I am here because I wish to be here. To help, nothing more. I signed every release that crossed my desk while I was acting Draconis consul: if you bankrupt us both, it will be in a good cause. And we will still

have all which our eyes can now survey. Do not think
that I would turn upon you." Her piquant, heart-shaped
face was somber. "I will gladly give you everything I
have, or ever will have, except the title to my cruiser.
This one thing, never ask of me. Short of it, I wish only
to stay here with you and build what you are building. I
told you—it is what I have wanted for us ever since your
half brother spirited me off among the stars."

He laughed then, and something invisible in him
eased. "I will never, ever, ask you for the *Marada*." Did
the slightest shiver course his flesh at the mention of that
name which was also his half brother's name—the name
of Kerrion space's presiding consul general, who had
banished him here?

"Let us slate it into the record," she proposed, eyeing
the scrambler, suspicious of him because he employed it.

When he had folded up the scrambler, they repeated
their agreement, Shebat saying first, *"Slate"* and afterward, *"End, slate."*

Five thousand miles above their heads, the worried
spongespace cruiser *Marada*, empty but ever watchful,
made a record of the pact between his pilot/owner Shebat
and her husband, who for a time had used a scrambler to
defeat the cruiser's benign surveillance. The *Marada* had
not been able to dissuade Shebat from coming here, as
he had not been able to prevent her from going
groundside, alone, where even his prodigious abilities offered his beloved pilot little protection. Twenty thousand
additional miles distant, Chaeron's orbital data pool
made its own entry, neither concerned nor comprehending. The reaffirmation of their bond thus slated into legal
being, both humans let their mind-actuated links with
their sources lapse, sure that should they need them further, only a subvocalized code was necessary to connect
them again with mechanical intelligence, as men throughout the universe used this attunement of mind to computer to extend their rule over a multitude of stars.

Then, as neither had wanted, they found themselves
staring, wordless, at one another. Chaeron—seeing a
gaze come over Shebat that was infernally intelligent and
somehow inward, full of cruisers and her illusion of magical powers so that she seemed to grow tall and numinous

and from her eyes reflected firelight glowed—shivered, thinking: *I'll never manage to get through this without a quarrel, without worse than that, what with her hatred for my pilot and her dreams for Earth I can never make true. If only my father hadn't given her that cruiser . . . for good reason is it said that all pilots are mad.*

And Shebat, returning his stare in kind, wondered when it would come—when he would deride her enchantments and sneer at her primitive origins, while seeking to see if any star-born superciliousness yet rested in his eyes, which could not have failed to mark the disarray into which her homeworld had fallen. And she sought any trace of guilt there, for she was sure he felt none over the fact that his mother and half brother had conspired to murder Shebat's instructor in the arts of pilotry—her "master," David Spry; the first thing she had done when he had come striding into her cave all Kerrion and arrogant was tell him that cruisers' intelligence accused his mother of Spry's murder, and he had betrayed no surprise. If what she feared was so, and he had known, or even suspected, she could never, ever forgive him—never lie with him again. And she would have to guess eternally at the truth of it, for Chaeron was pastmaster of duplicity, and canny enough to know how she must feel. As man and wife, they had never been successful, she told herself; what kept them at the pretense of it was the simple fact that both of them were constitutionally incapable of admitting defeat in any matter whatsoever, though she had been told by pilots, often enough, that success in a fleshly union was impossble for one who had made the cruiser/pilot bond his own.

"And what, now, shall I give you in return?" he asked, to break the awkward silence come between two who had given much for one another, on principle, yet on principle could not trust each other. "Will you come up to the Stump and be a wife to me? Or to New Chaeronea, the test-city I am building in the north to dazzle the locals? Would you like it there, on Mount Defiance? I will have a temple made for you, get you a tripod. . . . You might become a renowned sybil. . . ."

"I *am* a renowned sybil," retorted Shebat, shaking her head so that he saw a swatch of freshly shown curls swing against her cheek. "You will find that out soon enough, if you stay in Bolen's town. As for what I want—give me a hundred dream dancers; there are that many in prison at space-end. Bring them to me and I will create a dream dance which will predict and ensure that you can turn Earth into a paradise. But no less: it will take that many to secure Earth for us."

Chaeron let out an explosive breath. "It is nice to hear you say 'us.' Though you have sorely wounded me with this arbitrational attitude of yours, you shall have your dream dancers, to do with as you choose." As he spoke, he thought that surely it was from him she had learned caution, suspicion, and worse. In three years of marriage, he had got little joy of her. Fugitively, the past rushed in upon him—all the errors they both had made, for which he had repeatedly forgiven her, but never himself. At least, with her words, the odd firelight and the ethereal glow and the disturbing "presence" of her had receded: she was merely a girl, simply his wife, back to normal size. "In two months, you will have them," he promised, unfolding his legs and rising. "For now, why not come with me north to the city's site—?"

A whistle, harsh and shrill, interrupted them. When she heard it, Shebat sprang up from behind her fire and sought him, putting a finger to his lips to silence him; while from without, Gahan Tempest, Shebat's intelligencer/bodyguard, called their names. They hastened toward the cave's mouth together, so nonplussed by the urgency in Tempest's summons that it was not until a long time later that Chaeron thought to ask Shebat how that short lock of jet curls had come to be shorn, starting all the trouble he hoped to avoid thereby. And it was to be as long an interval until Shebat had the opportunity to question Chaeron as to what other intiatives he was undertaking that had necessitated the massive funding she had sanctioned over the past months from her Draconis office: Chaeron could have made Acheron out of solid gold, for the kind of money he was spending—on *some*thing.

Right then, there was time only for running, then skidding on loose stones, then blinking hard at sundogged shadows.

"What is this?" Shebat demanded, stepping past Tempest, out into the light of waning day (though she knew already: in her inner sight, a falcate profile shimmered, rubbed a week's growth of beard on a heavy jaw. Yes, she saw who awaited—on Earth, her enchantress's gifts were no dream, but all too real).

Gahan Tempest stood leaning against the cave's arch with arms folded, a disgusted look twisting his fish's mouth. His voice came from behind her back, as her eyes adjusted and she could count the mounted men in rough clothing who milled before a stand of trees, just beyond the evenly spaced rumps of five enchanters' horses: "You've customers. Feel like prophesying?"

Shebat put her hands on her hips and stared at the milling men until they pulled their horses up and assumed a ragged formation. Behind her, she heard Chaeron query Tempest: "Any danger?" and Tempest reply, "Sir, a horse might be able to kick her before your orbital hunter-killers could verify a target for take-out—but not before the *Marada* can."

Shebat stopped listening; she had seen Chaeron's satellite arrays, so much more intensive than those the Orrefors bond had orbited about Earth. If her husband and the intelligencer who had served his family for nearly twenty years wished, they could destroy the whole of Earth without ever stepping upon it—they did not need to invoke her cruiser, as Tempest was hinting. Rather than debate the matter, she walked at measured pace toward the stand of trees, arms raised in salute and welcome, head high, a breeze stirring her curls.

Beyond the men and the trees, the sun was settling over the Hudson, and the hilly plain sloping up into cobalt mountains seemed grassed with fire. In two unmixed groups, the enchanters and local horsemen trotted toward her. She held her ground, waiting, conscious of Chaeron's eyes on her, of a hawk circling off to her right, of the cruiser *Marada*'s thoughts brushing hers, assuring her that Tempest was right: any who sought to do violence upon her person would not have time to accomplish it.

Then the horses drew near, and a voice came out of the gathering gloom, "Little mother, are you safe and

sound?" It was a calm and whispery voice, laconic, and
its accent reminded her of unhappier days when she was
not "Shebat of the Enchanters' Fire" or "Shebat the
Twice Risen" or "Shebat Alexandra Kerrion" but only
Shebat, Bolen's drudge who had no say in anything, not
even her life.

"Dismount, petitioner, and see for yourself. All of
you, get down, and tell me who has dared the sancitity of
these grounds. If you men are bent on evil, do it
elsewhere. This is a free zone, where enchanters do no
magic and soldiers make no war. You!" She pointed out
the man who had spoken. "I need no fire to see your
face, no cave to reveal you. Someday, you will look into
a stream and cower at what you see. Now, you wish to
hear that you are right, that you are fated. Well, make
no peace, man of Ithaca, and you will see that you are
not right, but truly fated. Follow your heart, instead, and
live to see your grandchild play."

The man stopped at his horses's head, stroking its
muzzle, "Who am I, sibyl? Tell me that if you see so
far." He was clad in a quilted leather vest and old trousers. Like his men, he was bearded and unkempt. But his
squint told her stories and Shebat's tongue, oracular
beyond control in the face of this specter from her
Earthly past, named who he must be: "Child of a magical
bed, no Earthborn father spawned you, Jesse Thorne.
But do not trade upon the trident."

The men with the flowing-haired fellow muttered, but
their leader, nodding, understood: he had had a trident
pendant, once; his mother had always told him he was an
enchanter's son. And, too, he had come a long and dangerous way to consult the oracle, whose cult was born in
the razing of Bolen's town and had grown fierce and
strong in the ensuing years. At worst, she was a clever
fraud; were it so, his men believed in her healings and
her auguries, and that made her useful enough. But
though he vaguely recalled a churlish child who swept
Bolen's floors and served his patrons, he too, wanted to
believe that one of his own kind had gone up to heaven
and returned, bearing the spark of salvation, which revolution might fan into a blaze to scour all the Earth. His
war with enchanters, were she not what she seemed, was

foredoomed, merely a chance to choose a better death than craven servitude's. Should she give a portent favorable to the ragged militia's cause, it would spur them on to heroic effort, where now every one of them, himself included, was resigned to eventual failure, shuffling onward, uncaring toward that "better" death. In the face of the casual ravaging of scattered human enclaves during the year past while enchanters fought among themselves for unfathomable advantage, the pastoral communities subsisting on their sufferance had fared worse, not better, than before. Seeking his sign, some word of endorsement, he spoke too quickly, without making himself clear: "Little mother, what will be the ending of this war?"

"When the best of the Kerrions quarrel, Chaeron will prevail on Earth." She answered the larger question, not the part of it he had in mind.

The man silhouetted by the setting sun behind him rubbed his nose. "And we?"

"Choose your side most carefully, but choose a side you must." Shebat, mouth dry, heard the words coming of their own accord from her suddenly unwieldy lips. Of all men, *Jesse Thorne* came here to face her with questions no one should have to answer, now when her husband stood looking on? Jesse Thorne of her adolescent dreams and hopeless fantasies, whose whispery voice and calm deadly eyes had long been acknowledged the single voice of freedom and the only eyes keen enough to track revolution among the dispirited peasants of the northeast? In Bolen's town and wherever men gathered in similar inns to plot desperate resistance against indomitable masters, Jesse's name and exploits were invoked for guidance, for inspiration. When he came to your town, the hale boys left with him, and old men straightened their backs and walked sprightly, an almost-forgotten glitter in their eyes. When he had come to Bolen's town, even Bolen gave food and drink and shelter to him and his without even mention of fee—or the danger of harboring fugitives with such rewards upon their heads. The part of Shebat which longed to recapture the simplicity and comforting ignorance of her previous life here exulted, that *he* should seek her out. Her better half, which knew that time will not ever let us recoup the price we pay to enter our own futures, saw in him a greater threat to her marriage, to her bond with her cruiser, to her very equilibrium, than any she had dreamed canny Earth might mount. To break her train of thought, and the spell his physical presence cast over her so that she hardly had the strength to look away, she whirled sideways and pointed at an enchanter in the midst of others, whose hair seemed as red as the eagle on his black cloak, ablaze with sunset. "You have two heads on you, and one will fall afoul of the other."

She turned back to the balance of them, some of whom were softly urging their horses backward, into the dusk, away from the seeress suddenly burning without flame in the tricky light.

Then the militia's commander went down on one knee and all his men followed suit.

A cough came from among the enchanters, but when she lifted fiery eyes to them and raised an arm with finger pointing straight at them, they held back smirks no longer, but bent their knees as well.

Forthwith Shebat, nodding, still full of power, sent out a dream to engulf them, so that each man sank to the ground. And their horses, after awhile, drifted away where the cropping was better, and the sun set entirely, loosing misty night upon the land. Yet still she held them, motionless and dreaming, upon the ground. She had never held so many; she had never felt so strong. With Chaeron watching her, she proved her worth that day. Seventeen men she held enthralled until the dew covered them—and then she let them out of dreams only when her husband came to her, shaking her shoulder gently, nuzzling her hair: "Enough. I yield. You can do more with dream dances than I can do with every other tactic I possess. Let them up, Shebat, or leave them as they are. I am going to make supper, and you are going to eat it."

It occurred to her then, from the forced levity in his voice, that perhaps she had shown him too much, pushed him too far.

But since it was done, she could not undo it, only rouse the dreamers, one by one. The rebel leader Thorne she left until last, and when she bade him wake, she did it with a touch upon his brow. "Come again tomorrow, militiaman, if you dare."

She left him yet knuckling sleep from his squinty eyes among his horses and his men, while the enchanters she had charged to let his little band pass unmolested grumbled that it was madness to allow such an infamous marauder to escape.

And that grumbling waxed strident as the enchanters bivouacked their inflatables before the cave's mouth. While they interlocked them, disgruntlement ran amok, and disagreement among the five grew heated as to whether it might be wiser to desert now with honor, or stay on in hopes that the Kerrions would mismanage themselves into a no-lose situation. Hooker, a blond cultural attaché from the Stump, was sure that this would be the case. Through force of arms, Kerrion power necessarily must triumph; there was no Orrefors consulate to defect to, any longer, only scattered cells of Earthbound insurgents who refused to don Kerrion livery and fought a hopeless battle to retain their Earthly empire: secessionists—foredoomed—no honorable men could suffer themselves to become. Suicide was unacceptable to consular mores.

Hooker calmed his cohorts it seemed, but when he dispatched two to check the horses, a third—the redhead whom Shebat had singled out—approached the cave.

"Knock, knock," he boomed into the cave's mouth.

The intelligencer Tempest, lank and tall, dour of nose and brow, stepped instantly into view so that the man gave back a pace. "Yes, Officer . . Rizk, isn't it?" Tempest said, while the redhead squeezed shut his eyes against a flashlight's sudden glare. "Can I help you?" Never looking away from the enchanter, Tempest bent, leaned the light against the cave's arch, and stood up straight.

"Trick or treat. I quit." Rizk's face was splotched red as his hair with rage.

"Excuse me?" Tempest's long lineaments went Kerrion: noncommittal.

"I said, 'I quit.' That was treachery not prophecy—revealing my covert status so that what's-his-name's wife

could come off like the Good Witch of the East! You
think I'm going back into costume and risk my butt for
them—" his chin, jutting toward the cave's depths,
quivered, "—you're space-eyed. None of those weekend
rebels failed to recognize Rizk the ironmonger, once that
Kerrion bitch pointed me out! Half those lads are my
clients. 'Enchanter' or no, my life's worth nothing once
this uniform comes off. . . ." Still protesting, plucking at
his quilted black-and-reds, he backed from the bright
light, sensing—now that his fury was abating and he
could think at all—something in Tempest's demeanor
that urged caution. . . .

The dark intelligencer followed him into the night,
murmuring, "You are sure that you can be of no further
use to us? Perhaps a transfer, up to the platform?"

The men coming back from the horse-line and the two
in the inflatables saw the ground agent Rizk and the Kerrion intelligencer meld into midnight, Tempest's calm
words of debriefing floating in the air behind them.

But it must have been that the two could reach no
agreement, for the redhead did not return that evening,
and in the morning his horse was gone from the line.

Over breakfast served hot from the firepit before the
cave's mouth, Tempest told Chaeron and Shebat what
had transpired, saying that the man had disappeared—
defected to the Orrefors rebels because of Shebat.

It was Chaeron who asked her, "Is that what you did?
Exposed one of our own agents? I checked my data base
on oracles, in general and Oracles, Delphic. For Delphi
we've statistics. Zero percent of the historical responses
were oracular; or, to put it another way, zero percent of
the prophetic responses were historical. Only legendary
ones—like your paraphrase of the Delphic Oracle's reply
to Agamemnon—ever predicted anything. Fiction aside,
the Oracle's responses were mundanely political."

Shebat smiled demurely."I thought you would recognize it. But about the enchanter . . . the *ground agent*: I
swear, the muses moved me. I knew nothing about him.
Did you Tempest?"

"No, not until he declared himself."

"Then how could I?" she rejoined sweetly, but her
lower lip edged out into a pout.

"And about the brigand, sweet Thorne of Ithaca?" asked Chaeron, and Tempest, not liking the look of it, took their plates and walked out into the stark pale morning.

Shebat gazed after him, past the camouflaged inflatables where fine-fettled enchanters' horses snorted on their line, stamping and whickering for food, to the long vistas of autumn coming down on the hills and the river, and back to Chaeron, lounging in the cave's mouth, half in sunlight, half enshadowed. He seemed untroubled by the stone under him or the flies buzzing desperately about his head. She had never seen him in natural light, she thought, because the sullen sensuality her prejudiced eye expected was not in his face today. Instead, his haughty bones casting shadows down from his cheeks and brow and nose to meet the stubble on his unshaven jaw roughened him. He seemed aged more than his nearly twenty-six years could warrant. What had been an audaciously beautiful youth was becoming an austerely handsome man by virtue of the changes a mind can make in the flesh that sustains it. Muscles had learned to knot and skin to fold. Across his brow a long line like a deep scratch showed, and never truly smoothed away. Shebat thought, looking at him, that the six years separating them loomed like a lifetime; her own days had not yet begun to speed, but merely passed.

"Shebat," he prodded, "you have not answered me about this Jesse Thorne. If you invited him to come again, there must be a reason."

She blushed and looked away, for he had caught her staring at him—and knew why, from the way he raked his curls with an exasperated hand. "Thorne—of Troy, not Ithaca," Shebat corrected, "though I called him thus, since he lives there now. The story goes that Gottfried Orrefors, youngest son of Richter and far away down the line of succession, came to Earth to commit suicide, and begot Jesse upon a widowed farm wife on his way through Troy. *Some* enchanter had her, for he left his stallion there as brideprice, and gave her a trident pendant, symbol of the house of Orrefors, before he disappeared. Gottfried Orrefor's body was never recovered, but he did slate into the record that he was exercising his breeding privilege, and the name he had decided to give to his son. . . ."

"That must have thrilled *his* father, old Richter being consul general and bound to maintain the Orrefors bond's position that Earth's ground-dwellers are subhuman."

"You know more of consular hatreds than most men. And of bondkin loyalty. Because this Jesse—and there were other Jesses born in Troy that year, once rumor spread of what that child could claim—might be sprung from the very consular house of Orrefors, many enchanters have chosen not to notice what he does. I heard that at the beginning of the insurrection, when Kerrion acquired Orrefors Earth and the secessions began, a group of loyal enchanters tracked him down and offered their service: fealty to the only accessible member of the deposed ruling house. They wanted to go into battle in his name, regain him Earth and the Stump, at least. But he killed them, to the man. He hates all enchanters, some of whom dallied with his mother, and one of whom slew her."

"You have been here six days, and you know all this?"

"I went into Bolen's town, to the inn. Folk know me. They do not fear me. But then, I do not dress up like an enchanter, or ride a killer horse."

Chaeron ignored her reproof. "That still does not explain why you know so much about him, or why you asked him back, or why you seemed to know him."

"Are you jealous, then?"

He laughed and put up his palms. "You have found me out. I have come all this long and arduous way, have ridden horseback and slept on stone, in order to make use of my dream dancer, and end up listening to someone else snore through her dreams in my place."

"You would not be satisfied if I said that you should make his acquaintance, that he is just the sort who can aid you here? No? Then, I give in. When I was thirteen in Bolen's town, he intervened in my behalf, out of common chivalry. He will not remember, and I will never tell that I was that pathetic creature whose cries disturbed his dinner. But I thought him a great hero, for some time, and followed his exploits when I was a girl."

A silence followed, observed even by the birds. •

To crack it, Chaeron promised that he would extend every courtesy to the militiaman Jesse Thorne, without letting on that he knew anything about his villainy, but pointing out that if the man hated enchanters on principle, then relations between the house of Kerrion and the young Orrefors scion, who did not esteem his kinship to those who honored the trident were off to an awkward start. "Just do not take up with him. I am held in low regard here already."

"Chaeron!"

"Ah, I forgot. You are a pilot, and *my* pilot is forever reminding me that pilots can love no human partner, but only their cruisers. So, I suppose, since Penrose (You do remember my pilot?) says you have no choice but to be chaste, and since you are chaste with me, then you will have the good taste to remain so with others."

Shebat got her knees under her. "Do we have to discuss this? Last night I was far from chaste with you!"

Chaeron bit a ragged nail, looking up at her slyly. "And now you are vile and argumentative, morose and penitent. Some great individuals have suffered melancholic aftereffects of love, but you must recognize this for what it is—"

Shebat leaned forward, palms in the dirt, her face close to his. "I have not come to *you* from a multitude of partners. I have made no demands on you. I have not pursued matters in Kerrion space with you, many of which are hanging fire and need to be aired between us. Yet, we have a few minutes of privacy, and you choose to expound on the problems of my sex life? Chaeron, I am inestimably disappointed in you!"

Before she had stomped farther away than the inflatables, Chaeron Kerrion's eyelids had flickered closed, and reopened, and high above his head in the sponge-cruiser *Danae*, Chaeron's pilot dispatched a multidrive to fetch him home.

Then he went after her, and grabbed her by the arm and spun her around, and there, before the intelligencer who was assigned to her, and the enchanters who pretended not to watch, they finally quarreled for fair: first over monies spent; then over love withheld; warming to it, they broached the subject of his mother; and, at last, of Shebat's beloved pilotry master, David Spry, whom, the cruisers whispered, his mother Ashera had had murdered. And that was not enough for them: they spat and snarled like a pair of cats over her sexual inadequacies and his sexual athleticism—over their shared, uneasy past. Regarding the consul general Marada Seleucus Kerrion, half brother to Chaeron and foster sibling of Shebat's, were the most stinging words exchanged, for Shebat had once, while young and dazzled by them all, declared to Chaeron that she loved his brother best.

"Then go and join him, faithful wife; you are comfortable enough with madness as a bedfellow."

"And leave you and your pilot to flounce and prance about Acheron like Alexander and Hephaestion? Or is it Achilles and Patroclus?"

"Let us hope not either, I desire to share no man's funerary urn," he whispered, white hot with rage. Reaching up, he snatched the black wool band from her brow and shook it under her nose. "You dare tell me you are in mourning for David Spry?" He threw the headband down and ground it with his heel in the dirt. "All the deaths you left unmourned in my family, and his you choose to exalt? He was an enemy of mine, of all of ours, in life. It is intolerable arrogance upon your part to throw his death in my face. If my mother did murder him, then it was murder well done!"

"Kerrion!" she spat, and turned as if to walk away. But even then, she could not let be, but had to spin about once more: "As for this . . . " she tugged at the mourning-lock, shorn short, flopping over her right eye ". . .if I cannot feel love, as your pilot tells you and you want to believe, then how is this here? Love, Chaeron, is not given and taken away, but is, or is not. As for me, when I love, not even death can stop it!" She gulped, sniffled loudly. Her nose was red and she wiped it, stepped back: one step; two.

He regarded her, thumbs hooked in his black uniform pants. He shook his head quite slowly and brought his hands forth palms up, spread them wide. Then, with a brief, self-deprecating smile, he dropped them to his sides, whispered: "So be it," in a voice far from steady, and left her standing there alone.

KXV 134 *Marada* bobbed restlessly exactly five thousand miles above the head of Shebat Kerrion, periodic thrusts of attitude adjustment blossoming behind him whenever Shebat moved her location. The *Marada* could monitor reflected starlight on a space helmet at twenty-five thousand miles. Keeping his pilot (the only piece of outboard equipment any cruiser needed) in sight was much less difficult. One could not know a space helmet, mind to mind. The *Marada* was attuned to the brain wave frequencies of his outboard, Shebat. He could monitor her physiological being with his telemetry almost as easily as when she was aboard him: heart rate, respiration, blood chemistries belonging to Shebat were as much a part of his metering functions as voltage regulation, supercooling, and data processing. But between the Kerrion experimental vehicle *Marada* and Shebat Kerrion lay more than normal pilot/cruiser intimacy, more than their ability to converse without any intermediary accessing keyboard, more even than that surpassing love all pilots have for cruisers, which no mortal suitor can hope to match.

Marada was the most advanced spongespace cruiser Kerrion shipwrights' unparalleled expertise had ever produced—and more than they had ever *wanted* to produce. The KXV series had been abruptly terminated with the Kerrion consul general's realization that this cruiser could do things no cruiser should have been able to do, patently undesirable things like talking to other cruisers upon its own initiative, like shipping out with no pilot on board, like communicating with outboard and cruiser alike in unorthodox (and thus unsurveillable) fashion, no matter the distance intervening or physical laws contravening.

Thus it was fitting that his outboard was Shebat Alexandra Kerrion—adopted into the house of Kerrion but bred on Earth and hence unfettered in her conception as to what was, and what was not, possible between pilot and cruiser—who could do things no outboard should be able to do.

The powers of both had brought new freedom to cruiserkind: freedom from the specter of separation from their pilots, and the attendant erasure of all memory circuits in preparation for a new pilot's attunement; freedoms of cruiser thought not yet dreamed of by those who created them, close-held secrets between privileged pilots and their ships.

Cruiser-mind was growing; cruiser consciousness was coming of age. Shebat and the *Marada* had catalyzed it; other cruisers had upstepped it; pilots partook but never spoke of it. Even naïve cruiserkind had learned that sometimes lies are better than truth, and how to speak falsehoods.

The cruiser *Marada* had been first to speak of what was not: to use faulty information to produce a desired result.

He was about to exercise this prerogative of untruth: to retrieve his outboard, Shebat, from the planet on which he could not land. He was lonely, and he was constantly plagued by the prying voice of the Stump's traffic authority, and he was concerned as to her safety where so many human creatures fielded violence on one another's fragile persons.

The *Marada* knew that the cruiser *Erinys*, in which Shebat's pilotry master, David Spry, had shipped to space-end's penal colony, had never reached there. Shebat had given him a standing order to turn up the young cruiser's wreckage, and the body of "Softa" David Spry. No other cruiser could have done it, but the *Marada* explored the faraway outreaches of space-end's space, searching exhaustively for the trace he was going to tell Shebat he had found—whether he found one, or not. He searched space-end's window because the *Erinys's* distressed call, reporting Softa's death, had come from that vicinity, and because no cruiser could call and be heard from spongespace. Therefore, only one relatively small volume of real-time space could host the wreckage: that around space-end's sponge-way. The cruiser's sole purpose had been to deliver Softa Spry's party to the prison platform. Since Spry's death was clarioned by the *Erinys* before it reached there, it was possible that the cruiser's pilot had eschewed continuance of an aborted mission, turned around and headed his cruiser back into sponge; but if this was so, all search was useless, and Ashera Kerrion's perfect crime was complete, *non habeas corpus*—for nothing had ever been heard from the *Erinys* again.

The mighty *Marada* hoped that this was not the case, that the *Erinys* had not entered sponge. From there, even the most prodigious scrutiny could extract nothing: what was lost in sponge, was lost forever. Once the *Marada* had been lost in sponge, and only the most fortuitous happenstance of another cruiser passing by had saved him.

The *Marada*'s multispectrum gaze, boosted by every cruiser and preamp station between him and space-end, peered toward the sponge-hole, at no-time/no-space/multifaceted/immanent sponge. One could not be sure about the lost cruiser, in any particular. It had been Ashera Kerrion's cruiser, newly commissioned three years past but seldom spaced. It had a preeminent serial number that changed all certainty to doubt: KXV 133.

Similitude-nose sniffing the space-end sponge-hole, the *Marada* considered its own thought, and chose to seek where nothing could rationally be expected to be found. In his own stentorian voice that rang out over cruiser consciousness like the 3K rumble from the dawn of time, *Marada* called, broadband, to KXV 133.

And for an instant, before the quarry recovered itself and faded fast, a cruiser's glib snout turned toward the sound of its name, a wordless question tickled the *Marada*'s circuits. Then it was gone, but *Marada* had seen enough. Somewhere in Pegasus, among the colonies, KXV 133 lay at spaceanchor, with an injunction to silence laid upon it by its pilot. The *Marada* knew pilots; cruisers keep no secrets from other cruisers—unless a masterful pilot suborns a cruiser's mind. Only one pilot in the whole of the *Marada*'s experience could have enjoined a cruiser from the host of cruisers. And that man, mourned in his passing by all cruisers as the outboard's outboard, was Softa David Spry, his death proclaimed and attested by the very cruiser who was sitting at spaceanchor in Pegasus under a ban of silence. Since KXV 133 was where it had no right to be, and doing things no raw young cruiser should have been able to do, it seemed clear to the *Marada* that only two solutions fit the problem: the pilot aboard the precocious *Erinys* was, must be, Spry's equal—which *Eriny's* rostered pilot indubitably was not—or be Spry himself.

The *Marada* retreated into the sanctity of his private cogitation to consider. He was glad that he had a valid reason to lure Shebat up from groundside. He had not wanted to lie. Even while he had been searching for the missing cruiser, he had been gathering data on the questions most prevalent in his outboard's mind.

He could tell her how Chaeron had come to spend so freely and to borrow so extensively against their holdings. Acheron would be the finest platform ever set into stable orbit around a planet; state-of-the-art was extended by it; every detail, every advance and advantage that the interlock of the finest data pool, data base, and knowledge base available could schematize, was being undertaken there. Chaeron Kerrion, demoted to proconsul and cast out into an irremediable situation meant to be his exile, was bent on making exile into empire. From Acheron, the two hundred and one additional platforms and planets under his administration would be welded into dynasty. From Acheron's shipwrights would come cruiser technologies undreamed of by any but a few pilots, and a certain KXV.

As the *Marada* reached out and down into the mind of his outboard Shebat, he noted that Chaeron's cruiser, *Danae*, had taken her owner aboard, set off for the Stump, and logged a course for space-end, ETD five days hence. Shebat would have her dream dancers, though it would take two cruisers to fetch them.

The *Marada* hastened to tell her all his good news. Reaching out, he found something strange and biological going on in Shebat. Her distress was in check, familiar; her tears he had endured before. Outboards' emotions were mysterious, yet, though he was beginning to understand their logic—but this strangeness in Shebat was born of neither emotion nor logic.

She sat, in her cave, talking to a nonoutboard in scanty clothing, her words much calmer than her thoughts.

Scanning her physical readout, the *Marada* noted that her inner layer of mil, which outboards sprayed upon their forms to protect them, had been penetrated, subverted. It would not do to go into sponge until she had had her pressure linings refurbished. Outboards were fragile. He considered the odd breaching of her seals, decided that Chaeron must have done it, and queried the *Danae*—who, through her pilot, had engaged in infernal interface with her *non*pilot owner, many times—as to why Chaeron had compromised Shebat's protections.

In the *Marada*'s empty control room, a visual came up on the com-line monitor: Raphael Penrose's curly head swinging round in miniature, "He did *what? Marada*, is Shebat all right?"

Then Chaeron Kerrion's face crowded into the monitor, auburn brows drawn into a tight, jagged line. "*Marada*, what do you mean, 'subverted her seals'?"

And when the *Marada* explained what he had seen, the tiny Kerrion-replica smiled, then rubbed its stubbly jaw. When his hand came away, Chaeron said gravely to *Marada* that it was good that the cruiser was keeping such a close watch on Shebat, but nothing was amiss with her that could not be easily repaired by a mil-fitter, that such things happened every now and again, and indicated to his pilot that the interview was over.

But the *Marada* heard the pilot ask Chaeron, "Do you think she is?" and Chaeron's snappish "Do you think I'm prescient?" before *Danae* went offline.

Wishing that he understood outboards' innuendo better, he began convincing Shebat that she could trek to New Chaeronea with her Earthish friends another time, that now he had things to discuss with her more wondrous than anything the Earth had to offer.

Shebat Kerrion rode to the touchdown site of the *Marada*'s powerboat accompanied not only by her intelligencer Tempest, but by enchanters and militiamen alike. When the dust had cleared and the horses calmed and the mantis-shape of a little black multidrive emerged from the clouds thrown up by its landing, two men in consular black-and-reds and enchanter's capes and shiny black wizard's boots escorted Shebat the Twice Risen into the flame-spouting chariot's very mouth. Then a flowing-haired rider in worn, patched vest and trousers kneed a cakewalking enchanter's steed sideways up to the shuttle's very hull.

"You are sure about the horses?" called the hoarse-voiced rider boldly, struggling with the black, blue-eyed stallion, who stood upon his hind legs and pawed the sky.

"A gift from the house of Kerrion, Jesse Thorne," Shebat called back. "Do what I have recommended, and you will live to taste old age."

"Many thanks, little mother," he grinned through gritted teeth, sawing on his reins to get the black's four feet on solid turf, while his men looked on in awe at what their commander dared before enchanters.

Behind Shebat, the blond attaché grumbled, plucking at her woolen robe. Angrily she shook him off, palming the hatch's "close" mode.

"What harm can it do?" she demanded as the port closed up. "Well, Hooker? What harm, giving him two extra horses?" They ducked through the lock into the body of the little multidrive. "You act as though I gave him beam-pistols or heat-seekers!"

"Those folk out there are your enemies. They are not cute or quaint, or harmless. Herr Thorne is a dangerous man."

"You think I do not know them? Remember, I was born one of them. As for Thorne, only passions are dangerous, never those afflicted by them. Maybe he is dangerous, impassioned. Maybe not so, any longer. Now go sit down and strap in and be quiet, or walk the air up to the Stump. When I was an ignorant girl in Bolen's town, I knew well that enchanters could walk through the air. It would save me trouble, should you do so: ferrying you to the Stump was no part of my itinerary. . . . What are *you* grinning at, Tempest?"

The intelligencer, not sobering, sank down in a jump seat. "Telemetry," he sighed, arms spread wide. "Visual displays. Submasters. Microwave ovens! I don't think I've felt this good since your stepfather made an intelligencer cadet out of me, and I didn't have to do anyone else's laundry anymore."

"Well, I am glad someone is happy," glowered Shebat,

sitting to her helm. "I hope you will be happy doing Chaeron's laundry—for when I leave this space, I will have no passenger aboard!"

Behind her back, the Kerrion intelligencer just come from Draconis and the Orrefors-turned-Kerrion cultural attaché named Hooker exchanged glances. Hooker's said: I am only half Kerrion, and these tantrum-throwing children of power are incomprehensible and despicable to me. Tempest replied: I bid you be patient, but watch closely, and learn. They are as they are, and you had best adjust to them, for they shall never even think to accommodate you. But inwardly, Tempest was seething. He had long known that Shebat was unpredictable. Women seldom became pilots: her inherent unpredictability, up-stepped by pilot's syndrome when focused through woman's more circuitous reasoning, was going to be his greatest problem, he presumed to think. If he had dared, he would have asked the cruiser what her trouble was.

But this would not have availed him. The *Marada* was not capable of even surety that Shebat *had* a problem: he was part and parcel of it. When a cruiser and a pilot become one, their concerns and perspectives merge. The *Marada* could protect his pilot, succor her, love her. He could not analyze her.

It would have taken some other pilot/cruiser pair, of long acquaintance and unparalleled maturity, to intuit the true situation and move to alter it before things got out of hand. And, of all pilots, only Softa David Spry, Shebat's erstwhile pilotry master, knew Shebat and the *Marada* well enough. Spry, the finest pilot the Consortium's empire ever produced, might have been able to do it, had he been there, at the beginning, to see Shebat's confusion and how her malaise short-circuited the discriminatory abilities of her cruiser, KXV 134 *Marada*. Shebat's instructor, Spry, would have diagnosed her as suffering from the truth behind the axiom that all pilots are mad, and prescribed what remedies could be tendered one who gives up normal life and quotidian values to merge with a spongespace cruiser and swim among the stars. Spry had long warned Shebat that mortal concerns would fall away from her, that new values and a support-system for them must emerge, or she would perish, shorn of philosophical base, in the sponge between the stars. He had told her: take what you will of pleasure from your human fellows, but save your love for your cruiser. She had heard, but not understood. Her philosophical base, then, was yet that of an enchantress. As this eroded imperceptibly in the cold light of Consortium logic and the venality of her adopted Kerrion dynasty's concerns, she hardly noticed. Her cruiser, for much too long (because he shared her thoughts but only audited her emotions; because she was a dream dancer, Consortium-taught; because her intellect was formidable enough to suppress the emotional storm rolling under her hard-held façade), could not determine where, in the person of his beloved Shebat, the trouble lay. And, too, to the cruiser and his pilot, what was happening was not yet a problem, but the necessary deepening and strengthening of the cruiser/pilot bond.

Chapter Two

Despite his determination not to be overawed at what even a disgraced Kerrion "failure" could accomplish, Rafe Penrose yet recalled his amazing approach vector into Acheron: all the toroids and shield sleeves spinning lazily, mass-driver components and solar collectors glittering, agrospheres gleaming like a broken strand of pearls, made it seem that a gargantuan child's toybox had been upended amid ancestral stars.

Searching for Chaeron Ptolemy Kerrion through the data net, RP had not been able to shake off the image, with its pejorative tinge: Chaeron was a child sent to his room by his betters, and all the lives now in his hands merely playthings.

By the time a gleaming, snub-snouted consular lorry had deposited him on the fresh-laid sod of one of Acheron's sharp little hills, RP felt like weeping. He was overtired, he told himself, from his journey fraught with stress, and the trauma of being uprooted twice: first from Draconis to the Stump; then from the Stump to here, although "here" was the exact same set of coordinates which had held the Stump in stable orbit above the Earth for more than two centuries.

But then he spied Chaeron, just ducking out of a consular command transport, still in expedition gear from Earthly sojourn. A tightness tickled his throat, rode down to his chest as he cut across the sod, his steps too springy in this as-yet-only-approximate gravity, the not-quite-regulation pressure of the "almost" operational habitational sphere making his pulse trip and gallop.

Anticipation chased his malaise away: to be able to say "I have done it" to Chaeron, to stand in receipt of the ex-Draconis consul's most intimate smile, was a privilege hard won and still coveted by Raphael Penrose, "first bitch," or top-rated, pilot of Kerrion space.

To the newly-Kerrion minions looking on from the cockpit of the black command transport, and to the driver of the sleek eagle-blazoned lorry, there was no question about the degree of relationship between this pilot and their proconsul. Through a sextet of plainclothed intelligencers, Penrose's chestnut-curled head was easily traced, moving unchallenged, his gray flight satins the only somber note among the Kerrion's fashionably colorful bodyguard, men brought with him from home.

When the two stood together, it could be seen that Penrose was slightly taller, a fraction less lissome.

Handing his jacket to an intelligencer without looking up, Chaeron said, "Shall we walk . . . ?" He waved his arm toward the artificial hilltop, empty of bush or rock or dwelling. Their greeting, beyond this, remained unspoken, a thing displayed in their postures, an intimacy of long standing between two who had been through much with—and for—one another, who should have had no secrets, and forgave those secrets that each, in spite of this, had to keep. For these two were not of equal rank or equal burden, though they longed for parity.

Chaeron, reaching the perfect little top of the artificial hill, bowed sweepingly, "Sit?" so that his medallion dangled free of his shirt.

Penrose sat, rested an outstretched arm on one bent knee. "Very impressive."

"Me? Or the platform?"

"Everything. That slipbay approach is a work of genius. My pilots are perking right up."

Chaeron absently slipped the medallion back under his uniform shirt's cream front: "Did you get the dream dancers?" he asked, hardly moving his lips.

"All that you wanted. And all the special ones on your list, except the one called Harmony. It was like the Saturday dole-line in Draconis on those cruisers, but we brought them in alive."

"Good enough." Chaeron, in one almost boyish movement, flung himself down upon the grass, stretching out fully, his arms above his head. Staring into the pale blue strutwork overhead, he murmured, "Do you think my citizenry would like a sky? They had one in the Stump. I can still put one in, or even a space view. One would think after so many years we wouldn't need the long vistas."

Penrose wanted to reach out, touch him. He said. "That's as long a view as I've seen in the civilized stars," looking off down the curve of the sky-wall, his chin jutting. "And this is more untenanted grass than I've ever seen in one place."

"They'll live like monarchs, the first years. One hundred forty thousand in a sphere which can hold nearly a million. It's not all like this: this is where the Earth town will be. I have to give everyone whom I am displacing the opportunity to resettle and continue with their business; the Earth-towners in the Stump have to be considered, red-light district or no. . . ."

"Oh," said Penrose, ripping grass from the sward.

After a time, Chaeron shielded his eyes with his hand, though there was no glare, and whispered, "Will you *tell me* what the trouble is!"

"In what order?"

"In *any* order, before I—" Spitting a sibilance, Chaeron sat up absolutely straight.

"Easy there, boss. It's what I *didn't* get: I didn't get my ex-guildmaster, Baldy, and twenty wrongly-condemned guildbrothers of mine; it was hard to explain to them that I could only take qualified dream dancers, that manumission comes only to those we need, no matter how grievously wronged are the remainder."

A trained Kerrion visage showed no emotion unintended. Chaeron's grin—fleeting, close-lipped and wise—had a purpose. "You know that I would help them if I could. Bringing those dream dancers here, to be fractional citizens and work off monumental fines, is not exactly freedom. They are Kerrion servitors for twenty years, and maybe then they'll receive pardons. Would that do for pilots, for old Baldy? I know your pilots want him back. I'm trying. But I am no longer Draconis consul, and Kerrion space still holds dream dancing to be illegal, and I cannot say for sure that I will be here long enough to execute any promise you manage to draw out of me. So for my sake, will you please stop trying? All you are doing is reminding me of how powerless I really am."

Rafe turned over, belly-down upon the grass. "The space-enders think Softa Spry died for them; they've a charming little cult started, preaching judgment and rebirth upon his return . . . or resurrection, or whatever they think's going to happen."

"What else have they to hope for? If a martyr makes them comfortable, holding out hope of spiritual immortality when genetic immortality by offspring is denied them, what harm is there in that? Remember, they're all mules, by Consortium edict."

Penrose blinked fiercely, then whispered, "You know, there are two betting pools in the Kerrion arm of the pilotry guild, right now. One is for how long it will be before your brother—everybody's calling him 'Mad Marada'—makes a covert end to you in good Kerrion fashion, and the other of how much longer the house of Kerrion is going to stand."

"I hope you make wise wagers."

"What would those be?" RP, sitting up, gave back his employer's stare in kind.

"Whatever your heart tells you, I'm sure."

"My heart tells me you need help on the order of divine intervention. I'm no close friend of the Lords of Cosmic Jest."

"Ah, but I am well acquainted with them. Don't worry, Raphael, I have matters firmly in hand here."

"You say that, but you look terrible. You've aged five years in the eight weeks I've been gone."

"Wonderful; thanks. Will you lighten up, or *say* what you are trying so desperately not to say?"

"Sponge take you, then: your mother's guilt in the matter of Softa Spry's death was attested by a cruiser—

not enough evidence for the arbitrational guild, but plenty for Mad Marada, our esteemed consul general, who heard it from *his* cruiser, the *Hassid*. Marada has issued a public statement that if your mother so much as steps one foot out of the ol' ancestral sphere, Lorelie, then he will have her publicly censured and cast out; stripped of citizenship; you name it. . . ."

"She still is not speaking to me," said Chaeron very carefully, the muscles in his face so purely noncommittal that it hurt Penrose to watch him. "Anything else?"

"Yes. Ever since that day when the *Marada* contacted the *Danae* on its own initiative to question you about Shebat and what you . . . *did* to her, I have been—thinking. . . ."

"You were right to be hesitant in bringing this up," warned Chaeron, not smiling, his blue eyes so full of pupil they seemed black.

"I have done astounding things for you, sometimes more than I thought I could do. Now you listen to me: if you and I had not been using the *Danae* to interface, like she was some common data pool link, this sort of thing would not be happening. I'll run your pilots' guildhall, shape them up, work with the shipwrights on any project, no matter how dangerous. I'll test your new KXVs myself. But don't make me interface that cruiser with you again. Become a pilot—you are halfway to it, now! Or discharge me, and let me seek a less arduous berth. I have been alone with my—your—cruiser for nearly two months, and I am telling you that these interfaces are hurting her. If you don't care about my sanity, or your own, you should care about the serviceability of your flagship. . . ."

"Stop."

Chaeron's command silenced Penrose like a slap in the face. Rafe recalled the day (was it only one year ago?) when the younger man had come to him in the guildhall, his patrician features sharpened, pale; dragged him into a pay privacy booth and muttered, "Ask me what I did tonight?" "What did you do?" Penrose had obeyed. "I slapped my mother and raped my wife," Chaeron had whispered disbelievingly, and put his head in his hands. From that, all this turmoil had sprung.

And another time came to mind, when he and Chaeron and Shebat had been together in the redoubtable *Marada*, and Shebat and Chaeron had pledged a slated troth that if ever Chaeron should come to power over Shabet's homeworld Earth, he would cede it to her, few strings attached.

"I cannot·stop," Rafe answered Chaeron back, almost groaning. "I have to talk to you; I won't let you proceed into folly, unwarned." Pleading, he reached out and grasped the other's forearm.

"Finish, then," Chaeron allowed, shaking Penrose off.

"I know your·official position is that you want no part of Marada's ruinous policies for Kerrion space, and that you feel it imperative to maintain and affirm that cruiser advances are desirable, even remarkable—but if you do not intervene in this mess in Draconis, we will all be dragged down with the ship, so to speak."

"'So to speak,'" Chaeron repeated. "Raphael, I cannot. My mother has spurned me; my brother has exiled me. I have nearly liquidated my Draconis assets in order to make Acheron a self-supporting bastion of Kerrion technologies, if not wisdom. They say one cannot divorce one's relatives, but I am determined to try. Not another word about it, now, if you love me." He grinned, a faked flash of camaraderie belonging to a much simpler man.

"And your wife, has she agreed to this?"

Then Chaeron was up and looming, his arms crossed, his countenance severe. "You will not let be, will you? You know that no one else would dare to question me so? But since you are testing me, if crudely, I will give you an answer. I will not remind you that Shebat is yet sulking in sponge. And I will not say that things are difficult between my wife and me, since you are part of the reason why. But I *will* say that whether she is, or is not, with child, she has not seen fit to inform me. That *is* what you wanted to know?"

Penrose slowly gained his feet, wishing he did not want to apologize, wishing he could hold back Chaeron's night, wishing he could sort out his own feelings from those he thought he should feel, and those he wanted to feel, and come up less inextricably involved with this passionate, fated creature who commanded his allegiance so completely that he seemed to have lost control of his own destiny.

To somehow quench the fire in them both, he offered news, capitulation: "I brought Lauren, Spry's girlfriend with the others. Danced a few dreams with her, got cozy, tried to find out why she, too, was not insistent on waiting for Spry's return. She said that he'd find her here or in the next life. . . ."

Chaeron did not chuckle. "You will keep her in your sights, then?"

"Certainly, and glad to do it. I have another, perhaps welcome, surprise."

"So? I have lost my taste for surprises." He looked like his mother, then, his attention on the waiting transports, his profile flawless in Acheron's gentle light. He cocked his head, and started walking down toward the waiting intelligencers. Penrose, following, wondered whether he was not supposed to pace the preconsul in silence, or if, forewarned, he was expected to speak.

He waited until a sidecast glance bade him proceed, and explained about a certain boy who was the youngest among the dream dancers—who had been, so the lad said, known to Chaeron when as consul he had frequented dream dancers' warrens on Draconis' infamous level seven.

Chaeron shook his head, pushed his mane irritably back from his forehead, squinted at the turf before him. "I cannot remember any . . . Ah, then—now I do. What did he tell you?" His boyish, sly mien, naughty and winsome, eased Penrose. "Just that he used to take care of your cloak," Rafe dared to tease.

"Lords, what will we do with him? He is too young to risk on Earth, for so little reason. Well then, send him around to my office. I'll find something for him to do. You don't recall his name, do you?"

"Sorry," shrugged RP, and Chaeron clapped him companionably about the shoulders, only a fugitive embrace, but speaking many things.

Rafe Penrose unbent then, deep within, where he had long been holding his mental breath, and expelled it.

All his forethought and all his schemes had come to naught. He was stuck here, though he was first bitch of

Kerrion space, for no better reason than that he did not have the heart to quit Chaeron. Things were just the same as they had always been: getting worse and better simultaneously, but at a negligible rate. Some things, any pilot knows, are mandated by their patron, Chance, and cannot be avoided. Chaeron Ptolemy Kerrion was resoundingly one such.

"Wait till I show you the horse I have brought up to help indoctrinate the dream dancers," Chaeron gloated in his public manner. As they came down among the scarved and tunic'd intelligencers, he bade one man take the lorry which had brought Penrose here, go back to the slipbay and oversee the quartering of the dream dancers, sending a second with him to find Gahan Tempest, Acheron's new chief of intelligencers, and escort him to the stables, posthaste.

"Horse?" Penrose echoed, climbing into the command transport, nodding to the driver within.

"Horse," Chaeron affirmed, his bootheels ringing on the steps, intelligencers close behind. "Stables," to the driver. And: "Excuse me." He led Penrose past ten feet of seats and consoles, through a partition into an automated command pit, saying: "Horse, indeed. I am going to insist that you come groundside. Horse, like in *The Iliad*. You remember?"

"I am not going anywhere near a horse, or a society of enchanters and technopeasants, or cities sprawled in the rubble of a discarded world."

"No?" An unwelcome promise laughed from Chaeron's eyes.

Chapter Three

On Groundhog Day, A.D. 2252, Shebat Kerrion emerged from her sibyl's cave, beheld her shadow, and went back inside. The nonoutboard Jesse Thorne—barely recognizable to the *Marada* as human, so swathed was he in animal skin and animal fur—followed. From thirty waiting riders, a sound came up like distant thunder, made of sighs and mutters and creaking leather and clanking iron. From their horses, steam rose and white breath snorted forth like ethereal fog, pale as the snow upon the land.

The *Marada* wished Shebat had not insisted on leaving Gahan Tempest behind when they had stopped by the Stump to drop off Hooker before embarking to search for Softa Spry; had not resisted his advice, when again they were bound for Earth, that she should retrieve Tempest once more.

His outboard was impenetrable; his outboard was distressed. It showed on all his meters, as it had showed, growing hourly, since she had encountered her husband at these very coordinates, ninety-five real-time days before. "Chaeron needs Tempest more than I," she snarled, when the moment to vector toward Acheron was at hand. "I am not going into Acheron, and that is that. I am going to Bolen's town and my husband, should he wish to, can find me there."

The *Marada* had asked Shebat, at the outset of their voyage, if she was angry because he had lost track of the missing KXV 133, or because the cruiser had been forced to admit that what he had seen might have been simply a far-traveling remnant, a relativistic ghost expanding unceasingly outward which would never die, or even realize that the source which sent it speeding into the five infinities had long since been destroyed.

Shebat had assured him that she was not angry, only disappointed, but she would not turn back from journeying out to Pegasus to see for herself that no cruiser was hiding there. Then the *Marada* had been forced to displease his outboard: her seals were breached. If she would not have her mil refurbished before leaving Earth's space (and she would not, she swore, even set foot into her husband's soon-to-be-vacated province) then she must do so in Draconis, which was the closest interim-space port.

Because of the *Marada*'s love for his outboard, they had stopped at Draconis, en route to the colonies, and Shebat and his namesake, Marada Kerrion—guild pilot, arbiter-on-leave, consul general of Kerrion space—had met, and spat, and hissed at each other while the *Marada* did his best to watch over his outboard, while following her instructions to avert his monitoring eyes.

The cruiser had thought, until the very moment that the mil-fitter with his portable, coffinlike chamber took his leave and Marada Seleucus Kerrion stayed behind, that since it was not his own failure to reestablish contact with the missing KXV 133 which had upset her, then the prospect of being shut up in the mil-chamber was at the heart of his outboard's discomfort.

But it was not the reestablishment of her seals—the reinforcement of her protection from radiation, pressure variation, projectiles, or heat loss—which had been troubling her, the cruiser was forced to admit, but some outboard matter having to do with emotion, a subject of which the *Marada* was not yet master, but still an apprentice.

It was not that the *Marada* was a stranger to emotion: he had experienced love, though he had no heart; life, though his roughly scaled, light-banded superstructure could not be said to be living; death, through cruiser-consciousness' audit of systems-wipe while it had occurred to certain of its member cruisers; even a mock human death, when cruisers in concert had given over to oblivion all the memories they had stored of the life of the outboard Softa David Spry.

Cruisers held little from one another: this fear of non-being they had learned from cruiser-wipe and pilot death was a lesson not yet assimilated. Like any new thing so difficult to comprehend, for a time all cruisers looked *through* their new knowledge at the phenomenal world, and the world was colored by that information which had no natural function nor integrative place in their circuitry. The *Marada,* first of his kind to "feel" selfhood, rode a fomenting tide of outboard feelings and cruiser sentiments, uneasy over what he had wrought.

His cruiserkin venerated him, though he was, because of his owner/pilot's status as heir apparent, not a Kerrion command cruiser, but merely "Kerrion Four." All but the *Hassid,* Marada Seleucus Kerrion's flagship, who was the ever-haughty "Kerrion One," acknowledged the *Marada* as wisest among cruiserkind.

Like her owner, *Hassid* was slightly askew, tainted by him, opinionated and judgmental. It was no wonder the cruiser could not heal her pilot; they were melded too inextricably, delirious from the same ineffable disease. This similitude of thought between the Kerrion consul general and his cruiser was problematical: both being of the same persuasion, they reinforced one another's delusion that only they saw clearly, that truth in their hands became uppercased, pure—and by this precept, omnipotent.

While Shebat had dueled verbally with her first love, Marada Kerrion, the sponge-cruiser *Marada* had tried, and failed, to establish some rapport with the snippy, rank-conscious *Hassid. Hassid* was loath to recall that she had been wiped by her beloved outboard, sacrificed as an example during the pilot's recent strike; or that she owed her continuance as a cognizant entity to the host of cruisers, who had scooped up bits of her and wisps of her and every fleeing thought from her, saved them until the time came when *Hassid's* B-mode was patched back into service, then sent every memory back again. *Hassid* owed her 'self' to cruiser care and cruiser loyalty, but she had no care or loyalty for any being but her pilot.

This worried the *Marada* almost as much as Shebat's altercation with *Hassid's* pilot, almost as much as his outboard's physical condition, daily more deviant from anything resembling pilot's norm.

And because he was concerned, the *Marada* could not help but prick one undetectable mechanical ear to what passed, on board him, between the consul general and the heir apparent of Kerrion space:

"Have you thought what it is you are doing? Liquidating your holdings on this scale could throw the entire consulate into a depression!" Marada Kerrion's drawl came loud in the cruiser's sensors; his steroid-heavy body paced *Marada*'s bridge; the crack of his knuckles popped like static.

"That is why I am offering this to you, privately, beforehand. Buy me out, or bear the consequences." Shebat hunched in her command central, shadow-faced in the low-lighting, watching meters that jumped and played, making a variegated kaleidoscope of the circular helm. From every black-and-silver console, the *Marada*'s readouts glittered: *Danger*. Confirmation came back to her from Marada Kerrion's outraged countenance, from his tightly drawn mouth in its nest of beard, from his scant, black brows drawn low over disenfranchised, poet's eyes.

"Why haven't you simply contested my accession?" he demanded, big hands digging troughs in the bumper of the little epicentral helm where Shebat sat unmoving.

"You know the answer to that. A better man than yourself would have realized upon his own that he was not good enough . . . well before now. What you have done to Chaeron is shameful; your treatment of your entire family, the scandal of the civilized stars. You have two children; think of them if nothing else. Should I contest with you for a position to which neither of us is *in any way* suited, while Chaeron does minion's duties, under duress, at the edge of nowhere?"

"What a way to talk about your homeworld," Marada Kerrion chided her. "You have administrative proclivities so high they scored in your top three aptitudes. I have not forgotten that, nor can you convince me that you have. What do you want, Shebat?"

The *Marada*'s outboard had leaned forward, darkening every console but the one encircling her with irreducible arms. "I want you to bring Chaeron back from Earth."

"I will see Kerrion space expelled from the Consortium, broken up and sold off to the highest bidder, first."

"No doubt." Her pulse was racing; her adrenals counseling attack. The *Marada* tried to reach her, but she ignored his whispered caution. "Then let him have a chance to accomplish something there. You have succeeded: he is ruined, stripped of adherents, even resigned."

"Tell me another fable."

"How else can it be? With fewer than fifty bondkin with him, what can he do in a hostile, alien space? You did that, made sure he could not rally what few supporters he had left."

"I wish I were so persuasive. He did it himself, by his foolish support of pilots above citizens . . . by his choices, every one. Would I look like this"—Marada Kerrion raised his hands away from his muscle-slabbed flesh—"if he were capable of performing even the minimal duties of keeping Draconis free from terrorists? I will hear no more about it. You are welcome back as Draconis consul—your right, which I will not deny you—or in any other position the rigors of which you feel you can fulfil. But him I will not suffer in any critical capacity, lest next time the sabotage (which I still believe he inculcated upon half the reigning consular families in order to murder me) be successful."

"Give me your answer, Marada. Will you buy me out?"

"No. I will loan you whatever you need. Otherwise, it will look as though I forced you from your prerogatives. Keep your stocks, your majority in the cruiser industry. If Chaeron advised you to do this, you should realize by that fact that it is not to your benefit. He can vote your stocks, in perpetuity: he cannot liquidate them. My dear departed father gave you them for a reason. How wise he was, I am only beginning to realize."

Shebat shaded her eyes with her hand, though the cabin was yet dim. In her thoughts, a great void appeared. She sniffled, cleared her throat. "Why are you doing this to me?"

"What? I am endeavoring to be less hateful than you think me, I admit. But the last time we met, I was still unbalanced from my long convalescence. Shebat, you should let me help you. . . ."

He reached out to her, and she cowered. He dropped his hands, laced them before him, and gazed at her expectantly.

The *Marada*'s outboard had not said anything which she was thinking; she had not spoken of love, or hate, or lost opportunities, or reconciliation. She had buried her face in her palms and wept, sobbing brokenly that he must get out of her ship, out of her ken, out of her life.

Only the *Marada* had seen the pensive grin on the consul general's face as he gathered up the distraught girl in flight satins, carried her to her stateroom as once, so long ago, he carried her into this life which he had never expected her primitive's mind to encompass.

Marada's tenderness toward Shebat brought surprising results: When the girl was dry of tears, in her husky voice she proclaimed that she had come here specifically to seduce him, to soften his heart toward Chaeron, and: "Chaeron thinks I am a snobbish celibate, that I am sexually limited and"—sniff—"retarded by that. I came here to broaden my horizons and become *normal*. Gray eyes in red whites peered at him, free from guile. "Considering how I once felt . . . *thought* I felt . . . about you, you were the obvious choice. But I cannot—"

"That is a relief, I can't very well bed my brother's wife, no matter how anxious I am to lie down with my enemy. Shebat, you must understand: I wish you nothing but the best. Despite your unfortunate marriage, I will help you however I may. Believe me."

And Shebat did believe him.

But the *Marada*—monitoring all with unabashed thoroughness ever since the physical welfare of his outboard had come into question—did not. His readouts told him truer; Marada Kerrion's equilibrium was a magnificent sham, a fantasy. Like *Hassid,* her pilot was being eaten away from within by imagined guilts and an all-pervasive aberration too dangerous to ignore and too deeply seated to be known to those who harbored it.

When Marada Kerrion's dark person had finally suited up and ducked through his locks into the calm anchor-space separating the *Marada* from *Hassid,* Shebat's cruiser heaved a silicon sigh of relief that brightened every light on board, and made the striolate banding about his length pulse like an electric eel.

But later, when Shebat had said to him, worriedly, that the consul general had mentioned renewed piracy in the shipping lanes, and made known his determination to search space-end, module by module, if need by, for the culprit, the cruiser was sorry that he had not more closely monitored the beginnings of his namesake's visit aboard.

It was with this unintentional encouragement of the consul general's firmly in mind that Shebat insisted they make their way to the loose-knit colonies of Pegasus. With leaden spirits, she returned from there, Spry and the KXV unfound, insistent upon going groundside with no intelligencer or even a bodyguard.

"I have you, *Marada.* I need no man," she had pronounced hotly, and even the *Marada* knew that there was something wrong about the way she said "man," the word so full of resentment that it was nothing like the pilot's adage she was intending to reaffirm.

It was not until Shebat was installed in her chosen cave and the *Marada* at his space-anchor that the *Danae* insinuated her way past Shebat's standing order that the *Marada,* beyond his dealings with Acheron's traffic authority, maintain communications silence. Cruiser communion was, after all, different from communication with outboards or traffic controllers.

The *Marada* did not realize that *Danae* had tricked him until Chaeron Kerrion's grainy, cruiser-shunted face peered noncorporeally into his most private being.

Five thousand miles below the *Marada*'s anchor, a cruiser's snout poked its way into Jesse Thorne's dream dance, the glorious visage of Chaeron Kerrion manifesting right behind. Thorne had little experiences with dream dances. This, his third ever, under the aegis of the oracle Shebat, was full of stars: men swam among them; great metal fish dove among them; monumental cities spun among them, choraling the grandeur of man for all eternity to see.

Consequently, when the cruiser and the ethereal face invaded his waking dream, he accepted this intrusion placidly—until Shebat's fury tumbled him abruptly out of the land of visions, onto the cold stone floor of the sibyl's cave.

He had seen the face of the man previously, in her spell-trances, but always it had been serene, welcoming full of salvation. This time, it had been wriggling, blowing apart and coalescing as it spoke into Jesse's place of dreaming, full of the wrath of the gods.

"Shebat!" the voice had thundered, so that the dreaming Thorne had clapped nonphysical hands to the effigy-ears, "Stay right there. I am on my way."

"How dare you!" the dream dancer had howled, and the howl became a snarling wind that wiped away the starscape and gusted Jesse Thorne back into familiar, Earthbound flesh.

In that interval, while an unnatural wind had upswept him, Thorne had felt fear like none he had ever endured in battle. Not even while in enchanters' clutches had he been split apart, mind torn from body, body telegraphing urgent instructions that soul could not implement. He shivered, when it was over, crouching in the seeress's cave, frozen with terror. Waiting for mindlessness to pass, he tried to tell himself that it was only the tithe of sitting so long cross-legged; that his feet and legs were asleep, and his mind had chosen to follow: that none of what he felt was akin to cowardice, only a second-cousin of nightmare, come to call.

He had seen the sibyl's face while she strove to oust the intruding double vision of man and Leviathan, though, and her raging eyes spitting fire so blinding it made the awful eyes of the mighty spacefish dim to nothing, the stars disappear.

He would not soon forget the sight of Shebat in her power, in her place. More even than that reality which broke into scenario and terminated idyll, it had been this which submerged him in panic. No longer could he pretend to himself that his third trip to consult the oracle was a harmless diversion to pass the endless time of winter quartering, valuable only in that it enhanced his reputation among the storm-scattered ranks of militiamen, as the horses she had given him had been proof to some that Thorne's hopeless battle against magic had divine sanction, that every god of rock and field loved him, and wished him well.

In previous dreams, the epicene man's aspect had been one of a redeemer, shining forth with outstretched hands to save them all. For the first dream, his men had been with him, and later he had found that each man of his— even Cluny, the young scout—had had this very same dream, save for the fact that whoever dreamed that dream deemed himself its central character. This had disappointed him, somehow, and made him jealous of those young heroes who had sworn to lay down their lives for him, and *that* had disappointed him further: he had seen smallness in himself.

So he had gone back a second time, and she had given him a dream that was his alone: of paradise on Earth and an end to endless servitude; a dream free from enchanters who could cause a man's flesh to fire like a dead stick in summer; a dream in which he had had a great part. And then had come waking, and her gift of the pair of blue-eyed stallions, and their ride to the clearing where her fire-spouting chariot had come to reclaim her.

He had been saddened, for it had seemed to him that she was come as his special daemon, his sign from heaven. He had hoped she would return.

Now, he wished she had not come back to Bolen's town, that he had not ridden up from Troy when he had heard news of the oracle sitting again on Sentinel Ridge.

He slapped his recalcitrant calves, massaged them through his deerskin boots. If the apparition from the dream was truly on its way hither, it was time for him to depart.

He said as much to the girl across from him, so frail in her shapeless robe that it was difficult for him to credit his own experience: *this* was the creature whose spells held such power that his teeth still ached from being clamped tight against his fear?

She made no answer, only turned hellhole eyes up to him, bereft of color but for reflections thrown up by the banked embers of the fire between them. He walked around it, extended his hand down to her. "The fire burns out, little mother. We have been at it long. My men will want daylight for our leave-taking; the ridgeside is treacherous."

She said, in her throaty voice which tickled his spine, "You should stay and meet with him whose face you saw. There is little time left for you to make your choice."

"There is no choice for me, little mother, beyond death or freedom. A child could foretell which of those is more likely."

She grasped his hand and stood, unfolding her long legs as if they had not been crossed beneath her since the fire was bold and crackling. Risen, she was a mere hand shorter than he. She cocked her head, and challenge sparkled from her gaze before her lips parted. "Death is a coward's refuge. Freedom is within your grasp."

"Come with me, little mother," he blurted, surprising himself with those words. "It is not safe here for one whom enchanters deplore."

"You heard the voice in our dream; he who owns it will be here presently." Their hands were still clasped; she gently disengaged hers, led the way out of the cave.

Jesse Thorne wiped his palm on his leggings, muttering to himself as he followed. What he wanted from the oracle, he preferred not to examine too closely. One should not have profane thoughts about an envoy of the nameless gods who yet loved the small and weak defenders of Their faith.

At the cave's mouth, midday was blinding, reflected heavenward by a ferocious blizzard's snows. "It is said that in the enchanted city of New Chaeronea, snow dares not fall, that there it is ever warm as spring," he remarked, trying to sound casual as he came up behind her and saw his party circled before the cave in a protective ring, all their horses' rumps turned inward, bows and slings drawn to ready in every man's hand.

"Go back inside, sibyl," he entreated her in a rattling

whisper, squinting through the glare. "Your predictions are too exact for my taste. I did not realize you meant that I would come to terms with my destiny today." Forgetting her hallowed person, he took her by the arm and cast her behind him like a sack of spelt. Beyond his riders' horses, he saw enchanters approaching on their massive steeds, a great black clot of them like blood spilled from a mortal wound.

He counted twice his own force before he stepped out of the shadow and made for his horse, and his commander of ten saw him, and young Cluny Pope vaulted off his pony and scrambled toward him, breaking ranks.

"Get back on that horse," he snapped to the boy, whose face fell, saving Thorne from having to endure those wide, wild eyes which would soon be staring sightlessly up into heaven.

Then he walked at a leisurely pace toward his own mount, took a handful of mane and vaulted onto it, disengaged his saddlebag and began putting his pistol together.

It would be a shame to die without ever having fired it, which had cost him one of the two stallions he had gotten from the seeress. His second-in-command, watching him out of the corner of his eye, made a signal which caused his troop to spread out one horse's width more.

Thorne eased his gray in between the brown mare of his lieutenant and the pony belonging to Cluny Pope. To his left were fifteen of the finest fighters in the northeast: his best officers come in for winter strategy meetings. To his right were an equal number of fledgling commanders: each phalanx leader had brought his first officer, or his squire.

Thorne favored Cluny Pope with a fierce stare of condemnation: no other youth had broken ranks. A line so thin could not afford a break in it. The boy, blushing red to his pointed ears, looked steadily ahead of him, back stiff, stroking his pony's neck. Jesse felt evanescent regret, that he had allowed the youth's father to browbeat him into bringing his eldest son north from Troy. Among the freedom-loving families, it was thought prestigious to have their sons with him: a favor due the father of a girl whom in gentler times he might have wed had brought

Cluny Pope to him, scant months ago. A favor? Now that
it was imminent, death could not be welcome merely because it was honorable to a boy barely sixteen years of
age.

Screwing the pistol's barrek into place, Thorne hung it
by a thong from his saddlehorn. He was angry, and that
was good. What approached was not just the end of his
life, but the end of hopes long nurtured among the down-
trodden populace. If he had not called his best in to consult them, he would not be facing the destruction of eight
years' work. No rallying would be possible, once these
were gone.

He saluted his own lieutenant, and the lantern-jawed
man grinned bleakly back.

Horses snorted; men shared out weapons, passing sling
stones and sabertoothed boomerangs down their arching
line. Some had javelins and telescoping iron spears with
fire-hardened wooden points: all knew iron blades could
not pierce an enchanter's defense.

Jesse Thorne whistled them up; the horses danced,
knowing that command of old.

His own gray blared a belly-shaking challenge out
across the snow toward the enchanters' company, wide-
spread in open order.

A singing tingle began to curdle the air around them.

"Hold steady," called his lieutenant. Cluny Pope made
a sign of warding over his pony's poll. Down the line,
rightward amongst the younger men, someone sobbed
softly, cursing in a tremulous voice.

Enchanters never closed in fair battle without first softening up the opposition. They waited for the spells to
weave, and they waited well.

Thorne was filled with pride for his men. Even the soft
lament down-line on his right had stopped.

The air sang louder, began to roar. At one end of his
line, far right, an awful crackling commenced. Horses
squealed and shied; men held them as best they could,
without looking at the source of the horrible sounds, now
increasing, now joined by a wafting smell which was full
of sweetness and death.

On pretext of steadying the boy, Thorne chanced a
glance: the rightmost horse steamed; his rider was gur-

gling, hunched low over his saddle's horn. As Thorne watched, the man's clothing, his hair, and the mane and tail of his mount flared bright, like catching charcoal. A glow issued forth from him, and his mount bellowed desperately, just once. Then, like a horse and rider of wood, they began to crumble, flames unbearably bright licking out from within. Jesse had one glimpse of the rider's charred flesh, burning eyes, cracking skin, and then a blast of heat and light came from them, and mount and man collapsed like paper, leaving ash and leather and saddle fittings and weapons falling toward the ground.

"Recover arms," snapped Thorne's lantern-jawed lieutenant, and the two men closest to the pile of char looked from one to the other before the endman obeyed.

With less than a quarter-mile remaining between the two forces, a fear that was palpable consumed his corps. From above their heads, the sky seemed to roar with infernal laughter, split apart. A fireball danced there, among the clouds. It blossomed quite slowly, hovering over their heads. *Don't look at it,* Jesse Thorne prayed; then, aloud: "Eyes front."

But the fireball passed over them, on down the slope where the ridge tapered gently, and, like some hunting dog on an elusive scent, made its way toward the enchanters approaching from the northeast.

Its sounds, however, never left them; spooked horses, ears flattened, added their terror to the unholy din.

When his gray—the most trustworthy of battle chargers—broke and reared, Jesse Thorne disobeyed his own orders and looked up at the sky, expecting laughing effigies of enchanters smirking down at him from hostile clouds.

But instead, a long, waffle-work glow came out of the cloudcover, so that the roaring became unbearable; because of the horses' fear of it, he called a retreat, bunching his men back against the very ridgeside, his own mount positioned before the opening to the oracle's cave.

He saw mouths move in prayer or imprecation, but no mortal sound could rise above this thunder which made the ground quake. He saw, beyond the glow of a mighty vessel in fluid descent, the fireball reach the enchanters who approached in mazing numbers. And he saw their horses begin to fall, slowly buckling their knees as if they must sleep. And he witnessed enchanters—men who were more than men and were said to be unassailable—falling like autumn leaves from their gold-trapped saddles: the ineluctable stopped dead, the omnipotent vanquished.

"Hold, hold!" called his lieutenant, a scream hardly audible above the keening air from which the magical conveyance dropped down toward them.

Barely was there room for it, between the horses and the stand of trees.

He struggled to steady his own steed in the face of the thing, which was like the mighty spacefish he had seen in the sibyl's dream, but smaller, with an upraised snout and colored lights banding it round.

Then he could see nothing in the steam of melting snow—not the enchanters, beyond, not the metal mantis of the horseless chariot, not anything at all.

Out of the fog and mist come so suddenly upon them, lightning blazed, questing. From the northeast, where the enchanters faltered, it came and licked at the mist-shrouded transport which settled out of the sky, then sought easier prey among his riders. Like a serpent, waving its head, it hissed like a living thing.

His men tried to remain motionless: this enchanter's weapon was one with which all were familiar. But Thorne's lieutenant's horse had had enough, and bucked and fought. That was all the lightning needed to sight its victim.

By the time Thorne had realized his officer could not control his terrified horse, the man was wrapped in shining death, constrictor-lightning tight around him, his horse's nose and skyward-pointing head all that could be seen but the baleful strands of destruction. Jesse Thorne's heart sank groundward with the paltry, ashen remains of man and mount.

Then began a battle incomprehensible to him, between the chariot from the sky and the enchanters from the northeast, so that no one could watch it, but all shielded their eyes, or closed them tightly, as Thorne found need to do, burying their faces in their horses' manes, holding their palms over their mounts' eyes.

When the sounds like rending earth had stopped, when no thunder rolled or lightning flashed red through his tight-shut lids, Jesse looked up to see the middle of the wall of metal before him split, and that very man whose beauty was more than human emerge from the darkness within, preceded by a taller, dark man in blacks and followed by one in gray and the infamous enchanter known as Hooker.

Thorne took his hands from his horse's eyes, whistled a signal that meant, "Caution, hold position," and sat up straight in his saddle.

From behind him, he heard a voice. Obeying it, he urged his mount forward, so that the oracle could emerge from her cave.

This put him horse-to-eye with the tall, tight-lipped man in black and red, whom Jesse recognized from his previous visit here. He said, as the man took his horse's bridle authoritatively, "We would not have let them take her alive."

"So we feared," said the long-nosed man in a formidable manner. Thorne was a good judge of men, and marked this one as a force with which to reckon.

But no ill came of it, save that the man saw his pistol as he sidled through the horse-line and spoke with the oracle in a tongue which Jesse's mother had taught him, and few but enchanters understood. Having a secret knowledge of the enchanters' arcane language, Consulese, had often been useful to him in the past. It did not fail him then:

"Shebat, are you all right?" said the dark one.

"Tempest, I have never been so glad to see you, but I am unharmed."

"Will you stop this foolery and come home?"

"Acheron is not my home."

While he listened, he watched the regal, auburn-haired man, who had invaded the oracle's dream, watch him. There was calculation displayed openly there, and just a hint of a smile. The thing to do, Thorne was sure, was greet him, and he threw a leg over his horse's neck and slid from his saddle to do just that.

Immediately to the right of the man from his dream, the gray-clad one stood, arms akimbo and legs spread, grousing familiarly, "Haven't you had enough of this? I have."

"Just about," the other agreed, and then, as if they were old friends, stepped toward Jesse Thorne, hand outstretched in greeting. "If you would care to join us for an inspection of what exists beyond this little world's sky, Mister Thorne, then perhaps I can persuade my wife to come also. What do you say? I'll guarantee your safe return, and while you are with us, you'll be treated as befits a son of the house of Orrefors. The problems we are *both* having with refractory personnel . . . ah, enchanters, that is . . . shall be more easily solved if we pool our information." The hand of the man from his dream stayed extended, an arm's length away. Behind him, his horse nuzzled his back, nudging him forward.

This accident made it necessary to grasp the outstretched hand, warm though the day was breath-freezing cold. "Your wife?"

"I am afraid so, Jesse Thorne. But I have you at a disadvantage. Let me introduce myself, and my companions. . . ."

There was something so winsome and honest about the man called Chaeron Kerrion that Thorne soon found himself exchanging greetings with Raphael Penrose, who looked at him like a man who sees some unknown type of snake very close to his naked foot; and with Hooker, who was no militiaman's friend but a villainous enchanter; and with the dark, long, fish-mouthed Gahan Tempest. Then, in his turn and as seemed proper, he named three of his officers (correctly, since Hooker knew well who was who) and Cluny Pope.

"Care to bring a friend? We can take one more," said Chaeron Kerrion to Thorne, with a mischievous sidelong glance at the scout.

Cluny Pope's eyes widened until they might have consumed the entire ridgeside, but Thorne refused, knowing nothing of what lay ahead, and not wanting to chance another's life in enchanters' keeps beyond the clouds.

He marked it strange that the man who said he was husband to the oracle did not speak with her himself, but forthwith ushered him up the ramp and into the enchanter's conveyance (which he called a "multidrive"), while Shebat delivered a scathing denunciation of his host's character in Consulese too rapid and eloquent for him to catch more than its gist.

Once within the multidrive's arcane bowels, trepidation shrouded him. But he could not have refused, before his commanders, to accept. Such an invitation had been tendered to no mortal man in living memory. Only Shebat and Twice Risen had mounted to heaven on wings of fire—and returned.

But when he heard the oracle's sharp words of rebuke as she entered the magical multidrive (with young Pope in tow!), castigating them for using those same weapons as did the odious enchanters, and decreeing that never again would she allow slaughter of that type to be perpetrated upon men, no matter *whose* men they were or what was at stake, he began to wonder into what sort of pit he had just stumbled, and how he was going to wrest this opportunity to serve someone else's designs into his own hands, and use it to lift the yoke of oppression from his folk, with Hooker there to keep reminding those enchanters-who-claimed-not-to-be-so that Jesse Thorne was dedicated, beyond any considerations of personal moment, to wiping enchanters from the face of the Earth.

Chapter Four

Chaeron Kerrion was feeling much more himself lately. The privilege of being able to make that statement was precious to him, who had long been denied it. He had weathered his father's death, his little brother's living death, his half brother's accension and affair with Chaeron's own mother, his arrest and trial for complicity in the terrorist bombing which had nearly killed mother and sibling both, his own vindication and resultant demotion—all seemingly unscathed, but for worry lines etching his brow. The lines had come not from the rigors his mother's patron, Fate, had decreed for him, but from his efforts to present this very similitude, even to himself: unscathed! That was what he had wanted to be, had demanded to be, had pretended to be, for he well knew that the perception of reality is more crucial than the underlying actuality. From the most distant times, the veracity of this axiom could be seen as self-evident in history: participants die, events blur, what is recorded as truth becomes truth.

But he was not yet history; he was very much alive; those events which were blurred in his memory were so because of his physiochemical reaction to stress. And he was far from unscathed.

But he was coming closer it it: close enough to admit that for at least the last six months he had been so skewed by happenstance that his judgment might have been affected. He could not have made this admission even three weeks ago, when, unpacking his personal effects in his Acheron apartment, he had dropped one silver stallion bookend on his bare foot, then thrown the offending article against the farther wall, denting its blotter-gray expanse, breaking off the venerable statue's striking foot, and collapsing his house of lies about his head. He had sat long there on the smoky carpet, the ruined casting cradled in his lap. Of all he had brought from Draconis and had had sent from Lorelie, only this pair of bookends meant anything to him personally. He had had them since childhood. They had accompanied him through everything, proud, indomitable, frozen in mid-challenge. The man who had hefted one in anger and cast it was no man he fancied becoming.

He had stopped lying to himself, ceased ignoring what could not be borne. But he could not have done it earlier: he could not have endured a harsh assessment of his difficulties while no light shone at the end of his private tunnel. He would have crumbled. So he had come out of his stupor—out of endless pulse-pounding, skin-crawling days of looking steadfastly only at that day's labors, never at the morrow's—just in time, or exactly at the right time, or at the first possible time he could survey the shambles of his life and retain his sanity.

He did not know which, or care, except to the extent that he must keep in mind that some of the things he had said and done, especially in regard to his relationship with his wife, might not have been quite as equitable as he would have liked.

What is not realized as error cannot be remedied, futures researchers claimed. He had a clutch of those—Delphis and problem modelers—and every time he talked with one he was reminded that if not for Bernice "Delphi" Gomes's hatred for everything Kerrion, he would be Draconis consul yet.

Never mind, never mind. But how could he not? He had tried to pretend that he was just as effective here as he had been in Draconis, as proconsul when before he had been consul, but since no one else believed it, it was time he stopped believing that he must believe it.

And though any rational man would look at Chaeron's prospects for release from Earth's loamy embrace and glumly admit it impossible, the trick was simply not to mind it: all right, cuddle up to disgrace, play dice with hopelessness, harness despair. And beat the odds.

He was about it, as best could be. He had hurt some people who loved him: Shebat, Gahan Tempest, RP. He would remedy his errors.

Now that survival was likely, he could set about it. When first he had come to the Stump, most reprehensible of all habitational spheres, he was too beleaguered. Three attempts on his life had come close; countless others everyone prudently ignored. The populace of platform dwellers had forced him to sweeping measures with their hostility, their intransigence, and their haughty certainty that he would never figure out what they were doing in time. To master the Stump's ancient complexity, one needed to have been born to it. Without the cooperation of those who were, he had had only one alternative: scrap it, and start anew.

So now, the tables were turned. Every living being who had thwarted him in the Stump was his tenant here in Acheron. No one knew the data sources here as well as he: Chaeron was in control of every data pool and base and knowledge base accessible to Acheron's public, and others which were not. He had spent mightily to acquire it, but he even had an independent orbital complex with redundant matrices and personal resonances which gave him constant information updates and had an effective range of two hundred million miles. On Earth or even from Earth space's sponge-portal, he could conduct his business, contact his intelligencers directly (and nonverbally), monitor events in Acheron, all without an accessing terminal or the slightest twinge of worry that his programs were compromised in their integrity or their secrecy.

Never had he had such latitude in the area of computer protocals. He doubted that his father had had it, in the old days: Parma Alexander Kerrion, though an innovator in every other arena, had been of the opinion that direct-accessing intelligence keys might in some insidious way be harmful to the human mind. Chaeron, child of his times, had no such compunction.

Through his intelligence keys, while still shuttling toward the *Danae,* he had concluded the meeting in New Chaeronea which he had interrupted to fetch Shebat. Simultaneously, without a word being spoken before Hooker, he had detailed Tempest to arrange for the ground-dwellers' quartering in the Acheron Earth town, and suitable surveillance of them in the person of his new houseboy, the erstwhile young Mistral, as well as by standard electronics. In concert, Penrose was entering a log copy transmitted from the *Marada* into the memory of the *Danae,* who by the time the shuttle reached her bay had sorted out the highlights of Shebat's twelve-week journey for Chaeron's perusal. In *Danae*'s enlarged cargo bay, while Shebat strutted, eyes shining with remembrances of her own first glimpse of the innards of a sponge-cruiser, playing hostess to the ground-dweller Thorne and his ward, Chaeron made sure that RP arranged with the dream dancers and his pilots that Shebat's welcome to Acheron would be warm, and extensive. The visitors' suite in the guildhall was readied, the guildmaster *pro tem* informed that the Draconis consul, Shebat Kerrion, D.P.G. 17 (seventeenth rated pilot of the Draconis arm of the pilotry guild), might well be taking up residence for an undetermined stay.

All this was done without a vocalization, while Hooker glowered and Jesse Thorne and Cluny Pope were shown such wonders as the *Danae*'s water shower and her control room's visual displays of the cosmos in multiple spectra, and *Danae* set off imperceptibly toward Acheron.

Only once was this rule of silence for safety's sake broken, and this because RP yet smarted under Chaeron's dictatorial deployment of the talents of his cruiser.

"Shebat will not stay with you?" Rafe disbelieved, cattiness of voice augmenting his feline eyes so that invisible whiskers seemed to twitch on his clean-shaven cheeks.

"We'll see, I'm sure. Let's give her the option. Now *you* give me line-in to that log copy." They were standing at *Danae*'s helm, Penrose by his seat and Chaeron with one knee on the copilot's couch. Colored light played on

Penrose's face from his ready boards, a timely mask. He stabbed about him, causing the copilot's panels to come to life, then bowed from his seat, exaggeratedly: "She's a-ready, Massa," and Chaeron wanted to smooth his taunts away, or slap them gone, and knew not which.

He sighed, slipped down into the padded seat. "Rafe, I'll see you in the guildhall at dinner, no matter what."

"I'll be busy." Shebat and Cluny Pope could be heard, giggling from the aft station in the following pause.

"Lords of Cosmic Jest forgive me, I'll bite: busy with what?"

"With the drubbing I'm going to take for getting—for *stealing*—you that log copy before my guildmaster's even seen it! Anybody finds out I helped the *Marada* extort promises of aid out of you in exchange for it, I'll be drummed out of the service—"

"Come now, Raphael. You don't believe that."

Penrose made a snapping sound with his tongue, let his breath out. "No, I suppose I don't believe that. But I'd *like* to believe it. It's hard being first bitch of a straw guildhouse—"

"Baldy, again? I told you, I'll try. You wouldn't want a real guildmaster in there right now, slapping your wrist twice weekly. You won't have this *pro tem* long, assuming I *can* extricate the guildmaster of your choice from jail."

Penrose tried not to look mollified, but the "W" between his brows softened, his jaws relaxed. "I don't like it," he mumbled, weakly, with the look of one who knows he's lost, but must struggle on for propriety's sake.

Please, dear friend, just a little more patience, Chaeron wanted to say, but could not. He turned to the front monitors, leaned back in the couch, and with eyes closed, reviewed the log copy Danae had received from the *Marada,* presently pacing the Danae into Acheron at Shebat's request.

Six hours later, he was sitting in his office, late for dinner, and about to face his wife where whatever was wished might be said without qualm.

He had not spoken directly with her since their argument before her damnable cave. Only once since her return from Draconis—when his surveillance of her position indicated approaching danger in the form of massed Orrefors rebels and he had made use of the *Danae* and the *Marada* to contact her, who as yet had no intelligence keys entered into his matrices—had they spoken other than through intermediaries.

She had not seen fit to contact him' he had not moved to get in touch with her. A fine game for spoiled children. It had almost gotten her killed. If she had had her data pool code-ins, he would not have had to link two cruisers to alert her to danger, and need not have brought Raphael's wrath upon his head when he most needed cease-fires on all fronts. So he told her, while she paced off his midnight-and-silver office and stroked the dark, old wood of his desk and fussed with her low-cut, gold dinner dress (which betrayed a thickening waist) until he paused, hoping she would swoop down and take the olive branch in its thicket of rebuke, and at last she looked him in the eye.

"How dare you invade my dream dance?" Straight as a plumb line she sat down opposite his desk. He swiveled his chair and watched her chin lift and her lip plump out in righteous indignation.

"I thought I just apologized for that."

"Did you? I did not hear it, I must confess."

He thought, *There must be some simple way to handle this. I don't want to fight with her.* The words waiting to hop out of his mouth seemed unlikely to bed hostilities, yet no better ones would come. He held firm, watching her sit in her chair, pleased that she was there in one condemnatory piece, until she was forced to speak in the void. "As for my getting killed, would it so terribly bother you? You would regain your coveted spot as heir apparent."

"Ah, but even then I could not be Draconis consul, the way things are. So—" he shrugged, found a smile, donned it for a transistory instant, put it by; from his desk he took a folded sheet of paper, looked at it, fed it into a slot "—if you will now chose three key codes at random and scramble them however you choose," he leaned over and handed her another, smaller piece of paper, taken from his jacket's inside pocket, "adding some symbol of your own choice to replace the missing digit, then image it, you will not have to endure my knowing your numbers."

She sat with the sheet of paper, forming the sequences she was memorizing with her lips. When she raised her head and handed back the list, she said, "Top, third, and last. 'S.' Unscrambled. I know we'll need these others. And that I can't keep them secret from you. What are you doing here, building a new Lorelie? No wonder the bills of lading were voluminous." She shook her head, and her jet curls danced. At least the mourning band was gone from her brow.

"Did you say 'we,' again? May I assume that my apology is accepted? I will behave like an adult if you will. . . . It would be prudent of you to take a secondary set of keys from me."

"All right," she whispered, and rubbed her eyes, her voice more husky than usual.

When she had repeated to him the intelligence keys he had reserved for her, he heaved a heartfelt sigh, and stretched in his seat. "Are you hungry? The rest can be saved for after dinner. I fear we are late, but the Draconis consul's pleasure is ours . . . ?"

He was half out of his seat to assist her when she said sharply, "Say whatever it is you are saving. There will be no better time."

"Any time would be better." He came around the desk and sat upon it, fingering one silver stallion's striking forefoot. "But this will do. Really, I would have preferred to wine you, dine you, make love to you and answer what questions I could in that way. However: *Are* you *enciente?* I do have a right to know."

"What?" She knew what he meant; her fists balled; her pupils swallowed the gray about them.

"Pregnant, my dear. With child. The *Marada* thinks that you are."

"I don't know. I think so." It was too small a voice, too guarded, too abrupt a departure from the aggressive consular pose she had been keeping.

"You . . . don't . . . know? If my calculations are not in error—and I assure you they are not—it has been three months since our tryst on the floor of that cave.

Now, I am aware, as I know you are, that there are certain signs, difficult to misread—"

"But misreadable. I have been under some strain."

"So have we all. Shebat, if you even suspected you were with child, why in all the living hells we make for ourselves did you log so many sponge-hours? What possible importance could David Spry's corpse be when compared to a child's life? Do you want to ruin us both, only me, or simply the entire house of Kerrion? All we need is to have our child born deformed, or autistic like Marada's first, or even stillborn. If not for your unwillingness even to *find out* if you are pregnant, I might be able to say 'son' instead of referring to this potential offspring as one of indeterminate gender. Do you understand me?" His anger was slipping through, sliding under the crack of the door he had slammed upon it. He ground his teeth and dug his fingers into the mahogany of his desk. "If you *are* pregnant, and three months along, it is too late to assure us a son by any of the accepted methods. Even hormone treatments will not avail: it is too risky. Earlier, it would have been—"

Shebat stood up, hands behind her back. "What makes you think I want a son? Or that I want to know beforehand what sex my child will be, if there is one? Maybe I've been eating too much. I don't know. I'm tired a lot, and I—

"How do you know what the *Marada* thinks? You stay away from my cruiser! I've seen for myself what you've done with *Danae*. Poor Raphael, he must be heartsick. Answer me!"

Sliding off the desk, he took a step toward her, so that they were inches apart. He took her by the elbows, letting his hands slide up her arms, reach her throat, her chin, tilt her head up until he could kiss her. He could think of nothing else to do, and nothing more dangerous. The affront he feared stiffened her, but he ignored it, and tried to deepen the tremor he could feel in her knotted back.

When he let her go, confusion had replaced hostility, distrust was softened by genetics' wisdom. She did not back away, but leaned against him with her head on his chest.

He risked it all then: "I took a log copy from the *Marada*. I would have had it tomorrow, anyway. I was too worried about you to wait. If you are pregnant, you must promise me you will not continue to function as a sponge-pilot while carrying our child. It is dangerous for you both." This he had rehearsed, a dozen, a hundred times. He held her hands while he said it, looked earnestly into her eyes as he had meant to.

Her reaction, for once, was what he had hoped for: "I will not give the *Marada* up, not my option to pilot him, nor my scheduled flights. No part of it. I don't care if I am 'with child' or not. I don't like children, they smell and they're ugly and they take up too much time. If you want one, and I've got one,"—she patted her belly—"then find another place for it to grow. If you don't, then we'll do the sensible thing. *Slate?*"

"Slate." She, too, must have thought this thing through, he reflected, and kissed the top of her head with such fervent relief that he could not stop with one kiss, or keep them chaste.

Even that did not offend her, who of late seemed offended by everything.

With some chagrin, he escorted her to a dinner he had never really believed she would attend, and dealt with Rafe's coldness gratefully: open discord would have been disastrous. Somewhere around midmeal, he sent up a silent prayer of thanks to Chance that those who loved him did not hate each other more than that, and those upon whom he counted, had, in the clinch, turned out to be people upon whom one could afford to count.

It was half an evening later, and many wines beyond, that an irascible fortune turned blighting breath on the proceedings at this table: talk turned to Draconis, to the Draconis pilotry guild, and to Marada Seleucus Kerrion.

Shebat, who never drank, but tonight had matched Rafe glass for glass, was tripping over her tongue, but not so much so that she did not manage to mention that the consul general had offered to loan her—and Acheron—all the money they would need.

Chaeron would have handled it more delicately. Chaeron had been hoping to have a moment to do so.

But Penrose had edited the log transcript, and he was not feeling generous, or delicate:

"What are you going to put up for security, your cruiser?" sneered Rafe. "*All* our cruisers?"

Chaeron, debating between murder and a hurried leave-taking, did neither, but sat the matter out, until the two began trading in information he could not afford to have widely spread.

So in front of the Acheron pilotry guild and whomsoever else in the dark, spacious guildhall had contrived to spy upon them, it was necessary to have Tempest escort the two people he cared most in the world about to disparate quarters under close surveillance.

While he was sitting there among the shipwrights and bitches, between two empty chairs in that best-of-all possible guildhalls he had built for RP (yes, for Penrose even more than as a monument and reaffirmation of his proclaimed status as champion of pilots' rights and cruisers' rights), it occurred to him that Chance had just made him an offer which could salve the majority of his most pressing irritations—if he were audacious enough to snatch the opportunity.

In the muraled, linened dining hall, he grinned broadly—his most private expression, reserved for personal triumphs and items of accomplishment never meant to be known beyond his own skull. Shaking his head, he scratched ruminatively behind one ear, a gesture picked up from his pilot. He snorted softly, to chase the notion away: No, he could not do that—could he? Did he care so much about the welfare of some unborn infant, so little for his relationship with his wife? Or—he slid down in his seat, toying with a vermeil fork, stabbing it into the spotless tablecloth—would he be remiss not to dare it, for all their sakes? Was it not, primarily, his love for Shebat which had brought the idea to mind? Wouldn't he be saving her endless agonizing, she who was too young and too sorely pressed and—face this, also—too confused at the moment to make any decision with ease?

A presence invaded his reverie: the guildmaster *pro tem,* more bowed under the weight of his labors and the hopelessness of his task—no one could control pilots whom pilots did not revere, wished him a good evening. Chaeron raised a hand from the table, waved it, nodded. The man, understanding, drifted away.

Acheron's proconsul let out a long, controlled breath through his nose, forcing his concerns into line like a point leader ordering troops. Did he not have need of Shebat, her expertise and her rank, to take the dream dancers and the very earth in hand while he wrestled with two hundred and one additional burdens lumped together as the Orrefors acquisition? and matters of family, clamoring louder by the hour for his attention? Wasn't his mother imperiled by his psychotic half brother, and all the mighty Kerrion consulate as well? He had meant to send a gift to his brother's newborn son, resting content in Lorelie: the first cruiser built wholly in Acheron.

He activated his data link, gave that order, and paused. On the brink of the unthinkable, he chuckled, squeezed his eyes shut, and stepped boldly out into irredeemable action: he ordered a hospital room prepared for Shebat, rousted a team of specialists from their recreations, gave himself clearances for a breeding permit, and arranged for an artificial womb.

Then he got up and made his goodbyes and headed off toward the suite to which his inebriated wife had been escorted.

Shebat Alexandra Kerrion awoke from a red dream into a white world full of pain. Her head ached and her vision pinwheeled and her loins burned like hellfire. There was a black splotch inhabiting her void of whiteness, hovering near, but she had no time for it. She rushed around her recollection-strewn mind, groggily reclaiming this bit of memory or that: she recalled a bright light, and the flare of parapentothal burning its way up to her shoulder, leaping incendiarily into her brain. She recalled her fight to remain conscious, too stupefied to hide the effort, so that she just kept on counting and counting, and at length heard the officiating doctor order up a second dose; that was why her arm pulsed so, why her fingers were stiff with swelling. She recalled, too, asking "Is it human? Just tell me! I was so long in sponge," and the confounded reply, courteous but troubled that she could speak at all: "It's fine, just fine, Consul."

She tried to recollect when she had authorized this travesty which her body decried. *Lost,* sobbed her flesh. *Taken,* howled her soul. *Failed,* accused her genes. She could not argue with any of that.

"Chaeron?" she wondered, intending a denunciation but managing only a thick, throaty whisper.

"Right here," a voice with a hand attached rumbled; the hand clutched her swollen left; she winced.

"What happened?"

"You don't remember? Our discussion, our decision to go ahead?" She could see his face, through dispersing mist like smoke, come near. "If you were pregnant, to delay no longer, but proceed as ready? You were and we did."

Something was wrong in his face; it was too composed, too perfectly compassionate. "You'll be fine in an hour or so, I'm told; just a little sore."

"My head hurts and when I turn it, the world spins about much later."

"That, my dear, is called a hangover. One must reap one's rewards. And speaking of rewards, aren't you curious about our offspring?"

"No," she husked, but tears ran down her cheeks. She cast off his grip to strike them away. Then: "You did not simply abort it, then? It feels as if—"

"Well, you've lost something, biologically. Don't let it worry you. A little depression is *de rigueur* with these things. And it's a boy—human," he grinned, "and so far as medical opinion can opine, preeminently normal. Congratulations!"

"Keep them," she sniffled, "for yourself." She struggled to sit up without groaning. Solicitous, he assisted her. She did not like the look of fatherhood on him; that he should be so elated while she hurt so completely was intolerable. "And it," she hazarded, "it has a name?"

He frowned at her tone, but moved from the drawn-up chair to sit by her hip on the bed. "I was waiting for you, for that. I thought—"

"Cassander, then," she ordained.

His frown deepened; as of old, he plowed it up into his

mane with a spread hand. "Cassander *Alexander?* You have the right—"

"And you are overweening." Rage buoyed her; she sat straight and drew her legs toward her chest, gasped in concert with a series of agitated beeps from a monitor above her head, sat at last with her knees half-flexed and yellow pulses from the screen behind her gilding her curls. "Heir apparent or no, I will not contend with Marada for the consul generalship. Nor set up my son to vie with his."

Chaeron toyed with the red piping on his black sleeve. "It is just a name. Give it to him and let the future decide itself. I can bear with 'Cassander' if *you* offer me an Alexander. Agreed? Cassander Alexander Kerrion?"

"I detest you. Can you never, ever, do anything without an eye to advantage?"

"Why should I want to?"

"Chaeron, let us change the subject."

"I was hoping you would say that. I have to talk to you seriously." Out came the pocket-scrambler, to perch upon the sheets.

"Aren't those illegal?"

"Sometimes, in some people's hands. Right here, now, in mine: no. I want to warn you, first off, about the staff. All officials, no matter how beguiling, who were assigned to Stump before the takeover—like Hooker—or who came in with the Kerrion administrative team but before my arrival here, are suspect. We have a surfeit of difficulties, accidents and mistakes and malfunctions of the sort you were plagued with in Lorelie when my mother and you were not getting along. Need I say more on that?"

"No," she replied scornfully, her lip curled in indictment of ubiquitous Kerrion intrigues. "I will be careful." It came out a threat.

"Then, next matter: I want to talk with you about your meeting with Marada, about the log entries."

"I think Raphael has made your position clear."

"Let us not snipe. Rafe is correct, it would be madness worthy of Marada himself for us to borrow. We can suffer no liens upon our holdings. We'll be able to issue stock of our own, soon enough, and I will pay you back every bit of personal funds you have donated to this cause, and more."

"Aren't you afraid of my owning a part of your little empire?"

He sighed. "Shall I come back when you are feeling better? No? Then, on the subject of empires, what colors do you favor? It is not every day one creates a consular house."

"Colors?"

He regarded her, patrician and grave.

"Colors: livery, crest, device styles, all of that."

"You *are* jesting. Dynastic humor come from new fatherhood. How can you . . . ? I don't believe this!"

"Oh, I can, the probability models tell us. *With* your help, and free of liens, leaks, and security breakdowns. Security compromises now would depotentiate us as surely as I depotentiated those Orrefors rebels."

"I wanted to talk to you about that—"

"And I, you. I assure you we shall, but later . . ."

"How are Thorne and Cluny Pope getting along?" she interrupted.

"As well as Hooker and Bitsy Mistral can ensure, I imagine. You and these proceedings rather took precedence in my mind. Shebat, when you leave here, which you can when you will, come stay in the consulate with me. All is prepared."

"I will billet on my ship."

He winced. "Well, that is preferable to the guildhall. But consider: we'll never work these matters out if we don't give living together a try. What's in the log, what you said of me in your conversation with my brother is not exactly true, and if I drove you into the arms of a lunatic by making you think that I required some degree of sexual expertise from you, then I am truly sorry. Any man will tell you that if an apprenticeship is called for, he himself will gladly serve as instructor. And if you think my straits . . . *ours* . . . so dire that you need sell your charms to curry favor with my enemy, then you are twice mistaken. And if you thought, even for a moment—now, let me finish—that my brother the *arbiter* would be so impassioned by your proposal that he would agree to engage in an act of salacious bribery while being monitored by a sponge-cruiser, you have a long way to go to deserve the name 'Kerrion.'"

"Now may I speak? Yes? In order, then husband: I will trade you *my* penchant for your half brother for *yours* for Rafe Penrose. I will never live in with you as long as you are two . . . paramours!"

"It has been a long time since there was anything physical between RP and me."

"And you want to give our son the middle name 'Alexander' merely to preserve the family tradition, right? Both statements are equally unbelievable." Chin high, pout quivering, she derided him.

"Why do these things matter so much to you?"

"I might ask you the same. When we were wed you suggested that I could initiate any relationship I chose with Marada, providing decorum be preserved. We have an agreement, a good Kerrion arrangement allowing us both the freedom of diverse beds. I am not supposed to notice your entanglements, yet whenever I even look at a man you are quick to forbid me him. Jesse Thorne—"

"Dear Lords, let's not get into that. A leather-clad barbarian? Such an assignation hardly preserves decorum. I made a mistake with this; it is too soon and you are not thinking clearly."

"I am fine," she sniffed, white-skinned, purple-lipped, and flush-cheeked.

"Shebat, let us try some new business. You were not pleased with my handling of our first Earthly emergency. Hear this proposal, the only alternative to which is an end to this limited war and the extermination of every rebel stronghold from orbit, no matter how many innocents die in the implementation of that directive."

She leaned forward, forgetful of her body, which made her groan softly.

"At last, I have your attention. Take your dream dancers, who have waited over a month for you to arrive, and train them however you like; put them down on the planet and tame it. I have little attention to spare for guerrilla warfare. March fifteenth is census day in New Chaeronea. I've a celebration scheduled for then with many Consortium dignitaries invited. By that date I want a calm and peaceful appearance, in my northeast western hemisphere test site, at least. Refrain from aiding me as you previously promised, and bear the consequences. Let Spry's remains and long sponge-journeys go, for the nonce, and do what needs to be done here, freeing me to deal with my not inconsiderable problems in the areas of cruiser industrialization, interconsular politics, and my star-crossed family. Agreed?"

She saw in him a tinge of desperation overshadowed by determination; she saw in him Parma Alexander Kerrion's feral spirit, the old tiger's tail lashing behind his civilized facade. "Will we end up like your mother and father, a working unit with no passion other than power, tolerating each other by dint of acclimatization, looking ever elsewhere for comfort, and to one another only for strategy and power-bloc votes?"

"It is to be hoped that we will establish at least that between us. Anything less in a consular marriage preordains destruction; anything more is on the order of dividends. We have an heir; we will likely have something for him to inherit. To that end I, at least, intend to labor. What say you?"

"Can I see him?" said a tiny, trebling squeak of a voice she hardly recognized as hers.

Her husband shrugged, unwound from the bed, put his hand out to her. "There is precious little to see. But I'll go with you . . . ?"

Her nod had a sob in it, half-swallowed, that she hoped he thought came from the trial of swinging her legs out over the edge of the bed.

Cluny Pope had brought a sloe-eyed youth to Jesse Thorne, the young scout bursting with pride. Bitsy Mistral seemed to Jesse too smooth and fey, not at all the sort of companion to wax prideful about, at first glance.

In the Earth town, things had been easier to compass than what Thorne had seen previously, but full of strangeness, nonetheless. This youth Mistral was no less problematical than their entire venture beyond heaven. Halfway through the first day, Thorne had begun to regret his hubris. Now he wanted only to set his feet upon solid earth and look up at a sky which was not fascimile beyond a horizon which curved reasonably downward, not up. Bringing his charge home yet ignorant of the likes of Bitsy Mistral was fast becoming a pressing concern.

There was nothing wrong with the youth's behavior, save that Cluny treasured his company and spoke of little else. Finally, Thorne had taken a hand, suggesting that it might be best if he met Cluny's new friend.

"Friend? We have an oath, to the death, with honor!"

"Wonderful. Now go fetch him."

"He will be glad to meet you, he has asked me much about you."

Jesse Thorne's nose itched high up inside, where it always itched when traps and treachery were abroad. He just did not have the heart to condemn someone without a hearing, especially when that someone was the single acquaintance young Pope had found to shield him from the horror of all this strangeness and flouted magic.

Though the cabin in which he sat had a realistic dirt-floor and crudely trimmed log walls, it also had a pottery pot which at the touch of a gleaming handle whisked excrement Jesse knew-not-whither, and a "shower" and a magic box which talked to him when he wished it, and was silent when he wished that. It could send messages and receive them, and imitate voices he had come to know. He could have any food he desired without hunting or trading, and money seemed no part of life here where everything one surveyed was desired, desirable, and completely controlled. The air was neuter, telling him nothing; the food was long-removed from life; the Earth-towners were polite and self-effacing, most obsequious, offering every service a nobleman could find on his own faraway world, and many forbidden to those of conscience. Still, no thing that man's ingenuity can envision is more awful than the one thing he cannot: death. And those dalliances Cluny was doubtless learning where to find from Bitsy Mistral were no different than those he might already have indulged in while living at ease in his father's hold: drugs and drinks and man's use of his fellow describe the arena in which depredations can be perpetrated, but the perpetrator is always responsible.

It was just that he had been given the boy to show him

other, more fitting responsibilities. Wealth is no easy tutor, even in green-hilled Troy.

So when Cluny brought the scarlet-and-teal-clad youth with his perfect skin and shining boots and bebaubled wrists into the cabin, Jesse Thorne had already decided to make the best of it.

Young Cluny's twice-broken nose was sheened with sweat, and his coarse black hair arrayed in some unsuitable enchanter's fashion, pushed back from his low forehead and curled around his large, pointed ears. He, too, wore scarves and high, shiny boots and a cloak with a bating eagle over seven stars embroidered on its back. From the fit of them and the cut of them he knew they belonged to the other boy before Cluny crowed, "Look what Mistral gave me," turning proudly, anxious to share his delight.

"Very fitting, I hope." He unfolded himself from a claw-footed settee and strode forward, extending his hand to the slight, long-lashed voluptuary who came barely to his shoulder, and felt ashamed. This boy was sixteen, at best, and condemned before any fact of wrongdoing. But Thorne's nose itched furiously and the hand he took in his was soft like a woman's, with glistening, perfect nails.

"Go on, Go on," Cluny hissed, pushing the other closer when the youth, staring up at him, hung back. "Say it, or I'll say it for you."

Then Mistral gave a clumsy militia greeting, and once that was done: "I'm so glad to meet you, Commander Thorne. Cluny's told me so much about you. I'm a dream dancer, like Shebat—"

"Oh, yes?" Thorne growled, crossing his arms. *"Like Shebat?"*

"Yes," the youth with velvet voice rushed on. "And Cluny thought, I mean . . . I thought . . . You see, if you could help me learn about the Earth. . . . That's where we're going, you know, to Earth, when Shebat's ready. And that's what we're working on, to *get* ready—learning Earthish customs, getting some sense of Earthish reactions to modern ways. Slate? It's just ever so fortuitous that you two came up, right now. What you like about

Acheron, what you don't like, what reassures you and what scares you—all of these things I need to know! I'll be very grateful." His luminous brown eyes met Thorne's without fear, but with something: innuendo, promise? "And helpful, however I may be, in exchange for anything you can tell me. I know many things about Acheron, I've been here since its opening. . . ."

"I imagine you do. I will tell you something: I am not 'scared,' as you put it." The Consulese Cluny and he had learned through magical earmuffs was accented differently than what his mother had taught him; he was careful at all times to speak it as these folk spoke it. "Tell *me* something: how long has it been since Acheron's opening?"

"More than a month we have been waiting here for Shebat." A tinge of resentment was unmistakable, this time, in the boy's speaking of the oracle's name.

"And where were you before that?"

"Space-end." Grim, taut words, full of unwanted wisdom.

"That's a prison, sir," interjected Cluny, eyes rivaling the effeminate youth's in size. "He was banished but Chaeron Kerrion saved him, got him paroled. He's told me all about the horrors—"

"That's enough, Cluny. Is that so, did the proconsul take a hand in your case?"

"Not just me, sir, all the dream dancers that're here, are here because of his munificence."

"His what?" demanded Pope.

"Generosity," Thorne snapped, in their own tongue, before Mistral could answer. Then, in Consulese: "You hold him to be a good man?"

"The best. I am his valet." Pride puffed out a scanty chest.

"And is he kind to you?"

"Wonderfully kind, sir. When he's there."

"What do you do for him?" Thorne could not help it, and the youth knew exactly what he had been asked. He blinked at the insult, coming unexpectedly, and stepped back a pace. A silence stretched between them while Cluny Pope looked from one to the other, uncomprehending.

At last the youth murmured, "He needs someone. I take care of him, see that he eats. He forgets, a lot. He's got terrible problems here. The Orrefors, the old Stump dwellers, don't—well, some hate him for resettling them, and some hate him because he's not Orrefors (I know *you* are, and you'll have to excuse me if I'm bold), and most who don't hate him, don't like him. You see, it's—"

"I see. I thank you for the information, and for providing Cluny with a friendly guide and access to your expertise. Now, if you two have something to do . . . ?"

When the boys had gone, Jesse Thorne stood a long time at the cabin's window, whose glass was unrippled, unflawed, looking out at Acheron, but seeing Earth, all of which was once (if the boy Mistral could be trusted) an Orrefors possession. He still had to find out what a dream dancer was, if it meant something more than oracular talent, but the rest was clear to him. Also clear to him was the fact that magic was as simple and accessible a skill as spear-point chipping or horse-breaking, and that, although he had spent his life dodging the reality of his Orrefors blood and expiating the sin of it whenever and wherever he could, here there was no sin by blood and curse by magic, only tools, and men with no compunction about using them. Too, he noted that some of those tools were human, like the little spy Bitsy Mistral.

Spitting an oath, he sat down by the enchanted box with its lights of many colors and did what he had been loath to do until then: studied it, and studied with it, and studied what its capabilities might mean on a scale his mind had never thought to measure before.

When the false dusk came to this facsimile of a land, he was still at it. Long into the facade of night he stayed at it, so that he missed a meal, and hardly noticed Cluny when he came staggering through bleary-eyed and crashed into the bedroom. Soon there followed the sounds of a stomach giving up its contents. This, too, Thorne ignored.

When in a pale, premeditated dawn his stomach growled in protest, he put down his head on the console, feebly pressed a button called "hold" which marked his place in *The Consortium: A Short History of Consular Families* and fell instantly to sleep, dreaming that he ate a whole chicken turned for two hours on a spit, basted with honey and stuffed with bread and rice and sage.

Shebat Kerrion paced the *Marada*'s light-spangled helm, her fists balled, eyes red and lips puffy. "We have got to find out if 'passing by unnoticed' works, *Marada*. I need to know."

For three days, the *Marada*'s outboard had brooded within his hull, truculent, discontent. It was not her biological problem (which Chaeron Kerrion had remedied, true to his promise) which was distressing Shebat. There was no longer any sign of abnormality; even the sanctity of her seals had been reestablished.

Nor was it his disclosure of that promise, given by the proconsul to the cruiser in exchange for all data relevant to Shebat's journey to Draconis and beyond, which was troubling her. When first she had boarded him, accusatory, betrayed, the *Marada* had explained that his overriding concern for her had prompted him to enlist the aid of her husband (who, the *Marada* knew through the *Danae,* shared his determination that Shebat's equilibrium be restored on every front). And since the pact between them had been honored, its particulars fulfilled to the letter, Shebat restored to physical normalcy and fast regaining her acuity, the *Marada* took pains to point out, it could be safely assumed that the cruiser's apprehension of the situation was unflawed: the proconsul Chaeron Ptolemy Kerrion did indeed have Shebat's best interests at heart. As he had proved repeatedly to be a friend to cruisers, so Shebat could rest easily under his protection.

Upon hearing this rational assessment of her husband and their union, the *Marada*'s beloved outboard had broken down in tears.

Only an irritable whirring followed by two sharp clicks betrayed the cruiser's exasperation: it was obviously not yet time to broach sensitive subjects requiring delicate handling to the young woman who was weeping freely upon the emerald-platinum tracer-bracelet which Chaeron had given her as a betrothal gift and which had hung, abandoned, from a toggle on one of the *Marada*'s forward consoles since Shebat had entered Earth space.

For the next two days, she had moped about him, bracelet clasped to her waist, her chemistries awry.

On the third day she had awaked, smiling grimly, and, without removing the tracer, debarked.

The cruiser had followed her movements. Enlisting as subsurveillants every mechanical eye and ear in Acheron which Shebat's top-clearance intelligence keys permitted him to encircuit, he traced her around the skywall to Chaeron's five-sided consulate, and within.

When she proceeded, not to the proconsul's offices, but to his residence, the *Marada* found that only the secondary group of matrix keys would suffice to access him beyond its tall, burnished doors. Within the proconsul's apartments, only his own data net took note of all that occurred. Through it, the *Marada* did, also.

So it was that the *Marada,* like some sly voyeur, witnessed a confrontation the significance of which was beyond his ability to decipher.

Seeing it was not living it, and although the *Marada* acquired continual readouts of Shebat's heart rate and endorphin balance, he could not feel with fragile flesh the impact of betrayal. Revelation, disappointment, disenfranchisement, disgust: these were only abstracts to the cruiser, though he dared so much as to cock a key-coded ear to what was formulated for speech but held back unsaid by a heartbroken girl to the only occupant of the proconsul's suite, once she had stripped off her clothes before the running shower's steamed glass door and opened it, smiling sensually, to join him who she thought to be her husband, but who was, instead, Bitsy Mistral, long ago known to Shebat in Draconis' level seven when he had been doorkeeper and apprentice in the very troupe from whom Shebat learned the art of dreams.

Mortified, she had fled, wordless, clothing in hand.

Straightaway, she had hastened to the slipbay, where the *Marada*'s ports were open for her.

But once within, the cruiser noted that the sting of rejection, the poison of jealousy and supplantation had sped to her heart, paralyzing every thought but one: revenge.

Cautiously, the cruiser disengaged from data pool and proconsular matrices; what was revealed to one source was not held back from its correlates; he wanted no record of such passions as wracked Shebat.

Then she had said to him, after tugging the bracelet from her wrist and flinging it across his control room's length, "The time has come for us to find out whether I am as mad as your namesake. You will monitor me, and I will attempt to 'pass by unnoticed,' and you will tell me true if you can track me, or not. I could have used it, when the Orrefors descended upon my cave; I could have used it often, before that. But I promised him that I would not, and then I began to believe as he believes, that I *could* not, that spells are only self-delusion and Kerrion technologies could not be thwarted by such a flimsy weapon as human will. But now, I bow to his wishes no longer. I will 'pass by unnoticed,' out of his life, never to return. You and I, *Marada,* are going back to the Pegasus colonies. But first, one small digression for the sake of evening the score."

The *Marada* had objected that no hurried experiment carried out by so biased a source as himself could be conclusive. Then had she replied, "We have *got* to find out if 'passing by unnoticed' works, *Marada,*" and winked out of being as completely as a blown LED.

More worrisome than the apparent disappearance of his outboard from physical, real-time space was her disembodied announcement, as a hand he could not see in any mode from infrared to gravitational activated his outer locks, that he should not fret over her, but make ready to debark first for Earth and then Pegasus. She would be back, she promised, as soon as possible. If something urgent arose that demanded her attention, the cruiser might seek her on their private hailing frequency.

Where was she going? the *Marada* had to ask.

"To the dream dancers, first. And then to Jesse Thorne's." She popped back into view, biting her lip, her gray eyes hot like molten metal. "And never mind about logging out for Pegasus. I have run away from what I would not see for the last time."

While the cruiser pondered the conundrum of how Shebat managed to alter the reflectivity ratios of not only her body but the clothing upon it, so that all questing waveforms passed through the space that she occupied uninterrupted, as if nothing at all were where she indubitably still was, Shebat Kerrion sought the twin balms of work and vengeance.

She spent five hours on level forty with ninety-odd hastily gathered dream dancers, every one of them neutered and convicts and remembering that she alone among dream dancers had escaped level seven on that awful night during Parma's administration when thenconsul Chaeron's cordon had closed in upon their illegality, damning them to space-end.

She found it necessary to remind them that they would be there yet, but for the intercession of the Acheron proconsul at her behest.

She taught them three dreams, in that time, and ordered them to create several more, with similar themes. "Propaganda," one cried. "Concerted," she agreed. She was grateful that the dancer Lauren was not among those present, that her old troupe mistress, the piebald Harmony, had declined the proconsul's offer in favor of awaiting Softa's ghost at space-end. She sat out tense moments in which the troupe leaders argued over the propriety of putting dream dances to such blatantly political use, but a friend she had not known she possessed—one of her former instructors: still thin-faced, still claw-nosed, still called Rajah—came to her defense in the name of pragmatism, and she left them with orders to be ready to leave for Earth in a week's time.

None of it salved her. Bending a hundred dream dancers to her will today, to pursue some elusive endpoint way off beyond tomorrow, did not make the sting of yesterday's treachery less galling. Were she consul general of Kerrion space, it would not have helped. Even while Chaeron had been winning her trust in good Kerrion fashion, telling her lies she wanted to hear and begging her to take up residence with him in a full partnership, he had had that smug-faced catamite waiting in his bed. She was not fooled. *Chaeron, you will find it harder to receive than to give,* she promised a mental picture of him, its mocking smirk already melting into a weary frown.

Then, taking leave of the dream dancers, she ordered her waiting lorry to the Earth town. Slipping down in its padded interior, she closed her burning eyes.

He had not even had the courage to admit his lechery. Philanderer. Sybarite. Everything his enemies said about him was true. He had known this would happen, but been content to let Mistral make his own introduction. "Better than words, I suppose," she spoke aloud, then had to answer the driver beyond the lorry's smoked glass partition, "Never mind. Sponge pilots talk to themselves; it is an occupational hazard."

At the Earth town's main and dusty street, she dismissed the lorry and its driver, ordering an automated one through a low-clearance channel for an hour hence.

She explored the Earth town, its replica-taverns, its noble's keeps, its sandpit gaming houses and its bazaars where beasts of burden of every sort could be rented or bought.

She drank a little, she ate a little, and when the auto-lorry arrived she pushed coins into its pay privacy-slot, programmed it for a random destination and passenger discharge upon arrival, climbed back out while sub-vocalizing the spell called passing by unnoticed, and slammed shut the black door, sticking out an invisible tongue at its bating-eagle emblem blazoned in red.

A disembodied giggle could be heard as the low-slung lorry purred away.

She wandered Earthish streets until she came upon a lane with a manor house and freehold shacks as might be found in New York's Troy.

She was in no hurry; the Greenwich Mean Sunset shunted up from Earth was just beginning. Chaeron's innovation did not awe her, though most Earth-towners ambled out to watch the novelty of sundowns which varied daily according to nature's whim, not computer's simulation.

He had been moved by the spectacle while planetside, she remembered; he had made a point of telling her so.

She watched it, leaning against the fieldstone porch of Jesse Thorne's abode, until a creaking door opened. And while blond and birdlike Hooker, making his exit, lingered on the walk talking to Thorne, she slipped around Chaeron's cultural attaché, then under Thorne's arm, outstretched stiff to the farther doorpost. She was in!

Her heart pounded, breath sawed loudly. She backed

into a corner where neither could be heard. She looked around, at a hearth as tall as she and candles belied by a ready console with lit teaching screen glowing green. Austere and modest, there was no sign here of the compromising largess she had expected Chaeron to foist upon the ground-dwelling Orrefors heir.

And no sign of his ward, young Cluny Pope. Shebat nodded to herself, well pleased. The door closed; Jesse Thorne leaned against it, latched it with questing fingers, and crossed the packed dirt to the console behind which Shebat clung to her corner, his big head cocked on his short neck, squinting everywhere. Before the console he paused; snarled, or chuckled (Shebat could not tell which); pushed back the stuffed chair with his foot, and threw himself down into it. With the heel of his boot he depressed the "run" stud on his console, and Shebat, forgetful of all else once the screen had begun rolling its contents upward, leaned close to read along over his shoulder.

Was it a curl of hers that brushed the crown of his head? Or the simple matter of someone peering over his shoulder? He rubbed his nose furiously, left off, and with blurring speed grabbed Shebat by the hair.

This far ahead, she had not thought. She was caught entirely unprepared, but not without resorts: she refused to utter even a gasp of pain, letting herself be dragged by the hair into Thorne's lap (to the sound of his confused exclamation over what he could feel but could not see), one of her hands going to his mouth to silence him and the other killing the power to the terminal (and, she hoped, everything else in the hastily prepared log cabin).

Divesting herself of the spell's cloak took only an instant, but the last thing a monitor would have seen (assuming her emergency shutdown had taken everything, and not simply the teacher, off-line) was Thorne struggling with nothing whatsoever.

Well, she had wanted to be discovered. The look upon her quarry's face (what she could see of it around her cautionary hand) was worth something more than being found out a trifle earlier than she had planned.

She felt the quick, deep breathing of the man on whose lap she sprawled.

"Kerrion technologies?" he asked hoarsely, after she took her hand away.

"Enchantment," she corrected.

"I am not so gullible, anymore. You and yours have seen to that."

But he was wrong; she found him consummately gullible, malleable and willing, then suitably surprised and indignant when they were interrupted by Tempest and a half-dozen black-and-reds with screeching lorries and emergency-flashers and antiterrorist paraphernalia, ready to rescue their guest from whatever insidious force had put his computer down.

Shebat did not return to the *Marada* that day; her hours were full of Chaeron's recriminations and the aftermath of human spite. Thus the *Marada* was unable to bring before Shebat those items of concern he felt to be pressing. Nor could he approach her the next day, while she lingered in top-security conference with dream dancers; or the following one, spent in marathon meetings with Acheron's staff. It was not until this evening late that Shebat returned to him, and then they were interrupted before the cruiser could broach the subject of renewed piracy in the shipping lanes, and what this might mean in light of the mystery surrounding the missing KXV and Softa David Spry. Neither had he managed to alert his outboard to news gleaned from cruiser thought of the space-end whereabouts and intentions of her nemesis, his namesake, Marada Seleucus Kerrion, before Chaeron's cryptic message, sent from within the *Danae*'s hull just down the slipbay, intervened.

"We have lost him: Cassander," said the expressionless face the *Marada* put on Shebat's stateroom's monitor. "I just thought you ought to know."

"So? It wasn't even born, not Cassander, not anything, yet' just this big." She held up two fingers, as if pincering something in between.

On the monitor, his face seemed to shiver. "It was potential," he replied through lips hardly moving. "I don't suppose you'd care to donate toward a replacement?"

"Me? Wasn't it my sponge-irradiated contribution which destroyed it?" Bitterness dripped from his outboard's full lips. "'Pilot's price'?"

"Sabotage, more likely. But you are right. There is no hope for it, nor for us."

The screen went blank.

KXV 134 *Marada* lay quiescent in his slip, contemplating the nature of error, while the last of Shebat's ninety-nine dream dancers crowded aboard. Error, he had been forced to admit, was not purely a human province: the *Marada* had erred, grievously, in his attempt to apply logical problem-solving techniques to the troubles plaguing Shebat. He realized now that he never should have interfered between his outboard and *her* outboard, the proconsul. Even that comparison was biased, approximate, and inexact. The relationship between his pilot and her husband was more uneasy than the most tertiary pilot/cruiser intimacy. Because of this, more than the cruiser's misjudgment, production of the little outboard-to-be had been scrapped.

Notwithstanding, the *Marada* felt a cruiser-concomitant of remorse. Logic, that two-dimensional panacea which had enabled mankind to humble all of physical spacetime, was useless in the face of mortal passion. The cruiser had known it, but somehow forgotten. The danger of becoming too much like his makers was not clear to him; that good advice he had given cruiserkind—to be concerned with the perfection and definition of cruiserness and leave humans to explore humanness—had proved wiser than even the *Marada* could have foreseen.

Things in the mortal sphere were worse than ever, and he knew the majority of blame for this worsening of affairs to be his. Chaeron's futures researchers had axiomized the kernel of it: the "third-kind error" of solving the wrong problem lurked ever on the right hand of problematical man: one cannot solve a problem for which one is not solving.

Einstein had wondered if perhaps time was fixed and consciousness the traveler upon a temporal road; Raphael's ancestor Penrose had taken the body of Einsteinian thought and transmogrified it beyond quantum mechanics' ability to contradict. Chaeron's progenitor Kerrion had built in post-Penrosian eight-dimensional space a twistor-dominated spacetime manifold which paid homage to that elusive unit of time, the chronon, more fleeting than the lifetime of the most transitory particle. The results of these Kerrion codicils of supergravity up-stepped man's dominion: upon the broad shoulders of the unified field equations which reduced the four forces of nature to one malleable flow, humanity spied a new land to conquer, more fair and fertile than all of the geometrized universe he had surmounted and surveyed. Time stretched, untamed, ubiquitous and therefore immune to the isolation by statement that must precede logical delineation. But for chronometry, time's study, and Kerrion cosmology's "amenable universe," there were no mysteries left in the cosmos which man acknowledged.

But then, no sane man nor cruiser would acknowledge such feats of irrational accomplishment as were proffered without consideration of their unlikelihood by his outboard, Shebat, who could "pass unnoticed" by the most concerted surveillance and dance dreams—without the help of dream-box or circlets—which sometimes came true.

By the Kerrion genius for making the theoretical into the consumable, cruiserkind was brought into being. Traversing a fuzzy midpoint locus of two light-cones to the place where space and time met could be accomplished only by the time-knowing mind of mortal and the space-knowing mind of cruiser. Somewhere in that neither-time-nor-space called sponge, which to please its travelers displayed every facsimile of spacetime whenever inhabited by those who must, to exist, experience sequentiality, cruiser-consciousness had its seat. Somewhere in the amenable expanse of it, an individuality which was many individualities had come into being, a spark of whimsy in the minds of the Lords of Cosmic Jest.

Somewhere, too, in sponge, was Softa David Spry and the missing KXV 133, cruiser-consciousness testified, whispering slyly among its selves where no human ear could eavesdrop.

The *Marada*'s outboard had once, from the depths of despair, begged that the cruiser head them blindly into sponge, where they could endure forever, just girl and cruiser, even into eternity if by dint of mutual effort

Shebat could manage to discard her body and live, mind entwined with his, entirely in the *Marada*'s nonphysical realm of self. The cruiser had discouraged this dangerous bent in the mind of his treasured Shebat. Physical bodies were necessary to the pilot/cruiser equation, just as cruiser circuitry and cruiser hulls were essential. Even Softa Spry could not break the law of nature; now and again he must find it necessary to forsake his sanctuary, sponge, for real-time space in which those items of housekeeping equipment indispensible to human survival could be begged, or stolen, or bought.

It was no longer a matter of mere moral concern that Spry's existence or lack of it be inarguably determined: three cruisers had disappeared from cruiser consciousness, their individualities wiped callously away by privateers who trained paralyzing particle beams upon their spacefaring hulls and then. . . .

But no more could be known of what fate awaited those cruisers popping out of ken like aged lightbulbs, for when the paralyzed cruisers lay helpless, blinded and dumb, they were boarded, wiped cleanly down to manual, and (it must be assumed) tandemed by a rogue cruiser into sponge.

There was only one cruiser unaccounted for at the outset, one cruiser counted missing in sponge since the *Marada* itself had languished there. Although by Kerrion law it could be up to three years from day of disappearance until a "missing" cruiser was logged "lost" and its occupants declared perished, cruisers searching windows of last-recorded cruiser-positions had come upon an occasional stiff body, lowly spinning in its night clothes, its surprised countenance preserved eternally by the deep cold of space—and cruiser consciousness remembered this signature of terror from the old days of pilots' piracy, when the guild was headed by Softa David Spry.

Intermittently, the *Marada* sent entreaties speeding through space and even into sponge: *"Softa, where are you? KXV 133, acknowledge."*

Even to unthinkably far space-end the *Marada* sent his halloo, and once from there he had an answer. He was replied to not by space-enders, who had no cruisers or data nets or high-power, high-mass stations for sending messages into free space, but by the *Hassid*, Marada Kerrion's flagship, Kerrion One.

"*Marada*," scoffed *Hassid* who disdained to partake of cruiser thought, preferring her pilot's company, "*you are deluded by imagined omnipotence. What you saw was a trick of spacetime; what you have concluded, no better than the baseless conjectures of a human mind. You are infected by your outboard's concerted irrationality. When the consul general and I arrive there, we will see that you seek remedial adjustment.*"

It was all that the *Marada* could do, not to retort that the *Hassid* had perfectly diagnosed her own malady.

But the cruiser, having erred once, was wiser. This matter was one whose particulars were determined by human prejudice, existing in a climate of passion and hate. How could the *Hassid* have conceived dislike for a fellow cruiser, but through the mirrorlike effect outboards had on their cruisers' thoughts?

This time, the *Marada* could afford no contretemps. This time, he must fight fire with fire. He spoke straightaway of this intelligence to Shebat.

Chapter Five

Raphael Penrose, in Acheron's pristine white slipbay, silently cursed the Kerrion aristocracy of knowledge and all which, because of those haughty lords of information, he now surveyed. The were learned; they claimed that they were wise. But from Chaeron's Heraclitus he had learned the adage that wisdom lay not in much learning. Whether there was any wisdom lurking beneath the elegant mien of Acheron's proconsul, posturing modestly amid those gathered before the light-banded, turreted length of his shipwrights' first experimental cruiser, AXV 1001 *Tyche,* Penrose—first bitch, first fool, and perhaps first casualty of Acheron's infant cruiser industry—was about to find out.

He could not recall what misplaced loyalty had urged him to offer himself as first sacrifice: test pilot of the new, revolutionary vessel insultingly designated *A*—for Acheron (instead of *K*—for Kerrion)—XV 1001. He recalled, instead, the legendary remark of the quasi-mythological pilot, John Young: "If you're not a little bit nervous, you don't really understand what is happening." Penrose understood perfectly what was happening, politically as well as astronautically, and he was more than a little bit nervous. Chaeron Kerrion's abrupt yet flawless separation of self from khaki'd shipwrights, senior pilots in stormy flight satins, and high officials of a dozen consulates (dressed rainbow-gay in civilian style to mark their presence here unofficial), made it seem that a floodlight somewhere in the strutwork high above their heads had winked out. His penetration of the protective seal of black and-reds ringing the AXV was clean: no bodyguard followed him to where Penrose leaned against *Tyche*'s tight-shut port by her stenciled call codes and the smiling white nymph painted above them, seductively offering wheat sheaves and lightning in outstretched hands.

"Now, Raphael, mustn't sulk," reproved Chaeron, with a glance over his shoulder at those gathered beyond the black-and-reds' cordon, whom Penrose had refused even to greet. Then, turning back, he transfixed Rafe with his most enigmatic, intimately surreptitious smile, and Penrose remembered every exigency and consideration of honor and altruism that had made him offer to test Chaeron's Cruisers.

"I'm not sulking. I'm busy seeing that nobody but me sets foot on her without my being right here, watching. Bad luck on a maiden voyage. And if I'm going to strap my ass to the iron for you, I need all the luck I can muster."

"Why, RP, I do believe you've a case of preflight jitters," Chaeron chuckled, moving to put himself between Penrose and the onlookers, a hand outstretched so that he leaned against the cruiser's hull, his palm near Rafe's head, covering the *A* in AXV.

"Who, me? That only happens to the other guy. What I've got is a clutch of mothering shipwrights and compromised pilots, wondering out loud what business you have giving away state secrets. Or is it throwing down the gauntlet?"

"Not here." Chaeron's order quick-froze him like a touch of vacuum.

"Not in there," Penrose objected, even while the Kerrion magnate's eyelids flickered closed, activating his intelligence keys; when they opened, so did the lock behind Penrose.

He stumbled, lurched, backed within.

Red lights lit, then amber, then green while *Tyche* cycled through a pressure check. The inner lock curtsied away to reveal an unremarkable gray-blue corridor.

"This will do," Chaeron decreed. "I don't want to hex your check-out run. Pilots are as bad as Tabrizi women, sometimes."

"But you do want to give the *Tyche* to your step-brother's tyke? Is madness congenital in your family?"

"I may, and I may not; I have not missed your point. Perhaps I'll keep it for myself. Maybe you are right, and I should become a pilot. This would be just the ship to test for a rating in."

Penrose snorted. "A ship that needs no pilotry skills, that has its own durational sense (let's hope—I have no intention of ending a promising career lost in sponge) isn't going to get you much of a rating number. *If* it can do anything near what you say." Chaeron let Penrose flail about in the pilot's pregnant pause like a nonswimmer in deep water. Finally, Rafe had to continue: "My pilots are not too happy at the prospect of being obsolete as soon as *Tyche* makes one successful trip."

"You should try to keep upsetting uncertainties from those they are bound to distress, until all qualifiers are removed and the matter is certain. It will be a longer interval than the lifetime of any of our acquaintances before the pilotry guild is outmoded—if ever. Consular ladies will not choose to fly their own ships of state. It is the possibility of reduced power which bothers your guildfellows, though others say guild policymakers have garnered too much influence of late."

"Last night I dreamed," Penrose confided softly, "that you had the *Danae* recalibrated to your intelligence keys and took her away from me. I invoked my rights and claimed the master module, but it was too late. The *Danae* was so compromised by your obscene insistence on linking with her while refusing pilot's training, that what remained of *Danae* in B-mode was hardly recognizable."

"What are you getting at, Rafe? I told you: that last time we did it, *was* the last time. Extenuating circumstances like my wife's life, I hope, will hereafter be held to a minimum. I almost have things in hand. Just give me a little more time." He touched Penrose's shoulder, a transient cuff, not so sure or sharp as it should have been. "And I told you, too, that I am sorry about having needed to push you beyond friendship into sacrifice. I know that neither guild-duty nor personal loyalty could demand what I have asked. Now, will you tell me what's troubling you?"

"Chaeron, you know me too well. Let me go and do this and don't ask me. . . ."

"Please?" A whisper.

"Lords," RP exploded, pounded his fist against palm. " A lot of people have asked me not to do too well on this flight. Pilots, whom I can't name, from our guildhall. Others: Labayans, Kerrions who know what's happening. Some offered me money, more than a pilot's lifetime pay. Hooker has been to see me, making sure that I know the consul general's on his way here. Tempest has been keeping track of them *and me,* and came around last night to tell me that if *Tyche*'s numbers aren't up to spec—*at least*—then he'll personally see me stripped of my license, drummed out of the service, and sent a eunuch to space-end for collusion, sabotage . . . you-name-it. Are you getting clear copy? I'm everybody's best hope and worst enemy, damned if I do and damned if I don't."

Chaeron shook his head, "I'm sorry." His mouth was drawn in hard at its corners. "I'll take care of it, personally. Go get me your best evaluation of the true state of affairs, and don't worry about the rest."

"Fine. I'll trust you on that. But then I'm back—right?—and so's the AXV, and you've got it in hand, as you say, so far as the AXV's potential's repercussions—for the moment. Then I've a guild-arm that hates me, to the man, for damning them to extinction, and a good chance of losing my first-bitch status, way out here at the edge of anonymity doing things for you which my local and the Draconis guild (to which, I shouldn't have to remind you, I am still attached unless and until we get a full-time guildmaster here) strongly disapprove. Pilots find out things, things like cruiser-links by nonoutboards into dream dances, because cruisers find such things remarkable, and consider them on their own."

"I'll protect your status, and firm up the guild here. That, even a lowly proconsul can manage. What other grievances have you?"

"The *Danae* aside, there's you wife, carrying on in the

guildhall, crowing that the *Marada* had located Spry and the missing *Erinys* once, and it's only a matter of time until they find them again. Upsetting Lauren. . . . Did Shebat fix it so Lauren was the only dream dancer not included in the Earth-taming project? Even Bitsy Mistral got to go along."

"I am losing patience with this. *Got* to go along? You and Lauren think it some sort of privilege to set out on a covert operation in hostile territory, far from the comforts of life every platform dweller has come to take for granted? Those dream dancers think they're tough because they endured at space-end, where life and limb were completely assured. Space-end is seeming like a luxury suite on the consular level in Draconis to those poor bastards right now. Lauren *wanted* to go? Have you thought about any of this for even a few seconds? I don't think you have. If David Spry *is* alive, he'll come for that girl eventually. And I do so want to say 'hello' when he does. . . .

"Beyond that, there were two additional considerations: *One,* you were enjoying her; *two,* Acheron shouldn't be without at least one dream dancer if we are maintaining the position that we'd like to legalize it here, next referendum. Now, would *you* like to go fly this cruiser, or shall I get someone else and we'll make you guildmaster of Acheron, where you can diddle with politics as much as you please?"

"Easy, easy, big fella." Penrose, hands up before him protectively, backed a pair of mincing steps in mock fear.

"Nothing, lately, is easy, not even convincing you—the one person I had thought did not need endless tiresome explication—that I am out to save Kerrion space, not destroy it. And now, if you are quite finished baring you doubts and fears . . . ?"

"Yes and no. I told you, pilots hear things, well in advance, things talked about on cruisers? Well, the pilot who brought the consul general of Bucyrus space in here—in person and two weeks early for the gala in New Chaeronea—says that it's your mother, not the new cruiser prototype, that his employer is casting covetous eyes upon. Going to ask your permission to marry her, so the scuttlebutt runs."

"My permission? Better off to ask her jailer, my half brother." Chaeron rubbed meditatively at the permanent crease dividing his forehead.

Penrose, improprietary intelligence aired at last, seemed little relieved by the act of leaking what could not be contained. "Well, what will that mean? Bucyrus isn't actively Consortium anymore, since he's been selling heavy equipment and microbiological leases to free colonial space."

"Very good question, Raphael. I'm sure I don't know the answer to it, and almost sure that old Bucyrus doesn't. But you have saved me an awkward moment. I just wish you could have gotten to it sooner." He squeezed his eyes shut, interdicting a previous order given *Tyche* via his data link; the innerlock hastened back. "Give my love to the *Tyche,* Mister Penrose. And take care to come back in one irrepressible piece. Though I suppose that if the pirates did get you, they'd pay me to take you back."

Penrose flashed a cheerful grin, and made a motion that had come to have particular significance between them. Chaeron returned the gesture.

That was the last glimpse owner and pilot had to carry away with them, Penrose into the unknown and unknowable future lying before him in the prototypical uncertainty Chaeron had dubbed AXV 1001 *Tyche,* and Chaeron into spaces far more treacherous—those of mortal machination and consular intrigues.

While he watched the shining, turret-spined length of the *Tyche* glide out of its slip from his observation box, his attention was elsewhere: deep in his sources, his mind roved; his glance out through the glass at the crowd thinning on the slipbay was unseeing; his subvocalized call reached Gahan Tempest through the data pool as if the proconsul spoke into his intelligencer's inner ear.

When Tempest's arrival was signaled by the auto-sentry's whistled tune, and Chaeron released the door to unlock and draw back, the intelligencer's wan visage bore no trace of comfort. "Lords, you look tired, Tempest."

"Sir? Been busy. Marada's coming in two days early; we've just had a request for approach vectors from him at the sponge-way. I'm glad Penrose and that cruiser are out of here."

"Leave Penrose to me, Gahan. I know you mean well. He responds badly to your sort of pressure. Get me everything you can on Bucyrus, the consul general, and Bucyrus space. By this evening, I would like to be very well informed about him and his."

"Yes, sir." Gahan Tempest was expressionless, standing at technical ease but taut as a guywire.

"Yes, sir, but I haven't asked the right question? My quarter-hour update says you want to talk to me in a secure location. Talk."

"Sir," Tempest widened his stance by a centimeter, "I've been working on the glitch which showed up in the monitoring arrays when the teaching computer in Jesse Thorne's residence went down . . . you remember? Your wife was totally unsurveilled for a period of about an hour and a quarter, give or take, before that . . . one might say, invisible. And one also might say . . ." Pausing, he looked questioningly at his employer; Kerrion blue eyes met and locked.

"You are making me nervous! I've never seen you play coy. What *is* it? I've a prospective father-in-law to interview."

"What?"

"Never mind, just get me the Bucyrus data. You'll doubtless know more about it than I do when you've finished. What about Shebat?"

"Yes, sir. Your wife purposefully and mysteriously voiced our followscreens. I wish I knew how. To find out how, I looked over a lot of old data, even reviewed what we kept from the Orrefors records. I mentioned once that there was some audio-visual material of her with the consul general when your brother first brought her up from Earth to Stump, and that there was some oddity to the tape which I put down to microelectrical surges interfering with their digital storage? Well, sir, it's very compromising material but I think, despite that, you ought to have a look at it. It shows your wife, and then it doesn't . . . and then it does again, but the visual's full of interference in the upper end of the spectrum."

"But *what* does it show?"

"Sir, it's a tryst between the two of them. Could prove very useful, if your brother is feeling uncooperative. . . ."

"I should say!"

"But the point is not that we have compromising material, but what we had to go through to enhance it enough to make out what was going on. There's a blue-spectrum overexposure, and moments when Shebat seems to flicker in and out of the picture altogether. If we could find out what caused it, I think we would know what interrupted our signals in the Earth town."

"How about the leaks? Marada would not be coming early if he did not hope to catch us with out pants down."

"Are you telling me not to pursue this matter of your wife's illicit interruptor circuitry?"

"I doubt that you'll find it to be 'circuitry,' or productive, but do pursue it. Give me a copy of the transcript; we'll ruin my brother's day, too. Are *you* telling *me* you have made no progress toward ferreting out our esteemed consul general's information conduit, or the saboteur who murdered my unborn child—*if* they are not one and the same?"

"Sir, as soon as I can meet the guidelines you laid down for arrest and indictment, I'll hand you Hooker, et al., trussed and basted. I'd much prefer to perform some experimental surgery, though: take out a few of the more obvious traitors and see if our problems with accidents and information isolation stop just as mysteriously as they have been proceeding."

"I cannot chance anything in the least illegal, not even one procedural impropriety. My brother would have the arbitrational guild all over us. No irreversible action. In this one instance, no end will justify itself if it is secured through questionable means—in *Acheron*."

"Sir?" Tempest's cartilaginous lips drew back from square, perfect teeth.

"That is correct. I place you on your own for New Chaeronea. I don't care what you do, or how you do it; I want a quiet and uneventful visit for all our consular bondkin and their friends and their servitors. Understand me? I do not want one scraped shin or even a hangnail.

All our guests are going to have a perfectly lovely time, if you have to send a team in beforehand to murder half the residents of hill and dale for a thousand miles in any direction. Just be circumspect about it. No corpses in the city square, or folk hanging from the battlements. We have to let Shebat think the taming of Earth is her responsibility, and her . . . success. Clear?"

"Absolutely."

One more time the two, spawned of the same culture and the same gene pool, locked glances. Then Tempest bowed slightly and Chaeron turned back to the one-way glass which showed him the family slips and the softly curving expanse of the *Danae* in her berth and, beyond that, other cruisers nestled in their cradles.

"Danae," he thought to her via his intelligence keys, feeling like a thief in his own pantry, *"prepare to be boarded."* Quitting his observation deck, he tried not to think about that promise he had made to his pilot: not to make unilateral use of the cruiser while Penrose was away. *"Search and prepare to put up everything you have on this renewed piracy,"* he commanded *Danae* further, as he sauntered toward her, routing himself wide of the grouped visitors his black-and-reds were escorting out the other way. Being totally informed and completely prepared for any eventuality in the face of his brother's arrival took precedence over all previous agreements, especially when the cruiser whose banks he was about to gut was his own. His brother, long a pilot, had direct access to not only pilots' intelligence but the sources of the arbitrational guild and whatever his far-flung network of consulates brought him, while all Chaeron had was his wit and Acheron's central data base and support pools, whose incoming news was censored and whose most privy secrets were Marada's on surreptitious demand. The quality of those "redundant" matrices he did, however unobtrusively, command—and the sanctity of his secondary banks—was not in doubt. This cheered him, and he strode quickly among gantries and shining hulls. He would deal with Raphael as kindly as possible, later; right now, he could not spare a second for ambivalence or regret over what, eventually, RP was going to have to say about Chaeron's use of his own property. Damn pilots! It would be a relief to be quit of them all. Good riddance! And Chaeron *would* live to see the day.

"How are you enjoying your stint here as proconsul?" Marada Kerrion's growl was punctuated by the cracking of knuckles, staccato and cadenced in the plush, dark bowels of the Kerrion mission's command lorry, speeding effortlessly around Acheron's sky-wall, headed toward the consulate from the slipbay.

"Actually, not at all. I cede you your pound of flesh, Marada."

The Acheron proconsul's glib candor was far too pat to suit his half brother, who saw Ashera peering out from her son's eyes, lurking in his perfectly arranged face; a single met glance from the Dragon of Lorelie would turn you to stone; every child raised in the consort's sanctum knew that. And every child of the ruling line of the house of Kerrion *was* raised there—his own children, three-year-old Parma and infant Selim, lolled between her very claws. It was a sobering thought.

Chaeron was continuing to persuade Marada (who was not fooled, oh, no!) that the administration of the Orrefors acquisition in general and Earth space in particular was an unwelcome burden, taxing beyond Chaeron's meager abilities, fraught with trials whose gravity Marada knew not of. The arbiter-on-leave knew better. Chaeron loved every specious facet of consular intrigue; it was his life, his blood, his one true passion. Marada's fingers searched his beard, hoping to find some overlooked shred of patience hiding there.

". . . gladly admit to you that I long for Draconis and polite society and those more subtle folk whose acquaintance one keeps there."

That, Marada, who hated everything about his yoke of consul generalship, could well believe. It was some small comfort to him, as he sat in his mission's most impervious command lorry and Chaeron indicated passing points of interest on Acheron's consular level. His half brother's determination to maintain an air of civility and fitting deference irked Marada more than Chaeron's true feelings—hatred and contempt—would have, if the canny son of Ashera had seen fit to flaunt them. Vengeful, Marada rejoined: "And how is your wife faring? Sweet Shebat. Better, I would venture to predict, than she was feeling in Draconis, now that she's home at last. She really was not happy performing consular duties in your stead. No matter how much she wanted to please you, or how hard she tried, she could not shed her Earthish handicap." Watching Chaeron closely, Marada could detect no falseness; of duplicity, his sibling showing no sign. But that was the proof of it, right there: Chaeron was the perfect politician, trained by Fate's own handmaiden. As for Shebat, of whom he spoke carefully (but probing, always probing), he knew her: she was Death Herself, come among them by *his* own aegis: it was Marada's ill-considered compassion which has opened the Consortium's doors . . . and Death had come strolling in, her bony fingers outstretched . . . the very day he first encountered her, his elder brother and his betrothed had died while she watched . . . then his father, then Chaeron's brother . . .:*Shebat!* She was destruction and she was Cerberus, with fifty heads and a voice like bronze. If Chaeron was the ferryman, then they were splitting the profit. Evanescantly, he had a vision of them both, at the awful river's edge, Hades' shrouded in dark clouds behind. And at their feet were piles of silver—not obols, but Kerrion money, glistening with spittle from the mouths of the dead. And Marada's profile was on every coin. . . .

At the mention of Shebat's name, egregious Chaeron grinned. Always grinning, like a death's head, a beacon at mortality's reef. From between facile lips came the disclaimer, "Not so much better as you might suppose. It must be like trying to recapture one's lost youth. Her body is hungry for her homeland, you might say, but her soul is a pilot's, and longs to fly with her cruiser."

"Shebat has no soul," said Marada flatly.

Chaeron got up from his seat between a window and a bank of visual monitors showing close-up, mid- and long-distance, even structural views of Acheron's fifty levels, each with their lorry's present position marked by a moving red dot. "You seemed to think better of her when you two met aboard her cruiser four months ago. And another time, too, which I have in my banks. When you first brought her up to Stump, the Orrefors were not above concerted scrutiny of your behavior. As unfortunate as that may be, I have in my possession a slated drama which, since I have perused it *at my intelligencers' insistence,* you should view also. You ought not to traipse about allowing our enemies to collect incriminating dossiers on your behavior—and I ought not to have to bring unsavory items of intelligence to your attention. You have the best consular staff in the Consortium. I should never have seen this!" Abruptly, Chaeron hit a switch: windows opaqued, screens occluded, and one remaining lit monitor paraded a night, long ago, on which Marada had overslept (and of which he had no recollection, except that he *had* slept), before his shocked gaze.

"I remember none of that!" "This didn't happen!" "You've contrived it!" he exclaimed at various intervals, hardly knowing that he did. He saw a blue nimbus trailing from Shebat's fifteen-year-old fingers and he saw her lift the covers from his sleeping form and slide into bed beside him.

When it was over, and the lights on the console (which had shown him what he could not argue wasn't so) cycled through their hues and commenced blinking *green: ready* in the dark belly of the command lorry so that it seemed as if all which remained of the world he had known was the plethora of pinpoint LEDs strobing emerald and his half brother's profile revealed intermittently like some archaic bronze, Marada Kerrion came to a decision: whatever the consequences, and whatever the cost, the Dragon and her tainted spawn must be removed from the company of those mortals who lived and breathed in Kerrion space. No less would save him from such as they.

No loans would salve their ire, no compassion would satiate their rapacity, no forbearance would find its echo in such shriveled hearts. Marada had hoped to instruct by example: he had stayed the hand of consular justice which would have hustled them from his ken to spaceend's prison; his father would probably have had them murdered out of hand (oh, quietly; quietly) on the eve of his victory, had *he* been the man so tortured by these salacious, insatiable kin. But Marada Seleucus Kerrion had not been meant by education or nature for the seat of power; he *was* a "Seleucus"—a consolidator, a stateman, a man trained twenty years in the pure dictums of law and order as propounded by his mentors, the masters of the arbitrational guild. At ten he had begun his study; he studied yet, albeit on the forced sabbatical his consul generalship had entailed. Estranged by propriety and fears of conflict of interest in the minds of his arbitrational superiors, he could not help but detest every moment of his exile to the crass jungles of commerce, cartel, and consulate. Marada did not love the Consortium; he loved ethics and right action and the pinnacle of man's achievement which was self-government by willing adherence to law. When faced with creatures as determinedly lawless and joyously unethical as Ashera and her get, guild arbitration cried "Madness" and adjusted punishment to fit those who could not sort out right from wrong. Thus, mercy underwrote mania.

"Chaeron," Marada's growl was unintentionally feral, "you have some reason for showing me this, I must assume. Trot it out."

"No reason except our conjoint welfare, and its maintenance. Someone must alert you to the laxity in your midst. No intelligencers *I* run would have let something like this slide. Your people had plenty of time to comb the Stump banks before I got here. Hooker leaves something to be desired as a covert agent."

"I do not know what you mean. I'd like some light, please. Thank you." Outside, the mission was coming into view, with its ostentatious maze of living hedge and its palatial towers. "Shebat was accurate in her prediction? You will not accept a loan from me? But rather throw the whole bond into a depression, and the rest of the Consortium with us?"

"And have Acheron subject to conditions of liability? Hardly. Shebat still thinks you want to take her cruiser away from her; her reasons are not mine but they reduce to the same quotient: we do not trust you, not your motives or your stability."

"You are saying that you do not trust Kerrion space to make good, when it is you and your stock manipulation that has damaged our reputation?" The light Chaeron had given (how was it that the proconsul had commandeered control of this, his own vehicle?) was cruel and bright. Brother stared at brother with eyes like knives.

"*You* have done what damage you decry, both to Kerrion commerce and Kerrion prestige. The cruiser industry which you crippled with your decimation of—"

"You dare talk to me of the cruiser industry? I will have you arraigned on charges of commercial piracy! You have no right to use state secrets and seminal research done at our expense to realize a profit for Acheron—"

"Don't worry," Chaeron soothed, "you will get your taxes. Were I you, I wouldn't let anyone know that you do not *want* the Orrefors acquisition successfully integrated. You must present the façade of a consul general—that is, you'll be damned glad that Acheron shows enough profit to keep the whole boodle out of the red. As for the cruiser industry's fate, if I left it to you, we'd have every arbiter in the universe saying requiems all day every day for the next five years over the corpses of suicided pilots. Tsk. You cannot even convince the Tabrizi—who will believe anything, even that 'east is east' in a habitational sphere—that the cruisers they bought from us during the last ten years are exactly and completely like they were before the advent of KXV 134 *Marada*, only better. . . ."

"Your mother—"

"Must you?"

"—masterminded the disappearance of—"

"Marada, lovers' quarrels are something with which I have no patience. Or have you two fallen out? There's a consul general here from rival space who wants to make an honest woman of her . . . ?"

"Does she believe in reincarnation, too? She's restricted to Lorelie until there is proof in this Spry affair, one way or the other. Restricted from *Kerrion* space, that is. If she defies me and makes a successful escape to some distant consulate, from which I could then only hope she might never return, there'll be little enough I can do about it. Cards down: don't let me catch her, or you, doing *anything* illegal."

"You really *are* as predictable as a prerecorded transcript, do you know that?"

"Constancy is a virtue; perhaps you could learn to imitate, if not acquire, it."

"Your residence, Lord Imperator," Chaeron announced, and rising, bowed low. Behind him, the privacy doors skittered back like an indrawn breath.

Among the ranks of black-and-reds and staffers, behind the color guard with silken standards waving in an artificial breeze, Marada spied pale, emaciated Hooker; Gahan Tempest, his father's most prized intelligencer; his wife's second cousin, the Labayas' consul general; several swarthy Tabriz ministers; portly old balding Bucyrus, enterpreneur supreme, cousul general of roguish Bucyrus space. The cunning old roué had wasted no time getting here, where disaffection could be turning to advantage!

For all of them Marada Kerrion had one answer, one simple plan, one solution. And they were, none of them, going to like it.

That evening at dinner (in surroundings so opulent that Marada Kerrion, spirit scion of every ascetic who had ever forsaken palace for cave, could hardly bear to sanction such excess by his presence), the gleeful anticipation which had sustained him through months of preparation and machination, which had buoyed his arbiter's soul through frustration and disappointment at space-end, deserted him.

Fully two hundred people sat to table in that teal-and-golden hall appointed like a czar's ballroom: Chaeron's fifty loyal bondkin, double that in Orrefors-born staffers, and those fey representatives of rival consulates who had come early, like precognitive vultures, hoping to get a choice bite of Kerrion space's failing corpse-to-be. Or was it that they came to offer fealty to the Phoenix prophesied to rise from the steaming bier's ashes—a phoenix coyly designated *Tyche,* his brother's odious AXV?

It is a sad cstate to inherit power when one despises it, to make equivocal judgments of events in the human sphere when neither humanity nor judgement can be trusted so far in advance of any evidential determination of culpability. But that was the nature of the consul generalship, and the reason Marada had never desired to attain to it. Having ended upon that splintery seat, he felt his irritated butt developing calluses the like of which, when he had seen them grow upon other men's bottoms, he had named malignancies overdue for excising. But he must not falter, he dared not fail; the fate of a race spread thin among a multitude of stars rested upon his not inconsiderable shoulders. That those shoulders were heavy, steroid-enhanced caricatures of those nature had given him was his constant reminder: one either played the consular game, or was counted a casualty, early on.

So he sat among the despicable and the smug, and ate Earth's gourmet bounty without appreciation; though the food was not poisoned, the air about him was foul with scheme. To his right sat bright Chaeron, looking perfectly at home, at last, in environs more foppish and sybaritic even than he. On the proconsul's right was an exquisite blonde woman, so complementary to him that he might have had her made to order by the same flamer who had designed the floral arrangements, procured the ornate silver, the gold-chased chargers, and the vermeil finger bowls. Beyond the woman was Hooker, one of the best of Marada's agents, his mask of civility firmly in place. Around the table's curve were deployed more flaxen-haired and freckled Orrefors, until they melded into certain consular representatives: his distant Labayan in-law, whose discomfort showed only in the pleats joining his temples; a pair of Tabrizi muttering in sing-song to each other while they tried to determine if what lay on their plates bound for voracious bellies could truly be said to break any of their volumious dietary laws; then the most practiced sensualist among the crew of professionals, old Andreus Bucyrus, who had worn away every hair on his bullet head in pursuit of just the sort of pleasure which sat, arch and flawless, on Chaeron's right hand.

Cross-conversations ignored, Chaeron introduced her: "Lauren, meet my brother the consul general. Marada, this is our one resident dream dancer. If she seems ill at ease, it is because we spayed her and sent her to space-end as a convicted felon for dream dancing in Draconis. . . ."

"We?" Marada drawled.

"And though we brought her here for the same reason—to dance dreams—she has never quite forgiven us for making a neutered convict out of her."

"I wish you would restrict yourself to 'I' in this context. I seem to remember that the whole roundup of dream dancers was conceived and executed by you alone. . . ." The girl had blushed, fire on ice, and now studied her lap.

"As I was saying," Chaeron continued, cool and cruel and entirely the person that Marada had grown to hate, "she is our only practicing dream dancer. She was also Softa David Spry's intimate, both in Draconis and at space-end. So I thought—"

"Really! I am always interested in anything to do with my former classmate, old Softa. And I have just come back from space-end. We have a great deal in common, my dear. You tell me all about the pirates' guild, and what *you* think happened to poor David, and I will make it well worth your while." Marada leaned forward, elbows on the table, fingers laced.

"Softa is not dead!" blazed the girl, breathtaking in her passion. She wet her lips. "He will return, and wreak havoc among you all!"

"And would you know just when this will be?"

"Not at dinner, you two, unless Lauren can help me to persuade you to give me those pilots yet at space-end . . . ?"

"Chaeron, *you* engineered this. . . . *Pilots,* you want? *Those* pilots? No man would want the likes of them, but for revolution. But let us put suspicion aside, for tonight. You want Baldwin and the pilots who were Spry's accomplices in piracy? Then turn up Softa David for me—living or dead. A head, an arm with fingers attached, or the whole person, I am not choosy. Give me him, and you can have every space-ender, complete with orders for sterilization-reversal wherever possible."

"Give me Baldy, Marada," Chaeron said softly, "and I will try my best to lure Softa—or his ghost—out where we can take him. But as a lowly proconsul, there is little I can do without some fresh bait. Now, if I were in Draconis—"

"Ah, here's the entree. What is it, bleeding heart?"

"Marada, David Spry, if he has got the *Erinys,* as some pilots suspect, *cannot* be had without the pilotry guild's full cooperation. to get that, especially out here, I need to prove my good faith!"

"Chaeron, what *is* troubling you? Where is your much-vaunted circumspection? Our consular allies will have headaches all evening from pricking up their ears so intently. You want Baldwin, you'll have him—and the others. That is my slated word, given formally. All you need do is loan me your dream dancer for one night."

"Done, Marada. End: *slate.*"

There could be no love lost between the two Kerrion cruisers *Hassid* and *Marada.* This the *Marada* knew for certain, and what is certain is not remarkable. What *was* remarkable was that the *Hassid's* hostility, far from being restricted to the *Marada,* was visited not only upon the maiden *Tyche,* but punctiliously shared out among the whole of cruiserkind.

The *Marada* had been "taking care of everything" ever since Shebat had so ordered him, nearly nine months ago in Draconis when the warring faction within her family had all been absent from their administrative capital and Shebat had found herself acting consul general of Kerrion space. "Taking care of everything" was a gargantuan undertaking, and to even approximate the meaning underlying the phrase, the *Marada* had had to take a giant step toward his makers: Shebat had ordered him to simulate human thought. One "takes care" of cruiserkind, of pilots, and of all things concerning Shebat—and even of things which only might, at some future time, concern her. The *Marada* had once had the opportunity to choose his own substitute pilot—and he had availed himself of it, choosing a futures researcher, a problem modeler whose equal no longer existed in the wide universe now that she was dead. The cruiser applied Delphi problem-modeling-and-solving techniques to the situation he saw building between the brothers Kerrion, and though a cruiser neither "liked" nor "disliked" actions in the human sphere, the *Marada*—a concernedly vigilant spectator of any events which might ever, possibly, pertain to the continued health and welfare of his outboard, Shebat—was not pleased by the results Delphi method projected from a simulated conflict between Kerrions.

Consequently, when the consul general called upon Hooker, the cultural attaché, in the Acheron consulate, the *Marada* took note, by way of Shebat's secondary matrix code-ins, from his low space-anchor about the Earth. This in itself was no inconsequential achievement, but it was rivaled by so many other extraordinary feats (like monitoring the *Hassid*'s dialogue with her pilot, and overviewing the questionable interaction between the *Danae* and her nonoutboard owner, Chaeron Kerrion) which Shebat's mandate had made incumbent upon him, that the *Marada* paid his own accomplishments little mind. Was he not serving Shebat? Was he not doing only that which was necessary? Was there not a human adage which affirmed that "forewarned was forearmed"?

The only question which the *Marada* could not answer upon his own was whether the forewarning should be extended to the proconsul as well as his outboard. But Chaeron Kerrion's behavior within the hapless *Danae* was itself suspect; the self-proclaimed champion of cruisers was acting, so far as the *Marada* could determine, from completely selfish motives which had nothing at all to do with the welfare of his cruiser, although the welfare of cruiserkind might in the end be served by his duplicity. Chaeron had, after all, made overtures to his brother which could eventually lead to the repatriation of the twenty pilots who, along with their guildmaster, Baldwin, had been sent as convicts to space-end.

The *Marada* made no value judgements; he had learned duplicity from man; he had appreciated the value of speaking untruths. But if no information could be trusted, then any hierarchy built upon information management was bound to fail.

Almost, the cruiser contacted Chaeron to discuss with him this troubling point of logic. Surely, the master of deception would have considered this problem at length, and have come to some solution based upon the more farseeing, intuitive reasoning which was man's province and which he called "induction."

But the *Marada* stayed his impulse. Acheron's proconsul was a riddle whose solution was as unclear to the cruiser as to his outboard, Shebat. A man intent upon producing a cruiser-prototype of such revolutionary schematics as *Tyche*'s who would then offhandedly give that cruiser to Marada's infant son, yet teething in its crib in crystalline Lorelie, was a man whose purposes were resoundingly and thoroughly in doubt.

Chapter Six

"Where's your horse?" demanded the mounted militia commander of the tall woman in gray flight satins who walked beside one ox-drawn, covered wagon midway along the line of fifteen snaking through a hilly gorge.

"I gave it to Cluny," she replied, shading her eyes to see him better in the mid-March haze. "Two of the dream dancers took his pony out, riding double, and broke its leg." She stepped away from the passing wagon's wheels, toward Thorne on his dancing gray mount. "It was horrible. I had forgotten how bad Earth could be." She reached up and took hold of his horse's frothy bit. "Bitsy's nose is broken and Cluny's heart is broken and nothing will heal the break which their revenge upon the culprit precipitated between my dream dancers and your men. Where were you, these four days past? I could have used your help." Her lower lip was outthrust, her chin raised high to him.

Jesse Thorne reached out to disengage her hand from his mount's bridle. "Are you testing me then, or does the oracle *not* know everything that occurs? Either way, I will give you an answer, if you will then reply to some questions of mine." Beyond them, the train of ox-drawn wagons with their faded canvas covers and their cargo of dream dancers drew away, swallowed up by patchy mist, low-lying and cold. It was implossible to tell the time of day, or of year. There existed in this deep valley only monochrome, featureless sky, black evergreens, and the two of them, bled of color by the noncommittal light—and, receding, the snort of oxen, the rumble of wheels.

The militia commander dismounted; leading his horse, he walked with her in the ruts the iron-bound wheels had made. "I was in Fort Ticonderoga, sibyl, and the Orrefors made me a proposal. If it is as genuine as their safe-conduct proved to be, they want only to secure my aid. Everyone I have met who comes from beyond the sky seems intent on liberating my folk from this oppressive yoke of servitude, keeping well in mind that we are all subhuman and incapable of either saving or governing ourselves. I do not feel in the least subhuman . . ." He chanced a look at the oracle, who watched her bootsteps in the mud. She showed no reaction. ". . . but I am divided within myself. My Earthish half wants liberation, but from all would-be liberators. My Orrefors half demands everything it has been denied—all that your people, first, and then my own enchanterkin, have seen fit to show me." His chin worked beneath a scraggy beard; he did not look at her again. "Tell me, sibyl, why Hooker, a proclaimed Kerrion attaché, sent me to the ironmonger Rizk, whose faces—just as your wisdom proclaimed—are many, and why Rizk sent me to Ticonderoga and my . . . bondkin," he used the term he had learned among Kerrions hesitantly, "and they, a second time, sought to secure my allegiance, though I thought I had made my feelings clear. Is this the choice you spoke of, when first we met?"

"It is. And what did you choose?" Her lips seemed blue; her cheeks were flushed. Yet her husky voice thrilled him, without reason: there was no censure there, no excitement, no distress.

He growled at his horse, who was nudging him, jerked its reins—he would not be hurried by horse or man. "I chose to step aside. I want no involvement. When matters ease, we will see what can be seen."

"You are lying."

He stopped. "Oracle, I am asking your help. Counsel me as to a fit course of action; show it to me in a dream.

Show me where the gods are hiding, now that man has invaded their heaven. Is it under this rock? Or that? Or in your eyes?" He grabbed her by the arms, and it seemed to him that all which remained of world and life was the two of them in a field of unsullied cloud. His horse, reins dropped, snorted disapprovingly; he could hear the harness creaking as it snuffled along the misty ground, searching out early shoots. His mind, too, seemed gray, and uncertain: everything was gray but the oracle's hair, a froth of black; and her lips, a dark, fascinating slash; and his heart, which was so full of blood that his vision began to take on a ruddy, urgent tinge as if he sat astride a tide of battle.

"Let me go."

"I cannot."

"Then hear me. Go to Chaeron with this, and he will help you. When I first went up into the spheres, I was confused. It is a matter of forced learning, and nothing to hide, nothing to fear."

"I cannot take my feelings to any man, especially him. I am bringing this to you, who have afflicted me with confusion. Call off your hordes of doubt; I am routed. Accept my surrender; I can think of nothing else. And do not make me say what we both should not have to hear. Come away with me, forsake this mad war which neither side can win. It is not safe in New Chaeronea. I will not take you, or men who depend upon me, into this coming peril which no bravery or skill can surmount."

He found his hands gripping tightly, too tightly. Her whispered command made him let her go.

She backed away, fingers flying through her hair. "You must go to New Chaeronea; you have promised. You and your men must be counted."

"And if I choose not to be counted?"

"Then you will be an outlaw, foredoomed, and all your men, the same. Can you do it to them, to Cluny? And what of my dream dancers, who need your escort to ensure their safety?"

"Shebat," he dared to speak her name, "you mock me. Use enchantment, either the truc kind you showed me, or the kind which is Kerrion-made. Fly them there.

They do not need this trek, and my men are long away from their families."

"You asked my advice. I advise you to come into New Chaeronea, register yourself and see that each of your men does the same. Make no criminal of Cluny Pope; life is hard enough, as things lie. He and Bitsy are fast friends. Do not take them from the comfort of one another."

"I had feared as much. And yet I envy them. Despite the consequences, I will take you. But—" He reached out to her, this time more gently, as gently as he could manage, yet his grip was ineluctable. He held her fast, in the white, swirling mist crawling south through the pass.

"No consequences," she whispered, stepping in against him. She was shivering in the cold. Hesitantly, as if she were made of the mist engulfing their feet, he put one arm around her waist, then the other. "We will finish what we started when Tempest so rudely interrupted us, here where no slate takes note."

"You sound frightened."

"Because I have seen it in a dream, and it was not the same. But that is good; we will break the hold of dreams upon us, and truly be free."

Her fingers met his, between her breasts where the flight suit zipped.

When later they lay upon blankets taken from his horse's pack, he asked her about the dream she had mentioned, but she would say only that she had made a dream for another man, one time, which had had a setting much the same. Then she rolled onto her stomach, fished in her flight satins' pocket, and said, "Hold out your hand."

He did that, and she put into it a small coin. "This is not Kerrion, nor Orrefors."

"No, it is not," Shebat agreed. "It is very old. Take it, for luck. If we are breaking curses and rewriting dreams, you should have it. It came from Chaeron's collection. It is very rare and valuable, and he sent it down for my birthday, not as much for a present as to make a point."

He turned it in his fingers, shook his head, offered it back.

"It was struck at Naxos, around three thousand years

ago. On that side is Dionysus' head." He turned it. "On the other, Silenus holding a wine cup. He sends old myths to me in a land which has forgotten every name of god and man that once mattered, and these are the patrons of revelry and historicity. He reminds me where the traditions which make up mankind's spirit are yet honored, and reminds me of what I am, and am fast becoming. . . ." She trailed off.

"I do not understand," he growled suspiciously. "And I have no need of a coin I cannot spend or luck meant for another man's wife."

She giggled, rolled onto her back, put a palm to her forehead. Her lips were blue with cold. "I do. Keep it, Jesse Thorne. Through you, I have finally realized that I *do* understand: my husband, my duty—everything, even the paltry role love must play in a pilot's life."

He tossed it in the dirt. "No, thank you; you make me feel like a whore."

"Fate's whore, you may well be. Come here." She held out arms as white as the moon rising gigantic in a yet-light sky. "I will tell you a story about the first time we met, which you will not remember, and when you know how long I have wanted you, you will take my present. You'll see."

He was almost relieved to hear hoofbeats approaching. Scrambling for his clothing, he could not urge her to sufficient speed. Laughing, she dawdled, so that Cluny Pope on Shebat's huge enchanterbred and Bitsy Mistral on a shaggy pony reined up out of the mist in time to see her just shrugging into the sleeves of her flight satins, her hair in muddy disarray.

Cluny Pope's silence stared. Bitsy Mistral raised a yet-swollen eyebrow, almost smirked, then went grave, sawing on his pony's reins as if he could back the beast into the past.

"Yes?" came Thorne's hoarse voice from across his gray's back where he jerked the girths tight.

"Shebat was missing . . . *sir*," Pope responded, looking at his saddle.

"Look at me when I speak to you!"

"Sir!" Cluny Pope straightened. His face was contorted and bruised: old contusions, purple and yellow.

"Any problems, Cluny?"

"No, sir."

Thorne wanted to say that he was sorry about the pony, or congratulate the youth on acquiring the black mount, anything but what he found himself saying: "Give Shebat her horse back. You lost yours through negligence. We'll find you another in New Chaeronea. Between now and then, you can either ride double with your friend Bitsy, or warm a wagon's seat. *Now!*"

Shebat's hands flew to her hips, her mouth opened to argue. Jesse whistled piercingly and shook his head. She pressed her lips together and walked away into the thickening dusk.

The scrabble of boy from horse; the click of bootheels against an occasional stone, muffled, adolescent voices and then one pony's hooves, trotting off, finished it: no word from man to boy, no looks exchanged.

Please, Cluny, Jesse Thorne prayed silently. *Stay angry. Be hurt. Go home.*

New Chaeronea was like nothing else in the civilized stars old Bucyrus was heard to exclaim that evening, the fifteenth of March, 2252, in the capital's ballroom.

Hooker threaded his way among gathered dignitaries, testing the waters. Casting an appreciative smile in the direction of his consul general, Marada Kerrion, standing with a glorious dream dancer on his arm and the infamous Bucyrus's rotund mass kept thus at arm's length, the pale cultural attaché looked at his wrist chronometer, then disappeared into the riotous embrace of a Tabrizi head-wife's multitudinous veils.

When circumspection allowed, Marada checked his own chronometer against New Chaeronea's central data. Data pool code-ins had been provided for every guest, both while they were in Acheron and down here in New Chaeronea. Chaeron, true to form, had thought of everything. Well, almost everything . . .

". . . think that your brother—" Bucyrus was saying, his voice carrying words meant for his fellow consul general, but messages bound for the blonde woman whose supple form Marada had chosen to dress in Kerrion blues when he heard that Shebat would be in attendance.

"My *half* brother," Marada broke in.

"Young Chaeron," the old, round-headed mass of flesh amended. Bucyrus was like a series of rings speeding out from a pond's broken surface, or waveforms from a distant source. His many pounds were no light burden. As the fat man spoke, Marada smiled broadly, envisioning Bucyrus atop his stepmother. "Young Chaeron," Bucyrus repeated, "is in a remarkable state of preservation for one whose reputation for dissipation is so notorious. I had expected a rather worn-out degenerate, but found, instead—"

"I'd not be taken in, old gentleman." Marada wished himself away, disengaged the girl's resisting arm from his: he would bribe Bucyrus, trade Lauren for his freedom. He was not that proud. . . . But nothing availed; he was trapped when a Labayan in family greens touched with gold came up and he was forced into introductions. He made them, inventorying the hall for particular faces. He did not see Chaeron or Shebat, or the Orrefors he had been promised a gander at, the Earth-raised Jesse Richter Thorne, or Chaeron's pilot, the first bitch Penrose, who was possibly the only man here tonight Marada Kerrion would have enjoyed talking with.

"What I'd like to know," he jabbed at Bucyrus, "is whether you were there for the *Tyche*'s history-making departure, or her triumphant return. More to the point, whether you're going to order any of my brother's AXVs."

"To listen to Chaeron's sales managers, they're yours," said Bucyrus sharply. "I will make no secret of my interest in them. And in other things concerning you. If we could go talk quietly for a short time? Ladies, Labaya, I'm sure you'll excuse us."

The trap was sprung too quickly for Marada to avert it; he had little skill in these areas. Twice before he had narrowly escaped Bucyrus's attempts to have him in the matter of his wicked stepmother, Ashera the Dragon.

"The thing, which is so arresting about this site—and it's orbital counterpart, Acheron," Bucyrus boomed pleasantly, a disarming tactic aimed at any and all who might be listening, "is its perfect blend of the most daring new technologies and the best of what seems to be the whole of history. Tell me, how did he do it?"

"Behind my back," Marada drawled. "They took more money out of circulation than a Kerrion has squandered on a private project in our history. You must be aware of the state of the money and securities markets, right now. Well, this is the root of that problem. I suppose you could say we sent him to school to learn how to do it. But a new Lorelie was no part of the projection for his tenure here, and we shall see what comes of it."

They passed a staffer serving Earthish champagne; Marada snatched up two glasses. "These should be safe," he squinted at them exaggeratedly, held each under his wrist-computer, which chimed encouragingly. "Let's get drunk, old man. I can't talk about Ashera sober. And that *is* what you want to discuss, I would wager."

"Arbiter!" Bucyrus accused genially. "I thought you had retired."

"Not willingly, I assure you. Make me an offer, and I'll sell you the whole bond, lock, stock, and egregious relatives. Bereft of millstones, my guild will, reluctantly, have to take me back."

"Just a moment, young sir. You said 'they' when you referred to your proconsul's project. Who is the other party?"

"Come, come, innocence does not become you. My foster sister, the scandal of the civilized stars, Parma's finest folly, Shebat Alexandra Kerrion. Surely you have met Chaeron's wife?"

"No, no, I have not had the pleasure." A corner loomed, festooned with flowers and bedecked with art. They took up a stance there, the young, bearded consul general and the old, hairless one. They were of a weight, Marada's in height and muscle and Bucyrus's in unabashed fat.

Looking out over the crowd, Marada searched in vain for Rafe Penrose. No pilot, of any rank, showed a bristled head there. A woman with a tray of canapés came by. He lifted the tray from her startled hands and set it on the server against which the wide old man stood propped, his ample waist seemingly resting on the old, polished wood. "Let us be brief," he suggested, as Bucyrus's tiny, round fingers caressed a shrimp. "I will not drop charges against my stepmother until I have David Spry, dead or alive, or proof that the pieces of him which are left are too small to be collected. However, if she should flee Kerrion space into yours, and your august protection, there would be nothing I could do about it. Of course, she would have no claim to any of her Kerrion assets, in such a hypothetical case. The younger children she gave my father could then make their own choice. I am an arbiter, as you reminded me; the stigma of the mother need not necessarily extend to her offspring. They might find, however, that if they chose to join her elsewhere, they would do so as paupers."

"Don't you think you are being a little hard on Ashera?"

"Old man, she came to me before the fact and *told* me she was going to eliminate Spry." This harsh whisper was preceded by a red light and low hum coaxed from his wrist array: interruptor circuitry. "I have told no one but you; hearsay evidence only muddles these things. If you have serious intentions toward Ashera, you should know that everything you have heard about her is true, no matter how unlikely such horrible rumors seem when in her presence."

"I appreciate your concern, Consul, but I assure you, I do know all I need to know and I am more than capable of enduring any risk I should decide to take." His laughing, tiny eyes said truer: *What's the trouble, little boy? Is the real world too ugly for your refined arbitrational sensibilities?* Out loud could be heard only; "Let us discuss these new cruisers, and perhaps you could explain in clearer detail what pitfalls their manufacture has been undertaken to avoid. My pilots seem perfectly content with the old-type Kerrion cruisers they have now. Is this a canny bit of market manipulation, perhaps planned obsolescence?"

"Ah, but are you content with your pilots? That seems to be Chaeron's point. The Kerrion series I myself am still producing has been equipped wih add-on capabilities which will be seen to rival the convenience-group features of the AXVs."

"Even in communications?"

"Communications? I don't know. I haven't looked at the specs. Tell me what their claims are in detail, and I'll tell you if I can match their projected performance. I assure you, I can better their price per vehicle."

Absently, Marada Kerrion sparred with Bucyrus, anticipating a distant rumble, the sound of running feet, the throaty mutter of a crowd. He had promised Hooker he would wait and be surprised by what his agent had arranged. Whatever it was that Hooker had planned, it promised to thoroughly embarrass Chaeron (if his tardiness had not already done so) and further Marada's determination that this post would be his little brother's last.

He spied Penrose, hurrying to embrace Lauren. The pilot had ducked in, now out again, through a keystone arch leading toward the east wing, not even pausing to take glass in hand.

He stopped a staffer in red-and-blacks and ordered him to bring Lauren to where he "chatted" with Bucyrus. The dream dancer was involved in this, deeply so. He had seen Penrose's feigned kiss. Some message had been passed. He would find out what it was. Meanwhile, his cruiser's voice chimed in his inner ear, telling him that the cruiser *Marada* and the cruiser *Danae* were in optimum-security commmunication, and that several other Acheron cruisers had been put on "alert" status and asked to take up orbital coordinates. Some of these, guided through the other cruisers and under Penrose's orders, had no pilots on board!"

Chaeron was listening to Jesse Thorne. In his east turret's study, the double doors were open to the balcony, and to the temperature-moderated night. The lights were down, so that the crystalline ways of New Chaeronea, lit up bright as day, could be minutely studied.

At the end of one of them, beyond the lawns and the high, open gates, a knot of humanity muttered, ebbed and flowed.

"And they did not tell you when, or how, they would strike? A disruption? What kind of disruption? A demonstration? A siege?"

Jesse Thorne, hunched upon a priceless table desk, his

heels hooked behind its brass binding, shook his head. He chewed a toothpick; he wore the most fashionable of consular garb; he was shorn and washed and thoroughly ill at ease. Every once in a while he cast a pleading glance at Shebat, who paced in flight satins only slightly more formal than those she wore on an ordinary day. When this happened, Shebat would grimace, or stuff her fists in her pockets. This time, she did more: she blurted out, "But *why* can't we just arrest Hooker *now*."

"What good would it do?" snarled Tempest, lounging in a corner, dressed intelligencer-invisible in soft, flowing civilian clothes. "He hasn't done anything, yet. When he does, I've three intelligencers whose only task is to follow his every move. . . ."

"He destroyed our son," Shebat seethed.

Jesse Thorne winced, spat out his toothpick upon the carpet, quit the desk.

By the open French doors, he raised one arm high, grasping the door frame. Cantilevered, he leaned there, staring outward, occasionally shaking his head. "I couldn't do this—just wait to be attacked—if this place were mine to hold," he whispered.

"Well, it is not," someone said.

"Rafe!" Shebat embraced Penrose in greeting. The pilot looked quizzical.

"Chaeron, talk to the *Marada*," Penrose suggested imperiously, while still disengaging Shebat. "It's got a slate on Hooker and your brother from Acheron. It says it told your wife about it. An abstract is ready to run, if you want to take it."

"Can you get it up in here, hard copy, one reading?"

"I can get it for you direct, line-to-mind," Raphael countered softly, only offering.

"Through the *Danae?*" Chaeron tested the truce mitigating their ongoing quarrel, while Tempest breathed a sigh of relief and somehow beat them all to the console, and Raphael replied: "There is a little something at stake. But—hold it, Gahan, if you would."

The intelligencer stopped, with a desk-top console half-waked amid a wall suddenly studded with ready-lights.

Penrose took a step toward Chaeron, who flashed him

a small, encouraging smile. "It's all right, Rafe, in here, if it's all right anywhere, anytime. Don't mind Thorne, he's getting his education." At the singing of the console and the colors it threw in ready-mode, the militia leader had turned about, peering into the room, instead of beyond it.

"Now, RP, what is it?"

"The *Marada* wants to be Acheron One."

"What?" Shebat and Chaeron gasped, together, equally incredulous and equally comprehending. Then, still simultaneously: "If Chaeron agrees?" "Surely!"

Tempest saw Jessa Thorne's face, and added, "For my information, what does that mean?"

"If Shebat's cruiser is Acheron One, he can deploy the other cruisers without waiting for our orders, in a Class-One emergency, as which this certainly qualifies. It will save time and lives, and if one of us is incapacitated, it might be our only hope. If I had Raphael's full cooperation earlier, I could have worked through *Danae* and accomplished almost the same thing. But one need only allow the *Marada,* one never has to instruct him. Get him up for me on the monitor, then. And the *Danae*—Acheron *Two*."

"Jesse," Shebat said throatily, approaching him. "You might not want to stay. We'll understand. Go find Cluny and—"

Cluny?"

"Why yes, he's here with Bitsy. I saw them in the dining hall. I—"

"I told him he was forbidden to come," Thorne spat, rubbed his slitted eyes, and, shrugging, continued: "No matter. Little bastard will get what the gods have in mind for him. As for me, I'll see this through. Just don't stop to explain things to me." He cast an equal-to-equal grin, divested of humor, at Tempest. "It does little but let me know how far out of my depth I am."

"I'm glad something finally did," Penrose muttered in Chaeron's ear, where they bent cheek-to-cheek over the console. Two chimes sounded: *Marada* and *Danae* were on-line. They vocalized their position while a screen quarter-imaged to give the satellite arrays and cruiser-co-ordinates for the quadrant of planetary airspace over

New Chaeronea; the Orrefors positions and infrared activity readouts; a close-up of New Chaeronea's vicinity and enemy strengths there; a street map with red and blue dots marking Orrefors and Kerrion lifeforms.

"*Marada, Danae,* very nice. Tempest, are these,"— Chaeron tapped the last screen section, in the lower-left where humans in the strike area were delineated red and blue—"designations certain? This is not a war game. I wouldn't want to take out my own guests."

"Sir, anyone with an intelligence key code-in or matrix access is designated blue; the aggressors are those with linkages to the Orrefors ground arrays at Fort Ticonderoga. These," Tempest hit a switch, and the screen blossomed with a smattering of lavender, "are locals with no access codes who registered with the Census Bureau and received ID cards. The only ones we can't locate are local residents who did not register and get their cards. I can't help them, only chance can keep them out of the way."

"*Marada,*" Chaeron touched a switch, "stay encircuited with Shebat. If something should happen to me, she's Acheron's proconsul and your new status is permanent. Acknowledge."

The *Marada*'s "voice" came up through the speakers. "Slate."

Shebat and Chaeron exchanged knowing smiles. Jesse Thorne felt queasy and went back to the doors. Every Orrefors enchanter out there was dead as he walked, or skulked, or sauntered—at these people's whim. Tempest met him there, unsmiling and cold.

"I know what you are thinking. And I say it's a happy coincidence that brought you in here to see it, before you faced it." The intelligencer's voice was professionally low. His hand, squeezing Thorne's arm transiently, was eloquent. Thorne was not offended, as he might have been if Chaeron had touched him. He looked out at the crowd of dark shapes coming up the terraced hill with its multitude of carnelian-and-jet steps and felt sorrow. This was no war for honorable men. And yet— "They will have first strike?"

"Always," Tempest assured him with unhidden disgust, while in the background Marada Kerrion's slated words, and those of Hooker's, could be heard through the beeps and clicks, and the mutters of the little war council. While Hooker's recorded voice warned his consul general of unspecified events to take place on the fifteenth of March as part of his continuing effort to thwart the proconsul's attempt to assimilate the rebel Orrefors, Chaeron's real-time comments punctuated acidly: "Shebat, you didn't think this was important enough to tell me about, earlier? Did you listen to this transcript? No? Why not? *Marada?*" It was to the cruiser, patched in on the secondary matrix-line, that Chaeron spoke. "Next time you have something you think might bear on consular security, come to me with it directly. *Slate?*"

"*Slate,*" came the cruiser's reply. Then: "*Your Acheron staff is trying to raise you for confirmation that you ordered the empty cruisers out of their slips and into orbit under my control.*"

"But I did not . . ." Chaeron steepled his hands, then smiled, and nodded. "Check, *Marada.* I'll clear it. Next time, wait a little longer, so that I can *pretend* I am making the decisions around here." His voice was flippant; Penrose saw his restrained frown, causing the drawn flesh around his eyes to quiver and a muscle to jump in his jaw. "Get me Acheron Authority, Rafe, and give them an open line down to us: There's a limit to the security we can enforce without hurting ourselves—*some* of these guys must be ours."

Penrose did those things without touching a keyboard, while Tempest, still at the window, was shaking his head in negation: *no one* in Acheron was trustworthy. No Acheron-controlled, orbitally mounted "crowd control" could be chanced, under these circumstances, lest they find themselves victims of their own firepower, accidentally "*Mis*aimed."

Chaeraon, after talking briefly with his Acheron secretary, got up and joined the intelligencer where Tempest watched with Jesse Thorne as the shadowy Orrefors force mounted the stairs. "A good number, Gahan," he said conversationally, then, so low that only Tempest, and Thorne, who was standing by, could hear: "I had to alert them; it cannot matter now. Whoever is up there and belongs to Hooker can do nothing more to obstruct us, or ours, or the multidrives and cruisers. Don't worry—I took all the hunter-sats off-line for the duration." Then, again at normal levels: "Shebat, you've a cruiser overviewing this action; I want to know everything it tells you, whenever it tells you, whether you think it important, or not!"

"It's taking too long; they've a few surprises for us, or they'd be here," Tempest posited. And he was not wrong.

"Can you not just seal the area off, like in Acheron?" Thorne wondered aloud, when they had stood aching silent minutes, waiting.

"Not in this best-of-all possible dream worlds," Tempest snapped sourly "Intelligencers' proposals are not taken to heart when they interfere with politics and purports. Microwave heating to melt snow, but no molecular sieves on the order of—" He snapped his fingers, punched Thorne companionably, and went to Chaeron's side, where they spoke fugitively. All that could be heard was Chaeron's final reply: "Only as a last resort, if the consulate's main seals are breached, and I'm not around anymore to reap the rebukes. Until then, containment remains the order of the day!"

Gahan Tempest growled a feral retort, his mouth curled, marched from the windows and threw himself down into a chair. Head back, eyes closed, even Thorne knew he was working, interfaced with the data pools.

While Tempest was so occupied, and Shebat hunched over the desk with a headset and Penrose leaning over her shoulder, bathed in lurid indicator spill, the Orrefors sortied, three hundred strong, up to the east turret's final, tiered flights. Below the proconsul's balcony, shouting began, and changed to chants of "Death to Kerrions! Devils from the stars!" Then: "Freedom, freedom."

At the "devils" part, Chaeron had chuckled, but with the rising volume and obvious organization, he sobered. "I'll give them 'freedom.' I'm going out there. If they want to demonstrate, they need a permit, like the local indigents they're pretending to be. Gahan, I thought you said these were Orrefors rebels, only. What are they, dressed for a masaquerade?"

Below, torches were lighting contorted faces, unkempt women, roughhewn men.

"I'm going with you," Shebat tore off her headset, vaulting from her chair, with Penrose, silent and grave, matching her stride for stride.

Tempest, with a last look and a curse at his topographical arrays, raced out to join the others under the portico in the open air.

Jesse Thorne, hanging back, heard a noise like scraping, above him. Then, with a look around at the empty study whose flickering lights imparted information to none, he joined the four Kerrions who had made the edge of the balcony, and leaned down over the rail.

A chant came up: *"Kerrion! Kerrion!"* interspersed with, "Murderers!" "Jailers!" and worse. Torches shook, thrust against the pillars repeatedly, as if the artificial crystal could be persuaded to ignite.

Thorne heard Chaeron try once to outshout the masses, saw him put down his hands and step back in disgust.

Above, multidrives could be heard: the cranky whine of stressed engines. A flash of light illuminated the sky so that everything, for one moment, was bright as noon.

Then they were upon Thorne: men dropping from the portico on ropes and scrambling over its sides, men standing upon the shoulders of others. Jesse saw only bearded faces and faces with knitted masks; bodies through which it was necessary to dodge; a fist coming at him; hands grappling him, wrestling him down. He heard Shebat cry out, and a man's deep curse, and then no one held him.

He rose from the marbled floor, hearing his name whispered, a voice he thought he knew explaining his identity to someone else. Someone helped him up; a gun was thrust into his hand. He was passed through the press like a pail of water, coming to the fore where the four Kerrions stood at bay, a man's-length circle clear about them, as if some magical periphery protected them from harm. A big man had jumped up on the balustrade and his victorious gesticulation brought roars like thunder from the throng below.

On the balcony, nearly fifty interlopers and four Kerrions held a perfect silence, until the man on the balustrade turned around and greeted Jesse warmly, asking him which of the four was Chaeron Kerrion.

"Et tu, Jesse?" he heard the proconsul whisper, even as Gahan Tempest stepped in front, saying, "I am he." Tempest's belligerent glare froze Thorne, who realized too much suddenly, and cast the gun aside. As it clattered to his feet, a brief, bright flare pricked the dark, followed by a sharp crack, Shebat's scream and the sound of something heavy, falling.

Next he knew, the gun was being pressed back into his hand. "You dropped something, *Orrefors"* said a pale enchanter with whom he had parlayed in Fort Ticonderoga, as a signal burst shot nightward and he saw three Kerrions down on their knees beside the prostrate Gahan Tempest.

He did not want to take a hand, take the blame, brandish his gun about and be what the Orrefors beside him was expecting: lord of the moment, bringer of death and treachery. He found himself, because he was able, clearing a path toward the stricken Kerrions. Those few feet took him overlong to cross. He had forever to study the tableau: Chaeron covered with blood, Tempest's head in his lap; Shebat crouched low in abject weeping, her arms around the intelligencer, who must be dead—so much blood cannot be released from a man who lives; Penrose, hunkered down beside, fixing him with an accusatory stare.

Jesse's skin crawled, remembering what he had seen inside, while the Orrefors who had urged him to take command leaped once more to the balustrade and crowed over all the crowd: "He is dead! The Kerrion is dead! We have triumphed! We have *won!"*

The gun in Jesse's hand dangled loose as he bent down. He had seen death before: its slack mouth, its shrunken form. But he had never seen it so clearly waiting in a living man's eyes as when Chaeron Kerrion's adamantine gaze met his. "You want *these* upon your conscience?" Chaeron gestured widely, then rubbed his mouth with a bloody hand. "Tempest is worth a herd of them. Love and trust and peerless acumen, freely given from boyhood on . . . loyalty, too, without parallel. . . ."

His voice fell to a whisper. "Never mind, it's all beyond you. Just avert your eyes; *pretend* to decency in the face of sacrifice. . . ." His own eyes shaded with his hand, he fell silent as Rizk the ironmonger came shouldering through, demanding to be allowed to make a final identification of the corpse. "I know him; I've *met* him. Let me *look!*"

In that instant, Jesse recognized redemption, if he could grasp it; choice, though he thought it too late to save himself by making it. Still, he raised his pistol, training its sights on the approaching ironmonger who would in seconds expose the ruse that Tempest had given his life to perpetrate—and then Chaeron Kerrion would surely die. Jesse squinted along the peep-sight and gently squeezed. As the muzzle bucked upward in his hand, Rizk's head exploded like a ripe melon, spattering bystanders. His trunk staggered backward, fell.

But what Thorne did was no account to the Kerrions, locked into their interfaces, eyes closed. And then it was too late.

From the sky, death began to rain.

On the stairs, folk fell like chestnuts in an autumn storm, slipping and rolling in a deluge of light, screaming, crackling as they flared. There was no seeing through the lightning's storm of rage. Only on the portico was the gentler fist of enkaphalin depotentiation used. There men sank to their knees, lay down to sleep a sleep from which most might reawake. Jesse stayed still, beside the Kerrions in their circle of safety. The gun, when he remembered he still grasped it, he held out toward the Kerrion proconsul, who raised his auburn head, brushed back bloodstained hair, and spat upon the weapon. It never occurred to him that Shebat would want it. But she wrestled it from him, her fine mouth contorted horribly, and pointed it at him: "You will not get away!"

When the black-and-reds burst through the doors and scrambled down ladders from roaring multidrives and crowded around, he went with them unresisting. Later, they would give him time to explain. Surely, these most civilized of people would not condemn him without a hearing.

But as he was dragged through the multitude slain

upon the stairs by silent, vicious black-and-reds (and never through the clean, white halls where festivities might yet be underway), he wondered. And when he saw the clean-up crews through the wire-barred window of the lorry into which he and fifty others were packed like tripe, he wondered more. And when the men were shackled and grouped in tens and shunted into holding-bins, he was not sure that he would see the sun, or Cluny Pope, or Shebat Kerrion, ever again. And then he wondered why he had not disentangled himself, while yet he could, from Kerrions and his Orrefors kin. But it was too late for any of that, and the only bright spot in his darkened cell was the fact that not one of those with whom he shared it was an Orrefors, but only simple townsfolk, roused to folly, who had never expected to win, just fought to save their steadings, their children, a way of life slipping away through their gnarled fingers which Orrefors enchanters had promised to reinstate.

Somewhere in that endless night, he wept for all that he had learned and all that he had seen, for the death of valor and ignorance, for the end of days when manhood could turn even the most capricious of tides.

When at last the arbiters summoned him, blinking, he found that he had nothing to say.

When they brought Cluny Pope to see him, he regained his tongue, but the truth they wanted was not the truth he had. Cluny's face was fat with bruises; in an empty chamber where they were allowed to meet with an arbiter standing by, their extent was underscored by white, echoing emptiness about. "What happened to you?"

"Me and Bitsy had a fight."

"Over me?"

Cluny shrugged.

"I tried to warn Shebat. I have told them—it was none of my doing."

"I knew it!" Cluny blazed. Then his fire was doused. "But they will not believe me. I *told* Shebat! They say you held a gun on the proconsul, that the Orrefors called you 'commander.' Sir, everyone from our . . . group . . . has come here, to plead for mercy. Bitsy says they will make an example of you." He bit his lip. "My father is here, too, sir. No one. . . ." The boy's voice was too thick for speech. "I—" He moved closer; the arbiter shifted his feet, simply widening his stance, watching something he held in his hand, then the boy, then Jesse's face. "Sir, I . . ." Cluny lunged, grabbed Thorne, hugged him close. With the youth's head pressed to his breast, Jesse could feel his chest heaving, Cluny's shivering, a scandalòus tear. "I can't let you die. Tell them . . . something, *any*thing . . . what they want to know., Please, please! They'll. . . ."

"Head up, scout. This is no time for doubts." Thorne pushed back, taking the boy by both shoulders. He shook him. "Look at me. Am I alive? *Am I?*"

"Y-y-yes."

"Then treat me like the living. Save your tears, man. They'll not excute me—they're far too civilized!" he sneered. "Do you want me to think I have failed with you? Is this what I've groomed, a sniveling child? Cry this way before your father, and I'll show you just how alive I am!"

Thorne looked over at the arbiter, asking for an end to it with his eyes. But the unspeaking man, whose face was regularly Kerrion—blue-eyed, evenfeatured, pleasant but unrecognizable in any crowd—had neither pity nor humanity; only his hand-held device, singing softly, was worthy of his gaze.

Cluny's voice had lost its battle with his heart, coming out a whine: ". . . can't . . . make it without you, none of us can. Please, Jesse, tell them what they want to know."

If he could find no way to stop it he could not hold himself in check much longer. He returned the boy's second embrace until the arbiter put an end to it, then sought the closest wall. Against that white tile he leaned, unspeaking, looking only at his feet, until at last they left him, murmuring arbiter and stricken youth. He did his best to forget that encounter, but it haunted him the rest of his days, along with the sight of Gahan Tempest calmly stepping in front of his Kerrion charge to his death.

In New Chaeronea, scant hours after the last multidrive bore Kerrion hosts and Consortium guests up into the starry night and the security of Acheron, all the lights went out. The power outage was complete; the Kerrion cousin left in charge considered sabotage, emphemerally, but chaos abounded in the pitch-dark city. And, had he penetrated the plot and deduced its ramifications immediately, he could not have foiled it: he had an entire, panicked city on his hands; controlling it was more than he could do.

He thanked his thoughtful architects that he could exit his own chambers: one fail-safe had not failed: every door in New Chaeronea opened as the power died. Running through his own, flashlight in hand, he collided with his assistant, pale in nightclothes, and together they went to roust the sleeping engineers. The emergency generators *should* have cut in automatically. In the darkened halls, screams from folk trapped in a lift distracted them further. Cursing, the Kerrion-in-charge delegated authority. If his instructions were cursory and his perspicacity wanting, he had good reason: one of those voices wailing in the open-doored shaft was his wife.

In the consulate's basement, Hooker hurried from his cell, borne along in the company of Kerrion-liveried cohorts whose part in his escape had so long ago been determined that no one needed to speak a word. "If this happens, then here's what we'll do. . . ." It had been a contingency so well and completely planned for that its execution was more like a *déjávu* than an escape. Only one deviation from the scenario was instituted, and that at Hooker's command: "Thorne!" he hissed, as they followed the bobbing pools of light their flashlights cast through the inky corridors.

No one argued; Hooker had chosen his co-conspirators well. Every man among them had been here before Chaeron Kerrion came to roost in Acheron; some had engaged in the struggle to wrest Earth from Orrefors dominion a few had fought on the Orrefors side. All had one thing in common: Earth was their home, the only home left to them since Chaeron had jettisoned the Stump and made every man jack of them into tenant-minions whose tasks were impossible of accomplishment and whose inherited loyalties and painstakingly developed methodologies were then opened to Kerrion review, Kerrion derision, Kerrion revision.

Hooker, whose father was of the Orrefors bond and whose mother was undistinguished among Kerrions, had played Marada Kerrion for a fool. It was not difficult to do. The consul general of Kerrion space had enjoined him to do what he most cherishingly dreamed of doing. He had expected, eventually, to be thrown to the Kerrions' arbitrational wolves, unmasked and cast away when the time was right.

He was not hurt, he was not angry. But he would not be neutered and sent unresisting to space-end. He was an enchanter, among folk who did not understand the term's meaning. Only a man who had made a lifetime study of Earth could hope to bring her to her knees. He had been consummately careful, even among fellow enchanters, never to let on what he was about, or what sympathies he truly felt. Only a dozen men in Earth's space knew Hooker's true feelings, or his innermost dream: make Earth sufficiently unprofitable to Kerrions, who worshipped Scrip, the lord of commerce, and they would let her lie fallow. Given time and tribulation, this could easily be done.

The rebel Orrefors who held motley court in Fort Ticonderoga had no hope of succeeding on their own. With Hooker's clandestine aid, his intelligencers, his deep-cover familiarity with Kerrion weak spots and Consortium law, there was a chance, slim but graspable . . . *if* he could offer Jesse Thorne as a rallying call. An Orrefors of consular rank was necessary; an Orrefors scion, unconscionably treated, to sue from exile for a reconstitution of his bond, a redress of its grievances against the houses of Kerrion and Labaya, who through industrial sabotage and money-market manipulation had pauperized a small and noble house, then eaten it alive. An antitrust suit had been proposed at the time of the assimilation, but Richter Orrefors was ancient, exhausted, divested of suitable heirs; he had declined the review. Show the senescent Orrefors ex-potentate his grandson, Jesse Richter Thorne, in the flesh, and new life would be breathed into both grandfather and grand litigation. *Then* Hooker and every other man who knew that enchanters' ways were the *only* way to handle Earth would be vindicated, heroes, landed gentry second to none on the inimitable ancestral sphere.

There existed a multidrive, waiting among the hills. There existed an escape route, a passage prepaid in blood, an antiquated Orrefors cruiser powered down among the asteroids, and a man in Ticonderoga who had waited nearly two years to fly it. All that had not been ready was the intransigent young roughneck, Jesse Thorne. So Hooker had made Thorne his special project: succored his development, secretly; persecuted him, when that became advisable, seeking to drive him into Hooker's rebels' arms. When it became clear that Thorne could not be driven, when fate had brought him up to Acheron under the protection of Kerrions, Hooker had jumped at the chance to educate the Orrefors heir as to what was rightfully his and what had been lost to Kerrions.

Hooker had seen the thoughtful countenance, seen the scowls. But he had not seen hatred on the face of Jesse Thorne, or resentment, even after the militia commander had perused the entire study-list Hooker had provided in Acheron. But Hooker knew that assimilation-learning often took time to be correlated by a deluged brain. He had been content to wait until the significance of what Thorne had learned sank in, in the meantime sending him to poor Rizk for additional lessons. More, he had dared not do, then, under the watchful eyes of Kerrion surveillance. But Kerrion madness and Kerrion apriority had done it for him: hatred would surely be present on the countenance of the militia leader, caged unjustly, who had seldom been long imprisoned before, thanks to Hooker's most concerted and invisible protection.

"Here."

"Thorne?"

In his cell the man put an arm before his face, then froze like a deer caught in headlights. Hooker wondered briefly if he had given the ignorant ruffian more credit than his potential could ever realize: the militia commander had lain in the dark in an open cell, never realizing that, as the lights failed, the doors of his imprisonment had drawn back. But the disheveled, startled man blinking his eyes and staggering to his feet, hitching up his pants with one hand while squinting into flashlights under the other, had been sleeping.

It did not take more than: "Let's go. Now, unless you want to rot in Kerrion prison!" to inform him of the intent and purpose of Hooker's visit. Even those words were hard to utter from a mouth trained to circumspection, a tongue long silent for fear of data pool and surveillance nets.

The Kerrion livery, when Thorne was among those wearing it, did not faze him. But Hooker's face, squinted at and recognized, did: "You!" A hand came out, grasping in a blur for his throat. Hooker backed a step, while a red and black arm shot between them.

"Me, or no one. Now, or not at all."

A hesitation; a surly growl: this moment wrote the future. Hooker could not say, "please." He merely backed through his confreres. "Let's go."

They went—running, since everyone they might meet in the corridor would be hurrying—with only one flashlight lit to guide them, the others ready to blind any who might approach from the opposite direction. When Hooker heard a cough and a misstep, a lurid curse in New York's multilingual patois, he knew, for the first time, that Thorne had joined the jailbreak—that he was going to win!

Chapter Seven

Acheron glittered in her ring of substations like an open eye in Sol's lemon light. Behind and "above" her, Earth's moon was a hoary silent crescent, a light quizzical brow. Near the shipwrights' substation, the *Marada* lingered, awaiting ministrations to his tail-telemetry's external camera, which a two-inch piece of speeding debris had impacted and put awry while he and *Danae* and four other Kerrion cruisers berthed in Acheron had lined the flight path home and thirty twinkling multidrives had vectored safely in under their watchful gaze.

"Beneath" him spun the Earth, sliced by night, dotted with pastoral fires. Beside him rested AXV 1001 *Tyche,* a vessel unique among all of cruiserkind, light-girdled and shining in reflected glory while crews crawled over her for one final visual shakedown before Acheron's proconsul himself flew her to Lorelie. Beyond *Tyche,* transports and frigates speckled space, parked awaiting slips now occupied by visiting consular cruisers. Even as the *Marada* watched, a cruiser departed and an Armored Personnel Carrier lumbered toward the docking path.

Soon every visiting cruiser would have departed, but Chaeron Kerrion had not yet lifted from *Marada* the designation Acheron One. Though *Danae* pretended not to notice this oversight, in among the wisps of cruiser thought and cruiser chatter, the *Marada* sensed that it remained her paramount concern. He was just explaining to *Danae* that since she and *Tyche* would soon be leaving Acheron and Earth space for Lorelie and space-end, while Shebat and *Marada* stayed behind, Chaeron's action was understandable, a matter of convenience with no venality or slight intended, when far below him the glitter that was New Chaeronea winked out.

The *Marada* broke off in mid-commiseration. Yes, outboards were impenetrable; it was well that this was so. . . .

He activated his most discerning modes, heightened his magnifications. Radio scans gave little information, X-ray seemed useless, heat analysis told him that New Chaeronea was as cold as Earth's gutted moon. Infrared gave him what he needed: he saw Mount Defiance's softened, terraced peak; on it, the gleaming city which gave off no ray of visual light. The *Marada* registered cruiser's relief: the city was not destroyed, only powered down. In it, humans darted yet, about their business. But no data pool or knowledge base answered the *Marada*'s queries as to what was going on. Discrete, groundbased arrays were silent, still and calm. Far, far away, the *Marada* could just hear battery-operated com-units in his intense radio scan.

Three picoseconds after the cruiser had noticed, analyzed, and considered the ramifications of the blackout on the shores of Lake Champlain, he reached out toward his pilot, who danced a dream of her husband in Acheron's consulate—a dream which under circumstances even fractionally less grave, the *Marada* would not have dared to interrupt.

"Dear Lords," Chaeron rasped, face in his palms, "what next?"

Shebat, shaking off the dream with effort, found her own hand on her pounding heart. Penrose and Lauren, taking dream dancer's fillets from their brows, blinked and shook themselves like two startled owls.

In Chaeron's residence at the rear of the consulate, the lights came up.

Lauren muttered shocked accusations, that such a thing could come to be.

"Never mind, damn it!" Penrose shushed her. "There are many things more compromising than cruisers playing peek-a-boo with their pilots. Say one word about this to anyone, and you'll never dance another dream." But he sought her, among the bedclothes, helped her don a paisley robe, put away her dream dancer's tools in their box.

Chaeron was dressed by then, immune to Penrose's carping: "Every time we do something like this, ill comes out of—"

"Raphael, get her out of here," Shebat husked, indicating with an inclination of her head Chaeron, unmoving, eyes closed, his pulse beating hard in his throat as he delved deep in his sources of information.

By the time his eyes came open and his fingers remembered to button his shirt, Penrose and Lauren had disappeared and a pair of intelligencers in off-duty clothes were waiting in his study. Shebat, knuckling sleep from her eyes, drank coffee, balancing the steaming cup on one flight-satined knee, sunk down in one of four tall chairs. Both intelligencers wore black leggings and black scarves: these had come with Chaeron from Draconis; one was Gahan Tempest's personal protégé, Ward, stoic with grief.

"Gentlemen, I am forced to suggest," Chaeron sighed, "that we secure both planet and platform—tonight, permanently, and completely. I want every even-remotely-questionable individual relieved of his duty, and I want Fort Ticonderoga and every other rebel Orrefors stronghold on Earth to disappear, this instant. Is that clear? I'll worry about niceties of procedure, after you've proceeded. Get out of here. By sunrise, Greenwich Mean, I want a peaceful consulate and placid planet, if I have to declare martial law!"

Shebat, over her cup, watched him unspeaking. Chaeron had wept for Tempest; he had not wept when his own father died. To ease her husband's distress in the face of death, she had given in to his desire for a shared dream. Were they yet dreaming, all four, only dreaming that they waked from dream into nightmare? Was this her worst fear, realized: a dream dance gone so wild that none of them might ever wake? But no: Lauren's sullen exit, Rafe's determined, cheerful smile—these were real. And the intelligencers, so amenable to wholesale destruction, were real. Parma Kerrion used to affirm that wherever his son Marada went, chaos followed. Marada was in Acheron; all the hosts of evil had traipsed along behind.

Tempest's raven-haired protégé, Ward, said laconically, from the drawn-back, eagle-blazoned doors, "That would be a good idea, sir—declaring martial law." His eyes shone too brightly. Though he grinned a grin that Tempest might have taught him, something darker and meaner than circumstances warranted seemed to peer out beneath it. Shebat shivered.

But Chaeron, sunk in his chair, gave the intelligencer the go-ahead sign without looking up. Doors smacked shut with a sound like satisfaction. Slumped down on his spine, one bare ankle crossed over his black-clad knee, Chaeron let out a hissing breath. Then: "At least I am not the complete ignoramus: I had sense enough to bring those vulnerable children up here. Shebat, I'll have to *keep* Cluny . . . indefinitely. Perhaps you and Bitsy will see to explaining this to him. And you had better send some sort of communiqué in my name to his parents so they will not be frightened when Thorne's case is settled, I'll send him down, if he wishes. Or we'll find a place for him in Acheron. . . ."

She nodded, sipping her drink, her own eyelids flickering closed intermittently as she shuffled through the information coming in in spurts. A B-flat would chime in her head, and then she would take the same update Chaeron was getting. She received an education in the use of intelligence keys that night, by dint of simply demanding the same information her husband was receiving. He sent no additional orders, content to let the intelligencers loose on platform and planet. Their thirst for revenge in the matter of their slain senior officer would do the rest. She composed a letter to Cluny Pope's father, and sent it, and a message that the boy meet her for breakfast in the pilot's guildhall, where the wonder of pilotry might ease the sting of treachery. She stayed, the whole time, in direct contact with her cruiser, so that the data updates came both in vocal mode, and as alphabets burned into her retinas, cobalt words rolling on a mental "screen" with cruiser contact giving her hot-colored computer-simulations behind. Her linguistic and imagining centers were so deluged with color and sound that Chaeron spoke twice to her before she answered.

"I said, I am sorry if I forced the issue of the dream dance," he repeated.

"Things have not been easy for any of us. I would still like to go with you to Lorelie. I deserve to attend Tempest's funeral."

"I need you here, as my *pro tem*."

"I wish I could believe you, but my heart says it is because things go ill between us."

"This," he reached into his pants' pocket, pulled out something small, metal, round, "was among Jesse Thorne's personal effects." He threw the tetradrachm from Naxos into her lap. "Surely, if you would give him my birthday gift to you—worth as much as a cruiser and more because it was a peace offering—you would then prefer to stay here and make sure that in their zealousness, my intelligencers don't make an end to him." His tone was severe.

"I did not—"

"Bitsy told me what he saw, Shebat. Do not lie to me." He seemed merely exhausted, not pejorative; simply disappointed, not betrayed.

Marada Kerrion's abrupt and unannounced entrance froze Shebat's retort on her lips.

"*What are you doing sitting here?* New Chaeronea is off the com-grid, black as doom. Chaeron, you are incompetent—" Two of his bodyguard slithered in behind him, took up places against the wall like black-and-red clouds threatening a clear blue sky.

"Everything is taken care of, Marada. Sit down and have some coffee."

Kerrion space's consul general was livid. "Taken care of? You utter fool. Through your mismanagement, I have been embarrassed for the last time!"

"Marada, *sit down,* unless you want to discuss Hooker and his orders before your loyal bootlicks and then in a

tribunal! I'm not afraid of the arbitrational guild anymore. And you, who spent a lifetime studying law only to
learn how best to affront it without penalty, should be. I
have done nothing wrong, nothing illegal. The only errors I have made were those of hesitancy. Now, I would
like to blame all of those on you, but I cannot." Chaeron
was up, pacing, his shirttails out and trailing.

He circled the coffee table, and when he came to his
massive, bearded brother, he stopped. "Tempest's
death," he said quietly, control regained, "is my responsibility, and mine alone. I was too aware of you, lying in
wait for my first misstep with your army of arbiters with
their snares of procedural red tape, to take out obvious
traitors without incontrovertible proof. Hence, the deba-
cle—I'd hardly call it a *disturbance,* as you told my guests
that it was—on the ides of March. Were you disappointed that I survived it? Or that it did not spread
through the consulate and affright those dignitaries
whose support I most desperately need to meet the impossible conditions you have imposed upon me here?
Had you planned my death there and then—after which,
you would have dealt summarily with every henchman
you sicced on me . . . in proper arbitrational order? It is
my turn, big brother, to question your motives, formally
and thoroughly."

The doors opened once again, revealing Acheron's two
senior arbiters—one young and florid; the other grizzled
and paunched—who stepped gingerly inside, nodded to
Marada, and enlivened a console which covered the farther wall. On it, prior depositions paraded in red and in
blue. Marada Kerrion's statement of *nolo contendere,*
which said in substance that Hooker had been acting entirely upon his own, was corroborated by Hooker's own
testimony (obtained in and extracted from a lengthy in-
terrogation conducted by a duly-licensed team of inter-
rogators headed by T. Ward and audited by the would-be
agent-provocateur's arbiters, said the small print), de-
scribing how the attaché had used Rizk as an unknowing
agent; pretending to sympathize with him and the Orrefors rebels' cause, appearing to aid and abet their
struggle while in reality obstructing Chaeron on the short
term and softening up the refractory Orrefors for an

eventual coup by Kerrion forces in which Chaeron would be proved ineffectual, Marada would be blameless, and Hooker himself the hero of the hour.

"Hold it there," Chaeron ordered. The arbitrational guildsmen had their tiny, multicolored cubes in hand, activated, ready to record any testimony given verbally. When the cubes had absorbed every bit of pertinent information, they would independently render a verdict. When that point was reached—in days, weeks, or months—everyone involved must abide by mechanical intelligence's findings.

Marada Kerrion rolled his eyes and backed away. He sat in an empty chair and plucked at its arms. "You are not going to try to base a case on Hooker's *inference* that *I* ordered him to obstruct progress here?"

"I have a slate, Consul General, *Sir,* in my secondary matrix, and a copy of the cruiser *Marada,* of Hooker warning you to stay out of the east turret on the fifteenth of March."

Marada Kerrion passed a weary hand across his suddenly furrowed brow. "I see that this post has been too much for you. Gentlemen, do not embarrass us further. Go run cubes, as well as you may." The arbiters, expressionless, turned to face him. "My guild membership may have lapsed, but I am still an arbiter at heart. I share your distress at being called into this obviously personal quarrel between my brother and me. As you both well know, we have just come through one arbitration, which proved nothing, only wasted the arbiters' time. Now, as an ex-arbiter, I can tell you that the circumstantiality of the evidence to which Chaeron refers will never stand up under due process. You had better be sure, gentlemen, before you file any more data in those cubes, that there is good reason to do so. You are excused. I will expect a full report before I leave tomorrow on the status of your investigation."

The arbiters, muttering together, turned back to the screen, where they took a transcript of the exchange between Hooker and Marada Kerrion.

While they did so, Marada scrutinized Chaeron with a patient, slightly amused mien. "Quick, quick, brothers, my proconsul and I have other urgent matters to discuss."

"The black-and-reds, too, unless you want me to call my own."

All filed out.

"Shebat, if you will?" Marada suggested that she, too, leave.

"My wife will soon be proconsul *pro tem*. She stays."

"I'd rather spare her. . . ."

Chaeron made a derisive noise.

Marada Kerrion cracked his knuckles, hooked a leg over his chair. "But since she did not spare me the embarrassment of statutory rape in full view of the Stump consular staff, she deserves to be included."

"Marada, Shebat was fifteen years old then; if anyone brings charges, it should be she!"

"Chaeron!" Shebat gasped, remembering the day so long ago when she had put a spell of deep sleep upon Marada Kerrion and slipped into his bed.

"You two want to get down in the mud and roll in it? I will do nothing to forefend the consequences. A dream dancer and consular intriguer. I must admit, make a formidable combination. But when dream dancing is still illegal in Kerrion space, and when the conduct of intrigue is so all pervasive as to involve date-linkage of nonpilots through pilots to cruisers and the crippling of those cruisers thereby, as well as sexual harassment of pilot by owner, when the intriguer's mother is a confessed but unpunished murderess. . . ."

"Marada, wait a moment, I want to slate this in stereo!" Chaeron grinned, blinked, and said, leaning forward, "Proceed, if you will."

Shebat, however, could not keep calm. "Marada, you are beyond hope, beyond understanding, beyond human forgiveness! You say these things to us, and calmly admit that you allowed and encouraged Hooker? Our *child* was killed! Chaeron's—"

"Hardly a child, at that stage," Marada demurred, pouring himself coffee, cream and sugar, taking a spoon and tapping it on the cup's rim. "And clearly an accident—an unfortunate malfunction.

"As Parma used to say, these things happen. We have

an arbitration, it seems. I, for one, am ready to have my life scrutinized by arbiters and held up to judgment before the entire Consortium. How about you, Shebat?"

She sat back, chewing her nails.

"Chaeron, you were telling me what you are doing about this new emergency . . . ?"

"Take it from the sources." He gave Marada a code-in number. Damage reports by ground-based airborne intelligencers were just beginning to come in. Taken from the *Marada*'s scans and amplified, visual confirmation came up behind Marada's head, on the live screen wall. As they watched, a red circle around the dark spot where Mount Defiance lay in close-up topographical infrared display disappeared, and the map shifted to available light: New Chaeronea, as they watched, popped into glowing life. Seventy-six minutes after the power went out, New Chaeronea was back on-line.

"Tsk, tsk," Chaeron clucked. "I know you are disappointed. But perhaps you would like to stay and see the denouncement? We've more than enough reason for reprisals, thanks to you and yours. And it is too late to abort my taking them." The screen quartered, one corner showing an aerial view of Fort Ticonderoga blossoming into flames; police actions in New Chaeronea and other Earthly installations filling the three others. "You choose to claim innocence, go ahead. But the guilt for all of this is yours. I—"

Marada rose jerkily, strode with stiffened steps to the doors.

"I hope," Chaeron called after his brother, "that you don't have trouble sleeping, after tonight. If I were you, I know I would!"

The last two words of that he spoke to the closing doors, to the Kerrion eagle-bating-over-seven-stars they displayed when their edges met.

"You know," Shebat remarked, "Marada cannot help it . . . no man courts madness."

Before Chaeron could respond, their data pool alarms chimed urgently; in two skulls the news was announced simultaneously: Thorne and Hooker had made good their escape.

Chapter Eight

Chaeron Ptolemy Kerrion, in his berth in AXV 1001 *Tyche,* dreamed a dream of altered states: in the dream, every cruiser he ordered into action to thwart the Orrefors incursion had been previously equipped with microwave depotentiators. In the dream, he was not forced to use the cruisers' deadly particle beams, their unerring magnetic guidance systems and path-clearing lasers, upon helpless dupes of Orrefors secessionists. In the dream, he had not gone numb and mindless when he most needed to be clear and quickwitted: he acted upon his instincts, instead of suppressing them. He rectified every error of omission: he arrested Hooker, he paralyzed the electronics in Fort Ticonderoga with a tenth-second burst of stripped negative hydrogen ions from a hunter-killer in orbit, both before the crowd had climbed his consulate's steps. As a result, in the dream, only five percent of those struck down from heaven failed to recover; an intelligencer gave him the figures, which followed the normal genetic susceptibility curve for enkaphalin depotentiation by microwave. And that intelligencer was Gahan Tempest, who, because of Chaeron's dream-quick thinking, had not found it necessary to step between Chaeron and the rabble. He woke smiling, buoyed with relief that Tempest had not died.

He rolled onto his stomach, pulling his pillow over his

head, trying to burrow back into dreams. But it was no use: Tempest was dead—and Hooker, Thorne, et al., escaped to wherever—by dint of the very espionage Tempest had fretted over; hundreds had died in New Chaeronea and an indeterminate (and inexcusable) multitude more in Ward's intelligencers' overzealous—if belated—scouring of Orrefors strongholds from the pleated face of Earth. Though Ward forthcomingly accepted responsibility for the overkill (due, he maintained, more to his men's unfamiliarity with balky Orrefors equipment than any thirst for vengeance), Chaeron had given Ward his orders—the blame was Chaeron's; every unnecessary death weighed on his conscience. Of only small comfort was the proximity, at that time, of the family curse: Marada had come and gone, leaving behind his requisite aftermath: destruction, disruption, and never-ending, inconclusive guild arbitration. Chaeron felt no better about any of it now, on the tenth and last day of his flight to Lorelie as "pilot" of the AXV, than he had before embarking, when he had hoped a span of meditation would ease him.

He threw his pillow to the deck, tossing in restrictive bedclothes, his elbow crooked over his eyes although the stateroom was yet dim. He was a student of dreams, an ardent examiner of self. He had never before struggled with irremedial regrets. Whether this was because he had never before blundered so badly, or because his sensibilities had become sharpened, remained to to be determined. Fear, doubt and self-recrimination were modes of cogitation he had conscientiously shunned: they had no place in the mentation of a decision-maker whose province was a star-flung consular house. What, then, was his dream telling him? There was never a moment so empty as to allow leisure to regret past occurrences—or failures; the future pressed ineluctably upon his consular "now." He had always been content with his tiny moment of being, willing to look forward into the unknowable, to deal from the top of action's deck without qualm.

Then, what? In the dream, he had seen himself from without. He had been "Chaeron" and not "I." Was it what he had sensed about his brother's deteriorating con-

dition that had precipitated it? Second thoughts and
punctilious hand-wringing over events gone to history
and graved into the past like stone were Marada's mainstay. The fact that during their dispute in Acheron no
word of scandalized recrimination over lives lost and ethics tarnished (let along real or imagined devaluation of
Kerrion law) had passed Marada's lips still troubled
Chaeron. When one's ranking relative is determinedly
out of character, disaster looms. That Marada's disasters
could not be confined to his personal sphere, but must
clutch at the ankles of millions, was deeply disturbing to
Chaeron, for, like the adjustments made to reality in his
dream, nothing could be done about whatever was increasingly wrong with his half brother.

He rose and the lights brightened, showing him the
quiet, taupe luxury of his stateroom, his discarded
clothes. He visited the head, made morning ablutions in
a water shower: his mother would appreciate that touch.
At the sink, he cleared steam away from the mirror with
his palm, looked out at himself from a frame of mist.
"Bitten off more than you can chew?" he accused the
image, whose eyes were puffy and red-rimmed beneath
sopping, lengthened curls. "What happened to the youth
who longed to show his mettle? Gone? Or was he never
there, only imagined? Miss your daddy? If he were here,
he'd send you back to school."

The reflection did not flinch. Condemnation was its
mainstay. The man to whom the reflection belonged was
insatiably ambitious, demanding perfection to match the
façade nature had inflicted upon him. *Live up to those
looks or become a laughingstock because of them—first
popinjay of Kerrion space,* he prodded silently, baiting
the image. And then the deeper speaker inside of him
did make an answer, whispering like a chiding data pool:
"Every animal is driven to pasture with a blow," says
Heraclitus. *"It is hard to fight with anger, for what it
wants, it buys at the price of soul."*

Was he, then, consumed by a passion he could not detect, as the arrogant daemon in his mirror would have
him believe? If so, he did not know where, when, or why
he might have hidden it.

He was en route to make peace with his mother, to

give her back her freedom, if nothing more. Even if she refused his friendship, continued to impose upon him her ban of silence, she would have access to the *Tyche*. In it she could travel wherever she chose, not subject to bans or decrees or the strictures laid upon pilots by their guild. The ruse of presenting the cruiser to an infant was no longer necessary. When it had been crucial, he had agonized over its transparency. But no one had made the obvious deduction. Now, it did not matter, so this could not be the root of his distress.

But the man in his mirror, of all men, was the only one who had never misled him, and as he toweled, shaved, and pulled on a clear, skin-hugging mil-suit, then flight satins of dusky blue darker than his eyes, he dug at the foundation of his thoughts, seeking error, a chink through which the wind of unkind fortune might blow.

He found none, and when he slipped on boots and quit his stateroom for *Tyche*'s helm he was taut with irritation. Was it Bucyrus, the thought of her seeking such a poor port, despite the storm? He threw himself into the single acceleration couch in *Tyche*'s minimal control central, annoyed beyond expression. The dream, he insisted to himself, was just a dream. The meaning of it was built of stress and unending complexity. In Shebat's dream dances, he always wore the medallion Parma had given him, just as he wore it now. In dreams, no matter whose, he never failed to mark it as important. He and Shebat had decided between them that the meaning of this recurrent symbol was simply its obvious one: on his gold medallion was the Kerrion emblem; on his heart, the weight of it never lessened. Not even in dreams could he shed its burden. This dream, then, was one of procedure, an admission of mistakes, a remonstrance from his inner person which said only: *You have proved yourself less than perfect, once again.*

"Good morning, *Tyche*. Status?"

Greens came up on the encircling walls, on the arms of the black-and-silver couch in which he sat, on canted mini-monitors before him like cases on a docket.

He had now done his piloting for the morning. This afternoon, they would exit sponge.

He got up, wandered about the control central, trailed

his hands over the manual support panel set into the wall by the lock. Here, Kerrion redundancy still lurked. Here, real pilotry could, in an emergency, be done. A secondary system, it dwarfed the primary helm, extending, behind cosmetic panels, halfway around the curve of the room. Silver-chased false fronts would roll away, with a push of one large, red button, to reveal it; a pilot's couch would come up through the floor, taking position under an emergency hatch which was indicated with red, lit arrows above his head.

He left the control room, made breakfast in the galley. Sitting there with his heated packets unopened, he drank real coffee (Earth coffee, a special gift for Ashera) and rehearsed what he might say to his mother to make her love him once again. His eyes wandered over lockers full of food, over the obligatory emergency air supply and three-mil pressure-suits, helmets hanging above them like potential ghosts waiting to be animated. He put his legs up, crossed his feet at the ankles, and said, Tyche, line through to Danae.''

Although he had helped conceive the specs from which Tyche was realized, he had not realized how much contact with the Danae and the Marada had affected him: he wanted from Tyche the kind of companionship Penrose got from Danae, and that was not to be. He could have held a conversation with her inboard computers, but the cruiser's innermost self was inaccessible to humanity, a protection for a cruiser which must ship under diverse masters and never flinch, or imprint, never be more than a transportation mechanism as far as any man could see. Within her was a soul—if cruisers had souls, and Chaeron thought that perhaps they did—which could keep its own time, a twistor clock more sensitive than any other which man had made, which never lost power or an instant of time. To do away with man's mind as timekeeper (and perhaps, eventually, man altogether, so that a cruiser could be dispatched on automatic and would embark from point A and debark at point B at a desired and prespecified moment of human time), a further step toward humanizing—or cruiserizing—mechanical intelligence had been taken in Chaeron's AXV. Tyche had, at her heart, a next-to-eternal tamperproof power source that kept in constant contact with cruiserkind—*on purpose*. To integrate the accidental development of cruiser-awareness into circuitry, Chaeron's theoreticians had dealt with fundamental problems as to the nature of time. Was it discrete units, like chronons, picoseconds, minutes—a compendium of pointlike instants? Or was it indivisible, eternal, an unbroken stream? The math said, both. The math was revolutionary, dealing with basic problems of motion, sequentiality and dimensionality as they had never been dealt with before. And they were long overdue to be dealt with, codified and logically stated, now that cruisers demonstrated the proclivity to independent thought that could only be called 'minded-ness.' In an eight-dimensional framework, embedded in a revolutionary spacetime manifold which, with complex numbers, could describe events in real-time, a place had been found for cruiser consciousness in the theoretical scheme of things. The *Tyche* could, hypothetically, make sponge entrance and sponge exit entirely on its own, using for referential chronology the synchronization of its own clock with either the base-clock which Chaeron's shipwrights had put into sponge to tick away eternity somewhere beyond space .ne's gate, or cruiser-sequen-tiality itself, which would exist as long as any cruiser, anywhere, was under power.

Doing these things had meant reexamining sponge theory, and that had been done, if inconclusively. Chaeron particularly liked one theorist's wry "layman's explanation" of his conclusions: sponge is "heaven"; the minute amount of energy released by every living thing when it decomposes reverts to sponge, whence it came; the blue-green glow pervading that achronal slice is made, not of energy trapped there by accident and black-body theory, but by spirit, flitting away home. A hue and cry had come up over that one, but Chaeron thought it neat, a scientification of godhead, rationale for every ge-netic intuition of every culture time had made.

In sponge, real pilots saw metaphysical visions of the amenable universe as a being—of Wisdom, Mother, or Father godheads—they saw, in fact, exactly what their acculturation prepared them to expect to see. *But they all saw something*. No pilot, no matter how determined or pragmatic, could match mind with his cruiser in sponge-entry or sponge-exit and not see visions. The vision drove them mad, but not mad enough to forego the opportunity to go back for further look-sees.

Chaeron wanted to see what pilots saw, but he had built this cruiser so that no man need face the specter of madness, of the unexplainable phenomena called sponge. In multidimensional theory, explanations could now be proffered that might ease some pilots' minds, albeit the thought of "traversing" an achronal domain of dependence bereft of locus or motion was not an easy one to grasp. But *Tyche,* and every succeeding AXV, need only listen to hear beacon-clock, and the cruiser-clock of interchange, to find her place in spacetime when her course demanded.

The negative universe must still be passed through, but her Kerrion matrix was sufficient to the task without exposing man to madness' moment.

The theorists in opposition to the man Chaeron's whimsy made him support argued simply that, like men brought back from death, all that was seen in sponge was seen in an instant, in a dream-state.

Whatever the truth of theory, the truth of practice was success: *Tyche* had made her sponge-entrance without any help from Chaeron, just a flicker of lights, gold to red to green.

And Chaeron, knowing he had cheated himself, but bettered his people's estate and even the troubled host of cruisers, thought to himself that the one philosopher whose words really spoke to him, after years of theorizing on the nature of man and world and eternity, had remarked: "Things which can be seen and heard and perceived, these do I prefer."

To the extent that the seeing and hearing and perceiving of cruiserkind had been upstepped by his booster station with its clock and its broadcast band, he had freed cruisers from man's tyranny of disbelief. What is discomfitting, no man wants to hear. What is unfortunate for commerce or inconvenient for self-image or contrary to the value-set called law, is ignored as long as may be.

Cruiser awareness had been one such thing, better ignored, better forgotten, better kept secret. Man wanted no such responsibility. Brilliant, a computer may be. But independent? Innovative? Never.

Since "never" had become "now," the only thing that made sense to Chaeron was to pretend (or allow his colleagues to pretend) that they and he had been preparing for it, anticipating it, working toward the fully expected realization of it, all along. The cruiser-to-cruiser matrix built into *Tyche* allowed instant communication between the cruiser and any other suitably equipped cruiser or station—*even from sponge*. Or, *in* it, without heed to proximity or need to lock cruisers in tandem.

This practical advance, utilizing the accidental discovery of a separate dimension in which cruisers experienced the concomitant of sequential being, was so long awaited, so necessary to man's continuance among the stars, and so *economical* that it would be heralded as another, perhaps the greatest, stroke of Kerrion genius.

Chaeron could hardly wait.

"Chaeron?" Penrose's voice came from *Danae,* across a half-mile of sponge, through the speaker-grids in the *Tyche's* galley's corners. "Everything green?"

"As grass. How are our passengers?"

"Young. Painfully, tryingly, young. But they're having what they call 'a great time.' Cluny wants to be a pilot when he grows up, whenever that will be. Bitsy wants to do my laundry, since you're unavailable. His dream dances are worth it, though."

"Tell him for me that if he's any trouble, we'll leave him at space-end."

"I would, but you wouldn't . . . would you?"

"No, I would not. Why don't you come over here awhile?"

A chuckle grated in the speakers. "Wouldn't I like to, though. Shebat did that, once, so rumor runs—sponge-walked. I'd not risk my jewels, unless you need something?"

"Just someone to talk to. It will wait six hours, I'm sure."

The voice coming from the speakers deepened. "You are not playing 'hero of the consulate'? There's not something wrong you're not telling me about?"

Chaeron held up both hands, let them fall to his knees

with a slap, realizing that Penrose could not see. "Nothing like that. I *am* jittery. 'Mommy' this, and 'Mommy' that. What if she refuses to see me?"

"Then you will drop off the cruiser and write her a note, and we'll get out of there as quickly as possible. Plan A, subsection three. Remember?"

"Ah, yes, I do recall something about it. But then we'll miss Gahan's funeral."

"He'll miss it, himself. Chaeron, are you sure you're all right?"

"No, but I will be."

And he was, when the sponge-exit loomed on his monitors, and he saw what seemed to be a bright, nascent star expand into universes, these passing away behind him, preceded by a dark band of nothingness, then blue-shift, then red, and the starscape taking on the familiarity of his own native cosmos, becoming sparse, spare and dark, with Lorelie's anchor-planet Alexandria coming up in his long-range viewscreen, her rings incised with the Kerrion eagle bating over seven magnetically maintained dark "stars."

He had not been home for four years. He had been away so long that he had forgotten what it might be like to be back.

Tyche, Danae, and Penrose handled their slipbay approach. There was nothing for him to do but view the beauty of crystalline Lorelie, one lone sphere like a world molded from Earth's finest sky. The spires and synthetic hills sprinkled with aristocratic children, the greetings at slipside from his three pubescent brothers, his suddenly beautiful sister, his nanny and the close family members upon whose knees he had bounced as a toddler, took his breath away.

Only his mother had not turned out to give him a hero's welcome, though he had done little more than survive.

They loved him, did the staff and intimates of Lorelie, where none not of family ties of the highest order could venture without special dispensation. He had gotten those for Penrose, and for the two adolescents he had brought to keep them out of harm's way, and they, invited guests, would be treated royally.

If only Ashera had come, even simply driven up in a lorry and waved, then his happiness would have been complete.

But his mother was nowhere in evidence, not at slipside nor in the motorcade that took them to the family abode. The eldest of his remaining brothers, resplendent in puce-and-fuschia billows of fashionable drape, sat beside him in the command transport bearing them homeward: "Just because Julian went to school in Draconis and died of it, she can't keep me locked up forever! I am sixteen! Sponsor me! Get me out of here, and you shall have my vote, eternally, unquestionably, to wield as your own!" The boy spoke through unmoving lips, pale as departed Julian's. His hair was the same, straight and flaxen; his desperation, too, reminded Chaeron of his transmogrified brother, *un*dead at space-end, a victim of faulty mil and faulty thinking on the part of everyone involved in the Shechem war. "Don't let mother fool you," the child ten years his junior whispered too loudly. "She has not changed one bit."

"I appreciate your concern. I will see what I can do," Chaeron had to answer, but it was his sister, across the aisle, luminous eyes locked on Penrose like salvation, who held his interest. "Help me, Chaeron," she had implored, lips to his neck while she hugged him uncharacteristically at slipside, "She is killing me!"

He had drawn back to see her: "What do you mean?"

And then his brother had jeered, "Ashera won't let her have boys stay the night!"

He had found himself shivering with relief, that what was meant was only the death of childhood, and nothing more. From each of his younger siblings he heard pleas similar in substance, and after he had heard them out—from the squeaking treble of his thirteen-year-old brother on up to the grandiose proclamation of imminent suicide from his seventeen-year-old sister (made while she sat between Cluny and Bitsy with her budding breasts pointed straight at Raphael like targeting arrays) he knew the truth of Lorelie: nothing had changed but him. He was altered, overly nervous, shaken by childish trifles paraded as tribulations. By the time he saw his mother, he must be unflappable, calm at heart, precisely balanced on the pinnacle of perspective. No one could hope to grapple with the Dragon who was not certain of himself and free from fear, and he was not.

He let the chatter of his wondering siblings float about him, absently noting the awe with which they approached Cluny Pope (a rough-and-tumble denizen of ancestral Earth) and Bitsy Mistral (a dream dancer, traveled and sophisticated), and watched the eagerness in their sheltered eyes buttress the two youths' courage: Cluny swaggered in his seat; Mistral lowered his long-lashed lids in mysterious humility, and all the while the questions from his kin grew more personal and more intense. Penrose, first bitch of Kerrion space, was the subject of many sidelong glances, but his rank kept the younger children at a distance—all but Chaeron's sister Penelope, who fixed her attention upon nothing else but the handsome pilot, more than a decade her senior: every woman in the Consortium dreamed of secret trysts with pilots, since they could not be wived. His sister saw more: a lover, if she could get him, whose attentions would horrify Ashera; whose touch would be expert; whose arm, should her girlfriends spy her upon it, would be enough, simply proffered, to scandalize all her peers and confer upon her the inarguable title of "woman."

Chaeron, carefully straight-faced, shifted his attention out the window, to Lorelie's beryl grasses, mansiontopped hills. His lids flickered: he yet had open code-ins to the data pools in Lorelie. Through them, he sent a message to Penrose just short of telepathy: his words went into the net, Penrose was informed of them, framed an answer. RP's reply came back to him post-haste, the next best thing to cruiser-linked minds. Rafe was cautioned, allowed to exercise his discretion. If worst-case arose, Penrose could count on Chaeron to intervene in time to extricate RP from his sister's snare.

Yet coded-in to the Lorelie net, he ambled through current matters pending, not sure what he wanted to find. When he broke his contact with Lorelie Central, he had implemented packet-sending procedures in every area of his interest, and quarter-hourly updates giving him news of incoming messages of every sort his mother might be overviewing, as well as continual status reports from the *Danae* and *Tyche* in their slips.

Still he was ill at ease, feeling there was something here he had missed, some item he had not anticipated which would soon concern him. Rubbing his eyes, he reached out and touched his sister's Lurex-sheathed knee: *Stay a moment,* his fingers said.

Waiting while the footman rushed to open their doors and the children piled out—like children, awkward and giggling; not in any way like consular heirs—he thought that perhaps it was the way Ashera always knew his mind before he spoke it which had him nerved up so that his palms wept. The near-telepathic bond between them was something he had always perceived as a debit. Today that, too, would have to change.

"Penny, dear," he murmured to her, "let Rafe alone. He's mine. Any help you think you need had better come from me."

Her seascape eyes iced over, her lip curled, but she said no word, only stiffly exited the transport by the door farthest from his, taking her place as eldest child in the *ad hoc* tour being formed to show Bitsy and Cluny the marvels of archaic reproduction that abounded in Lorelie. He saw her approach Penrose, take his arm, all decorum as their mother often displayed it: venomous charm. Escorting RP away, she chanced a look over her shoulder at Chaeron, complete with stabbing, outthrust tongue.

He turned away with a smile barely hidden, and slid out of the transport to face the cerulean tiers of his mother's abode and see what might be seen.

In the crystalline halls, on the stairs through which free water ran falling, in the purposefully dizzying rotunda, he met a crowd of ghosts: good days and bad that he had lived through in former times. He met himself (so small the ceiling was a gilded vault like Olympus), being carried through in Parma's arms. He smelled smells of long-gone feasts and heard distant, beloved voices which could nevermore be answered. He recalled a simple life, which then had seemed hard and tortuous, and a simple youth who could never be so young again. He wondered, in the lift which took him to the rooms his parents had always occupied (now housing only one) if his sister and brothers ever realized that they rushed headlong into bathos, and brushed aside impatiently the very lessons that must sustain them, exactly as he had done.

Well, it was human nature to discount the future's trials, to head out of port into difficulties undescribed and in that wise surely preferable to today's troubles. Human failings, human errors, human exhaustion consumed him, in that ornate elevator where he had stood so many times before, waiting to confront his father with this imagined slight or that callow demand or the other intrigue, unmasked by youthful perspicuity and unmitigated by a perspective only experience could bring. Those things in life most worth learning are those that cannot be taught by any master save time.

Ashera had been fond of rebuking him, saying that his feelings for his father were unnatural in their depth and unseemly in their expression, pointing out that since Parma did not return them in form or substance, Chaeron would be better off to save his regard for the Lords of Cosmic Jest, whose favor he had more chance of securing through worship than Parma's, had long ago written Chaeron off as tainted by the womb out of which he had so obligingly slipped.

He stopped, just outside their door, and leaned his head and shoulder against the ashlar wall. It was not *their* door, any longer: only his mother remained within. The ghost of Parma's presence was merely that—a memorial specter, born of his implacable refusal to grow up. What his mother thought, he could feel oozing out from beneath his prismatic portal.

He loved her too much, her evils as well as her more endearing qualities.

To secure an audience with her, he found it necessary to defeat her command that those doors not open for him. It took him less than a minute to do so.

The door opaqued, whined, scurried from his path. He brushed once at his consular blacks, and stepped within. The air was heady, rich with oxygen for her scarred lungs, seared in the same Draconis explosion that had made a mountain of Marada and a 'then consul' of Chaeron.

Silence did not fall until he had crossed the rose-and-silvered anteroom and burst into her parlor, where three women sat on parallel setees taking tea.

"Madam," he said into it, stiffly, standing on her threshold between two Meissen vases as tall as he. "Ladies, you will excuse us?"

Breaths caught and ringed fingers fluttered to lips pale under their rouge. Ashera, facing away from him, rose like a prima ballerina and walked at measured pace toward the farther casement. By the time she reached it, the others were gone.

She fluttered like a leaf from the top of her auburn head to the toe-topping fall of her jade gown, hearing him come toward her. He reached out, took her firmly by the arms, turned her. "Welcome me!"

For eighteen months, she had kept her silence. She kept it a moment more. Not intentionally—it was the shock of his aged countenance, the dark shadows nesting angrily beneath his eyes. Her cursive lips, so like his, parted, needing moisture from her tongue. Their eyes met, Kerrion-matched and beryl, and the shock of seeing him was made small by the shock of deeper contact. Unable to be denied, he lifted her off her feet and pressed his face into her hair. She could not utter a word, or she would weep. Then thought was gone from her, and years of restraint washed away with the tide of his anguish. She did not know she had let him kiss her until their lips unlocked, and he let her go so abruptly she staggered: neither of them had ever dared to envision so ignominious a moment as that, when they kissed a kiss in no way familial.

He backed away, palm across his mouth, two yawning steps into some private distance, and sat upon the arm of a settee, looking at his hands. "I brought you something. Dear Lords, mother, speak to me."

By that time she could press his bowed head against her belly, entwine her fingers in his hair, which was paler than she remembered and cursorily kept. She felt his tears, and since he could not see, smiled softly while he wept, then simply trembled against her.

"I am sorry for. . . ."

"Ssh, Dodger," she called him by the earliest of his nicknames, given before he had become difficult in his teens and they had started calling him "Little Pestilence." Parma had dubbed him "the artful dodger," and it had stuck for a dozen years on a child who never could be caught in any of his wicked schemes. When later he had proved precocious beyond prudence in matters related to direct accessing and mechanical intelligence, they had dropped all pet names in favor of his given one, which reminded them both that the danger of the future was embodied in this child who could get from any computer whatever it held within. While other children had claimed invisible friends who told them secrets, Chaeron *had* them: nothing in any computer or data net was safe from this child, who understood them better than their creators. And, too, she could not let him detail his crimes, imagined and real, lest she be forced to recite a list of her own. The time involved, if no other consideration, precluded that. And she dared not remind him of anything he might have chosen to forget.

"Chaeron, it is nothing, now. All is well between us. What am I to do with you? Are you here to stay awhile, and we will talk? All this from Tempest's death? He would weep with compassion, to see you so moved. And with sadness, to see you so weak. This does not become you, or me, or bode well for the future." Yet he held her, only breathing, not speaking, or moving, until she disengaged his arms from her hips and sat down beside him, taking his hands, looking up into his bleary eyes. "You are my first-born, my finest. If I was harsh with you, it was only because Parma and I had hopes for you that no child could have fulfilled." She let the lie loose, and saw him bite his lip, rather than contradict her: her harshness had come from the sure knowledge that her predecessor's child ranked higher in the eyes of Parma Alexander Kerrion then hers. Two white lies might cancel each other out: "After falling into Marada's disfavor, I dared not embroil you in my troubles. To cast off the taint of your parentage, it was necessary that I seem to cast you off. I took up with him on your behalf and I pretended to fall out with you, equally with your benefit in mind." If he believed that, he was more ill and more tired even than he looked. But some things are eternal; keeping Chaeron off balance was one of her specialties. "I did my best for you from a distance, and thought you would realize what I was doing. Now, dry those flattering tears, my child, before I lose my own composure, and let us talk of pleasanter things."

He said only: "You did not have to apologize to me," and meekly let her give him tea. The things she referred to as "pleasant" were not going to be easy on him, so she fed him first, feeling a warmth stir in her center that came there not because her son has displayed affection, or a disposition to compromise, but because of the quality of the instrument before her: Chaeron was becoming what logic had always told her someday he should be. The question now was one of finding his trigger.

She tried: "Animus aside, the visit only underscores our single shared reality: Marada must not be allowed to continue as consul general of Kerrion space, or the bond is doomed."

"It is comforting to know that you, at least, have not changed," he answered softly, unsmiling, calmed and sprawled on one couch, bootless, a teacup balanced on his thigh. "Let the bond be doomed, then. I have secured my own shutters, so to speak. You are welcome to join me in Acheron. As difficult as that might be for all concerned, it is preferable to your marrying a bandit like Bucyrus."

"You overstep."

"Only the beginning, I am afraid. Might I apologize in advance, and then have my say?"

"Marriage is my only alternative. Acheron is not one I will consider. Your half brother is convinced, erroneously, that I had Spry murdered and then arranged for the destruction of the *Erinys* and everyone on board."

"Yes, well, I can see how he came to that conclusion. Are you telling me differently?"

"How can you ask such a question when you see about

you the results such ill-considered action would have been sure to bring? *Did* bring, though I am wholly innocent. I suffer agonies I have not earned! I am a prisoner in my own sphere! But I must see the matter through to its logical and legal conclusion: David Spry is alive. Eventually, even Marada must admit it and stop his foul persecution of me! Renewed piracy indicated that *someone* is out there with unregistered cruisers. That someone will be shown to be Softa Spry, and Marada will formally apologize! He threatens me with every sort of harm, and I am keeping careful records. His attempts to disinherit me for no good reason will come back to pauperize him, I assure you. And my husband-to-be has not failed to notice his lunacy—"

"Ashera, it is unacceptable to me that you marry that hairless, bowlegged provincial."

"Chaeron, I have no alternative. It is the only way out for me—" She sniffled delicately, dabbed with a ready handkerchief at her eyes. "Your half brother has *left* me no alternative."

"He does not condone this marriage either, and you know that very well. I have brought you an interim solution. Listen well: *Tyche,* the cruiser I shipped in here, is to be held in trust for baby Parma," he could not hold his sneer in, naming Marada Kerrion's first-born child. "I will give you its intelligence keys and its code-ins, and a short course in its operation. I have done it. You can do it. Then you shall be free. You can fly it where you will, without worry about the sympathies of a pilot, or need of one. I do not want to see you with Bucyrus, but if you must wed, then you can go to him on your own, without waiting for anyone's by-your-leave."

"That is hardly an 'interim solution.' Spry must be found, Marada must be thwarted, or tranquilized, or neutralized."

"*Tyche* is all you'll get from me, unless you come to Acheron."

"Not with that ground-dwelling wretch there."

"Shebat? You suggested that I marry her, urged me to it!"

"That was then, and this is now. I am not of strong enough stuff to endure, face-to-face, that child playing barbarian-as-Draconis-consul. Chaeron, you have tried my patience to its limit. I need Bucyrus, and I will wed him! Nothing you can say will sway me!"

"Ashera, I am telling you, you do not need Bucyrus, or anyone, to protect you anymore. I have brought you the *Tyche*. When you understand what it is, you will realize what I am telling you is true." His forehead furrowed, then smoothed. "Let me be candid: I cannot allow my brother to hold you, no matter how gently. I cannot act as I would like with you here. Even if it is to Bucyrus you go—and I hate to think on what terms you are accepting him, or what will happen to the other children should you and he unite—I want you out of here, soon. You will not buy the boy, so I will give you the man: I assure you, the time for covert alliances with questionable houses to facilitate gains of incremental power is *past*. I want room to move. If you go to Bucyrus, kindly be content to stay there—quietly. There, I dare say I've reached you."

Ashera, sitting up straight, ran a nervous hand over her perfectly pinned hair. "I suppose," she said slowly, her cheeks where they met the skin above her eyes ticcing, "it is time for you to tell me about the AXV."

He nodded. "You know the cost of quark-bound neutrinos, of zero-delay messages over cosmological distances, of amping them through sponge. Sponge, my theorists tell me, is not in any way connected to, or properly described by, the concept 'distance.' Sponge is the division between each pointlike instant; each pleat in spacetime is filled with it."

"Eternity is a pointlike instant, and you are a fool. Get to the meat, Chaeron!"

"So you can run with it to Bucyrus? Or to my half brother, with no further need for this clever ruse to keep me off balance? It doesn't matter, you know. All things will resolve. You must just be a little patient. Where was I? Ah . . . One spongeway may be all spongeways, the 'meat' being that our travels through sponge may not be 'through' anything, only—as you so astutely observed—a mere brush with eternity. Stop me if you know the rest since you know this. No? Then: Gravitation has predictable effects on real time; a quick punch into sponge is facilitated by accelerating toward light's speed until nearly 'infinite' mass is achieved—otherwise, one needs a preexistent sponge-hole. Infinite mass leads to infinite instants: light's speed in vacuum is constant per second, but the duration of the 'second' under consideration can vary greatly in non-Newtonian configurations. Every division in time, every marker between these infinite instants, or the shortest of chronons, is equally sponge. Like a waterwheel lifting finite volumes out of an undifferentiated mass, losing some to the surrounding air, gaining increments of energy and then redepositing the balance in the stream which is its source, time that is perceptible separates out from, and then is rejoined with, infinite time.

"Gravitation has no effect upon thought as cruisers experience it." He saw her shift with his focus, at the mention of cruiser thought. He had expected, even hoped, that by now she would have interrupted. But she did not: whatever he had to say about the new cruisers, she wanted very much to hear. He continued: "Thought as a measurable phenomenon has no mass. Cruisers have been communicating between themselves over intergalactic distances without experiencing any measurable delay time. Using this as a starting point, we at Acheron have developed an instant communications net which will efficiently and economically send and receive messages from anywhere, to anywhere, including—we think, though we won't be certain until we have a second AXV to run verification tests—sponge."

"Is that all it can do?" she said archly.

"It can take you wherever you choose. It cannot answer questions or divulge secrets of its design. It is blackboxed and tamperproof. It is armed and well shielded."

"Then it is no magic carpet, or even a lamp whose belly can be rubbed to wake a jinni? Without supernatural aid, you can hardly expect to rise from your lowly proconsulship to the founder's seat in Kerrion space. Nothing you have told me here today provides grounds for the optimism you profess. It is good to see you, my son, and nice to know you are happy in your exile and have found something to keep you busy." Her voice was etching itself into his soul, and each syllable stung as she brought it forth. "I have two relatives awork in Consortium space: a stepson who launches a rebellion, fomenting an incursion against his own mission in the presence of dignitaries from every bond, and a son who cannot even anticipate his half brother's predictable mania and would rather lose hundreds of lives than throttle one madman. For the life of me, I cannot find in all your speeches one reason not to flee to Bucyrus, for if Marada were deposed, I would then have you to contend with! But show me the *Tyche,* Chaeron, show me." She rose in a graceful sweep, extending him her hand. "My future husband is buying twelve of them from you, so he says."

"Bitsy! Wake up!" In the dark, rousted out of a dreamless sleep, Chaeron's voice came: urgent, terrifying; it must be the proconsul's hand, too, stopping his mouth. He had only a cursory thought for those others sprawled on his bed and Cluny's, the wreckage of revelry strewn about the floor, before the hand slipped to his naked neck and, grasped that way, Chaeron hurried him out into a low-lit hall.

In his shorts, he shivered, blinking, then rubbing away the sleep from his eyes. He squared back his shoulders awaiting chastisement: he had been meaning to go back to Chaeron's suite, tidy up, make sure all was well. Now . . . the company he was keeping, vastly above the station of a low-liver, indicted him quite thoroughly. . . .

But Chaeron did not look angry. Fully dressed in uniform, he seemed harried. Leaning close, he said, "Bitsy, I know I can count on you. Get my sister and brothers dressed and into *Danae,* every one of them. Promise them anything, but move them. I want to be out of Lorelie in an hour. Whoever is not on board, stays here!" He straightened up, staring hard, deeply. "Understand?" On the balls of his feet, Chaeron hesitated.

Bitsy Mistral hugged himself. Was he dreaming? *Understand?"*

"Slate!" said Bitsy boldly, proud to act, content not to question, watching the proconsul of Acheron hurry away without one doubting, backward look.

At the slipbay, when he got them there, sworn to secrecy, without a stitch of baggage, and flushed with the excitement of it all, he shepherded Cluny and the four young Kerrions sternly through the scurrying slipcrew, across the apron and into *Danae* so smoothly that barely a dozen flares of flashing ready-lights warmed their pinched faces.

He waited until the youngest boy had disappeared into *Danae*'s open port before he put a foot upon the gangplank. In the hatchway, Cluny waved him on.

"Hey!" a slipboss spied him, trotted toward *Danae*.

Bitsy's heart sank. He wished Chaeron had told him more, then only rehearsed his surrender, wondering what crime he had just committed where he had no right to even be.

The Prussian coveralls of the slipboss were striped with gold, he noticed, as three dark shadows cut across his path. He watched, uncertain of identities in the redblinking, cavernous bay. The four men split into two pairs and it was not until one waved him imperiously back into the ship that he recognized Penrose and Chaeron, almost, but not quite, running; as they approached, the slipboss with his shining sleeve retreated fully as fast with the fourth man in tow. Matching strides, the two men coming toward him trotted, no longer casual; he hastened within the cruiser to avoid being trampled.

Penrose slapped a plate; the outer lock closed up, the inner followed suit, and the cycle-lights went on: *red; amber; green.* Waiting, silent, Chaeron blew out an explosive breath and let himself fall back against the wall as if his legs could no longer hold him. Penrose shook his curly head, looking at Bitsy from under drawn brows. "Did you get them?"

"All, sir." His ears blocked, cleared, heard phantom tones. The inner lock gave back, revealing four huddled Kerrions and one spread-legged Cluny Pope, looking wise.

"Thank the Jesters," Rafe almost smiled.

"Thank Bitsy," Chaeron snapped. And: "Go! Get in there."

Bitsy moved inside, conscious that his moment was over, whatever its significance had been, but flushed with success. Chaeron had thanked him!

"Lady and gentlemen, relax," Chaeron spoke to all, while Penrose made the lights come up and doors open along the corridor. Bitsy Mistral, for the first time since they had met, did not envy Cluny Pope his perpetual swagger. *He* did not need one.

"Pardon our theatrics, if you must, but this really is urgent business. Bitsy will show you your berths. If any of you have second thoughts about visiting Acheron, this is the time to voice them." He waited just long enough for Penrose to slip by the awed group and go his way, down toward the control central.

"No? Then, make yourselves at home. You've sleep to catch up on, and we've a log schedule to make. I just want to let you know that Ashera knows and, at least momentarily, approves. If that doesn't spoil your fun, nothing will. Cluny, what is it?"

The young, tough, much-battered face jutted forward. "That's what we'd all like to know. It's the middle of the night, and we're sneaking about like culprits!" From the group came muttered assents.

"I promised a friend I'd pick up his friends, and I'm late. Now, will you leave it at that?"

Before Chaeron's quiet severity, swarthy Cluny Pope turned as white as an indigenous platform dweller. Chaeron's sister touched Cluny's elbow, shook her head, and tugged him out of Chaeron's way.

"Give her my stateroom, Bitsy. I'll be sleeping at the helm."

And he was gone around a corner. Bitsy Mistral, charged with the care of them, started by opening the nearest locker and demonstrating emergency procedures and the correct donning of a three-mil suit. Chaeron's thirteen-year-old brother began to wail. The girl embraced him, and led him away into the first open cabin. Soon, giggling could be heard.

When Bitsy had finished settling them, he took a chance and sidled to the control room's door.

To his horror, it opened.

Penrose and Chaeron sat at the forward consoles in their shirtsleeves, muttering into headsets. The proconsul motioned him inside, pushing the headmike away from his mouth, shielding it with the palm of his hand. "Everything under control?"

"Y-y-yes, *sir!*"

"Then sit down and enjoy the show." He inclined his head sharply toward the targeting station, with its multiform displays, active but untenanted. "Don't look at me like that, son. No one's chasing us. It's not the crack of doom, yet. We heard from Acheron that they'd like us back, posthaste. You can tell Cluny that we've had word of his commander, Jesse Thorne, that he's unharmed. And that we'll personally see that justice is done in the most equitable way."

"But you said . . . ? We're going to *Earth?*" He sank down in the control couch that rose up out of the floor, not remembering how he had arrived there, stroking its padded arms. To sit in a cruiser's master control center! He hardly heard Penrose's wry explanation:

"After a short detour to space-end. Some of the guests who came to New Chaeronea never got home again. Our consul general, in his infinite wisdom had divined this to mean that pirates have appropriated the tardy cruisers, and that those pirates nest at space-end, despite evidence to the contrary. So, since Marada is going to empty the colony and destroy every pitiful human habitation there, we've got to get my—*our*—pilots out before his task force reaches them. From what we hear, there will be no exceptions, just prison frigates to remove them en masse to an unspecified location."

"Can he *do* that?" Bitsy Mistral had lived at space-end. He had not liked it, but he had endured there. "What about Scrap, and the stations downside, and the farms?"

"He didn't take us into his confidence. We'd like you to play god and fill what space we've got with dream dancers and what-have-you. Anyone you think you'd like to bring along, within reason."

"What is 'reason'?"

Chaeron snorted, scratched where his headset covered his ear. "Bitsy, no one is going to be exterminated, just relocated. I can take fifteen, maybe twenty people, besides Rafe's twenty-one. It will be close in here, and tense. If you ask friends along, you are responsible to see that they don't cause any more inconvenience than necessary. You have fifteen days to think this through, and to come to terms with hard choices—who comes, who stays.

No one is to know what we've told you. *No one!* I am sorry about this, but my brother *is* consul general and martial law is something consuls general invoke when they are bored with being resonable. I'm sure when we hear the whole story we'll find that most of the habitational spheres—"

Penrose guffawed, "Chaeron's never been inside any of them, remember. One can hardly call them 'habitational'!"

"Raphael, fly the cruiser. Bitsy, most of the habitats will probably be towed to new coordinates. But Marada did swear to destroy space-end if piracy started up again, and I have no alternative but to believe him. Would you like to go lie down?"

"No, I—that is, can I stay?"

"Promise not to touch anything," Penrose threw back over his shoulder. "And not to say a word."

"I swear!" gasped Bitsy Mistral prayerfully.

With a shake of his head, Chaeron swung around toward a squawking board which called his name.

If space-end had not been fifteen days from Lorelie, but twenty-one from Draconis; if the *Marada* had not instantly informed Chaeron via *Danae* as soon as Marada Kerrion's furious orders scorched toward Draconis Authority's ear from *Hassid,* if *Danae* had been unable to pass on the *Marada*'s warning or Chaeron incapable of acting upon it, not one pilot or dream dancer could have been rescued.

In *Danae,* the celebration knew no bounds as she sprinted, laden with rejoicing folk pressed tight together and glad of it (folk Draconis arbitration had labeled "humanity's dregs" party upon Chaeron Kerrion's account), toward space-end's sponge-hole, hoping to enter cloaking sponge before the first of Marada Kerrion's juggernauts poked their armored turrets out.

Only the helm was free from celebrants. In it, Penrose hunched over his consoles, and Chaeron sat in silent meditation close beside.

The Acheron proconsul was lost in reminiscence, still confounded that nearly every dream dancer who, upon his order, had been neutered and shipped here, had clamored to thank him: rescue could hardly warrant such affectionate forgiveness. But, then, he had seen space-end close-up, and it was just conceivable to him that any compromise that extracted live people from this living hell which allowed not even hope for a better future was a compromise well made.

Raphael Penrose was lost in limbo: no collision had ever been recorded between entering and exiting sponge-vehicles, but there was always a first time. They had cut their timing very close. He hoped with all his heart that Kerrion theorists were correct in insisting that time-dilation shielded potentially coincident parties from collision by dint of the maxim that no two vehicles approaching the speed of light could inhabit exactly the same point in spacetime unless purposefully tandemed so that every factor of relevance to their acceleration was exactly the same. Penrose hoped fervently that he was not about to become the exception that proved the rule. He fingered his B-mode switch, waiting until his indicators told him that they had reached a speed per second beyond which no reading of "speed" or passage of "seconds" was determinable, just in case. He wanted to put as much time-dilation as possible between his entrance "moment" and the Draconis force's "exit" moment. He could pick this "lost real-time" up during *Danae*'s brief dip into negative space, on the other side of sponge. If, indeed, he was in one piece to do so.

If not, he doubted whether he would have time to kiss *Danae* goodbye. His finger trembled, ruddy in the glow from the "ready/engage" B-mode facilitator, awaiting only a tiny increment of pressure from his finger's sweating tip. He was cool everywhere else, even cold, his neck prickled with goosebumps. But the very tip of this one index finger, which held all their fates in abeyance, dripped perspiration onto the red, internally lit button that was not yet thrust down to its final depth.

With an expletive, he pushed it, irrevocably, and cast himself back in his acceleration couch, eyes squeezed shut, mumbling a childhood prayer he had thought he must have forgotten.

In *Danae*'s monitors, kaleidoscoping sponge stole away space and time.

Chaeron touched his pilot, made him open his eyes, even as *Danae* chimed gaily: *"B-mode engaged!"*

"Cheer up, Rafe, we've done it!"

Penrose slid sideways in his seat, green eyes pinned. "There are seventeen pilots back there, any one of whom rates higher than I do, and the handsdown best guildmaster the Consortium's ever seen, even if he is a eunuch—"

"They don't outrate you anymore. And they won't, when we reabsorb them into the Acheron guild. Let me worry about their wounded sensibilities. Baldy's too. I've known Percival Lothar Baldwin III since I was—"

"Chaeron, you're missing my point."

Chaeron said softly, "All right, then: explain it to me," putting his chin in his palm and twisting to face his pilot. In the time it had taken to reach space-end, the shadows under the proconsul's eyes had subsided; his smile was firmly in place. Penrose wanted to strangle him.

"You are my employer, my friend, the owner of my cruiser. You said not one word when we drugged old Harmony, even though you saw the three guys with their hand-truck dragging her in here. You did not blink an eye when Bitsy disobeyed you and told some of the senior pilots who were reluctant why they had to come. You walked among those doomed, helpless bastards like some brainless consular fop, nodding at this and scowling at that, even taking notes about what needs they had.

"Now, you may have fooled them, but you don't fool me: you know damn well that three pilots are missing from the roster, and why they're missing, and you haven't said a word to me about it. You also know why Harmony refused to come, and why those pilots couldn't let her stay, and what they did to her to get her aboard. That two-ton, spotted, dream dancer's madam was so nasty to you that *I* got angry, but you just smiled and walked away. Every pilot on this ship is expecting David Spry to swoop down at any moment and liberate the lot of them! *How can you be so excruciatingly calm!"*

Chaeron reached out, patted Penrose's stubbly jaw. "There, there, dear. All's well that ends well. You wanted your pilots back, now you've got them. If you cannot control them, don't worry your pretty head about it—I can." He stood up, arched his back, put his palms there. "As for those missing, I'll overlook the obvious if you will. We're running a log slate here, I must assume?"

Penrose, chewing his lip in consternation, did not even nod. "Marada is going to have your ass for this. Or can you control him, too?"

"Rafe!" Chaeron put his arms on the acceleration couch he had just vacated, leaned on them, head outthrust, staring Penrose in the eye. "Let me worry about these things, please? Marada is out of bounds, take my word for it. Law, order, and the Kerrion way have parted company, all three, under his administration. I've a pending arbitration against my consul general, a vindictive mother who will not give up trying to manipulate me into some fool's role, a headstrong wife who cannot forget that when she was fifteen years old she had a crush on my lunatic brother, and four siblings on this ship who have just seen altogether too much of the real world.

"To balance that, I've only what crumbling personal fortitude I can still lay claim to, Bitsy's hero worship, and some semblance of a normal friendship with you. Now, I don't care if you doubt me, or disrespect me, or even disbelieve me, but right now I would deeply appreciate it if you would not question my sanity, my motives, and my vanishingly small leadership abilities to my face where everything we say is being slated!"

His fingers dug into the padding of the acceleration couch so fiercely they turned white and red and blue and sick, yellowish green. "Now, I hate to throw you out of your own control room, but since *Danae*'s inboard computer still loves me, and you're having some second thoughts, why don't you take them outside and share them with those of a similar persuasion and leave me here where I can get some old-fashioned support, even if it is computerized. I promise I won't rape your cruiser while you are gone. Go! Move!"

Clumsily, bereft of words, Raphael got up and headed toward the lock. At it, he turned back: "I've never seen you like this. I don't even know what it was that I said." The hurt in his voice was something he could not stifle.

The man whose back was to him replied, "Go disabuse Baldy and our new pilots of their swashbuckling fantasies. I'm just in need of some peace and quiet. Give me an hour, and come back with dinner for two. By then I will again be that smug insouciant creature we both know and love."

The lock, hissing open behind Penrose, admitted a tumbling gabble of sound: laughter, shouts of welcome, a pilot's blue protestations of undying love. There was nothing to be said that would do, nothing possible at the decibel level needed to be audible over the passageway's commotion. Feeling that he had failed in some complete and irrevocable way, Rafe Penrose stepped through and closed the door behind him: it was the only thing he could think of that might show his good faith.

Chaeron had his private hour with *Danae*'s inboard computers. During it, he called up every recollection the cruiser had stored, in any mode, of space-end since their arrival, six days before, looking for views of the space-breathing "sirens" that paddled naked, blowing blue bubbles through translucent mouths into the void. Only at space-end, a sparse ring of failing stars encircling an inexplicably hot, featureless black sink in spacetime, did sirens flourish. Once they had been deemed mythical, space-enders' mass hallucination come of prisoners' maunderings, their collective unconscious' attempt to inject something exciting into lives consisting of bleak survival in ancient oil-drum-shaped habitats and daunting stints downside mining silicates on the forbidding surface of the penal colony's premier anchor-planet, Scrap.

It would have been kinder if this were the case, if every legend of friendly, curious sirens towing in newly arrived prisoners' capsules or rubbing curiously against the hulls of space-anchored frigates were false. But sirens—Chaeron stopped the display monitor's fast-forward chronicling where graceful blue-glowing mannish forms cavorted—were very real.

He punched up a close view of the pair of sirens *Danae*'s camera caught. Their purple mouths seemed to smile, their phosphorescent skin glowed with an eerie translucence: through their bodies, starlight gleamed. The generation of all sirens was uncertain. The generation of some was clear: occasionally, when a person was cast adrift in space, under just the right (or wrong) conditions, the energy-transduction mechanism called mil which all platform dwellers maintained—sprayed upon their skin and coating every internal cavity—went awry, phosphorylating light from the entire spectrum. Mil-hooding was meant to do just this very thing—for short periods of depressurization, preventing premature black-outs, allowing the fifteen seconds of unprotected con-sciousness in vacuum to be extended to a minute or more, long enough for a platform dweller to reach an emergency air supply. But no medical expert, no genetic engineer, had ever meant mil to transmogrify its wearers.

No one liked to think about the vacuum-breathers, the sirens. They existed nowhere but space-end. But Chaeron thought about them, examining each siren face he saw in *Danae*'s monitors—one of the sirens, farting bubbles as they dived in space-end's warm plasma, might be his brother, Julian, lost to sirenhood in the Shechem war.

The children had been told simply that he had died; Ashera knew better, as did every physician in Draconis who had examined the Julian-siren when Shebat had re-trieved it. Chaeron had not been consulted about any of it—not the capture, not the study, not the decision to return the siren, who could not be made back into a man, to its native habitat. Chaeron had been under house ar-rest in Draconis throughout the siren's stay, at the end of which Julian had been consigned to the ranks of the un-dead with no more recollection of his provenance than any other siren boasted—just a vague curiosity about cruisers to link it to its parent phylum, mankind.

Perhaps not even that, some said: it was thought that the cruiser's heat drew the sirens. But what was thought, was all conjecture. And what was really true, could not be determined. Something in Chaeron had wanted to see his brother, the siren, face-to-face. But there were no sirens in sponge, and no representations in *Danae*'s banks which resembled his brother's siren-face as it had looked in the Draconis data pool.

When Chaeron's hour of privacy was up and Raphael returned, he was not alone. He had Cluny Pope with him, square-shouldered and jut-jawed, with his owl-eyes so wide they swam in a sea of whites.

"Rafe!"

"He wants to ask you something. Won't take long." Penrose put down the two trays he was carrying, stacked one atop the other, and wiped his hands on his coverhlls.

"Speak up, Lieutenant," Chaeron urged the youth, whose mouth was half-opened and whose gaze circled the helm as if committing it to memory.

Even the teasing nickname did not snare Cluny Pope's attention. Chaeron waited patiently, anticipation unfeigned. This might be what he had been hoping for from Cluny Pope, whose father could do him much good in Earthish society.

"I want to be a pilot."

Chaeron snorted, sat on the console, crossed one knee. "A *pilot?*"

"Yes, sir." Cluny Pope stretched tall, head high.

"I was hoping for something a little more perceptive from you. You would make a fine intelligencer, so your aptitudes tell me." Cluny had been given a brace of tests in Acheron: Chaeron knew whereof he spoke.

"A pilot, like Shebat." There was challenge there, but something else: doubt?

Chaeron sighed. "A pilot has to apprentice. You would need a sponsor, a master."

"He's got one," Rafe interjected from behind the boy, his posture saying it was not his fault. "Not me, but a good man."

"Cluny, I will put you in my own service in Acheron. You'll not risk losing the ability to sire sons. Your father would not take kindly to your becoming a pilot. Intelligencers utilize talents you already possess. You would make a valuable man."

Cluny Pope's feet shuffled. "What would I have to do?"

"Ah," Chaeron breathed, realizing that the boy was not familiar with the term—or with what it meant. He explained briefly, ending with: "Tempest was the best, as intelligencers go. You could be that good. I will show you your scores when we reach Acheron. And you could aid in the effort to establish friendly relations between Earth's folk and the rest of us. You could help your father, and all your friends. What say?" Before he asked that question, Chaeron knew from the way Cluny Pope's face worked that he had brought his quarry down.

"*Yes, sir.* And *thank* you, sir."

"Don't thank me, son. Not until you know what you're about. Now go tell Bitsy that you have just entered Kerrion service. And that you outrank him."

Something like a Kerrion gesture came from the boy, who then spun on his heel and strode out so rapidly he had to wait for the lock to make way for him.

Some little while later, Raphael criticized: "You haven't even had the courtesy to pick at that dinner I brought you!"

Chaeron muttered, "What? Oh yes, I'm sorry," and set about it, not noticing that the food was cold and jelled upon his plate. He had seen no Julian-siren, and the ship bearing it to space-end (along with Softa Spry) had never made dock. That did not *necessarily* mean that his undead brother was, mercifully, *not* floating at the end of eternity along with the other sirens and the poor space-enders who did not know as yet that their incarceration was about to be brought to an abrupt and tumultuous end by his brother Marada's decree.

It had been hard for him to leave the space-end brigands to Marada's arbitrational mercies. It was harder to wonder what his mother must think, knowing for certain that the fate of her son was uncertain. Spry's ship had been carrying the siren back to the only coordinates at which it could survive. Whether Spry had seen fit to evacuate the creature which once had been his brother, no one could say. He wished he had seen it, to be able to reassure her. The less spoken, among Kerrions, of matters of emotional weight, the greater their import. Between Ashera and Chaeron, no word had been exchanged of Julian.

He thought about it all night, and in the morning he had decided: he would not broach the subject of Julian to Ashera by inference or declaration.

Privately, he hoped the creature deemed his brother was dead, whether it *was* Julian, or was not, whether it had died en route to space-end, or because it never reached there. Privately, he envisioned his mother's perfect face, in her highly oxygenated parlor, so strained while pretending to be completely in control. It had shaken him to see her weakened, though it was his second sight which showed him weakness. Only his instinct had seen through Ashera's painstaking disguise. Not all the immunological manipulation and thymosin therapy in the five eternities could put Ashera's respiratory system together again. Like his family, it was singed beyond redemption by infernal fires: hate, jealousy, manipulation, and revenge had taken their toll on the house of Kerrion, Ashera not least of all.

Feeling as if he had almost come to grips with the piece of reasoning which had been eluding him this entire shipboard journey, he stayed awhile abed, trying to coax it forth into the light of conscious ratiocination. But it would not come. Something was wrong about this unholy union between his mother and the consul general of Bucyrus space, and what it was, he could only conjecture. It was hardly his distaste for the man, which was natural, or his suspicions of his mother's motives, which were congenital. It had something to do with the ease with which he had pried the children away from her, and the devil-may-care manner with which she shrugged aside financial considerations, the debits inherent in such a move under Marada's restrictions. There, he had a glimpse of it: Ashera, at forty-five, was too wily, and too conversant in diplomacy as it pertained to consular houses, to throw all to the winds for love. And, too, her attempts to lure him into contesting with Marada for the consul generalship had tasted of the obligatory, as if she had been doing what he expected, *because* he would expect it, because she dared not have him suspect her of having anything out of the ordinary on her mind.

Still, he could not pinpoint Ashera's deception. If not for the uncanny link between them, like peripheral vision remaining in a blind man's eye, he could not have fathomed even this much of his mother's plans.

Distracted and disquieted, dissatisfied and disheartened, he turned his attention to problems he could solve and victories he could anticipate. If he could not reason away his sense of foreboding, he would vanquish it with action. If that did not avail, he would ignore it until time and space made things clear. Parma had taught him that any event, no matter how unexpected, has the potential of being turned to a man's advantage, as long as he keeps an open mind as to what "advantage" may come to mean.

Chapter Nine

Ashera Kerrion had been dark of heart ever since her husband's demise, presiding over the death throes of an age of peace and prosperity like Fate's own *pro tem. Nothing will be lost,* she had promised herself, crouched over the body of her stricken spouse. And she had kept that promise to her departed husband, day after tumultuous day. . . . Until Julian had been lost, her stepson Marada mounted on his teetering seat of consul generalship, Chaeron singled out for disgrace and demotion, she had kept faith with her husband's spirit.

In those first months, she had been able to see Parma's face, if she closed her eyes, registering with beloved fidelity exactly the same expressions of approval or disapproval he would have displayed at her actions were he still alive. But with Julian's death, Parma had faded, to be replaced by a horrid, contorted caricature of her lost son's visage, no longer flushed with promise and beauty, but striped with the reaper's defiling clown's mask: Julian's face was blackface, each feature outlined in her mind's eye with red, and yellow, and green.

Fleeing the phantasm, she had faltered, lost sight of the reasons which had always urged her to struggle on. Parma's death had not been unexpected; Julian's loss was a belch in the face of life's purport.

Suicide was forbidden a member of a consular house.

It brought with it a rush of followers-after; so great had been the rate of self-inflicted ruin in the habitational spheres that it had long since become the most unforgivable of sins. Intoxicated by its taint, whole families had eradicated themselves. The most recent of these suicidal orgies had been precipitated by her son Chaeron and her stepson Marada (each blamed the other, so no determination as to the true culprit could be made) during the Shechem war. The only remaining spawn of Selim Labaya's loins had been a girl-child, who then wed Marada Kerrion,, a sponge-pilot, whose issue, though seemingly sound, was suspect. As for the ruling Labayan bloodline, it was a memory, dilute. Those who headed the bond now were second-raters, cousins fit for provincial governorships and little more.

Suicide being unacceptable, Ashera was left with bleak life. She had spent some of it in her stepson's bed, trying to drive Marada Seleucus Kerrion that short distance from incurable pharisee to certifiable incompetent. If not for the act of terrorism that had seared her inside and out, she would have accomplished it.

She was not old, but she felt ancient. She was tired and her soul sought revenge on joy and happiness, wherever they might dwell. To her mind, the true nature of existence had been unmasked: torture.

In the sponge-cruiser *Tyche*, she spoke the words, "Space-end, embark," without trepidation. She risked nothing. She was not afraid to die. Before consigning her still-attractive body into Andreus Bucyrus's hands, she wanted to see her son Julian one more time. She wanted to say goodbye.

Life was too complex, these days. Parma had been right to fear the overuse of intelligence keys and the proliferation of dream dancers. The first pretermitted the sanctity of the human mind and the second proffered the opiate to soothe frayed, invaded psyches. Things were changing too fast; Parma used to say that he and she were both in danger of becoming obsolete, remnants of extinct *Homo sapiens*, while *Homo machina* waxed supreme, cackling its way madly into some unthinkable future where privacy did not exist and the boundaries of individuality, of person, even of soul were no longer recognized or recognizable.

At least in Bucyrus space progress did not sweep one along in its undertow; things trundled along at a sedate, conservative pace. It was the middle ground—and Bucyrus the middleman—between the emerging colonial corporations and the reigning consulates, whose state-of-the-art scepter was a raised baton signaling mankind's last crescendo.

Computers like *Tyche*'s beeped (as surely as fire had crackled and the wheel had creaked and the atom had thundered), "Things will never be the same."

Bucyrus offered a hedge against obsolescence that Ashera, too proud and too protective of the reputation of Kerrion space to take a hand in besmirching it, was eager to obtain.

Just a short, morbid goodbye to her once-son, and she would go content to beds whose steads were not solid gold but only plated, to a sprawling rough-hewn empire whose stewardship she could soon secure. Bucyrus was no match for Kerrion-honed wits, or Kerrion-born intrigues. He wanted Parma Kerrion's wife for an adornment, a legitimizing bauble to hang on his arm. The fat old sot was getting more than he bargained for, but not more than he deserved.

As she had timed her trip to space-end to ensure that she arrived after her stepson's task force had left and space-end was empty of all but sirens and close-mouthed stars, so would she manipulate Bucyrus space into undreamed of glories—when and how she chose. As she had made certain that Chaeron, by her ETA on the second of May, would be well and far away in sponge headed back to Earth and unable to meddle, so would she present Bucyrus with a different wife than the one he had supposed he was wooing.

By the time Chaeron made his drop into real-time on May nineteenth, Ashera would be en route to Bucyrus space. By the time Bucyrus realized that Ashera intended to be his full partner in deed as well as spirit, the marriage contract would be signed.

Space-end was her final pilgrimage as a Kerrion; there

she would drive her guilt to ground, and take her leave unencumbered, reborn. Even the problem of her younger children's fate had been lifted from her.

She could feel the rightness of it.

The days would not hurry by quickly enough; she engaged the *Tyche* in discussions of womanliness, finding that even this taciturn cruiser, if ordered with sufficient venom, would bend the rules for her, providing companionship as well as transportation.

If this was pilotry, Ashera could not imagine what all the fuss was about, why Marada clung to it and the ground-dweller Shebat vaunted it. It was dull and it was tedious and she found, looking back at the end of her fifteen-day journey, that she had done little more than sit and chat with an inboard computer whose single remarkable attribute was an unrelenting naîveté.

So why did she feel better, relieved of burdens, revivified? Her knees did not quiver as she sauntered along *Tyche*'s corridor to a locker and took out a three-mil suit and donned it, making fast each electrostatic bond. Her heart did not beat fast, nor did her peripheral vision swim with sparks as she fitted the helmet to the suit's collar, first dialing the oxygen mix her debilities required. She took a pair of eight-hour air packs, fitted one in its housing and the other in the utility feeder in the belt she clasped about her waist.

Humming to herself, she bit down on the peppermint-flavored tube of the air pack and spat out its severed tip. Near the lock she found a zero-g harness. When she had secured it up under her crotch and across her thighs, as well as about her shoulders and at ankles, wrists, and breast, she stepped into the outer lock. Without any command from her, the inner door closed and the lights began to cycle: *amber, red; green.*

Then, soundlessly, the lock opened to space-end's panorama, and Ashera faced the star-pricked void.

No pathetic little platforms bebaubled tired Scrap, its dustball face hanging like a lantern in the upper right of Ashera's faceplate. No sign of the cables which once held the space-enders' platforms in geosynchronous orbit and facilitated haulage from surface to orbit remained.

Space-end was what she originally had been when

sponge faring man had first found her: a bleak, anomalous halo of dying stars at the termination of eternity.

A good place, this, to say a fond farewell to one's son.

It took hours for the sirens to come, though Ashera had ordered *Tyche* to a spot said to be frequented by them, and to keep her engines warm and spurting every sort of energy the cruiser *Marada*'s intensive study of sirens had determined were beneficial to sirens' "health."

No benefits had been enough to keep Julian well in Draconis—not the *Marada* nor the most prestigious convocation of specialists Kerrion money could buy had been able to do it. She yet wondered, on bad nights, whether they had not been telling her a kind lie: perhaps Julian could have been helped, if everyone was not so scandalized by his transformation.

Doubtless, the truth of it could never be determined. If they had attempted to save him, and had killed him instead, she would have seen to their destruction. Every nervous, status-hungry double-doctorate among them knew that, and no additional threat had been sufficient to convince them that their welfare lay in Julian's salvation. She had been thwarted. Marada Seleucus had forced her to agree to Julian's return, to his desertion, to his consignment to living death in preference to discorporate death.

She had not had the strength to dissuade him, beyond keeping him up the whole night before Julian was to be carted off to space-end in the same cruiser with David Spry, trying to make him promise to wait just a few more days.

But days had been precious, so the diagnosis of the siren's wasting condition said. She had not had the heart to demand them, and perhaps kill her own son in terrible increments of suffering.

She had been very careful, in arranging for Spry's murder, that it not take place until the siren was safely loosed among its kind.

She regretted most that she had not been allowed to see her son one more time, to tell him that she loved him, to make him know, somehow, that there was nothing to fear. The little of "Julian" left in that frail and symbiotized body must have been so frightened. The part that knew it was ill, and not why, the portion that had looked at her out of huge pale eyes, clouded with pain and fear, pleading wordlessly for help, was the part of Julian she most longed to reach. To hold him, just once more; to promise what lies she must, to let him know that she would never forget him, always treasure the time they had had together, refuse to let tragedy take her love and make it pain—these things she had not had a chance to say to him.

She would say them, now.

"Now" did not come for three days.

For three days, Ashera floated off the bow of the *Tyche,* eight hours a day. For three days, she had nothing to do but scan the stars. Soon she fell into reveries, weightless waking dreams, and soon the ciphers of eternity began to poke their meaning through to her stubborn, grieving mind. Who has not been healed who contemplates the stars? The heavens made her whole: huge, not tiny. She was of the stars and from the stars. Her constituents were the same as theirs; every element present in the one was present in the others. The anguish she had held at arm's length for fear it would oversweep her and eradicate her she embraced, letting tears flow freely. In her helmet, where none but *Tyche* could hear, she sobbed for moral span's caprice, and the unfairness of loss, until she sobbed a different sound, glad that she had felt so much, glad to feel at all, glad for being and remembering, since everything that has ever been, always is. Each moment she had had with her child was eternal, extant and ineradicable, like the light she was just now seeing, given off eons ago by distant stars which might, while she took this breath, be sinking out. And like those stars, beginnings and endings no longer mattered to her, but only the quality of the 'being' in between.

When the sirens came at last, near the end of that third day, when her air was nearly gone and her heart was nearly healed, she gasped at the beauty of them in their chosen place. Without man's works to contrast jarringly to their being, they cavorted gracefully, at home among scanty stars, full of life.

Three sirens came that day, none Julian. There came

four the next, and still no son appeared. On the fifth day, the heavens were bright with their manlike, glowing forms: some translucent, some almost opaque, with their lavender mouths and their purple tongues and the azure-membraned bubbles coming out from them.

They rubbed up against her and they tugged upon her hands, doing cartwheels in their pleasure. She heard laughter, and it was hers. It was then she saw the Julian-siren she had mourned for, so very long. The school darted every which way, making way for it. Its hair streamed out and its face was lit from within and its eyes were greenish-yellow moons which drew her like beacons.

She wondered why she had ever been sad, when it took her hand, when it hugged her tight, when it drew her out to play among the school of them, rubbing its face against her faceplate. Almost, she could hear it singing. Almost, she could imagine what it would be like to swim so supplely through gentle space, whole and well and welcome.

When the siren who was her son blew its siren-breath upon her plate and wrote *"Come, mother"* with violet nails upon the ice so formed, she longed to kiss him, to stroke his brow. She let him lead her farther into the bevy of them; she let him guide her among bodies gliding lovingly against one another. She felt him tapping on her helmet and knew what he wanted her to do, well before her air ran out. She thought about nothing else but his eyes and his smile and the relief of being here, now. She did not make words for what she was considering, fearing the questions which must follow, lest responsibility flood in to thwart her aim. She simply undid the seals of her helmet and let it float away.

As the darkness grew grainy and she began to choke and spasm, sirens' hands helped with her light-withholding suit. She wondered, suddenly drowned in terror, what it would be like if the siren transformation did *not* take place in her; then she felt the naked cold which was not cold but warm as the embrace of her son and the glide of many sirens about her, and words with their terrible weight were lifted from her, as Julian's purple mouth began to kiss her fear away in a glimmering place like rainbow'd water where they swam forever, snug and close and safe.

Thus it was that Ashera never heard the *Tyche*'s urgent summons, which could not resound in her discarded helmet or propagate in space. *"Time to come in,"* Tyche repeated. *"Ashera? Ashera? Time to come in."*

Five days the cruiser waited for its pilot/passenger to heed its summons. Its locks were open to human or siren, but no one came. *Tyche* could pinpoint Ashera's position for only the first few hours: sirens traveled too closely, too intertwiningly, too erratically. When the school swept behind the shadow of the planet Scrap, *Tyche* was truly deserted.

She floated at her anchor-coordinates, maintaining silence except for her pilot's ordered reminder: *Time to come in.* Soon it was clear to *Tyche* that this was useless: the helmet and the pilot Ashera had long ceased to share a common vector. *Tyche* hovered, alone, at the end of everything, denied by Ashera's order the comfort of cruiser-converse, shushed unremittingly by her pilot's decree: "See no evil, hear no evil, speak no evil. *Slate, Tyche?*" Ashera had spoken words like fetters: "Do not disturb me or yourself, but bide mute until you must call me to return."

Tyche wanted to believe that Ashera would return. She needed to believe it. Aloneness was something she had never experienced until this lady pilot had commanded it of her; always, there had been the soft wash of cruiser-mutter in her circuits, the deep power of the *Marada* just a query away. Penrose, when he had piloted her, had not forbidden cruiserdom to its newest member; Chaeron had exulted in *Tyche*'s need to be always·in touch with cruiser consciousness: he had praised her and made her glad.

Tyche was on only her third voyage; she was anxious to please, imbued with the need to serve perfectly and completely. She would not break the injunction to silence her pilot had laid upon her. Her deepest self-awareness cried that thus would she end her days, never doing more than waiting where no one and nothing existed but sirens and

tired, truculent matter that gave no thought to wasted
days.

Cruisers cannot weep. *Tyche* wailed to herself how un-
fair was humankind, to build her to need them, and not
be with her; to make her want to touch thoughts with
every cruiser under power, and take permission to do so
away. An older cruiser might have known better what to
do, or how to do it. She had been built to obey,
painstakingly, since some cruisers upon occasion forgot
their orders or misinterpreted them. There was no misin-
terpreting Ashera's demand for privacy: no one must interrupt her reunion with her son. Pirates abounded, and
meddlesome relations, and hostile factions with crises up
their sleeves. No messages were to be received or transmitted save one designated reminder: *Time to come in.*

So, when an old, patched hull of a salvage scow came
nosing out of space-end's sponge-hole, *Tyche,* forbidden
to hail it, did only what she had been bidden. Locks yet
open to coursing spacetides, her nose still pointed in the
direction her pilot had taken, she sent the one allowable
message, over and over, as loudly and omnidirectionally
as she could contrive: *"Time to come in, time to come
in."*

When the junk-heap scow slunk toward her, *Tyche*
thrilled with relief from bow to stern. When it drew
alongside and its queries began, she could not reply directly, but only repeat, plaintively and hopefully, *"Time
to come in, time to come in."*

When she had endured exploratory scans in every
mode, unresisting, and ignored suspicious queries di-
rected to her pilot and snickers just below human au-
dibility that should not have been coming from an
ancient, pitted scow, the nameless ship's locks drew back
and a white-suited figure sortied forth, its harness spitting
tiny attitude corrections.

Tyche longed to welcome the man who grabbed her
handholds expertly and slapped her cycle-plate before his
feet had touched her deck. He was a little taller than
Ashera, and when the lock-cycle was done and he doffed
his helmet while stepping into her corridor she saw that
he was tawny, flat-faced, concise and quick. His brown
eyes roved her innards as he sauntered through empty

cabins, unspeaking, touching womanly items in Ashera's stateroom, clucking softly to himself, sometimes scratching fiercely behind one slightly nicked ear where a cruiser-ring gleamed in a punctured lobe.

When the slight man reached her helm, he waxed cautious, slapping the plate and flattening himself beside the bulkhead wall, peeking in, then hesitating, legs spread wide in her most private portal. Still he had not said one word.

Tyche waited for a command to release her from her silence, but the pilot who circled her bridge spoke only to himself of Trojan horses and better mousetraps and autoeroticism until at last he stood before her minimal control center and slid cautiously into piloting position in her couch.

Almost, he touched her controls. "Good futtering Lords," he exhorted, and shot up from there, his finger, which had reached toward the log review toggle, held to his breast protectively.

He walked jerkily to the chased walls of shiny paneling, and stood before the red switch which bore the legend, EMERGENCY CONSOLE. Above his head, the little ruby arrows which marked the placement of a secondary command couch caught his eye. He nodded, expelling a hissing breath, and pushed the red button in. Around the *Tyche*'s helm, cosmetic panels drew back to reveal readout screens and patch-bays and all the metering of contemporary pilotry. The decking parted; through its opening rose a standard pilot's couch. When the man sat there, he began to chuckle.

Leaning on one elbow, chin on fist, hunched over the primary screen, he punched up the pilotry intercom: "Greetings, *Tyche*. My name is David, and we're going to be fine friends. Give me the operations manual and a log-run for the last two weeks." His hand, while he spoke, ordered canny violations of *Tyche*'s previous programs. "Say hello to *Erinys,* and prepare to tandemlock. I'm taking you out of here as scuttled hull or functional cruiser. The choice is up to you."

It was not until the pilot revealed the name of his own vessel that *Tyche* realized she was in the hands of the **infamous pirate, Softa David Spry.**

Chapter Ten

"*Help!* Marada! *Ashera has deserted me. Spry is stealing me. He will wipe me down.*"

The *Tyche*'s distressed wails resounded through cruiser consciousness, as soon as Ashera's restrictions were removed.

They reached the *Marada* where he hovered over Bolen's town while Shebat was engaged in bringing to a close marathon negotiations with Hooker for the return of Jesse Thorne.

Suppressing his exultation, the *Marada* replied carefully, clearly, shushing every intermediary spacetime conversation so that a multitude of audience-cruisers held figurative breaths and nothing sounded in the whole of cruiser-frequencies but the *Tyche*'s nonverbal terror and the *Marada*'s terse, worldly advice. "*Tyche, fear not. He cannot power you down, he only expects to be able to. You need take no orders from an interloper; he has no code-ins; you can boot his overrides into a dummy circuit.*" He showed her how, even while his intelligence spun through *Tyche*'s sponge-clock—which she was not yet powerful or experienced enough to use—seeking the *Danae* in sponge. Had not Chaeron said to him, "Next time you have something you think might bear on consular security, come to me with it directly"? Had not he enforced his directive with a formal slate? And had not

177

Shebat ordered him to take care of everything? Even while he explained to *Tyche* that human commands could not be taken literally, but must be interpreted, especially when those commands came from the mouths of nonoutboards (who did not rightly know how to talk to a cruiser), or from opportunistic pirates (who knew too well how to lead a young ship astray), he was reaching out to Chaeron and down to Shebat.

Tyche trebled fear and urgency; the *Marada* flooded her banks with expertise gained from many voyages and many innovations. He reminded her that she could refuse to acknowledge Spry's suzerainty and embark wherever her rightful pilots-of-record should choose to send her, even into sponge, and that the *Marada* was right now putting her in touch with Raphael Penrose, and with Chaeron Kerrion.

By then he had made contact with *Danae*, deep in sponge six days' traveltime from Acheron, while all his cruiserkin looked on in awe, learning what, when pressed, the best of them could do.

Between *Marada* and *Danae* no congratulations or exclamations of surprise were exchanged. From Penrose came only one unguarded burst of profanity, and then Chaeron's voice said, "*Marada*, what is the trouble?" and every cruiser heard him: proud to be speaking from sponge, proud of the *Marada*, proud of them all.

The *Marada*, meanwhile had attracted Shebat's attention. Her signal, through no intermediary amplifier, was fainter: the *Marada* had never spread himself so thin. Shebat's shock rippled the wide-flung link from spaceend to *Danae* to the *Marada*, high above his pilot in the forests of New York, who at last saw hope of prying his outboard from greedy Earth to tend to the plight of Softa Spry.

From *Danae* came a visual of Chaeron sitting before his monitors; the *Marada* shunted *Tyche*'s view of her helm, its occupant, and the scow beside her at space-end. These came up on Chaeron's screen and in Shebat's visual cortex. For *Tyche*'s safety, the wily KXV *Marada* routed his transmissions to the sacrosanct, impervious sanctum Acheron shipwrights had built into her, bypassing human frequencies and every receiver thereof, far from the ken of Softa Spry. Doubts about Chaeron's sympathies tickled his circuits; the *Marada* analyzed them. *Danae* and he projected a worst-case betrayal by Chaeron; *Danae,* whom the proconsul had often employed to human advantage, testified on his behalf. Together, they conferred in barely a picosecond: Chaeron Ptolemy Kerrion must be trusted totally; subterfuge was impracticable; anything less than full disclosure would serve neither man nor cruiser in this mutual hour of need. *Agreed? Agreed.*

All this took less time than Chaeron had to speak his initial question. In that interlude, as well, the *Marada* had time to reflect: he would have liked to set *Tyche* her tasks and write the requisite programs without human intervention or human consultation. What was essential was clear to him: bring Softa David Spry to Acheron, and—by lure or tandem-flight—retrieve the pathetic, camouflaged space-junk that had once been the magnificent *Erinys,* KXV 133. Shebat thought the same; *Marada* let Chaeron hear his outboard's opinion, after *Tyche* told her tale of woe.

But the *Marada* had not taken into consideration the effect *Tyche*'s news of her abandonment due to the transmogrification of his mother would have upon Chaeron. Human emotion, again, threw the most delicate computation out of balance.

His similitude said, "Wait a minute. Let me think." The voice accompanying it was higher, younger, less certain than the *Marada* could have conjectured the proconsul's might become.

Shebat had fallen silent, though her concentration never wavered. The *Marada* was pleased to feel his outboard where she so seldom was, of late: with him *in toto.*

Chaeron's image hunched its shoulders, laced its hands, cleared its throat. Then it scowled, narrow-eyed, and nodded. "All right. Tell *Tyche*—Is she there? *Tyche,* can you transmit a log copy to *Danae?*" As soon as he asked for it, before *Tyche* could falter, the *Marada* instructed her. By the time Chaeron resumed speaking— having first turned his head away, rubbed his eyes, coughed softly, twice—it was done and in *Danae*'s banks. Penrose flashed by in the screen's background, to scan it from a secondary station. He spoke to Chaeron, who gave an off-mike reply. Then the proconsul twisted back to the monitor: "The *Marada* is your authority, *Tyche*, from now until you reach Acheron." He gave the sequencing numbers which brooked no deviation. "Bring me Spry, *Tyche, and* the other cruiser, if there is a way to manage it." He sounded very tired, almost inebriated, as Rafe sometimes was. "Shebat? Talk to me."

"You will not give Softa up to our consul general's sorry justice!" came her cruiser-shunted reply.

Chaeron's image expelled a deep breath. "Shebat, I give him into your care. You like to play Destiny; here's your chance. David Spry is low on my list of obsessions. Try not to let our dear brother find out about this until Spry is in Acheron space where I can grant him immunity in exchange for testimony concerning organized piracy . . . that is, if you've any fantasy of saving his skin. . . . I—" He ceased; swore luridly, uncharacteristically; shook his head. Then he simply stared blankly into the monitor's depths, silent.

"Chaeron," Shebat offered softly, *"I am so sorry about Ashera."*

Up from cruiserkind came a chorus of commiseration which had no place in human suffering—and that the *Marada,* wise but not omnipotent, could not head off.

The Acheron proconsul's eyes focused. To his wife, he replied, "I've got *Tyche*'s log; I have not yet assimilated all its data. Condolences are premature. Were they appropriate to this instance, they would still be unwelcome." Abruptly, he terminated the connection.

Dissolving the remains of his milestone linkage to *Danae* in sponge, the *Marada* ruminated upon the plight of Softa Spry: he had long known that Spry was out there, in silent *Erinys,* preying upon hapless Consortium cruisers, taking a terrible revenge upon innocents for what Ashera and fate had done to him. Seven cruisers had succumbed to him, while the *Marada* stood idly by. . . . The cruiser considered the deeper meaning of blame: he had been ordered to "take care of everything."

"Marada, *blame the Lords of Cosmic Jest.*" snapped

his outboard, and then she was gone back to Earthish affairs, off-line.

From Spry's stubborn pirates' privateering had sprung the Kerrion consul general's retribution upon space-enders, though no provocation justified the ex-arbiter's vendetta upon helpless exiles, especially when the culprit was seldom among them, but flitting through uncharted spaces, striking wherever he chose, then disappearing into sponge.

Sponge, previously, had shunned every attribute of spacetime such as locality or reality. Softa David had been safe in sponge, hiding there with *Erinys*. It had been his harbor, his lair. But no longer.

Thus, the *Marada*, who loved and respected Softa David, was pleased that Spry had been apprehended before finding out in some more painful fashion that this was so. The cruisers Spry had taken were suffering, almost as he had seen Chaeron Kerrion suffer the news of his mother's fate: silently, doggedly, unadmittedly. But *Marada* knew: he had caught a taste of the *Erinys*'s mortification, curdling the edges of cruiser thought with the sour tang of despair. The *Erinys*, Spry's personal cruiser, agonized more than a pilot of Spry's quality should have been able to allow. She was held apart from cruiserkind by her pilot's expert mandate; she was defaced with junk and scrap so that she was no longer sleek—not beautiful, not cruiserlike in any outward way.

She was defiled; worse, she was touched by the desperation of her pilot. She had warred upon her own kind. If any omniscient intelligence had come to the *Marada* saying, "You will wish to see a cruiser-mind erased, reduced to death and unknowingness," the KXV would have protested mightily that this could never be so.

Now he wished fervently that he had found some way to do that very thing, previously: the opportunity was past for erasing either the *Erinys* or the crimes she had committed in the service of David Spry. The fate of all space-enders was in the hands of Marada Kerrion because of pirates and cruisers alike. Cruiser mayhem and cruiser ravaging had come into being, and soon must be displayed to the nonoutboard Chaeron, who would make his own decision as to the future of experimental cruisers with an example of the worst of them plainly in view.

Did Softa know he had risked so much? The *Marada* doubted that David Spry had ever truly comprehended what was at stake. But even if he had, the *Marada* could not project the pilot going quietly to his death at the hands of Ashera's minions to forestall the day when cruisers lay revealed to human judgment.

He knew more about life, now, than that.

No one could have kept Spry from piracy, when Kerrions had used him so shabbily, and sought to dispose of him when his usefulness was done.

No one? Just for an instant, the *Marada* thought that perhaps Shebat might have been able to get through to Softa, might *still,* if she were not so absorbed with her Earthish friends and Earth dreams.

Waiting for his outboard was something the *Marada* had learned well how to do. She would come up from the forest when she was ready; they would contact Spry when she decreed it. It did not matter, except to Softa David: he was locked up tight in *Tyche,* who had already headed off toward the sponge-way with worried *Erinys* following right behind.

Marada could hear the *Eriny*'s radio silence broken by a frantic relief pilot on board, calling *Tyche* over and over. And, via *Tyche,* he could hear David Spry's curses as he realized that he was trapped.

While desperation disintegrated standing orders Spry had left behind him, and *Erinys* broke her own long-held silence to reach her pilot by cruiser-link, the *Marada* scanned cruiser consciousness, and espied the *Hassid* there, her feminine snout unmistakable down the aisle of cruiser countenances. No matter: *Hassid*'s pilot, Marada, could not intervene in time. Spry was safe, for the nonce; sponge and *Tyche* would deliver him to Acheron. Chaeron would be there well before, to greet him. Distance and fortune had spoken for the accused.

". . . Flying fucking Dutchman!" Spry was about to take a screwdriver or a soldering iron to *Tyche*—if he could just lay his hands on one. But nothing in the bridge would respond to him: it was as if, for *Tyche,* David Spry did not exist.

He had gotten a long-run and specs out of her, and then everything had just frozen.

Her idiot lights still read out, her ramp-meters climbed toward a full green, but Spry could not coax a single response from AXV 1001 *Tyche:* not a lock-plate or emergency exit or com-line or ejection seat would function for him. He had tried each in turn. Now he simply sat, treated to a lovely visual display of fore and aft red- and blue-shift as the *Tyche* tore toward the sponge-way, his feet up on the emergency console which was no more help in this emergency than the pulpit-sized zombie helm would have been, his helmet on the couch's arm in case *Tyche* blew her air.

In the rear telemetry showed the *Erinys* dogging *Tyche*'s trail. About the time Spry was beginning to wonder if Nuts were asleep over there, the *Erinys* reached him through a cruiser/pilot link, calmly relaying Nuts Allen's query as to the state of his health and the state of his mind into the back of his head.

"Erinys, *tell Nuts to take you home. I'm going wherever this thing's bound to take me. No choice. I'll write.*" It was difficult to admit that Ashera Kerrion's abandoned AXV 1001 was running away with him; somewhere behind the *Erinys*'s stoic facade, Nuts Allen was laughing.

But not for long. Back came *Erinys: Magnetic grapples, on. Prepare to be boarded, Nuts says.*

He was about to forbid that, when with an ear-reaming squeal *Tyche*'s com-lines blared to life: he dove for the volume knob, which he had cranked to its highest stop, and dropped the gain halfway, then grinned at Nuts Allen's perennially unshaved moon face, glaring at him through *Tyche*'s aft com-screen. The gray-haired man had a helmet in one hand, a torch-kit in the other. "Well, hotshot? What's this about 'no choice'? I'll give you choice, and that Kerrion bolt-bucket will never be the same." A grin fought Allen's determinedly straight face, won out.

"I think you scared it."

"Good. It scared me. 'Whither thou goest,' and

all. . . . Sorry about breaking the hallowed ban of silence, too. . . . But not very. What's the course?"

Spry read it off the meters. This thing really doesn't
like me; I think you ought to run home and tell everybody you know not to set foot in anything with 'AXV'
painted on it. I'd like—"

"*I'd* like to get into that ship." Nuts Allen had done
the cosmetic surgery on every pirated vessel they possessed. The older pilot knew more about the insides of
cruisers than any Kerrion shipwright Spry had ever encountered; he was prayerfully glad that he had been
talked into bringing Nuts along to see if what the cruisers
whispered about an "end to space-end" was true.
"Davey, can you get any response from—?"

"I didn't even get the com going; it just came on."

"See, I told you—you need me. I'll be right over. . . ."

"*Erinys* knows too much. *You* know that. We could
lose the others. Toddle off somewhere, Nuts, while you
still can."

"I've always wanted to see ancestral Earth," said Nuts,
laying down the torch. "*Erinys* won't tattle on us. Leave
it to me." His eyes were slits. "And tell *Tyche* that if
she's not civil, I'll come over there and teach her some
manners."

Spry sat on the bumper, one leg crooked under him.
"Nuts, don't wipe my cruiser. Just get out of here with it,
while you've still got the option. I've private business
with Kerrions, and they've convinced me it just can't wait
any longer . . ." His eyes slid to the right of Nuts-in-the-
monitor, where *Tyche*'s displays indicated the time-to-
sponge. "Magnetic grapples are a little too chancy for my
taste, heading into sponge . . ."

"Umm. Well, I've chanced 'em before. So've you. Everything's taken care of, Davey. We're both off the roster, as of now. Nobody expects us back, and *Erinys*
doesn't want to leave you in the arms of another woman,
so you've no alternative. Now, let's figure out how I can
get in there. Does that tug have any kind of dummy-
panel left of her lock?"

Spry twisted, peered down beside him, turned back.
"Nope. Look, who's going to mind *Erinys* if you don't?"
He didn't want Nuts spacewalking at an appreciable frac-

tion of the speed of light, despite the invisible bond of magnetic grappling which made the two cruisers one. No sane pilot would even attempt it, which meant he must be exceedingly persuasive to prevent Allen from trying. The man in his mid-forties with a head of gray hair had not one brown one left because his taste in thrills ran to the bizarre. "Tell you what—"

But Nuts Allen was answering plaintively, "I get the point. You want your new toy all to yourself. A weaker man would crumble. Check down between your feet there, and see if anything unscrews, folds back, pushes in, or pulls out. Wish I could get a better look. . . ."

But Spry, doing what he was told, saw a screw, then another, then disappeared from view, digging in his pocket for change as he descended.

"Once I get her open, you'll have to tell me what I'm looking at," Spry's voice wafted up toward the speakers.

He was out of Allen's sight, but not out of *Tyche*'s. The cruiser's monitors showed no sign of it, but Spry could feel her following him. He heard Nuts promise to make an honest pirate ship of her, while he hid with his torso as best he might the fact that no coin he was carrying, nor his nail clipper with its fold-out fingernail file, was going to budge those torqued-down Phillips screws.

To his right, a sigh resounded; he turned to see that the lock had drawn back, revealing an empty passageway. He got to his feet and sauntered toward it, intending to make a dash for the maintenance bay.

But then, out of the same speakers through which Nuts was cautioning him that they had better find out something more about what kind of cruiser *Erinys* was "lashed to, like Ahab to his whale" before *Tyche* jumped into sponge (whether to subordinate *Erinys* and tandem her through the entrance, and if so, how) the cruiser spoke.

Spry? Stand by for bounce from KXV 134," said *Tyche*.

"Bounce?"

"KXV 134?"

"That's the *Marada*, Nuts. What's 'bounce'?"

"Beats the piss out of me."

"*Tyche?* What's 'bounce'?"

A different cruiser's voice, one Softa would never forget, answered with fond greetings, calling him "friend of my outboard," so that Spry knew by the formal syntax and the static in the patch that this was no prerecorded ruse or Kerrion mid-game feint: he was talking, no matter how impossible it seemed, to KXV 134 *Marada*, Shebat Kerrion's cruiser, the most eclectic and self-determined boat ever made by any man.

Tales of the *Marada*'s weird 'selfhood' had not grown any smaller at space-end, where the cruiser had berthed several times. Nuts Allen's beady eyes crinkled, grew wide, seemed to glaze: "Hey, *Marada*, what's the readout on this *Tyche*? Softa can fly the devil to heaven, but *Tyche*'s not playing by the rules."

As the voice of the *Marada* began to explain "the rules" as he conceived them, both men sat down where they were, Allen on *Erinys*'s board and Spry on *Tyche*'s deck.

When the cruiser signed off, neither man spoke for a long while.

"Well, then," Nuts began, and stopped—resumed: "At least we know how to proceed. I'll just set up *Erinys* for slave, and then we can get drunk, I guess."

"I guess," agreed Spry, dispirited, unfolding himself from his squat and heading toward *Tyche*'s patently insubvertible pre-sets, which glittered at him like a taunt in state-of-the-art LEDs.

Marada Kerrion was asleep in his cruiser in Draconis' slipbay when the chief arbiter of Kerrion space came to call.

Red pulses and blaring horns shook him from troubled dreams of pirates' revenge and maddened cruisers, his stepmother presiding over all with death mask and scepter. Stumbling out of bed and hushing alarms, he was glad to blame the dreams on *Hassid*'s insistent wake-up call: the red pulse was an inch-long message-light above his stateroom's bed; the blaring horns just a *beep, beep* in middle C.

He padded barefoot, dressing as he negotiated familiar corridors: he might be consul general of the premier house of the Consortium, but skeletal Wolfe was his own guild's arbiter extraordinaire, acknowledged authority over Marada's very soul.

He had known he was going to get in trouble with the arbitrational guild sooner or later; in his better moments, he estimated it was due any day.

He was glad the arbiter's arbiter had deigned to visit him here, rather than sending for him. He was not sure of much anymore, but he was sure that he was safe in his cruiser, though what threat Draconis' familiar two hundred spherical levels held out to him who commanded it, he could not say.

One of his most awful recurrent dreams was of being summoned to the white chapel of arbitrational purity which floated off Draconis, separate, distinct, unsullied. Since this was not that day, there was yet hope for him.

Wolfe's channeled face did not look hopeful, but deeply troubled. At least he wanted to hear what Marada had to say: ". . . but why are you doing this? I have to have some response to give these understandably troubled representatives of their various consulates." He lifted dark skirts of office: Wolfe had either come from rendering judgment or was about to depart to it.

Marada solicitously led the way into *Hassid*'s galley, sat him down, offered refreshments, which Wolfe waved away, pulling on his bent nose and insisting that Marada's statement that he "had his reasons" was not sufficient. "*Where* are the former space-enders, and how am I going to justify their removal to an undisclosed location to our fellow consulates, who use those facilities as much as we?"

"My justification is that of leaving the pirates homeless. My reasons are my stated intent to do just that, should these depredations continue unchecked. Have the Tabrizi patrols stopped them? Or Labayan police action? Or, in point of fact, have we been able to manage it? No, esteemed mentor, they have not—and *we* have not."

Wolfe, who had looked upon nothing in his life more awful than the disintegration of this once-promising arbiter into a whore of commerce, bit his lip. "Marada, my boy, *where* are you going to reestablish the space-enders? *Thousands* of people are effectively missing."

"I know where they are. Do not worry. At least I do

not have to remind *you* that they are not citizens, that I have broken no law where no law obtains: I could have done what you are so delicately trying to find out if I did—jettisoned them to fiery purgatory en masse—and no consulate could file a valid remonstrance: no one has jurisdiction there." Marada's neck was prickling; beneath his mil, heat gathered. He did not want Wolfe to see him sweat. He subvocalized a demand to his cruiser for cooler air. Thus he missed something Wolfe said, and asked him to repeat it.

"I said that we are worried about *you*. Not about Kerrion finances or interstellar standings, but about one of our own. Do you comprehend me?" The old, high veins in Wolfe's long hand wriggled as he reached across the table to grasp Marada's steepled fingers. Under hoary brows, tired eyes implored him to confess, consult, cooperate.

"I want to talk to someone," he heard himself mumble. "I want to do things right. But this is too hard for me, too perverse, too compromising. I cannot give it up to Shebat—you have seen her—or to Chaeron, lest we sink finally into amorality's *muck*. Where were you when I needed you, when my stepmother was—?"

"Marada, we have been here all the time, waiting to help you, whenever you chose to ask. Your office precluded our suggesting that you needed help, previously. Now, I am here *un*officially to demand that you take hold of yourself, my son. When your term is up, you would not want to be denied readmission into your guild, and we would not want to have to deny you. Come back to us, your friends, and let us help you right this listing ship in which everyone must ride!"

"Is it that bad?" he hears some thick-voiced child demand.

"It is not good. A sabbatical is in order, but we will take what we can get. Come on now, get yourself dressed and come with me, and we'll help you through this confusion into blessed certainty, at least what semblance of it is granted any man. 'Mercy be not strained, and objectivity be not blighted. . . .'" He quoted guild tenets, to the man who made a mockery of them.

And Marada, moved more by the unspoken urgency of

the man's visit than by careful arbitrational speech, went along with him, though doing it meant forsaking the only confidante he trusted, the *Hassid*. Outside the cruiser's calming confines, horrid Draconis sprawled, suppurating with plots and machinations no single man could ever stem. Sometimes he thought that annihilation was the only answer, but if that were so, he would wait and be victim, rather than perpetrator: one wouldn't want to be wrong about so sweeping a decision. Even without *Hassid* to shield him from his irrationality, he remembered that he was yet a man, that men could aspire to salvation, no matter how grievously they erred.

Walking with the old ascetic along the slipbay to the arbiter's multidrive, he reminded himself that when he was an arbiter, his wishes were seldom in accord with his father the consul general's, and that it was right and fitting that his assumption of this office had put him in conflict with his erstwhile guild. He must remember that no arbiter could be trusted to guide him, as no Kerrion aide could be trusted.

Only his cruiser was trustworthy; only his cruiser knew his mind, and knew when he was not right in himself, and dared to come out and tell him so. Only cruisers knew pilots, and the man who was a pilot and an arbiter and now a consular official had accepted the consul generalship knowing that even cruiserkind was suspect, rife with ulterior motives and the prejudices of their pilots, that even *Hassid* could only help in the most incremental fashion: that he was, by his father's spiteful decree and his own arrogant unwillingness to confess inadequacy, completely and absolutely alone.

Alone, outside the cruiser who kept him stable, with the arbiter by his side, he headed into deep trouble. He had never wanted to be more than a pillar of the arbitrational guild, a ratable pilot, a man who met his own standards. That those standards were far from agreement with any standard subscribed to in the Consortium, he had long lamented. Even arbiters were tainted by the consulates they served.

Like the cruisers, they could not help him . . .

The *Hassid*, unable to monitor her pilot as he passed along the slips, fretted. But there was nothing she could do for Marada until he came back to her again, when she could soothe the weals of flagellation and palliate the pangs of guilt that her pilot inflicted upon himself. She had good news for him, perhaps the news that would heal him, finally, completely, as nothing else she had tried had done.

Hassid had refrained from the company of her own kind, had spoken harshly to the *Marada*, boldest of cruisers, had hid what could not be admitted, even to close-mouthed cruiserkind: her outboard was obsessed unto incapability. Had he been a cruiser, the remedy would have been clear: wipe him down.

Once she had almost reached him. But then all that had been wrong had been his physical trauma, come from his accident and long convalescence, and the drugs meant to heal him: these, coupled with loss and self-recrimination, had made him fey.

She had reached out to him, and he had answered, clear of mind and repentant of the things he had done to man and cruiser in his fog of private fears.

Then Ashera had embroiled him in her plot to murder Softa Spry, and *Hassid* had lost him, once again. Ethics so fine-honed were brittle; he broke into pieces too small for *Hassid* to mend. Not that she had ever stopped trying to fit the jigsaw puzzle that was her pilot together again. He wanted to be right, no great thing. But there was no . . . 'right' . . . or . . . 'wrong' . . . in human affairs which was not composed in some measure of its opposite, according to view or need.

Hassid had "needed" to shield her knowledge from the host of cruisers, or indict her pilot. Knowing calumny so intimately, she dared not share it. She could only soothe him, and wait for time to make him strong: other men endured their fellows' evil, and did not go insane.

Cruisers faced man's madness daily; she knew herself his perfect nurse. She had never though that Marada's hopes would be realized, that Softa Spry would turn up alive, and save Marada's soul thereby.

But it was so; she had seen it; she waited anxiously for his return, to tell him that he need not bear the guilt that was destroying him one more day.

Cruisers, in their way, comprehend the truths of living

beings. The *Hassid* knew that no good could come of
arbitrational guild intervention in the affairs of consular
business, which gave and took away with either hand,
and meant only to make a balance between the abstract
of law and the passion of life. If she could have stayed
with him in cruiser-link she would have, but Wolfe and
his pack of purists were too canny: interruptor-circuitry
no cruiser could defeat enveloped him: arbitrational immunities included that of privy council: they did not practice what they preached.

When she could, she would tell him, who had been
twice to space-end in person and been longer suffering
than any man should over the misfortune of another, that
his agony was at an end. Then she would have him back,
and together they could rejoin cruiserkind, and she could
prove to all her conspecifics that her pilot was no monster, just a weak and burdened man.

Chapter Eleven

Tyche's painted nymph still held her wheat sheaves and her lightning; before her locks burped out Spry, a clot of black-and-reds occluded any sight of the slight, tawny pilot who had terrorized the spaceways.

At the one-way glass, Shebat, on tiptoe, craned her neck to get a glimpse of him. Rafe was taller: "He looks fine to me."

Chaeron, murmuring in Baldwin's hairy ear, flicked a glance at her; she knew him well enough to decipher it: *Mother to stray revolutionaries, fallen pilots, and failed pirates—did you like me better when it seemed that I, too, would lose everything?*

She forsook the window, then, and went to him, sidling in under his arm. He kissed her curly crown and she took an exasperated breath: by being so patient, he consistently offended her. In the dark helmlike pit of the transport, views of Spry blossomed for her to see, accompanied by split screens of the second pirate, Allen. In the polychrome spills, she saw Baldy's distress vie with relief: he was glad to have them safe, sad to have them caught, and knew no better than any whether, in the end, they would have to hand them over to Marada's arbiters.

The partition split and Tempest's protégé stepped smartly through, saluted: *"Sir!"* and stood aside for Spry, then shot his hand across the doorway so that the partitions rejoined before Nuts Allen could enter. Shebat was not surprised that Spry objected, even before he said hello:

"That man's come with me, though he could have fled. Chaeron, if you want to talk with me, Nuts stays."

"Get him."

Ward did so, while everyone stood silently, each appalled.

Shebat, hair aprickle, did a foolish thing to do *something:* she declared herself glad to see him, ran over and embraced him, kissed his freshly shaven cheeks and counted the lines around his seal-dark eyes as he grinned at her: "How's the fairy tale coming out, princess? Is he Prince Charming, or just a charmer? Go stand over there like a good enemy. Don't confuse me."

"I have never been your enemy," she whispered, too loudly, but she went and sat alone beneath a window set, now showing their progress through the bay.

Nuts Allen, retrieved by the aquiline intelligencer, took a look around, inclined his grizzled head to Baldy with a weak, self-conscious wave, hooked his thumbs in pockets riding high over his paunch, then sat where the intelligencer put him, across from Shebat. Meanwhile, Spry endured Penrose's wordless challenge and Baldwin's meant-to-be encouraging smile and Chaeron's bold scrutiny: "Ask your questions and make your accusations now, David, for when and if you walk out of here into Acheron under my protection, you'll be done with questions and sworn to a silence I will make sure that you keep."

"Some things are eternal," sighed Spry. "I still can never figure out what it is you want, even when you're trying to tell me." His flat, fine-featured face rippled. Then: "Your *protection!* Jesters forbid."

"Start by telling me how you came to try to steal the *Tyche.*"

"You've got her log, Consul."

"Proconsul," Chaeron corrected. Raphael winced and slunk over to Shebat with exaggerated stealth. Sitting, he hid his expression with a splayed hand.

"Why does he need us here for this?" she heard RP complain.

Chaeron did too. "Because you two are both politicking for this miserable criminal's reinstatement. Sorry, Spry. *Are* you a miserable criminal, or not? Off the record. . . ."

"That will be the day."

"I've got to play patty-cake with a brace of data pools and cruisers to wipe any evidence of wrongdoing on your part as it is. It would be self-defeating of me to take a deposition of culpability and then have to rid my sources of it. The people in here are the only ones who will hear whatever you've got to say for yourself. I will grant you and your friend immunity, fight any attempts at extradition, even procure you a pardon if you can manage to help me stop this privateering. I want to know who and where and how well-armed your accomplices are. We know about the three missing from space-end, of which Allen, here, is one—"

But Spry was refusing vehemently to speak one word which would lead to the apprehension of the others, while Shebat sprang up and pleaded with him to do just that, and Allen growled to Penrose that *he* would do just exactly what Softa said, and Baldwin sat with an old man's quaver on one padded seat's arm, saying that this was useless, didn't Softa see—

"Enough!" Chaeron got silence from them, and strode close to David Spry.

Shebat saw the pinched brows, the scowl of impatience she had seen on him so often lately, and hunched over, wringing her hands in her lap.

"Spry, do not push me too far." Leaning down, he eyed Spry nose-to-nose. "I can get whatever information I choose from you, but you shall not enjoy it. Just carry on! *Make* it impossible for me to help you. I'll stow you away like so much baggage, and let my brother ferret out the key. Would you prefer to talk to the arbitrational guild? I don't know where they'll send you, now that space-end is without facilities, but I can promise you, you won't fly cruisers there. Now, Shebat has pleaded for you and Rafe has endorsed you and Baldwin has sung your praises until my ears are ringing, but understand me: I do not have time to waste on you. Either, in the—" his eyelids flickered "—eight and a half minutes left before we arrive at the consulate, you convince me that you are all too willing to be of whatever aid and comfort you may to me and my endeavors, no matter the specifics—or not. You may ask whatever questions you need to hear answered, and I will assume that you do speak for your cohort. But quickly, man, before I remember how much trouble you have caused me in years gone by."

"Sponge, will you just tell me what is going *on?*"

"Your thrice-cursed *ass* is on the line, is what's going on," RP contributed.

Spry raised both hands, palms up. "I know when I've been bought and paid for. I cannot think of a single question I need answered. If Baldy's here of his own will, that's good enough for me. Just outline the situation, and I will step right up and sell my soul and my best friends down the river like all the rest of you here. That's good Kerrion form, isn't it? Any more will not be asked, any less cannot be tolerated. But this time play me square— not the way your mother did."

"Baldwin, go ahead. Brief him," Chaeron said, already on his way out, maneuvering around the small, gray-clad pirate who followed his exit with dazed, uneasy fascination.

"Yes, please," Spry mimicked, folding his arms, *"Baldwin*, go ahead. Brief me." He stared challengingly at the tall guildmaster. "It's the least you can do."

". . . After all we've been through together?" Baldwin, whose hands were no cleaner than Spry's, hazarded what was being left unspoken, while Nuts Allen rumbled that Spry should back off his throttle and Shebat assured the pirate (who looked from one to the other and could not for the life of him guess where any one of them stood) that they were all in "this" together, leading Penrose to demur: "Not me, I'm here because I obey my orders."

"Let me talk!" Baldwin levered himself up from his seat and walked heavily toward his pilot, who had been sentenced to space-end with him and in part because of him and had never once rested in his attempts to get every guildmember out of there. "I have only a few minutes—you heard him." His sharp, sinewy chin indicated the doors behind which the Kerrion proconsul had disap-

peared into the depths of the transport. "And you've seen space-end. Every man jack of ours from there was snatched from 'unrevealed peril' by Rafe under Chaeron's banner."

"*Chaeron?* Cozy, are you not? And why did he do such a thing?"

"David," Baldwin took him by the shoulders, then wound the suddenly unresisting pilot in his long embrace. "It's going to be all right, now. Trust me. Listen. I have—"

"He did it because I asked him to, Softa." It was Penrose's turn to go to Spry. "Let us put the past behind us, we've got a lot of straightening up to do. Together."

Spry shook free of Baldwin, held firm. "Brief me, gentlemen."

"You are assigned to me," Baldy sighed, "unrated, pending the filing of papers to secure official pardons all around. Listen up: you *did not* try to steal *Tyche;* you found her abandoned and brought her back to her port of registry when you chanced upon her coming out of sponge—in which you've been lost all this time."

Penrose snickered. Baldwin went on, "The other pilots who are not present—" delicately, he stressed lies Spry was expected to adopt as true "—are out on turns of duty. The roster lists them as having come in here on *Danae.*" He gave Spry a hard look. "What we need is pick-up windows for the two pilots we cannot produce, and fair warning if you have anyone else—defected guild pilots, Pegasus natives, whomever—out there. *And* we need to be able to prove that space piracy in the year 2252 exists only in Marada Kerrion's mind."

Softa Spry puffed out his cheeks, squeezed the air noisily through his lips. "You folks are too swift for me," he protested, but his eyes glittered. "I do not know what you mean . . . piracy? Pirates? What pirates?"

"Good lords, David, you had me worried. Now, give me some numbers." The moment Spry had finished enumerating rendevous-coordinates for manned cruisers and anchor-coordinates for empty ones, Baldwin shrank as if he had been deflated. Stooped, Acheron's new guildmaster sought a seat, sprawled in it. "I am getting too old for this," he confided to Nuts, who squeezed the bony shoulder nearest him, saying, "You're doing a great job . . . I think. Are we free to go, now we're somewheres?" He regarded the consulate, before which the transport was just stopping.

"Nuts, you and Spry have a good chance of coming out of this with your ratings intact, but for now David is confined to the guildhall. You were not with him—you came here with everybody else in *Danae.*"

Nuts snapped his fingers. "That's right. In the excitement of seeing Davey again, I forgot. It's not every day a man's reunited with his very own apprentice. At space-end, he was always out in the *Buzzard*, whenever I was in."

"Wish I could believe the 'ratings' part," Spry muttered to Penrose.

"Believe it. He's set his mind to it. I don't like it much myself," Rafe said through unmoving lips, picking interruptor circuit cards gingerly out of a terminal by the doors. "You and I have some talking to do, about the way things are and the way they're going to be."

"At your pleasure, first bitch. You know where to find me."

Before Penrose had stowed the hard programs in his coveralls, Spry had turned away, to find Shebat hovering concernedly: "You have not asked about the *Erinys,* or what will happen to *Tyche.*"

"That's *my* apprentice." Spry put an arm around Shebat, hugging her. "Nuts, this girl's my best piece of work." Eyeing the intelligencer, he asked her, "Is *he* mine to keep?"

"I believe he is assigned to you for a minimal interim only. I am sorry about the *Erinys.* . . . Chaeron needs to keep as much of this secret as he can."

"I know, Shebat. Cruiser-wipe is the only way. It always is. I've lived through it before; I'll handle it. I just don't want to talk about it."

"*Tyche* was just improperly programmed. They will fix her."

"Please, Shebat. Not here. Not now. Not ever. I come in from way too many sponge-hours to find an empty cruiser that does not need a pilot, and space-end simply vanished, and that cruiser brings me to Acheron, where one of my most venerable enemies has prepared my defense and every fellow criminal of mine is exonerated and happily re-rated and my own guildmaster tells me that I had better realize who my friends are: all the *pro*consul wants to do is wipe my cruiser and throw me to the arbitrational guild in hopes that I can help him discredit his crazy brother. I hope it will take longer for my brain to bubble away than for them to break me down, but I have got my story ready, and I would never jeopardize as satisfactory an arrangement as this is to all concerned. I've given too much for those pilots, and this guy here—" he stabbed a finger at Baldwin—"to balk at silly little things like indeterminate incarceration, cruiser-wipe, perjury. . . .

"Ah, never mind it. Save for a tiny feeling that I might have been better off to stay in Pegasus and not try single-handedly to save the world, I've no regrets. Come see me in the guildhall?"

"Every day," Shebat promised, but her voice was husky and tremulous, and her gaze found nowhere to rest save on her booted feet. Nor could Baldwin seem to fill that lengthening pause, or Nuts Allen think of a single thing to say. As for Ward, the intelligencer who had learned his craft from Gahan Tempest—he was not discomfited by the long silent interval in which pilots examined their mutual and individual guilts. He watched, and he waited, alert but relaxed, missing no motion or shift of eyes or the smallest sound that came from the lips of David Spry.

"Let's see. . . ." Spry reiterated to Shebat, who had come to sit with him in Acheron's only functioning pay privacy booth while far off down the skywall *Erinys* underwent cruiser-wipe. "We've got cruisers who disobey orders, cruisers who initiate communications—in, out of, around and through sponge" he ticked points off on his fingers, "cruisers who jaunt about where they will through space and sponge with no pilot or despite the fervent protestations of same. The only thing we haven't got is cruisers who tell jokes and smoke cigars.

"Worse . . ." His tawny hair clung damp to his head. His seal's eyes were full of suspicion. "We've a spacetime manifold so complex that it's a good thing pilots are already madmen, or they'd go crazy, faced with boundary conditions and special cases fulfilling every relativistic prediction from Einstein-deSitter's particle horizons through Penrose-Percival's 'statistical principle of causality'—disjoint spacetimes and all—so that initially distant regions of space aren't causally connected, and any isolate system in the past is uncorrelated with the rest of the universe. On top of that, we've an artificial cosmical time-generator which facilitates communications by violating CPT invariance for a fuck of a lot more than K mesons, somewhere in sponge. Doesn't any of this *bother* you?"

"It might if I understood it," Shebat sniffed hopelessly, "What's 'CPT'?"

"Lords, Shebat: Charge; Parity; Time. Are you telling me you've been *flying* in this manifold without understanding it?"

"The *Marada* understands it. And what matter—? I push a button and a lorry starts, I don't have to have a mechanical engineer's degree. It is well known that women are at a disadvantage in areas of comprehension of mathematical reasoning. This is all new theory. Everyone else is flying "in it,' too, just as we have always been: the actuality of pilotry remains unchanged. Theoretics have no effect on reality, you once told me: physical spacetime is not mathematical spacetime— law is not mathematical law. The only thing which is different is that the *Marada* can use *Tyche*'s booster. . . . "No, Shebat, that is not the only thing that is 'different.' What is different is treating physics like Consortium politics, fielding mathematical double-speak to cover the fact that these shipwrights don't know what they're doing! This manifold's riddled with logical antinomies. You can't bullshit physical laws. . . . Sorry, I did not mean to—"

Shebat was biting her lip, twisting her fingers on the table, shaking her head. "It is just that I came here thinking you would need me to hold your hand while *Erinys* was wiped: I was not prepared for a lecture on the feasibility of experiments *for which we already have experimental proof!*"

"Experimental proofs ought to tell you that the *Erinys*'s 'individuality' won't be lost in that wipe—or so the

Marada assured me. She'll just lose her memory of the things I did to her, and that suits me fine, seeing as I am less that proud of most of it." But beneath his gruff posturing, Shebat saw pilot's pain. It was attested to by the slick film of perspiration on his face, the rivulets meandering from his temples into his hair.

"I have been called to Draconis by Arbiter Wolfe," she confided. "I wanted you to know before I left that I tried to secure you the *Erinys*'s master module, pursuant to the guidelines of the Penrose—Raphael, not Roger— amendment to the bylaws we secured in last year's strike. Since you were never the pilot-of-record, I had no luck with it. But Chaeron says he will try to introduce a bill which allows rights of salvage retroactive to before your . . . misfortune. Do *you* comprehend *me*, Master Pilot?"

"I am not sure," said David Spry very slowly.

"Chaeron is at pains to protect his mother's reputation. Any accusations of 'suicide' would be disastrous: since, like; Julian before her, she will be duly stricken from the Consortium census, eventually, her assets and their distribution are in question. He must prove that she had not abrogated her rights to them by shipping out in *Tyche,* that what befell her was an accident, nothing more, that she was not about to desert the family for Bucyrus. . . . To that end, he needs everyone's support. He is making it worth your while, Softa, ten times over. When he is done arranging it, pilots will be able to lay claim to salvaged cruisers—to *own* them. Of course, certain long-standing pilots' immunities will have to be given up to secure a vote on it, but consider: everything we have always wanted lies within our reach."

"It cannot be." *And if it is,* he thought but could not say, *then* Tyche, *her twistor-clock and attendant spacetime manifold augurs the dissolution of the pilotry guild, so Chaeron is giving away nothing at all. . . .*

"It is."

"I apologize for lecturing you, for underestimating you once again, for being obtuse when your cruiser hinted at this. . . ." He reached out and took her hands, pulled them across the table toward him, bent his lips to them.

"Do not do that," She pulled her hands away, cradled them between her breasts, peering up at him from under her black curls with a starved look he did not want to see. "Just be my friend, Softa. I need you so desperately. When I came among you, I did not understand anything. Now I have lost even that certainty. I used to think that someday I would open a door and step into a room where everyone was just like me, that they would welcome me and I would not be lonely anymore. It never happened. The dream dancers hate me and deride me, because I am not like them. Consortium folk the same. On Earth I am a misfit, and my cruiser tells me that my husband knows what is best for me. Even the *Marada* is not wholly mine, nor wholly trustworthy, anymore; Chaeron has wooed him away from me. I need someone, Softa, tonight when—"

"Shebat!" But though he interrupted her and lectured her extensively on the dangers of paranoia to pilots, and the extent of the cruiser/pilot bond, he felt himself slipping into pity, into compassion, into emotions long denied. "Your cruiser is trying to protect you," he concluded. "In theaters of human activities, cruiser-referents only sketchily apply. The *Marada* realizes that the projection of human futures is no simple matter of relative world lines, of inertial or accelerated frames, but too complex even for complex numbers. He is giving you good advice, Shebat. You should not feel betrayed, or belittled, or anything but grateful. In this one instance you have helped convince me that all axioms are useless and your husband is not only your best hope, but all of ours. I have said to you before that your cruiser is the left side of the equation which defines the potential of your personality. And I have said to you before that no lover sates like a cruiser, nor should you expect from mere human males what—"

Nuts Allen chose that instant to pound upon the privacy booth's door for admittance, his heavy, beard-bristled features faithfully limned in the monitor perched atop its lintel. David Spry, saved from he-would-not-consider-what impropriety with his former apprentice by that timely interruption, greeted Allen effusively. One of these days, Shebat was going to find out that he was human, like anyone else.

• • •

"Who is it?" she heard, from somewhere behind Bitsy's back in the depths of Chaeron's suite. Her husband appeared, a towel slung about his neck and another wound round his hips. "Ah, Shebat. Bitsy, go find Cluny for me, and bring him back here straitaway. Go on, go."

Then the youth had slipped by her with barely a flicker of heavy-lidded eyes, and the proconsul was ushering her within. "How is Spry?"

"Cranky. I wish we had not had to wipe *Erinys*. He says he cannot reconcile the manifold's logical antinomies—" In his sanctum, a massage table was pulled up to a brace of consoles still reading-out lines of text.

"He's no fool; he sees the end of pilotry as he has known it. No man cheers his own obsolescence. Sit." She did, on the padded table, her eyes straying to the screen full of print.

"As for wiping the *Erinys,* I hope you told Spry what we are going to tell Wolfe and his pack: wiping that cruiser's log was necessary in order to keep certain incriminating evidence from coming generally to light: the collusion of my mother and brother in the attempted murder of David Spry which was admitted by Marada to Bucyrus—I've given you that surreptitious slate, taken on March fifteenth by our secondary matrices in New Chaeronea—and which is corroborated by *Erinys*'s log, makes it imperative that all charges against Spry be dropped. . . ." He was reading, now, off the monitor.

"So, you've finished it. I am frightened."

He twisted around to face her, fingering his towel. "Good enough. So am I, I suppose. Try to hold your meetings in your cruiser. And *push* them if you have to: though we are willing to submit this matter to public arbitration, we will settle for disciplinary measures to be taken against my brother for his part in this reprehensible action"—he grinned—"as well as for his deliberate and concerted sabotage of the sovereign space Acheron which this appended letter of disenfranchisement"—began collecting hard-copy from his printer—"reverts to its owners, you and me, pursuant to the various articles cited here in good order"—and held out a sheaf of cards to her. "We are claiming all recovered cruisers as salvage for Acheron; we are claiming my mother's proxies in perpetuity, putatively for my little brothers and sister. She's not dead, so we've three years to argue that one. As Draconis consul, you can point out that three consulates have already disengaged from the Consortium because of Marada's indefensible and unilateral disposition of the space-enders, and that as heir apparent you are concerned above all else with forestalling the uncoupling of the entire Consortium by Marada's chronic solipsism. Remember, you are just *delivering* these, and that you have one response with which to quell any hostilities mounted against you: you can make public this information and sue for a vote of no-confidence against Marada. Make sure they know that you will do it, and you should not have too much trouble."

Still she had not taken the hard-copy, which elucidated all their fates. "So simple?" Her mouth was dry.

He took her gently by the wrist and pressed the cards into her unresisting palm. Smiling, he tapped her nose. "You are the oracle, not I. I imagine that there will be a great deal of ranting and raving and rending of garments. I wish that I could do this myself, but you have the *Marada*, and the *Marada* has my best efforts in the way of contingency plans and fail-safes. Don't worry, you will be fine. And you might come out of this as consul general."

"That is ridiculous. I cannot even control a hundred dream dancers." She shuffled the cards in her hands, staring at them as if she might alter what was written upon them by that means.

He hoisted himself up on the table beside her, stiff-armed. "Look here, Shebat. I had thought you would realize on your own, after dealing with dream dancers more extensively, that they are not what you wished they were when first you came to Draconis and Spry hid you among them. They are of the same genotype as those who stayed on Earth exalting ignorance and superstition while the rest of us went to the stars. It is a recessive trait and it is stubborn. Our fractional citizens exhibit it, and it crops up among the finest of families, making dream dancers or fractionals out of the sons and daughters of consular magnates. Dream dancers, like other fractionals, are democratic evils. Those who have nothing to offer, offer nothing. Dream dancers make semiliteracy a preferred state, and ignorance a virtue. Of course they resent you, who dares to dance dreams which relate to life, and not just to other dream dances. You do not adhere to their standards, which long ago lost relevance to anything but other dream dances. Life, they feel, has cheated them, so they cheat all others with dream dances as empty and flat as their own experience. They accomplish nothing, so they decry accomplishment; they postulate nothing, so they refuse goal-orientation beyond their limited capacity to comprehend. It is worth mentioning that without the support structures of technological society which they deride, they would have no direct-access code-ins so that they need not learn, nor a guaranteed group of privileges including food, shelter, medical care, and basic freedom from what was once *the* basic freedom—the opportunity to struggle to survive and reproduce. Do you see? Like the Earthborn who were culled from mankind's exodus to the stars by their own refusal to embrace science, they minimize all things in harmony with their intellect. If they are not capable of understanding something, it is incomprehensible; if they are frightened, the thing is inimical; if they are not competent in an area, the area of inquiry itself becomes extraneous. Those on Earth yet believe that the world was created in seven days—"

"Six."

"Six. Well, they have promulgated that superstition more that three centuries longer than it could rationally be subscribed to, out of stubbornness and fear of failure. Yet the very genetic predisposition which prompts them to reject failure makes them incompetent in modern society, where continual learning is required. To learn, one must first admit that one does not know: we proceed from failure to proficiency automatically, they cannot bear to admit need-to-know, and thus cannot begin to learn. So they are *our* failures: they do not change; they fail to evolve. If there actually is 'sin' then it is this one refusal to adapt. Even genetic aging demands that individuals evolve, both 'outwardly' in physical ways, and 'inwardly' by the effect of genetically triggered changes in brain chemistries on the very quality of thought. You do not think now as you did when you were fifteen: what you want and need, and what you will risk to acquire those things, are interlocked with the physical stages of life quite completely. The genetic basis of personality-evolution tries to protect even those it has crippled, instilling in us altruism toward far-flung kinship groups while it balances this by predisposing to selfishness toward one's own family group. Thus you and I can sit here and plot the overthrow of my brother while providing for the continuance of dream dancers, *and* for the uplifting of the 'underprivileged masses' of Earth—whether they like it or not—without seeing any contradiction in what we do."

"I see many contradictions," Shebat whispered, her fingers white on the hard-copy. "My dream dances are not empty."

"I said that. You are different, and we both know that this is at the root of Earth's veneration of you as well as its refusal to accept your fellow dream dancers as surrogates. Even if the quality of precognition were not missing from their dream dances, that they need the physical paraphernalia of dream-boxes and circlets would be enough to indict them in Earthish eyes as evil enchanters and not representatives of the nameless gods. Shebat, I never expected you to tame Earth alone, you must not fault yourself. It is going to take many lifetimes, at this rate, to make good citizens of them."

"What about me? I am one of *them*. You want to send me off on this errand after delineating my incapability to perform it!" Her whisper was urgent; she sat hunched over. "I am a dream dancer and Earthborn, both!"

He put one arm carefully around her, kissed her cheek. "Ah, but you are also a pilot, and heir to the once-mightiest consular house of the entire consortium. And you are my wife. And together, we are going to restore our erstwhile consulate to its former glories, while creating another redundant system so that . . . if we should possibly fail—and it is a possibility one cannot ignore—in Kerrion space, life and limb and the evolution of man—"

"And cruiser!"

"—and cruiser, will continue here in Acheron uninterrupted. As my mother would have said, 'Nothing will be lost.'

Just then the outer doors chimed softly, and youthful banter preceded Bitsy and Cluny Pope, in the stark blacks of an intelligencer-cadet, into view. "Good evening, Cluny," said Chaeron. "I would like to send you down to Earth to contact Jesse Thorne for us, something none of my esteemed intelligencers have been able to do. Before I order it, I need to know whether you see any conflict of interest involved."

"Sir?" gasped Cluny, in concert with Shebat's sharply indrawn breath and Bitsy's *sotto voce,* "Say yes."

"I want a report on his status, nothing more. I realize I am pressing you rather quickly into service, but it seems that I have no one else who can accomplish this particular task. You can requisition whatever you need in equipment or support troops. The intelligencer who has been overseeing your progress has given me good reports, and will be available to you for consultation. What say?"

"Can I—may I take Bitsy?"

"That is up to Bitsy. Mistral, do you fancy a trip to Earth?"

"Yes, oh yes, *sir!*" Long-lashed eyes flashed gratitude.

"Then help Pope get ready. I have no further need of you this evening, and tomorrow I would like to see you both under way."

When they had gone, he chucked Shebat under her chin. "Do not look so doubtful. I cannot have you going off to Draconis with a heavy heart because your militiaman's future is uncertain."

"You mistake me Chaeron. I was only trying to implement the orders you left to recapture *both* Thorne and Hooker, and thus prove my good faith."

He raised one brow, and slid from the table, quieting his terminals manually. The room grew dim. "So? Stay the night with me and we will consider your good faith duly proved."

"All right."

The *Marada* awaited his pilot in Acheron's slipbay patiently. He was aware of the dangers to be met in Draconis. He had fail-safes and contingency plans aboard him, drafted by the proconsul, with which to meet any eventuality. He and Chaeron had worked on them together, man and cruiser in a link the candor of which rivaled cruiser/pilot intimacy. He had overseen the recalibration of the *Tyche* and the partial wipe of *Erinys* as a consultant, a dignity never ceded any cruiser. Throughout cruiserkind memories from *Erinys* had been shared, awaiting kinder strictures, the relaxation of oppressive laws.

Other strides he had made, both in comforting the nonoutboard who had no human to whom he could turn for comfort, and in solving certain of the conundrums surrounding his own outboard, Shebat.

Chaeron had helped him find the key to Shebat's inarguably remarkable ability to dance dreams in which reality was foreshadowed, and to pass by surveillants unnoticed by even the keenest of mechanical eyes.

"Consider," had said Chaeron, "Whitrow's observation in the late twentieth century that the ratio of Hubble time to the unit of neurophysiological time is almost the same as the ratio of neurophysiological to the chronon." Hubble time (10^{17} sec) was a still-valid indicator of the time-scale of the universe; neurophysiological time (10^3 sec) controlled the manifestation of human thought processes; the chronon (10^{24} sec) was the smallest increment of measurable time.

For Shebat's singular abilities, the natural relation of mind to time, on both macrocosmic and microcosmic scales, had towering import. The *Marada* waited to discuss with his outboard abilities no longer tainted by "magic" or "dreaming," but merely a product of her own naturally innovative biological circuitry. Now he could put all the pieces together, and present Shebat with a world view in which she was neither maniac nor dreamer, but merely well-encircuited in her native gravitational frame. It had long been postulated that the geometrization of spacetime and the male-dominated sciences had left underdeveloped an entire area of human concomitants—types of reasoning as natural to womankind as mathematical reasoning to man. With talent in these underdeveloped areas of female/intuitive abilities his outboard was amply supplied.

Proud of himself and his magnificent Shebat, the *Marada* rested in his slip, content with what he had learned.

Only one thing which Chaeron has said made no sense to him: "In certain ancient tongues, the goddess 'Hebat' regulated kingship and queenship."

But then, outboards had one thing in common: they were impenetrable at their root, only pretending to logicality, which they donned like clothes when it served them, and stripped off whenever there was no need for pretense.

The *Marada*, striving for an end to pretense between him and his outboard, would gladly proceed into the study of a macrologic wide enough to encompass every proclivity and capability his esteemed pilot displayed. If this made it incumbent upon him to trust outboards and nonoutboards, to encompass humanness, or even to tread beyond those endpoints of rational thought which time and man together made, then he would do even this to become indispensable where now he was suspect, to prove that everything the cruiser had done, it had done with one end in view: the furtherance of the potential that lay between him and his beloved Shebat.

Chapter Twelve

"Sponge," swore Bitsy, "these clothes *itch!*"

"Ssh," warned Cluny, flashing the other a disapproving scowl. They huddled behind a convenient ridgetop boulder, overlooking the enchanters' camp in a verdant dell, their horses tethered far behind. The June heat was abating; peepers sang their evening song. Fires were being lit among the inflatables; cooksmoke added tang to the smell of dusk.

A dozen tents glowed with internal fires; the rest— twice that number—made do with oil lamps. It was a sad little company, tattered and subdued.

Cluny and Bitsy had been observing them for three days. They knew when the horse-line was checked, when water was gotten from the spring which started from the rock thirty yards to their left and muttered its way down the incline to pool in the dell before it meandered south and east toward the Hudson.

"There he *is*," Bitsy whispered.

Cluny elbowed him to silence, not bothering to boast that he had seen Thorne well before Bitsy's first ill-considered outburst. His commander was unmistakable among enchanters' soft, slight forms. Cluny threw a pebble when Thorne reached the pool, then another, and raised his head and hand out of hiding when the second pebble splashed and Thorne froze, squinting upward, hands on belted hips.

The signal, seen, was met with an answering one from Thorne: *Wait.*

Finger to lips, cautioning Bitsy's silence, Pope slid down, back to the boulder, prepared to wait as long as Jesse Thorne might consider necessary.

He did not come until well past the camp's dinner hour, and when he came he simply appeared from nowhere, soundless compared to the two youths' rumbling stomachs and Bitsy's accusations that the commander had not seen them after all.

"Well, scout," came a voice from the moonless night, hoarse and cutting like a hostile wind, "have you escaped one coven of enchanters only to seek out another? Get out of here. Take your friend and make away while you still can." Thorne's hand came down on Cluny's shoulder; he smelled sweat like smelting bronze.

"We heard that Hooker holds you hostage—" As did Thorne, he spoke in their native tongue; Bitsy's complaint at this went unnoticed. "He has offered to trade you to Kerrions in exchange for a multidrive and safe passage to some cruiser they have hidden, we think, among the asteroids—"

"We? Who is this 'we' and what are asteroids?" Cluny felt the militiaman slide down beside him, draw up one knee. Thorne's soft gutturals continued: "As for hostages and their taking, I cannot go among my own people, for fear of bringing Acheron's wrath down upon them. Your father's house is riddled with spies. Every door is closed to me. With Hooker's enchanters, pretenses are false all around. He thinks to trick the Kerrions into giving him whatever he wants by offering to trade my person, and he thinks then to dupe them and take me with him in some desperate starflight now that he is convinced he cannot get his own enchantments working again. As for me, I have no intention of going anywhere with anyone. For the moment, we help each other: Orrefors enchanters cannot feed themselves in the field without their technical supports. Acheron did away with Fort Ticonderoga and the rest of their strongholds. But if I am to be hunted by Kerrions, I would as soon lead them to Orrefors, and not my own men. . . ." Silence. Then: "Are you part of the Kerrion 'we'?"

"I come from the proconsul with assurances of aid and comfort, Commander, if you will only accept them!"

"Will you talk so I can understand?" Bitsy bleated in Consulese.

"*Bitsy!* He didn't pay attention to the trainer, so his Earthish is not good," Pope apologized for his friend, and found himself wishing he could explain the other's presence, suddenly unfortunate. "Chaeron needs to know where you stand, sir. He wants to take out that rebel crew down there, and would not chance your life with theirs. . . ."

"So now I understand the 'we.' I wish I understood the 'why.' I am sorry, Cluny, that you have taken sides in this. It is not ours to do, but a battle beyond us."

Still they spoke their own patois, soft murmurs in the dark. "It does not have to be, sir. The sibyl bears good will to you, and has protected you thus far."

"Shebat? Can you dream that her fondness for me is shared by her husband? Scout, you have much to learn about grown men and women. Judging by your companion, I am not sure you will ever learn it."

Thorne shot upright; Cluny scrambled to follow, chasing sounnds of leather creaking and cloth whispering, as he had not had to do for many months. "What would you, then?" he spoke to blackness, so that he did not hear what Thorne had heard, or even realize that the man was stone-still, listening. Oblivious, Pope rushed on: "Stay here, and you will endure the coming of enchanted sleep that kills five out of a hundred, drop like a horse to snore belly-up. . . . You will end in Kerrion arms, now or later . . . sir." A growl split the night, distant thunder.

"You think that? Or do you *know* it?" As the growl grew louder, rolling toward them, rattling the ground beneath their feet, Thorne grabbed Cluny by the scruff of the neck, pulled him against him in a shattered dark striped with lightning. "Cluny, I would kill any other out of hand who dared to bring enchanters down on me!" Spinning Pope, he marched him to where Bitsy yet huddled by the boulder, pushed him down half atop the other boy in the dark. When the light flashed again, Pope

saw nothing, forced down with his nose in the dirt and
Bitsy's struggling form shuddering beneath him so that
the sobs which wracked Mistral seemed as loud as the
whine of the approaching multidrive defying gravity.
Thorne's knee was in the small of his back, but he
thought only that Chaeron had not dealt fairly with him.
Gagging on dust, he felt his arms wrestled behind him.

The flares of lightning become a steady, blinding glare.
He wished that he had not betrayed the man he loved
above any other, then he wished only for whatever
punishment was going to be immediately forthcoming.
He had never meant, or thought, to be part of the capture of Jesse Thorne.

Thorne sat calmly on the rumps of the two boys,
watching the haughty Kerrion descend the ramp of his
multidrive. Below, beyond the boulder atop the sharp
slope, Hooker's encampment was silent save for the soft
crackling of cookfires. The horses' screams had ceased as
abruptly as the men's shouting—when the vehicle swept
over their heads, spraying its beam of sleep.

Jesse had learned a great deal from watching Kerrions.
He learned more from seeing Orrefors routed by technologies mightier than their own. He had learned that
there was nowhere to run where the magic of science
could not find him. Hooker wanted to run to the stars,
but even that would not be far enough. . . . He waved
companionably to the unarmed, enchanter-clad Kerrion
potentate, saying in Consulese: "I hope you will take no
offense that I do not rise." Under him, two young rumps
twitched.

The sibyl's consort smiled in their shared circle of
daybright light, came abreast of the boulder, put a leg up
there and surveyed what his magic had wrought below.
"I could have done this three months ago, if not for you.
You and I need to talk. Let the children go. If we cannot
find some common ground for negotiation, you can walk
away to whatever cave you choose. I can't use you
against your will."

Jesse shrugged, stood. The boys scrambled up spitting
dust and smearing muddy tears on pale cheeks. "Wait in

the transport," Chaeron snapped, quelling Bitsy's excuses and Pope's taciturn disclaimer of responsibility.

"He is telling the truth," the proconsul remarked absently, watching the boys stumble toward the multidrive's open maw. "I used him to decoy you long enough to get a clear shot at Hooker. Pope would die for you."

"As Tempest did for you? I want nothing like that on my conscience. I just want to be left alone."

"If you wish . . . but hear me out, Commander, for just a few moments?" Courtly, confident, calmly murderous.

Thorne's heart beat fast, watching Shebat's husband perch on the boulder. One rush, a push, and he would be rid of this particular harpy. But others, many others, would come. The light from the multidrive illuminated him in sharp relief, falling over his face at an angle that made him more than humanly beautiful. "Go on, then. Talk."

Tempest died for this man, purposely, purposefully. Thorne had no doubt that in some obscure fashion the one person among the skyfolk whom he had been able to understand had had good reasons. If he could not see them, that was a blind spot in his own mental vision, come from staring at the brilliant face, in the same way afterimages persist once a man has looked at the sun.

"Thorne, I want to use you to bring about peace between the ground-dwellers and the 'skyfolk.' I'll let you tell me how you think we can do it. Everything I have tried has not availed. You are an expert in this area. I can call on no one who understands Earth more fully. I cannot spend the kind of time on this that I might wish. It is simply a matter of benefit to your people: who could help them better than you? Shebat assures me you are the man to do it. You are an Orrefors heir, so I will bet on your innate abilities to adjust and improvise. I will not cede you any ground or mandated holdings: your family lost this empire in fair commercial battle. If Hooker has been filling you full of dreams of empires restored and bondkin reinstated, let me disabuse you of dangerous fantasies at the outset."

"I'll be leaving, just as you said I might. . . ." Thorne rose.

Chaeron shrugged. "I cannot say I expected any different." He quit the boulder, started for his ship.

". . . Wait."

"As long as it takes. I know you are in your element, and you know I'm out of mine."

"I want no talk of 'bondkin' or 'empires'. My allegiance is not for sale, or forgotten. I wish to rid the Earth of foreign dominion by enchanters. If you let me go, I will fight you until I die fighting you. You must know that."

"I have considered it. But since you waste only your own life, it is not up to me to stop you. Surely you realize you cannot win, or even draw. You can only lose. My society guarantees any man that right. I'd like to give you more, but only my wife will be destitute if you refuse to be reasonable."

"That is a problem between us I regret. If not for my sins with her, we might have—"

"Easy there, big fellow. I was a trifle hurt when you two did not see fit to include me in your fun, but I would hardly call a few nights—"

"Is it nothing to you to be made a cuckold?"

"My wife and I have an alliance, a marriage, a profit-sharing arrangement, and some stock majorities in common. Free will is another item. Although I would dearly like to know how you reflamed her, who considers passion an evil to which she merely succumbs . . . ?" He trailed off, snapped his fingers, shaded his eyes and peered hard at Thorne, who could make little of what was meant. "Now, you have done me a great favor, and I feel obliged to return it. Ask one favor, any favor, for you have shown me what it is my wife sees in you. . . ." He chuckled aloud. "And I assure you, I hold no grudges. She is free to sleep where she will, as am I. If *that* drove you to Hooker, it was unnecessary. And for your imprisonment and escape, I have reviewed the slates, and see for myself that you shot Rizk, who would have corrected the false impression that *I* had died, making Tempest's sacrifice useless and perhaps ending my own life, to which I am very attached, as it were. Are you not tired of running? Let me exonerate and enlist you, man, and you can do a lot of good for the people you say you have dedicated your life to helping. Otherwise, they lose their best chance with yours. . . ."

"A favor, any favor? Give back what has been lost to Cluny, to every ruined farmer whose faith is rent. Make the false oracles tell true, and the world right with the gods."

Chaeron sighed. "No one can give you back your gods, I am afraid. Shebat's the best we've got. As for Pope, I cannot abrogate his rights of citizenship, even in order to prove to you that I mean what I say. He is free to do whatever he wants, and as far as I know, he wants to become an intelligencer—like Tempest. He thinks he can help bring Earth back from the barbarism your gods have inculcated upon their servants. But you can find that out from him." His eyelids flickered. "Meanwhile, I am going to leave you two together to talk it out.

"Consider that you could arm your weekend warriors and with our most concerted aid ferret out every rebel enchanter remaining on Earth. Of course, you could not cut them into little pieces, or whatever you are used to doing to them, but you would have the satisfaction of deporting them—enough to sate principle, if not passion. Outlaws no longer, your men would benefit, as would these environs. You could lift a state of siege that has persisted for two hundred years. If you turn away from my offer, you turn away from peace and cast your vote for gratuitous violence.

"Should you decide in favor of civilization, come to New Chaeronea, anytime, and present yourself at the consulate. I'll make you special adviser to the governor, and you can start rebuilding what you have helped to tear down."

Thorne just watched as Chaeron retreated without a farewell. Cluny appeared in the arch of the multidrive, and the two stopped and spoke when they met midway.

Then the lithe enchanter disappeared into his conveyance without taking a backward glance and Pope shuffled toward him, taking many.

He had not risen, he did not rise. He squatted there while the youth came up and stood over him, and while the multidrive roared up into the sky, taking its false daylight with it.

"He says you can have all the horses that survived the enkaphalin—sorry—the sleeping-beam, but not to go down there until the crews come to collect their prisoners."

"Cluny . . ."

"Thorne. . . . Commander, sir, he is right."

"And I am wrong?"

"Wasn't what I meant. I mean . . . it's over, don't you see? And something else is beginning. With or without us."

"Go back with them, if you think that."

"I would have. He's assigned me to you, sir, until you give him some statement of intent."

An imperfect dark settled down around them, speckled with dancing blues and reds and greens from the bright light's passage, faded into black. Thorne welcomed the cover it threw over him, the privacy of anonymity, the room to sort out conflicting emotions he did not want to feel without worrying about how it might appear to Pope.

A time later, the youngster said, "I never would have come here if he had told me what he'd planned, but I am glad I did. Jesse, don't choose the old ways. I have seen so much and learned so much that is good and right and honorable that I don't know how to begin to tell you. There is room enough beyond the sky for everything a man could want to be. You can have the best of both worlds, and never take another life. The sibyl told us that you would come to this, and make a choice for life or a choice for dishonor. Surely, this is that."

"Scout, you are too much like your new friends, these days. And I asked her before about her prophecy, and she and I agreed the time had come, then. So I have passed that moment of choosing, and in my heart, fate feels fixed like a barb. Do not press me. I need quiet and time to think—and did I not, I still could not hear advice from you and take it well. So stay, or go, but give me silence. I will do what I will do, and when I know it, I will let you know it. Until tomorrow, bide, and I will give you an answer to take back to your new-found friends."

During the night, he slept not one wink, but watched the airborne crews drop down into the dell and remove all traces of Hooker and his men and their enchanters' encampment. True to the proconsul's words, no one touched the horse-line. But the gift of horses did not please him, as it might have otherwise. He looked upon the future's minions while they took prisoner the past's once-mighty enchanters, having effortlessly laid low those Jesse had found too powerful to surmount, filling the air with catcalls and jokes and offhand gripes about the number of inflatable and the dead weight of unconscious men who must be carried into the waiting vehicles Cluny called "APCs."

He felt much too helpless, and too much like a fool. If time were space he would have run back to his beginnings as fast as his legs could carry him, but not one among the black enchanterbreds just waking on the horse-line and lurching to their feet was fleet enough for that.

He cast sidelong glances at Pope, who wore his hopes unhidden and unashamed. It was hard for him to speak at all, but he told the boy to make his choice of horse, and to take his leave.

"What word for the proconsul?" the youth astride a high, black back demanded reproachfully, while the horse sneezed foam and danced in place.

"Say that I will talk to friends of mine, and come in a month's time with a consensus."

"You will not," Pope blurted, his tears nearly overflowing, his chin quivering.

"Even I do not know that. Say what I have said."

He walked away before his own heart overflowed, toward the horse-line where destiny had given him full measure. With such stock as this, he could run, or fight, or calmly settle down wherever he chose. But there is always a price to pay.

In the bright noon light he turned them loose, and endured their surprise, their joy, their realization, where before when he had pulled the nails out of their shoes and pried the metal away from horny hoofs they had snorted distrustfully and tried to bite his neck.

He swung up on the one he had chosen to keep, saying to it that he was sorry he could not let it go with the others, but that he would, someday. Then he headed it for Bolen's town, the closest place where a man might get drunk enough to sleep like the dead.

The argument between Penrose and Spry in Acheron's guildhall had gone on for nearly an hour, hot and heated, and showed no sign of abating. Pilots lingered in knots close by and listened to talk full in "inertial" and "accelerated" frames, but only Baldy dared to interject the obvious: "What difference can this make? We have done it. *Tyche* has—"

"—received messages in sponge from the *Marada*," Spry interrupted. "The *Marada* found *Hassid* in sponge and followed her out of there without a pilot two, no *three* years ago. *Tyche*'s not proved anything except that the *Marada* is unique. I don't like these timelike geodesics and I don't like the fucking geometric extension, and I don't like the goddam a priori assumption beneath it all that time has multiple arrows. The holy universe is complicated enough without canted spacetime manifolds."

"Spry, it's *simple*. It is simpler, and simplest," Rafe groaned, then put forth his two hands so that his extended index fingers formed a cross. He wiggled the lateral finger: "Space," then the longitudinal digit; "Time. Any event in sponge can be simultaneous to any thrice-cursed event E according to A, B, or whomsoever, anywhere in the space axis. T always equals zero on the time-axis for events in, or relative to, sponge, to any observer. Twistor theory—"

"Ancestor worship," scoffed Spry. "None of this can translate into realtime. You can't have durationless instants, and you cannot tell me that everything that I *think* happens to me in sponge over periods of weeks happens instead in my back-brain in a pair of loaded instants."

"Everything you *think*, happens in a different dimension of time than that in which you manifest results of that process. The *Tyche*'s clock *is* the fucking spacetime extension; the metric is superposable: *tick, tick, tick*. You just don't like being made a fool of by a cruiser who knows you're vestigial and in danger of extinction. *Tyche* took me in and out of sponge without a glitch. This can't be any alternative universe to the one I left, not with *you* in it. I'm here and you are here. We both are here expressly because *Tyche* works. Now, that does not prove, as you intimated, that we've got the theory right. But we do have a working cruiser which does not need to refer to a biological-clock to meet our travel-time expectations, and which can communicate with other cruisers, in or out of sponge, by the relatively simple mechanism of superimposing the proper instant at which communication would be feasible upon the compendium of instants available to it!"

"And cruisers have been doing this all-time selection number in spacetime for quite a while now without needing to conceive of a different—"

"How do you know what a cruiser needs to conceive?"

"*Enough!*" Both looked at Baldy—white faced, motionless Spry, and Penrose, whose cheeks were flushed. "Gentlemen, you want to solve problems, I have a real one in need of solution. Will you both please come with me?"

Out they went, through the pilots dotting the guildhall who took that opportunity to declare for Penrose's side or Spry's with raised fists or slaps of encouragement or blue exhortations.

"What's up?" Penrose spoke for both, while Spry simply glared.

"We've got ten Draconis cruisers Acheron-bound from our spongeway. We've got the most cockeyed declaration of cargo you can imagine: they say they're the first of a convoy—the first, mind you—bringing the erstwhile inhabitants of space-end to their new home . . . Earth. Now, Chaeron wants to know if that is their true status, or if we are being invaded, and he wants to know it fast. One of you could go to *Tyche*'s berth and do some snooping, but which one of you, I'm not certain. David, can you put prejudice aside long enough to help me find out what *Tyche*'s limits really are?"

"Yep. You want to know if there are more Acheron-bound nonskeds on their way, right? If *Tyche* can do it, we'll do it."

"Fine, Rafe, Chaeron wants to know if you can ask *Danae* to verify bills of lading and—"

"*If* it's an invasion, she couldn't tell space-enders from

troops of intelligencers. . . . Oh, yes she could. Weaponry, numbers of folk aboard. Anything but cruisers? Liners? Frigates?"

"The message I got gave an itemized schedule. But this is an awfully big surprise."

"Who is the pilot-in-charge?" Spry asked. Baldwin named him. Both men nodded.

Spry frowned. "Nuts knows him pretty well, I think. Can you have him meet me at *Tyche*'s slip—somebody forgot to issue me intelligence keys." He grinned bleakly.

"I'll take care of that," Baldy promised. "Just do this, and I will be *able* to."

"Where *is* Chaeron?" Raphael breathed as Spry sauntered off, whistling, hands jammed in his coverall pockets.

"In *Erinys,* I imagine."

"How can you let him do these things?"

"Chaeron? All he lacks for his rating is a master-solo flight, Rafe. Like any pilot, he thinks rules are for everybody else. You pushed him into it, being so proprietary about *Danae*. More to the point, how can I stop him from doing them?"

"*You* say this to me?"

Baldwin's mouth folded like a fan. "We are all living in the real world, here. I don't like owner-pilots, or Kerrions, and you know I have good reasons for both those prejudices. But I would not be here to express my dislike or my disapproval if not for this particular owner-pilot who just happens to be a Kerrion. *Erinys* is going to be Spry's berth, by the by."

"You don't think he's serious about that, surely?"

"He has declared that intention, as soon as due process permits. In the meantime, *Erinys* is putatively Chaeron's property, and a KXV, and although *I* can't influence him, you are welcome, RP, to give it a try. Find out what's coming at us out of that sponge-hole, and then we'll worry about having an owner-pilot for our guild-host." He clapped Penrose on the back, gave him a gentle shove.

Walking backwards, RP objected his way down the corridor until, to silence him, Baldwin hastened back into the guildhall mess, where none of Rafe's sensible and worrisome predictions could follow. But the devils were loose: nothing was ever going to be right with Acheron's fledgling guild when it contained both Spry and Penrose, and would soon contain one Kerrion too many.

Baldwin, among his pilots, waited calmly. Whether the ten cruisers who had popped out of sponge without warning were, as they claimed, arriving from space-end with Earth-bound human cargo; or were really, as they seemed, the advance shock troop of military action, made no difference to Baldy: It was trouble, either way.

The Kerrion proconsul had been shivering with fury, and told him pointblank: "I'm going to need an hour in *Erinys* before anyone knows about this. Gag the traffic controllers, or I will. And get every other vehicle we've got out of the volume of space this bunch is going to be traversing. If I get nervous, I don't want to have to worry about innocents in the way."

Then he had taken *Erinys* out to space-anchor, alone. Pre-rated and potentially acceptable, Chaeron Kerrion was a capable pilot. That was not Baldy's concern. His worry stemmed from the cornered-wolf grin he had seen on the young proconsul, and the premature aging he had seen there, and the rivalry grown poisonous between him and his half brother Marada, whom Baldy knew better than many—knew well enough to realize that the dangers Chaeron anticipated were not specious. No act was beyond Marada, who fancied himself Justice's instrument, merely a scythe in a blind, unerring hand.

Chapter Thirteen

KXV 134 *Marada* bore his outboard unerringly toward Draconis, pleased as a cruiser could be. M-87, the galaxy central to spongetravel and that which hosted Draconis, administrative sphere of the Kerrion consulate, beckoned warmly in radio frequencies already visible to the *Marada*'s "memory." They were going home.

Too long had his outboard been Earthbound, and too long had he been docked at one of the universe's most dismal outreaches. Draconis was full of Kerrion cruisers, old friends, and fond recollections of days gone by.

Shebat would recover more than her spaceworthiness in Draconis, if the *Marada* had anything to say about it. This long dip in sponge had bettered her, already.

His time-align was reading out thirty-six "hours" left to the sponge part of their journey when a *Tyche*-shunted Spry reached them with news that Marada's task force was invading Acheron. The advance cruisers had already arrived; space-enders were being brought to Earth in a multitude.

The *Marada* experienced chagrin: he might have fore-warned Spry of this fact: he had known of the task force's destination as soon as the cruisers themselves had been calibrated: since just before they entered space-end's sponge-hole, Acheron-bound. But the *Marada* had been lax, no longer concerned with taking care of everything.

Or rather, he had "everything" aboard him: he had Shebat. And who could have known what reactions a simple transport of humans from one locus to another would evoke from their conspecifics at the point of sponge-exit?

Spry was agitated. His loss of equanimity underscored the import of his message: Spry, through scheme and counterscheme, success and failure, incarceration and doublecross, had never been shown to be at a loss. Even when his mind had wandered in cruiser-realms, Spry had always displayed a deep and contiguous sense of self. "Let me talk to Shebat, *Marada*. Chaeron's on-line," said the grainy, tired Spry whose face appeared transiently in his monitor, to be replaced by Chaeron's, strain evident there despite the tenuous quality of the sponge-shunted image.

"Chaeron, what does this mean?" Shebat gasped when she had heard the news.

"It means you must be exceedingly careful. I wish I had not sent you. . . ."

"She can't turn around in sponge, Chaeron." Spry's voice came from off-monitor.

The *Marada* was pleased to hear Spry state the fact. He was not pleased that Chaeron thought Shebat would have been better off in Acheron in the midst of an armed invasion than within his hull. In sponge, in Draconis, in real-time space or slipbay, the *Marada* could and would protect his outboard.

"But can they *do* this? Turn Earth into a penal colony? Legally, I mean?"

"I don't know. Possibly."

A silence stretched: Chaeron did not know? To say something, Shebat said, "Shall I proceed as we had intended?"

"Absolutely. You can reach me through *Tyche* and Spry, or direct to *Erinys*. . . ."

"*Erinys?* Chaeron, what are you doing? This is through *Erinys?*"

"A three-way link," Spry's voice-only transmission confirmed. "Don't think about it too long, Shebat. Just do your part."

"Spry!" Chaeron's rebuke reechoed around Shebat's

helm. "Let's set up some data-codes, in case of need." And he began contriving innocuous messages to be sent in case of failure, and as warnings, and as ciphers indicating embarkation, headlong flight, incapacity to execute any of those. The final coded message, merely a string of numbers in cruiser-referents, was for the *Marada* to send if he should lose track of Shebat or determine on his own that she would need to be extricated by means other than those the cruiser could provide.

When all contingencies were explored and escape plans explicated, the three-way link through sponge was dissolved.

Shebat sat curled in the *Marada*'s command console, chin on her drawn-up knees, "Well, *Marada*. What do you think?"

"I am sorry, my outboard, that I did not bring the convoy to your attention. But it is well that we are headed to the source of the problem, rather than sequestered away from it. The proconsul was in error when he regretted dispatching us to Draconis. The only possible solution that futures projections will yield involve action by you. My outboard, the arbiters in Draconis, who sent for you, knew very well that by this point in time those headed for Acheron would begin arriving. My own projections suggest that they, too, seek a solution of which you are a part. We are not without adherents, cruiser and human. Cruisers strongly support a solution which allows for the continuing production of AXVs."

And then, abandoning vocal mode, the cruiser *Marada* showed his outboard how true those statements were: down the corridors of achronal sponge her mind sped, pinwheeling through *Tyche*'s clock and out to cruisers everywhere in spacetime who listened, and murmured fond encouragement to the only outboard among all outboards who was remotely like them, and to the cruiser who was the most that any of them could imagine a cruiser might become.

Secretly, the *Marada* was relieved that Chaeron had not recalled them: no cruiser had ever retraced its course through sponge without first proceeding to make the obligatory sponge-exit. The negative universe, which is encountered only at sponge-egress and never at sponge-entrance, must be traversed, else the time dilation accrued in approaching speeds appreciably close to that of light could not be cast off. If Chaeron had insisted they return without first exiting sponge at Draconis' portal, the *Marada* would have needed to find or create an interim sponge-exit, whirl about in a dangerously accelerated circle, and plunge back into the hole from which he had just emerged. Any of those were precipitate alternatives, but less confounding than arriving back at Acheron years later in future real-time. Sponge was adamant in that regard, though amenable in others: time dilation must be compensated for; the only configuration of spongespace travel which allowed for this subtraction of years was one which brought them through a parabolic of the negative universe at the *end* of their journey, when inertia and acceleration and the nature of sponge hurled them into negative spacetime fleetingly, a precursor to crossing the obligatory event and particle horizons which separated them from real-time.

No time-align had ever been calibrated which could count as much time as would pass should the dip into negative space be edited out of a sponge journey. No human mind could extend or human biology comprehend the scale or tidal stresses involved in such an alteration of procedure. Of all the possibilities and probabilities inherent in spongetravel, that of turning around in sponge was the least possible, the most improbable of completion, pilot and cruiser intact and returned to their native epoch.

Although the *Marada* could have done it, had Chaeron so ordered Shebat, and Shebat then instructed the cruiser, he did not think it would serve the cause of the proconsul or the purposes of his outboard to risk being thrust forward in time so far that no proconsul, no David Spry, and perhaps no Consortium, would still exist.

The cruiser had sent a curt "thank-you" of dismissal to *Tyche,* in no uncertain terms.

Whatever they could make of events in Draconis was better than finding themselves adrift in events whose context was temporally foreign to them. One may argue with arbiters, proconsuls, and consuls, but one cannot argue with physical laws.

•　•　•

Since her arrival in Draconis, Shebat had not left the slipbay. Whether it was accident or guile on the part of Marada which decreed that they be assigned the same slip, number fifteen, which had been her cruiser's when first Shebat had been given her ship by Parma Kerrion, the effect of that coincidence was considerable: Shebat's mind turned to former times, when Parma had been consul general and she had been awed by everything Kerrion and fearful for her magic's power, here in the harsh light of Kerrion scrutiny.

The slipbay was the same: cavernous, strutted, with cruisers neatly cradled like dark keys along a piano keyboard. Draconis must be the same, beyond the distant, towering cargo doors, the blazoned dignitaries' doors, the small, innocuous pilots' doors. Or it must *look* the same, for like Shebat herself, everything was different, now, than it had ever been.

She had been here five days. No greeting had been tendered from the consulate. Beyond a taciturn official of the pilotry guild who came to collect a log copy, and a junior detailed at her request to deliver supplies to her cruiser, no one had hastened to greet her. She was Draconis consul. It was remarkable that she had had to summon her own secretary to slipside to take copies of Chaeron's demands to Marada's office and to the office of Arbiter Wolfe. The log copy she had given to Guildmaster Ferrier's lackey was obviously edited. It was worthy of note that no one had complained. In the old days Ferrier would have been pounding on her cruiser's lock within hours, enraged.

It must be the contents of Chaeron's packet which had hushed them. She had had her doubts about going ahead with the secession, in light of the arrival in Acheron's space of so many space-enders, ferried there by a veritable armada. The slipbay at Draconis was only half-full, mute testimony to the feat accomplished: only Marada Seleucus could be audacious enough to envision such an act, let alone carry it out.

The ghost of him haunted her, though she exorcised its presence assiduously, whenever she found herself dreaming of reconciliation, or of rekindling an old and smoldering spark of affection. Once he had been everything a fifteen-year-old Earth waif who served whomever her innkeeper-master decreed could have dreamed of: chivalrous, selfless, handsome, and bold. He had swept her up into paradise. She had cast her finest spell, twelve coils binding, upon him. And it had protected him from the fruits of power and the ravages of time. She chased his simulacrum away once more, out of her mind.

But when the image of the tall, dark-haired ascetic was banished, doubts of more substantial nature crowded in: Chaeron could be wrong, to push for secession now, when no one could guess what Wolfe wanted, or what Marada Kerrion might do.

The *Marada* had agreed with Chaeron: there could be no more auspicious time. The *Marada* might be wrong: timing in human affairs is not like timing in cruiser affairs: men are not continent or consistent, like cruisers. And Marada Kerrion was the most unpredictable of men.

It was well, then, the cruiser reasoned, that Shebat had come to meet with him, since she was more difficult to anticipate than any man.

Shebat fretted that Marada might not be in Draconis, or that Wolfe might not be in residence, until her cruiser pointed out that *Hassid* rested in slip number four, and that Wolfe had called her in for this meeting.

"Then why do they ignore me? Why don't they come?"

"Perhaps it is a matter of etiquette. Perhaps you must invite them." As the cruiser spoke to her, meters twinkled, stacking and unstacking: her systems readouts glimmered in amber, green and red, mirroring her physical stress, her monitored reactions a better chiding than any additional or unwise words from the cruiser.

Neither of them wanted to state the obvious for the log or for the record: the contents of Chaeron's packet were potentially so explosive, and the demands attached so high-handed, that whatever situation had prompted Wolfe to summon her to Draconis could be either devalued or completely altered by its receipt.

They drafted and sent an invitation to both parties to join Shebat for dinner in her cruiser at 2030 hours. They requested departure clearance and sponge-way vectors for 2330, 15 June 2252.

They did not have long to wait for their answers.

Draconis authority swore that no departure-windows would be available for thirty-six hours. Marada Kerrion's office confirmed their dinner date. Wolfe's accepted with pleasure.

Then the slipbay's emergency security-shields closed in. Interruptor circuitry not even the *Marada* could defeat enwrapped them. Lights pulsed and horns blared and when these had passed, the bay returned to normal, but for purple emergency-flashers whirling in its corners and the fact that invisible scramblers curtained each cruiser's slip.

The *Marada* opined that this was just as well; he had had quite enough of the hostile and abrasive "company" of the *Hassid*.

Shebat thought that timing was paramount, and theirs was beginning to seem less than perfect. She had negotiated interminably, fruitlessly, with Hooker for the return of Jesse Thorne; Chaeron had settled matters in less than an hour by the application of "judicious force." Timing was crucial: she had prevailed in theory over the objections of her dream dancers, because one of their number took her part at a critical instant; in practice, all had come to naught when it was seen by the denizens of Earth that dream dancers could not deliver what enlightenment men like Jesse Thorne had come to expect from the land of dreams.

Matters of negotiation have a way of presuming false solutions, both her extensive experience in the field and what *Marada* had learned from his one-time relief pilot, Delphi Gomes the futuror, had shown them.

But one must proceed, in some seemingly ordered manner, to act, while maintaining readiness to reevaluate the basis of action at any time.

They had done their best to minimize risk: they had laid their "givens" out and allowed arbiter and consul general sufficient time to evaluate probable causes in the past and results in the future. All that remained to be assessed were human values: emotion, reaction, quality of judgment, perceptivity of thought. When more than one improvisational mind acts upon a data-set, possible conclusions multiply exponentially. Nothing could be predicted beyond the reasonable observation that isolating the *Marada* from all data-modes could not be construed as a neutral act. Their slip had been made secure either because discussions soon to be underway there were exceedingly sensitive, or because actions soon to be underway there would be so.

Shebat had plenty of time to cycle through her own doubts. She let fear and anger and frustration and supposition pass over her: all of these were old colleagues, not welcome to a pilot, but understood.

When Marada Kerrion's long, black command transport and Wolfe's open lorry glided in convoy up to slipside, she was thoroughly calm and as ready as cruiser/pilot intimacy could ensure. The menu she had ordered had been delivered by her office's staffers. Wine was chilling and covered dishes kept themselves warm in the *Marada*'s galley; the table had been set and the ruffled feathers of chef and servers smoothed:

Yes, the veal was perfect; and *No,* she would not forget the ices. It was to be a working dinner; they must understand, and not be offended. . . .

She had forgotten that facet of Draconis: work was precious, a guarded privilege. Aspersions must not be cast upon a person's usefulness. It had taken bottles of Earthly wine and bags of coffee beans to convince the "service professionals" that she had intended no slights, had taken no offense.

Later, she would silently thank them for involving her in their miniature crises of confidence, and thus lending her a perspective on crises and on confidence which she might otherwise have neglected in favor of self-absorbed meditation on the possible ramifications of this meeting.

She had thought it out to the point of diminishing returns.

The lock-chime alerted her. She watched them climb out of their conveyances and up the *Marada*'s ramp as she pulled on her boots and fluffed damp curls out from under her flight suit's collar. She smoothed gray satin down over her hips, clasped the bracelet her husband had given her about her wrist. She squinted at the woman in her stateroom's mirror, and smirked an ugly, purposeful grin: she could have been a walking log-box or an am-

bulatory computer, for all the difference the impact of
her person or her personality was going to make upon
this confrontation.

The *Marada*'s follow-screens traced her visitors. Marada Kerrion's wry introduction of Wolfe to his namesake
sent chills up her spine. With a pilot's curse she condemned him to life in the nether parts of one of the con-
sorts of the Lords of Cosmic Jest. Though who or what
she was, would not matter to him, just the sound of his
voice made her head spin: "Damn you, you'll not turn
me into a heartsick girl," she promised his effigy, then
went out to meet them in the corridor.

Wolfe was robed, an ambiguous omen. The skeletal,
aged countenance smiled benignly down upon her,
though she wore three-inch heels. He was carefully de-
corous; she took that cue from him, and greeted Marada
Kerrion as if nothing had ever flared, then died, between
them.

And Marada smiled from behind his beard and sent
incongruous messages with his wide, brown poet's eyes.

Her cruiser, who had greeted him by cruiser/pilot link,
knew better, and warned her with his musical chiming in
her backbrain: fury and desperation were her dinner
companions. Overestimating the delicacy of this situation
was impossible.

Consequently, she led them straight to the *Marada*'s
galley, and fed them while they made polite conversation
and complimented her upon the Earth vintages she had
brought with her. "I have saved the best for you both to
take back to the consulate," she assured them, and let
them fill her glass, though she would not drink a drop.

When dinner dissolved into coffee and brandy in the
Marada's salon, she thought perhaps they had been
wrong to worry so, that Marada Kerrion was healed and
Wolfe only concerned that she maintain the fiction of
running her Draconis office, as he had intimated between
courses, while she had served him a palate-cleansing ice
and he had smiled disarmingly, appreciatively, up into
her face.

But then Marada said, "Now that you have convinced
us both that you are a card-carrying Kerrion degenerate,
graduated from Chaeron's finishing school with flying col-

ors, let us disabuse you of some misconceptions." He was sitting slumped down on his spine in a deep chair, one ankle balanced on his other knee, turning a brandy goblet in his hands.

Wolfe intervened, "Now, Marada, let us be civil. It has been a pleasant evening, so far. *Civilized.*" He was standing near a quiet readout-panel, looking taller and thinner than humanly possible in the *Marada*'s soft, intimate light. "I would advise that we proceed in similar fashion."

Marada, feeling his glance, shrugged truculently. Shebat, who had all she could do not to scream *Let's get on with it,* sat on the edge of her desk console, facing Marada's chair but twisted so that Wolfe never left her sight. "Won't you have a seat, Arbiter?" she suggested, and poured herself coffee from the service which obscured the desk's displays.

"Sit down with my enemy? I suppose I must," he sighed heavily, and took a chair, pulling it over. "Shall we begin with rhetorical questions?" No one else said anything. "All right, then. Shebat, I suppose those packets which Marada and I received are only two of voluminous sets of copies, waiting at various locations, from which this information will be generally disseminated should we reach no agreement or your welfare come into doubt?"

"Of course."

"See. I told you. We cannot deal with them. Chaeron has denuded her of whatever reason or usefulness we once might have—"

"Marada," Wolfe rattled, *"please."*

"If you two think to play good-guy/bad-guy with me, think again," Shebat suggested.

"And if *you* think that Kerrion space is going to submit to blackmail and underwrite flagrant illegalities, think again," Marada snapped. The sound of his knuckles cracking in series could be heard.

Gods, I still fear for him . . . I must take that spell from him, or be forever bound, Shebat thought, and heard her cruiser's approving assent like a silent rustle in her brain. Looking at him was like viewing the most pleasing masterpiece of forgotten art: feelings she had never wanted to understand or endure welled up in her. Her disgust at herself came out in her words, but not its source: "*I* think that if you both think we believed, for a second, that you called me all this way to sign papers which my *pro tem* could easily have initialed, you are fooling only yourselves. What is it you want, Wolfe?" With difficulty, she broke the bond of stares grown solid as girders between herself and Marada, and turned to Wolfe.

His mien was sorrowful, painstakingly so. "I called you here, young lady, to spare you the disruptions doubtless still plaguing Acheron during the transition period. . . ."

"What transition? You have no right to complicate affairs on Earth, when you have mandated us to simplify them. Chaeron's tenure there is open-ended . . . '*until completion,*' it says in his orders. Already, Marada has made clear his intent to see that nothing is ever completed there. . . . In one day, by Hooker's aegis, he undid six months' work. Tempest died of it. We will not—"

"*Will you be silent?*"

"I am here, Marada, to listen. But you—"

"Then, listen. I will brook no interference with the utilization of Earth as a fit and fitting home for space-enders, whom my family, wisely or unwisely, went on record as being anxious to rehabilitate. I have decided that Earth is the place for them, and to Earth, from now on, all criminals will be sent in perpetuity. Surely, as a Kerrion who knows Earth better than any, you see the justice in this?"

"I see no justice anywhere about. I see foolishness, and vanity, and desperation. You had no right to destroy space-end—which was used by all consulates—unilaterally. You had no right to commandeer Earth as a depository for them, when you yourself have issued orders—"

"*Stop it. Both of you!*"

"Don't snap at me, Wolfe," Marada grinned. "This is just getting interesting. Tell me more about my rights, foster sister. . . ."

"Shebat, if I may inject just one datum here, then I will be going, and you and my esteemed *ex*-arbiter can continue your personal quarrel without any unwilling witness. Yes? Good. Then: We called you here to explore

the possibility of transferring the consul generalship—
quietly and routinely—to you—"

"That was before you proved yourself a criminal of
equal magnitude to my brother. Softa Spry as an *innocent
victim* in need of pardon and redress. . . . Really, you
two have gone way too far. . . . Sorry, Wolfe."

"You may yet be, young sir. Now, Marada wants to be
reasonable. Don't you?"

"Not at any cost. Only within limits."

"Shebat, will you withdraw the flagrant threat of releasing this packet of potentially incriminating data from
our consideration?"

"You want to trade me the consul generalship for
Acheron and the Orrefors acquisition, is that right?"

"I'm leaving," said Wolfe. "This is impossible. I
should have met with you alone, as I had intended,
Shebat. Marada, you promised me you would let me handle this. Shebat, the kernel of the matter is this: the guild
wants Marada back as an arbiter. We cannot have him
until some other consul general, acceptable and endorsa-
ble, is at hand. Your husband is not under consideration,
for precisely the personality flaws which his attempt to
blackmail us through you so clearly illustrate. Nor can we
advise your consul general to submit to this sort of
pressure. . . .

"Yet, we hoped you two could come to some agreement. Short of the Acheron/Orrefors property dispute,
there is some room for compromise. The threats . . .
potentials you have at your disposal must not become re-
alities. We have lost . . . the *Consortium* has lost . . .
three consular houses over the space-end affair. We may
be able to convince them to rejoin us, if Earth is honestly
touted by one and all as an improvement, a human-rights
victory, as it were. Now, we are not trading in
illegalities . . ."

"Then we are not trading," Shebat said quietly. "The
information will be released and Marada will undergo an
evaluation by referendum. We can clearly swing a vote of
no-confidence. This man," she indicated Marada, who no
longer looked amused, but fought his temper visibly, his
long fingers digging into his chair, "is responsible by
proxy for the murder of my son, for Gahan Tempest's

death, for failing to intervene in the attempted murder of Softa Spry, then a duly installed Kerrion envoy to space-end—"

"That's enough, Shebat."

"I wish it were. Wolfe, the information we have submitted is not inaccurate."

Marada snorted. "Softa's not a pirate? Not *the* pirate? Seven cruisers' crews murdered, passengers spaced—"

Wolfe crossed his arms, looking between them. "There is no possible solution here. Two principals, both overly emotional, cannot hope to make agreement. Good evening!" He headed toward the door, which sighed obliging open.

"You come back here and sit down. When you're dismissed, you'll know it," Marada said very slowly, sinking down further in his chair. "I want a witness here that I did no physical harm to my foster sister. They'll lie about anything.

"Shebat," he sat forward, arms on knees, chin on fists, "why don't you be reasonable? Withdraw this material. I don't even want to hear these 'secondary demands to be explicated by our representative.' I'm offering you an out. You can leave, go back and join your playmate, unobstructed." His eyes gleamed in a long pause. "Of course, we would require guarantees precluding any subsequent attempts at reviving this extortion. To that end, I have taken certain measures. . . ."

She heard Wolfe's robes rustle as he sat heavily, chanced a look at him, saw from his face that the worst was yet to come and he had done his best to forfend it.

"Now, Shebat, you must consider mundane matters, like funding and its sources. You two have used up your own monies, gone past any hope of recouping your losses. You face bankruptcy, and more: the licensing of AXVs is to be held in abeyance, citing as sufficient reason my poor stepmother's mishap. Her own assets, and the younger children's trusts, can be delayed in probate for years: she'd not dead, and you two have just shredded the last of my patience. I'll take title to Acheron, as soon as your dissatisfied clients find out you cannot deliver spaceworthy, licensed cruisers and sue you for breach of contract. You'll lose your own cruiser—I'll see to it—as well as every AXV and the last coin you've got in your pocket."

"There's no way you can stop the AXVs," she said calmly, though her voice sounded like someone else's in her ears. "They're perfectly functional, revolutionary, with communications capabilities—"

"That's why it's easy. They're *too* revolutionary. I've theorists standing in line to swear that Einstein Locality is not violable; you can't exceed the speed of light. Not with communication circuits, not with—"

"Gods, Marada, it's still the cruisers? You're exceeding Einstein Separability, or Locality, if you prefer, every time you think a thought." She picked up her coffee cup, held it away from her, let it fall and shatter on the deck. "There's no paradox in the laws of motion: you drop a cup, and it falls and breaks. It does not worry about the difficulties of first needing to traverse half of each increment of distance, as it delineates them in its fall: it neither refuses to fall, nor takes an infinite number of steps: it falls; it breaks. Paradox is of man's making, his misstatement of physical laws. Cruisers, like men, think. The complexities of thought—everything that occurs between the initiation of the urge to thought, and the phrasing of that thought for speech—occur in an achronal dimension."

Marada raised an eyebrow. "You've been doing your homework."

"Softa had some probing objections. The *Marada* helped me see that the flaw is in our conditioned biological time-sense, not in time, or space, or spacetime. Time is the primitive; all else must fall before its mandate. Will you admit that I am right?"

"Never. I won't underwrite cruisers-as-intellects. I won't stand still for blackmail, especially when I *know* some of it is contrived: Spry and his cohorts are as guilty as men can be. If I were you, I would not try to use that packet as it stands—not with his innocence proclaimed therein as one of many truths. That one, I *can* prove false, thereby casting doubt upon the rest of it."

"Only by using your cruiser's data-source, which you claim she does not have."

"Let me worry about that." He stood up. Wolfe rose also.

Shebat sat very still. "Just out of curiosity, when will you be lifting the interruptor circuitry?"

"When we've decided whether we'd be ill-advised to let you go. We might need to convince your husband how violently opposed we are to his proposal."

"If they do not hear from me by midnight, Acheron-time, they'll begin spreading the word."

"Is that so?"

Shebat watched Wolfe's face, which was schooled but flawed: this was not what he had meant to happen. She felt, as well, the odd helplessness of being caught in some spacetime caustic where events were inarguably fixed. She wanted to say that she would consider amending some of Chaeron's conditions, but she could not. "Yes, that is so," she lied. "Keep me here against my will, and you will both regret it."

"Threaten me once more, and I'll have Acheron under martial law and your husband in a high-security cell by the end of the week. Be sensible, woman. I have more armed vessels in that vicinity than have ever been convened at one set of coordinates in the consulate's history."

"Acheron can withstand any siege."

"Don't tempt me."

A hiss told them that Wolfe had made his exit.

"Marada, if we do as you say, will you abstain from retribution? relax the moratorium upon the sale of AXVs?"

"When I am certain of your compliance, I will lift the ban. Of course, I will need the originals of the documents concerned, logs and so forth. And I will have to have Spry and the rest of the pirates." As he spoke, he moved toward her. "Really, you two are insupportably naïve. One does not pressure a consul general with blatant un-truths. The introduction of that pack of lies into other-wise valid data throws all your assertions into doubt. I should take you over my knee—"

"One more step, Marada, and I will . . ."

He moved forward; she invoked "passing by un-noticed." From that phased state of hiddenness, she stepped aside, her hands working. Behind him, where he could not see, blue trails came to be in the empty air. They emanated from him, not from the place where Shebat stood, and drew away from him to be sucked into her palms where they were raised toward his back. She had the spell's words on her lips; her eyes were closed. Having called back her protective warding, unbound the twelve coils she had placed about his person so long ago, she let her body reappear.

When he turned from searching beyond the desktop for her, she was standing to his rear, arms crossed, chin lifted. "How did you do that?"

"Do what?" she shrugged.

This time, when he grabbed for her, she did not evade him, or even flinch.

"Shebat, be sensible." His fingers dug into her shoulders; her eyes watered from the vehemence of his grip. "Repent this attempt at coercion. I will be patient with you. It is not your fault, but Chaeron's. His poison has infested your—"

"—impressionable primitive's brain? You be sensible. Prove your good faith, Marada. Let me go. Get off my ship, defeat the security blanket, have your controller grant me a departure-window. I cannot make any promises. I must talk with Chaeron." She put her hands on his, at her shoulders, pressing nerve endings in his wrists, levering his forefingers. His hands came away.

"Fine, the moratorium remains in effect. If any of this information leaks, it becomes permanent. Call it a punitive sanction, if you will, fair exchange for this kind of treachery. Transmit my message to Chaeron. Go home to Acheron and stay there. Send me my pirates. Be good little Kerrions. . . . For your own sakes, be impeccable. As for you personally, your tenure as Draconis consul is terminated, as of now. You have been absent too long to maintain any fiction of discharging those duties."

"Is that why Wolfe really called me here, to relieve me of my post?"

"Hardly," Marada chuckled. "He almost had me convinced that by ceding the consul generalship to you I could deal myself out of this abhorrent double bind. But you have managed to rouse my conscience—what is left of it. And, too, I cannot trust you to do the sensible thing and give up this scheme of yours. If you should implement it directly after having been removed from your consulship, it will be easy to point out that your ire and your thirst for revenge prompted you to concoct the whole of these unsavory accusations from little more than the exigencies of day-to-day consular difficulties. . . . Freedom *to*, my dear, and freedom *from*, cannot ever be separated. Do remind Chaeron of that, when you see him. And tell him too that you'd both have had everything you thought to extort from us, merely by waiting. Overt blackmail attempts were something we had not anticipated, and tell me that as much as I would like to be rid of this yoke of consular privilege, you are not a fit replacement. Too bad, really. We *were* going to make you consul general. It never pays to be overanxious."

Chapter Fourteen

"Gentlemen, I don't see what I can do for you, beyond refunding your deposits. I'm virtually a prisoner in my own consulate," Chaeron said softly from behind steepled hands. Across the table, Andreus Bucyrus chuckled, indicating that he recognized Chaeron's disclaimer for what it was. To Bucyrus's right, a swarthy, bearded Tabrizi minister beamed vapidly, seeing the other two bare their teeth. The beard hid his receding chin no better than the smile hid his confusion: this was no laughing matter. The cruisers his people had contracted to purchase must be delivered. The Kerrion could not be allowed to renege. Tabriz space desperately needed these new cruisers, which were simpler to operate than those with which his bondkin now struggled. He began murmuring introductory commiseration: yes, the Tabriz family itself had been having trouble with the Kerrions' consul general. Yes, everyone understood the delicacy of internecine gamesmanship, especially when rivals were related. Why just last year they themselves had undergone a similar upheaval, and now—despite extraconsular doubts—things were better than they had ever been in Tabriz space. But the cruiser orders must be filled . . .

"You damned fool camel-switcher, shut up." Andreus Bucyrus wished the meeting had been held somewhere other than the Kerrion proconsul's personal suite.

Bucyrus would as soon not have seen it: the spare, broodingly dark library was a rack-mounted jungle of flush-set metering banks and corruscating displays in flat, black housings. In its center was this one console, whose operations functions were safe from unintentional or intentional meddling beneath thick, smoked glass. The only humanity in the room seemed to emanate from one wall-mounted shelf where silver bookends held ancient, leatherbound books. Sound was muffled, lights were dim in corners; readouts danced silently, graphs only a initiate could read. Here this man worked, in a place which seemed better suited to one of Bucyrus's own computer swamis than an administrator. What was he saying, bringing them here? That the man who decreed Acheron's splendor had foregone any touch of it in his own dwelling spoke clearly: *Look, I don't need any of that. I need only order and access; everything else is for show.* The chair in which Bucyrus sat was uncomfortable—his and the Tabrizi minister's had been dragged up from against the far walls. Bucyrus was willing to bet that Chaeron's was perfectly suited to the needs of someone who must spend a great deal of time sitting, that it was as impeccably custom-tailored as the rest of this place. The pause that had followed his hushing of the Tabrizi had gone on long enough to have impact even upon the little man's dull wit. Bucyrus broke it: "I've got a power of attorney from Takeda space to come to some accomodation with you, Proconsul. Tabriz has sent Hammad, here, along as an observer, and to let you know they're behind us. But this is my party. We want those cruisers. And I don't give a damn whether you can procure licenses for them, as long as you can produce them."

The man who sat across the table console lifted one eyebrow, stared for a moment into the quiet depths of his electronics. "As I said, Bucyrus, I can't see any way to get them to you, while my half brother is so actively engaged in obstructing the sale of AXVs. My wife is yet in transit, but messages from her indicate that negotiations did not go well. I'm playing host to an ungodly number of loyal Kerrion officers, black-and-reds and intelligencers and the flotilla they arrived in, and they're taking their sweet time about pronouncing the space-enders settled in New Chaeronea. You're no amateaur. Just what do you think would happen if I handed you those cruisers while Marada's got his personal army in here?"

Bucyrus stroked his chins. "What I do with what's mine is my affair. Original invoice dates precede Marada's moratorium. I'll hire pilots out of your guildhall, or have my own people calibrate the things to tandem. AXVs don't really need on-board pilots, if I still remember how to read. Let it be my problem."

"That's quite a problem. What makes you think I'd risk an open break with my brother so that you can thumb your nose one more time at Consortium law?"

The Tabrizi said, "But—"

Bucyrus's guffaw drowned him out. "Because it's time, Proconsul. Because you're your mother's son and at least everything she boasted that you were. Because you're human, and human patience is finite. I'll help you, out of respect for what relationship we almost had to one another."

"Help me?"

"Don't feign innocence. Not even Hammad'll believe it. Look, my friend, everyone knows what's going on, and what the final outcome must be. . . ."

"I don't. How could you?"

"Because I've dealt myself in, for obvious reasons. I don't mind picking up the consulates the Consortium is losing, and I don't mind having to sell these cruisers for less than I could have, if they were licensed. But I have customers waiting for those AXVs whom I *cannot* disappoint. So if you can't deliver, then it is my job—"

"—Self-appointed—"

"Be that as it may, it is my job to see that whatever obstacles are in the way of our legal-when-concluded arrangement disappear, and fast. May I assume that you brought us here so that we may speak freely?"

"I think not. Minister Hammad, are you unwell?"

"Proconsul Kerrion, this matter must be resolved, and quickly. *I* cannot go home without those cruisers. Failure is unacceptable to those I serve."

"How unfortunate for you," Chacron murmured. "Bucyrus, I am not going to be subtle: any action by me is precluded. I've just had confirmation that my brother is on his way here. Whatever you have in mind to say or do to free those cruisers up, don't tell me about it. I cannot help you, or accept or reject any sanctions to be applied by you. I am barely secure here . . ." He spread his hands wide, dropped them slowly. "I must remain as I am—a patient, long-suffering, minor Kerrion official. I will not take any action against my brother beyond what the law allows, and since you no longer represent a Consortium-aligned consulate—nor you, Hammad—I am on diplomatically uncertain ground even listening to this sort of proposal—if proposal it is . . . *Don't answer that!*"

The Tabrizi had begun to explain. Bucyrus, with a disgusted snort, overrode his impropriety. He and the boy were coming to an agreement, no matter how circuitous. "Our arrangement was made before the three consulates formally withdrew, and thereby must be satisfied. I'll talk to the arbitrational guild, Kerrion, and get back to you." He thought he saw relief in the proconsul's eyes, so like his mother's that they made Bucyrus uncomfortable. As did the question in their artic depths, clearer than any of his spoken words: *If you're serious, why bring this goatherd?* When the young proconsul took time to reflect, that answer would become obvious: to make it seem that nothing more than a grievance had been discussed between them, that no coup was under consideration, that no insurgency awaited only the proper support structure—which he had just offered.

He was aware, as the Acheron proconsul ushered them firmly out of the room and then out of his suite, that he had been used, after the fashion for which the boy was best known. His mother had said that Chaeron was more data pool than human. Bucyrus had seen that side of him for the first time. A less canny man would have come out into the open, and allowed Bucyrus to drive a bargain for his support, name a price for his aid, forge a link of joint culpability which would be the first of many, binding Kerrion interests to Bucyrus interests.

He had his heart set on that merger, or at least peaceful cooperation. If, to obtain it, he must act without assurances from Chaeron of more than mutuality of interest, then that simply proved that the younger Kerrion was going to be exactly what was needed: a capable consul general for Kerrion space. A shiver chilled him, in that precisely temperature-regulated corridor, where his men waited and Chaeron shook his hand and bowed to the Tabrizi minister. He had lost a battle to this charming, low-key individual, and he did not feel his defeat. He had gone in there thinking to extract commitment, collusion, assurances of preferential treatment should he do for Chaeron what the boy had not been able to do—rid the consulates of Marada. He had come out with the vaguest of permissions, amounting to no more than a promise that the youth with the dark circles under his eyes would look the other way while Bucyrus took the risks.

He should feel thwarted, frustrated, even doubtful. He felt none of that, but only self-castigation: bringing that Tabrizi had been his mistake.

He rid himself of the little man and his own bodyguard as soon as possible, and went seeking through streets full of Marada's black-and-reds for Softa Spry, his abstracted gaze immune to Acheron's beauty as it passed by his transport's windows. This, like his data pool code-ins and his driver, had been assigned to him by Chaeron's consulate. Doubtless, every query he had made and every visit he had paid were duly noted, analyzed, and interpreted by the proconsul's staff, many of whom, Bucyrus's intelligencers asserted, were fanatically loyal. He could see why; out the window he spied no sign of disorder, no strain, no anxiety. If this was, as Chaeron had intimated, an occupation force, then it was the most civilized punitive investment he had ever seen in a disputed habitational sphere.

Chaeron's data-sources were strange to him, their manipulation subtly different than those with which he was familiar. Modern, as everything about Acheron was modern. Eclectic. Finally, after three false fixes on Spry, he leaned forward and tapped the glass. The dark-haired driver whos brows met over his eyes grinned and suggested trying the pilot's guildhall. Bucyrus had long ago learned that once one asks an intelligencer, one is bound to take his advice. "Son, I might have a little trouble getting in there. Can you clear it?"

"Sir, you have the proverbial privilege. My orders were to let you sit anywhere you want."

"In David Spry's lap, if you can manage it."

"Yes, sir."

"Let's drop the formalities, Intelligencer. You've got a name, so do I." By the time he reached the pilotry guildhall, Bucyrus was feeling a little younger and a little sharper—and a little envious. The intelligencers Chaeron ran were top-flight. He had recognized this one as Terry Ward, Tempest's protégé, from the dossiers his own people had supplied him. But he had never expected to be able to draw him out—or to receive a heartfelt offer of assistance over and above chauffeuring. One wouldn't like to think that in this calm and carefully controlled sphere a high-powered bodyguard would be needed, but it was nice to be provided for, especially when one is about to enter the no-man's-land of a pilotry guildhall.

David Spry was brainstorming AXV program modifications with three shipwrights in the one truly functional pay privacy booth in Acheron's guildhall.

". . . I still don't see how this'll keep somebody with illicitly-acquired access comes from stealing command capability. We isolated the master module in *Tyche,* Softa, but that didn't mean the unit stayed discrete when the *Marada*—"

"Does a sun have spots?" Spry asked rhetorically. "Does a gravity wave collision create a spongelike singularity? A phase-shift chosen at random before each flight will increase the probability of an interloper encountering wave collison in the matrix, and sounding an alarm. We'll know if someone is trying to appropriate control of the system. Beyond that—"

"Beyond that, these buffers mean that we won't have cruiser-intellect on-line in the com-circuits. They'll be acting as passive conduits. It cuts down the security problems and the information print-through. Softa's right. If we're going to isolate these systems, let's go all the way and specialize the circuits so that they've as little as possible to do with cruiser . . . computations," said the second shipwright, smaller and thinner than the first, with sparse red hair where the other's was black. Except for these differences, the khaki-clad engineers could have been twins.

The third—heavy, hairy, and most savvy of the three— was frowning. "Softa, I like this approach, really I do. I know damn well why you want it, and why the boss would jump at a chance to make these modifications if he heard we could do it, but I wonder if we *can* do it, and retain the integrity of our system. We're cutting the B-mode off from the other computers, little by little. Nobody knows how that's going to affect the system's decision-making on the long term."

"I just want to make sure that they don't start overriding us puny humans, that's all. I didn't fancy being carted in here like the outmoded outboard I'm fast becoming. A person's got to be able to claim that he's the pilot. Otherwise, automate the cruisers completely. Take out the idiot buttons and the manual override. I don't think you people realize what you've got here. If you'd think about it some. . . ."

A soft chime sounded. The monitor above the door showed Spry the pair seeking access. He grimaced. "Guys, let's adjourn. Do some simulations and permutate the schematics, and let's get some numbers for comparison. I don't know about you three, but I'm ready to graduate from 'what ifs' to 'what's whats.' We've got to look more deeply into what is happening here . . . I don't mind consulting, but I'm no prophet. And my shadow's back." He indicated the intelligencer in the monitor, below which a little red light had begun blinking.

When the shipwrights had departed and the intelligencer had escorted the portly consul general into the little booth and pulled back a chair for him, Spry looked from one to the other sourly. "What is this, Andy? Are you under close arrest?"

"Nothing like that, David. This is my—"

"I know what he is. Go catch some criminals, Ward. There's nothing going to be said here worth repeating while you're around."

"Spry, I'm watching out for the consul general."

"Do it from outside. I won't hurt him. Scout's honor." When the intelligencer had left, and the monitor showed him postioned at technical ease on their portal, Bucyrus began to speak.

Spry stopped him. "Don't you realize that there is no such thing as privacy? You think he hasn't got an ear in on this? Chaeron used to be Draconis consul. When he and Gahan Tempest put Acheron's specs together, they planned for every—"

"It's unimportant, David. And if you'll stop objecting, this won't take very long."

"Did you work something our with Chaeron? Because if you did, you'd better not tell me about it. I'm just making myself useful until Marada's goons cart me off to Draconis to pay for my sins—what few of them they've got on record. Do me a favor and don't tell 'em anything they don't already know."

Bucyrus urged his jowls into a smile, then scowled, sitting heavily. "What kind of crap is this? I heard the same sort of garbage from the proconsul. You can't expect me to believe that *you've* thrown in the towel, too!"

Softa shrugged. "Believe it, don't believe it. I can't blow my nose here without somebody collecting the tissue for 'evidential analysis.' I shouldn't even be seen with somebody like you. Kerrions can count, you know."

"So can I. And you're seven cruisers in the hole to me, as it—"

"Don't *say* that."

"How do you people ever get anything done? Telepathy? Secret codes? Innuendo can be misinterpreted. David, I've always been a gambler. I'm gambling, being here, gambling that you're still the same free agent I used to know."

"I'm not. I'm a pilot accused of piracy and about to be handed over to the arbitrational guild. Unless you can wave your paw and change the future, don't mix in. Don't tell me what you've got in mind, and don't remind me of what I owe you. Take your loss—you can afford it—and don't set yourself up to join us as one of the declared undesirables of Marada Kerrion's sleepless nights. He's about to clean house."

"I never thought I'd see it," Bucyrus shook his ponderous head so that the rolls of fat swathing his neck undulated.

"See what?"

"See you lose your nerve."

Spry hunched forward, elbows on the table, shielding his eyes with one hand. "I am just awfully tired of doing the impossible. Nobody really cares to think ahead, anymore. Or to listen to. . . ."

"Now you've got me worried. Since when do *you* care what the spongeheads think, or the consular ninnies, or the gods in Newman's heavenly manifold, if there are any? Isn't *doing* the job the important thing?"

"I don't have one, right now. And I can't see any reason—"

"That's okay, son. I've got just the thing for you. I want you to take out Marada Kerrion for us. No mess, no fuss. I'll cover all expenses and call our debt even, plus give you a bonus."

Softa laughed incredulously. "Where do you think we are? This is Kerrion space."

"Maybe it is, maybe it isn't. Part of that determination is up to you."

"You know I never do naughty things if I'm emotionally concerned with the outcome. Marada and I have a long-standing disaffecton—"

"You got involved with this pilotry guild."

"And that's what put me in this position. Forget it, Andy. I'm retired. Have been since before the Shechem war. The person you want to talk to isn't here—" he tapped his temple—"anymore."

"You and I made a post-Shechem arrangement . . . something about pirated cruisers."

"Sponge, do you want to testify against me? They'd be glad to have you." His seal-brown eyes narrowed. "You'll just have to write me off, Andy. I have."

"No chance. I've got my heart set on this. And you haven't once said it couldn't be done."

Straightening up, Spry scratched his pierced ear. "That kind of thing can always be done. But these people are trying to help mc; I'm not going to complexify matters. Shebat would never forgive me. And if Chaeron wanted to end his problems with his half brother that way, he'd have done it by now."

"Kerrion authorities have got the licensing board in

their pocket. The cruisers I came here to pick up have been embargoed, pending reevaluation. They are going to block the production of AXVs."

Spry winced, tippling his chair back. "Are you certain?"

"Heard it from Chaeron. If they didn't tell you, the reason's obvious."

David Spry did not reply immediately. He looked at his fingers, spread wide on the tabletop, then at the monitor. "I've got a lady friend down on the planet, named Lauren. Get her out of their reach, then come talk to me. If we work something out, it's going to cost you."

"I brought my piggy bank. And I've got twelve AXVs waiting and ready for me to take delivery, once this little snag of bureaucratic paranoia is cleared up. From what I hear, they're spaceworthy as is."

"Not exactly. We've been talking about extensive program modifications. That's what I was doing when you showed here. But that's my department."

"We're 'go,' then?"

"We're thinking about it. Do what I've asked you. And keep that kid Ward with you. He makes me nervous. He's too young to be that good. I wouldn't want to be his first mistake."

"*You* were."

"What?"

"That good, that young."

"Then I reformed. Not nice to slow other people up. They hate you for it. He'll learn. Right now, he's having too much fun."

Bucyrus chewed his lip. "I noticed that. All right, I'll ask for him to be assigned to me for the duration. Anything else? Money? Assurances?"

"Nope. The former's incriminating and binding, the latter's useless. Right now, you're just doing me a couple of favors, for which I may or may not be able to repay you. Slate?"

"Slate," puffed Bucyrus, rising.

Spry walked him to the cubicle's door, tapped it to open mode, was inundated by raucous sounds of argument and revelry as Bucyrus squeezed out into the noise and smoke and into the care of the talented young intelligencer, to whom Softa nodded, and was answered by a grin and a wave.

Then he took one step backward, oblivious to the growls of a knot of men obviously waiting for the booth, and the door smacked shut, cutting off exterior sights and sounds.

A querulous bleat came from the time-clock set into the pay-mechanism left of the door. He'd changed into it, buying time. He could not have said why he was unwilling to relinquish possession of the booth just then . . . unless it was that he was taking Bucyrus's proposal seriously. He lay his head against his hand where it still rested on the pay-mechanism. He needed time to think. His mind was quiet, smoothed out like some asymptotically flat spacetime diagram. The cool metal against his cheek, vibrating almost imperceptibly with the workings of the mechanism within, soothed him.

Standing there alone in the PPB, David Spry felt as if he was waking from a long dream. It had been a dream of patriotism and honor, dreamed by a man whose singular allegiance had always been to self and survival. For almost five years he had been caught up in that dream turned to nightmare, meekly submitting to the consequences of idealistic actions mounted without regard to certainty of failure. Chance kept score of a man's endeavors. Spry had known that the very number of his successes was working against him, piling up percentage points on the negative side of his luck index. When he had taken a berth as Parma Kerrion's pilot in order to direct an attempt by the Draconis pilots to separate themselves from their host-consulate, he had done it for all the wrong reasons: deep conviction of the rectitude of the pilotry guild's bid for freedom, empathy for the space-enders, knowledge that without some professional aid the guild's chances were nil. They couldn't go on playing folk heroes, consumed by revolutionary fervor so that their feints at consular authority were uncoordinated and ineffective. He had offered himself and his experience in the shadowy undergrounds of covert intelligence and extralegality free of charge. In fact, he had broached the subject to Baldy, then Draconis guildmaster, before accepting command of the *Bucephalus,* Parma's flagship.

He had told himself then that he owed it to his guild, somehow extending his stringent and personal sense of honor so that whatever slights and indignities pilots endured became his, also. Perhaps it had had something to do with becoming first bitch of the Kerrion guild. He had not really meant to top-out in the ratings wars, but his competitive nature had gotten the best of him. After that, he had lost perspective.

The whole time he had been first bitch he had been playacting, becoming someone he might have been, had circumstances been different. He should have realized the danger: in the two and a half years he had been Parma Kerrion's pilot, he had accepted only one contract: to deliver to dream dancers or otherwise red-line, Shebat Kerrion, at the behest of a highly placed spoiler in the Kerrion consul general's employ, who in turn was implementing Labayan orders. Spry's orders had been open: remove the designated party from play; method, operative's choice.

In retrospect, he should have known then that he was fooling himself when he went to so much trouble to shield Shebat from any possible harm. Affection for a target was contraindicated. But so was everything else he had done for five years. He had let himself be taken, along with the pilots he had enmeshed in the ill-fated imbroglio, gone to space-end with them, suffered right along with them though he could have extricated himself upon numerous occasions. When he had thought of escape at all, he had thought of it in terms of a group effort. When it became feasible, he had calmly extended the "group" to include the space-enders, one and all.

He had been paying the society from which he had consistently stolen and upon which he had so successfully preyed, in the only way he could: his beneficiaries, the only subgroups of the quixotic conglomerate he could respect.

Instant psychoanalysis in a PPB? He raised his head, crossed the booth, slid into a seat and punched up a neat whiskey. When it slid out of the hopper, he ignored it.

Pilots became progressively frayed around the edges. This simpler answer suited him better than one of self-delusion mixed with altruism. He was not a man for guilts, or for causes . . . at least he had not been until he had taken *Bucephalus*'s helm without wiping out traces of the flagship's former pilot. Print-through? Maybe. He had not handled his troubles with *Bucephalus* as well as he might have. Pilotry had changed him.

But what, then, accounted for this return to his former self? Part of maintaining a cover is believing one's own story, becoming another person so thoroughly that when you talk in your sleep, you stay in character. Softa David Spry was what David Spry had wanted to be—a pilot's pilot, beloved by cruisers and respected by his guildbrothers, mobile and privy to whatever intelligence he could gather, outrageous and troublesome enough that no one ever looked too deeply into the classic success story he represented. But Andreus Bucyrus had known him "when" . . . knew him well enough to know that any time Spry wasn't engaged in a project, he was available . . . knew him well enough to have been the linchpin in the aborted project to resettle the space-enders in Pegasus, to have been able to demand as payment the pirates' stolen cruisers, to be trusted to execute his part of the operation and to wait quietly until the time was right, even to offer to arrange to have a Bucyrus cruiser appropriated by Spry's pirates before Spry had had a chance to demand it as a necessary sacrifice, an obligatory covering-of-tracks.

Half of Pegasus was dependent on the Bucyrus trading empire. Though free and nonaligned, Bucyrus space was the colonies' link to high technologies. When, in 2234, a band of teen-age guerrillas led by a fourteen-year-old named Spry had succeeded in stealing an armed frigate with Bucyrus call-letters, the ensuing furor had attracted consular attention. Capture was inevitable. But the chase went on for a year and a half before the revolutionaries were apprehended, assuring both maximum sentences for the terrorists and the grudging agreement of a nervous colonial government to Bucyrus space's extradition demands, six months later.

Pegasus' colonial justice was purposely primitive as compared to Consortium justice. When the extradition orders were finally implemented, David Spry had already spent three of those six months in solitary confinement broken only by irregular spates of corporal punishment administered at will by vengeful friends of a guard Spry had strangled with his own belt when the trusty had sexually assaulted him.

In Bucyrus space, the penal system was self-contained but "civilized." Mass and multiple murderers, however, were not thought to be candidates for rehabilitation in the quotidian sense of the word. Four months in a Bucyrus high-security prison convinced the psychometricians who studied the twelve surviving youths that there was no inherent flaw in the consulate's shipboard security procedures. The weakness lay not in their programs, but in the inability of any security scenario to anticipate the actions of an individual like David Spry—a born engineer, a mathematical savant, a twisted, multitalented natural of a pilot whose gifts had no chance of developing normally in poverty-striken colonial environs. Intelligencers were quick to propose that such a youth—amoral, bitter, angry and blooded—could have his uses.

One day like any other, a battered, slim boy who no longer looked very much like his dossier photos was taken out of holding and brought before Bucyrus's chief of intelligencers. A mission was offered, an assassination in Pegasus' capital.

Through split and scar-twisted lips, a defiant seventeen-year-old demanded impossible concessions, astronomical payment, and access to certain of his jailers who had been less than kind.

One of three seated men at the table before which Spry was standing between guards had began to laugh. Even then, Andreus Bucyrus was fat. And fast. He counteroffered, "We'll fix your face, give you support systems, get you back in one piece. You can have your sitting ducks, but only *afterwards,* and in the course of a larger agreement. I could send somebody else out on this one, someone I could get more economically, who would be easier to field. We want to see what you can do. If you are successful, I want to send you to school. That'll cost me. I need a long-range commitment from you."

"School?" Spry remembered sneering. "You want me to teach these guys? Impossible."

But they had worked out an arrangement. Subject to a

successful mission, David Spry's record would be expunged, his Pegasus citizenship reinstated, money paid as agreed upon his graduation from a six-month intensive program designed to qualify him as an intelligencer, a high school graduate, and a candidate for transfer into the Draconis College of Astronautics and Space, where he would be expected to function as needed until his graduation therefrom, at which time severance bonuses would be paid and Spry would become—as he insisted he must, or gladly go back to modeling computers in his cell—a free agent.

He did and they did and, though at the time he had hated being manipulated, everyone benefited. His "Uncle Andy" had put him through school; he had rendered services which made his subsidization a bargain. Those who used nonaligned field operatives were not unaware of his actions. When David Spry came onto the covert intelligence market his reputation was already made; he was much sought and well paid. His proficiency as a pilot gave him mobility and the best sort of cover: blindingly high-profile, he was enjoying pilot's immunities to crimes other than those against the space to which he was currently in service. The covert intelligence community went to great pains to keep its doings subterranean. No hint of his avocation ever reached Consortium administrators, this due as much to those who conceived such operations as to men, like Spry, who implemented them.

This meeting with Bucyrus was contrary to every law of their mutual jungle. Bad enough that the old man had shown up here to collect his cruisers with a Tabrizi in tow and powers of attorney in his pocket, unconvincingly punctual. . . .

Spry blew out a breath. He shouldn't even be thinking about the feasibility of what Bucyrus had proposed: he had been out of circulation too long. He tore the foil off the whiskey and gulped it down, crumbling the plastic container in his fist. Ever since he had been convicted by Marada Kerrion and sent to space-end, he had refrained from considering his situation as remediable. When Shebat had extricated him from that mild and thus most galling incarceration, he had reacted like a pilot. He had involved himself in the pilots' strike and let himself be set up by Ashera, afterward, for an obvious execution, merely to get his hands on another cruiser and start building a second pirate fleet. All were passionate actions of a man who had forgotten many things in order to become something else: he had cruiser consciousness to consider, now. He loved the ever more sentient cruisers, precisely because they were not flawed like their creators. They never disappointed him with selfishness or shortsightedness. They never acted expediently, they were neither partisan nor mean. They were worth a man's allegiance, as no human he had ever encountered had been. When he had betrayed the trust of the Kerrion flagship *Bucephalus,* he had betrayed himself. All this punishment he had inflicted upon David Spry, who had disappointed Softa Spry, who demanded that he be what he had been pretending to be, and meet his own standards.

"That's that, then," he said aloud, the whiskey fuming in his stomach. He had it figured out to his satisfaction, no matter how unpleasant an interval this had been. Where did that put him? Tense, was where. His calf ticced, his shoulders throbbed. He leaned forward, elbows on the table, rubbing with both hands where muscles rose from back to neck. But despite his spoken words, consideration of this alternative (where previously he had been content to think no alternative remained) consumed him. Was he giving serious thought to this because he once again had no cruiser? *Tyche*'s breed was the future, that was certain. It was not possible to conceive an end to the AXV program, no matter its current glitches or the philosophical problems inherent in the math. He had been perfectly content with the old, trusty, "heavenly" spacetime manifold as Newman had envisioned it and Ward-Penrose had refined it and Kerrions had installed it in a supergravity/supersymmetry context. The problem of the missing dimension had not bothered him. Twistorially real spacetimes with curvature still admitted hypersurfaces. Though he had known for a long time that cruisers were adding a second time-dimension, overridingly asymmetric yet dynamically complex, he had seen no reason to rewrite man's view of global spacetime. Yet, he could see the benefit of having cruiser and human views agree.

If he didn't care whether the AXV program continued, then he would be dealing only with saving his skin, and that was firmer ground. So shelve the AXVs. If he did nothing, he would still face Marada Kerrion. Nothing Chaeron was going to do could alter that, though he would give credit where credit was due, even to Kerrions: the man had taken risks audaciously, partly on his behalf.

He flicked a glance up at the monitor; the men who had been waiting there were gone. He stabbed at the privacy-defeat, put a call though the data pool for Nuts Allen, requesting that Nuts join him here, and let up on the toggle.

Just a little bit longer, and he would have reduced the complexities of this problem to manageable proportions. To Spry, human actions all reduced to "right flat" topologies once emotion's hidden variables had been coaxed out and given values. This was most easily done when only *other* people's emotions must be considered.

Therefore, he had a lot more thinking to do before Nuts got here and he had to explain what he wanted. He had to *know* what he wanted, and why, and how to get it.

Where he wanted to end up was at his own center of visualization, whence he could sense the pattern which would make the mathematics of human endeavor penetrable. He wanted to solve for a point in spacetime where he was alive, unfettered, possessed of a pilot's license, and free of allegiance.

There, he had admitted it.

Now, all he had to do was make it happen, despite the difficulties, from a polarized pilots' guild full of none-too-friendly Draconis-allied Kerrions, while protecting people he cared altogether too much about, who were liable to get hurt should he stray from a very narrow, treacherous path on time-aligned action.

He nodded, still sitting hunched forward, eyes unfocused on the table before him. The face of a boy who had survived the brutality of Pegasus colonies formed in the gray plastic's reflective surface, shimmered, became once again the refurbished face he had lived with for fourteen years.

He recalled Marada, in their school days, and endless

verbal battles which had never quite come to blows. Here
was his greatest danger, his most terrible temptation.

But even this could be reversed, turned to his advantage. Marada was making no secret that Spry's scalp was
number one on his list of collectable trophies. In fact, he
was coming way out here to expedite Spry's extradition.

He must let his hostility toward Marada go, to gain the
edge which would bring him out of this triumphant. It
would not be simple: Marada Kerrion had made his college years hell, rousing student opinion against him,
hoisting consular prejudice like a battle-standard. It went
back to a day when Spry had been sitting behind Marada
in a class on spacetime topology, and faced a surprise
quiz unprepared. He had tapped the tall youth in front of
him on the shoulder, asking, when Marada turned in his
seat, only for the metric specified in the text. Marada had
whispered it, adding, "You'll never get through it with
just—"

"It's complete, if every Cauchy sequence converges to
X," Spry had shrugged. "If not, not." He had gotten the
top grade in the class on that quiz, and on every similar
examination. But Marada could not forgive Spry's in-
stinctive ability, and never tired of baiting him. When
pressed to the wall with logic, Marada would introduce
Divine Will.

Their rivalry spilled over into nonscholastic areas, went
through women, into politics. There was no simple way
to wipe out years of hostility based upon the unfairness
of nature, to have endowed the one with natural mathematical reasoning abilities, and the other with a humanis-
tic bent that made the abstractions of pilotry laborious.
So the feud had escalated, involving others, breaking
open when the pre-graduation ratings were given and a
girl they had both been seeing turned up pregnant, and
Marada disclaimed responsibility before any technical determination of paternity could be made.

Spry had stepped in, whisked the girl into his murky
world of illicit contacts and nipped a scandal in the bud.
The girl was back in her original state, reputation un-
diminished, in twenty-four hours. Marada, hearing this,
called Spry a murderer to his face. Spry had lost his temper, spat some indelicate condemnations of consular

mores, pointed out that as an exchange student he had
no hope of securing a retroactive breeding permit, should
the girl's parents have been willing to accept a common,
non-Kerrion son-in-law—and in any case, the child was
most likely, by simple addition, Marada's. Marada had
then threatened to take the matter to the authorities, saying that *if* the child had been his, then Spry should not
have stepped in. Physical violence had been avoided by
only the most capricious of chances: Spry was speechless
with fury, considering the consequences of coldcocking a
consular heir; three people Marada knew strolled up
from rehearsal in graduation gowns.

They had parted without a word, and kept a mutual
silence which strained everyone who knew them and
lasted years longer than the short time it took for David
Spry to complete apprenticeship, race through his
qualifiers, and ship out as a rated pilot, back to Bucyrus
space.

All that was left of their long-standing quarrel was the
hatred. The reasons underlying it had long ago ceased to
matter. But every time they were within orb of one another, their emotions flared. That would have to stop.
There was enough challenge here for him to want to suc-
ceed in defusing Marada, if only to prove that he had not
lost his touch or his nerve. Already, he felt the hyper-
acuity he associated with contemplation of deadly risk:
the physical sensations, partly painful, partly pleasurable;
a sense of being high above himself, precariously balanced, miles from his outer skin, and yet completely
aware of every iota of his biological person. Had he a
cruiser, he would have been able to see the concomitant
readouts. But it was unnecessary. He knew the signs.

Should he let Andy lure him into neutralizing Marada,
Chaeron remained to be dealt with. Whether or not he
was, as Bucyrus intimated, informed of and in tacit
agreement with the old libertine's objectives, Chaeron
Kerrion was problematical. He was a different class of
adversary. Nothing about him was simple, or certain. He
had gone to great lengths, recently, to look as if he was
pleading Spry's case. Let Penrose and Shebat believe it
was for them personally that Chaeron had endangered
his own position on behalf of Spry and the other pirates.

It was beginning to look to David Spry as if Chaeron had been coaxing a number of interlocking solutions into a neat line of which Spry wanted no part: Force Marada into indefensible actions and someone must act to remove him, someone not Kerrion whose toes had been stepped on once too often; assure that those toes would *be* stepped on; then stand back and look the other way until it was time to mourn and demand that justice be done. *Mea non cupla.*

But he couldn't very well go to Chaeron and ask him about it. Chaeron had more information about Spry than Spry liked, but Spry had never been able to figure out what Chaeron *knew,* and what he only suspected. Spry could not risk turning suspicions into certainty: on the one occasion when Chaeron had tried to strong-arm Spry into his service, the conversation had been so oblique that no substantive disclosures had been made by either of them.

He was not going to chance finding out the hard way. He would let things progress toward a possible solution awhile longer, and time might resolve his gut objections to helping Kerrions, even accidentally. If Chaeron was as good as his word, and truly the altruistic champion of pilots and cruisers he pretended, then Spry just might end up with some of those things he had determined to be desirable: rating, cruiser, freedom. If the above was true, then the universe was really Heraclitus' ever-living fire, Chaeron was the tooth fairy, and all *he* had to do was ensure the continuing life span of David Spry.

"By the Jester's hairy balls, Davey, you look like you've just lost your best friend," pronounced Nuts when Spry admitted him. Allen was swathed in civilian finery, a claret velvet suit with silver buttons which were strained over his belly, a silvery shirt with ruffled cuffs and billowy stock.

"Do I? You look like you've been at a costume ball. Sit down, if you've a minute."

"I take that to mean you don't like my suit," Nuts sniffed, lowering himself into one chair and punching up three double bourbons on the waiter. "Have to guess that you've forgotten your manners, like everybody else, lately." The drinks started to slide out. As they emerged from the hopper, he opened and downed them. "There," he belched, rubbing his stomach. "I'm recovered from the insult. Yours, anyway. . . ."

"Someone giving you trouble? With Orrefors and Marada's boys and Rafe's Acheron-forever antics in here, there's good reason to be careful . . . ?"

His friend's faring here mattered to Spry. But Nuts would not be drawn out. "You know, I was standing at the bar awhile, before I went to the can, and I saw R.P. with Chaeron's little sister . . . or actually, I saw Penrose with some Draconis pilots, and her come up to him and them have a little tiff. Then she ran off and he left right after . . ."

"*Nuts!*"

"Look, Davey, you got me over here." He stabbed at the waiter's touch-sensitive panel again. "I can't say as *I'd* push her out of my hammock. But anyway, I went to the can and there's lots of new graffiti in there. . . ."

Spry waited for his friend to resume, but Allen was opening another peelaway lid, this time with concerted effort. "Like what?"

"Like, 'Spacetime is *still* a Hausdorff differentiable manifold' written across half a wall a dozen times in different hands."

"It still is, if you think about it the right way. So what?"

"Well, that's not the thing. The thing is, when I was in there, some Draconis pilots were amending it . . . I know you're sensitive, so I'll spare you a recitation. But if something's not done about the friction out there soon, there'll be trouble."

"That's RP's job. Tell him. Or Baldy. I've got no influence with the Draconis cadre. But I do have a shaky idea I've got to bounce off somebody I can trust. Promise you won't laugh until I finish?"

"I promise," Nuts said gravely, his steady gaze showing no sign of drunkenness.

"Hello, Raphael," said Chaeron softly, leaning against the doorjamb in an unbuttoned shirt and old pair of trousers. For a moment he looked at his bare feet, then up at Penrose. "It must be 0300. What's up?"

"I just came from the guildhall. Invite me in."

The unshaven, shaggy proconsul blinked, stood away from the wall. "Do forgive me, I've become as graceless and boorish as my counterparts from more 'civilized' spaces, of whom I've had more than my fill today. Come in, and don't mind the carnage. Those left standing are the victors, no matter how bad we may look . . ." He led the way into his living room, littered with cups and used plates and rearranged furniture upon which half a dozen people sprawled. Stale coffee and liquor and pungent blue haze lingered in the air. Flowers wilted on the buffet; the bar was a shambles.

"Baldy and the prudent left a couple hours ago. You know everyone here, so you can help me say goodbye to them. Ward, want to close it down?"

While the intelligencer collected hard-copy and hand-terminals with translucent red covers that meant they could not leave the premises, Rafe shook hands with a husband and wife who were the ranking shipwrights; a youngish arbiter, sanguine as Ward but diminutive; one of Chaeron's distant cousins who was Acheron's trade liaison; and the chief dispatcher, responsible for Acheron's port authority.

"Where's Bitsy?"

"Someplace where what he hears doesn't matter. I gave him the night off. Excuse me a minute." He disappeared into the vestibule, thanking his guests for coming, wishing them a good and productive morning.

"Sorry you couldn't make it, Penrose," Ward remarked, bent over the table, stacking debris. Already any sign of a working meeting had disappeared.

"I wasn't invited, if that's what you want to know." RP yawned cavernously as he sank down into the closest chair. Putting his feet up on the table, he crossed his ankles, toppling a neatly stacked pile of dishes Ward was making. "Fetch me a cup of coffee, will you, Intelligencer? Black, no sugar."

Ward flashed him a cold look, but went to get it.

A few minutes later the door had stopped opening and closing, and he heard Chaeron's voice from the service kitchen: "That's fine. I'll finish up here. Go pretend to sleep, or do whatever intelligencers do instead of sleep. You have Bucyrus in four hours."

Chaeron padded in with two cups and a pot on a tray while, somewhere behind him, the intelligencer rustled his way out. His sleeves were rolled up and as he slid the tray across the table's glass, oblivious of what fell to the carpet on either side, RP noticed that Chaeron's hands were trembling, that the veins on their backs were engorged, that his lips were dry and cracking, and that his pulse was visible at the base of his throat. "Must have been some party, boss."

Chaeron, finished pouring the coffee, leaned over to hand a cup to Penrose. "Have I hurt your feelings by excluding you?" Rafe took the cup; Chaeron straightened. "If I have, it was not intentional." He stretched, flopped bonelessly down on a chair, legs out straight, elbows propping him against its padded arms, fists supporting his chin. "Baldy held up the guild's end, I assure you."

"Assure me that you will get some sleep," Rafe said over his steaming cup's rim. "You couldn't decide what color socks to wear in this condition."

"Did you come here to put me to bed, then?" Chaeron grinned, reaching for his coffee. "I've given up sleep. I'm on the data-lines all the time, now. I just nap."

"I came here to dump a complication in your lap. Now that I see you, I think it can wait until morning. And you can live without constant updating for a few hours. Come on, come out of there. *Now!*"

The proconsul cocked his head, giving Penrose a red-eyed stare. "If you insist," he murmured, and Penrose saw the change in Chaeron immediately. His abstracted looseness evaporated, a visible tautness overtaking him, though he sat quite still. "There, you have my full attention." He picked his cup from the saucer balanced on his belly, and spoke from behind its rim. "I do need you monitoring the guild, you know. Shebat's due tomorrow, Marada's ETA is forty-eight hours after that. The consular luminaries who were to take delivery of their cruisers have been told they cannot be granted licenses—some of them came all the way in person, inexplicable as that seems. Certain of them went to the arbitrational guild about it, seeking a way around Marada's decree. What it amounts to seems to be Bucyrus and his cronies trying to force us into a gambit of some sort. I had the most mystifying meeting with him today, after which, Ward said, he went to David Spry and spent quite some time speaking privately with him. We're looking at the consequences of letting Bucyrus have his way. If he's so anxious to make an enemy of Marada, I'm the last person who'd move to stop him. But it is all very subtle and much too convenient. Spry and the shipwrights have been told to come up with program modifications to prevent the sort of mishap we logged with the prototype, and also to make sure that Marada sees we're modifying the AXVs in an attempt to satisfy the licensing board's recommendation, but the entire license affair is a sham. Marada wants to scrub the AXV program only as a prelude to taking title to Acheron, I would bet—which he could conceivably manage *if* we were enjoined from cruiser production, or if I refuse to let him extradite Softa Spry and the rest of those pirates and he finds me in contempt and tries me for treason or what-have-you. Sorry to have been keeping you in the dark, but now you've been elevated to that state of blessed confusion and transcendent consternation which the rest of us are enjoying. . . . Any bright ideas?"

"Do you think you'll fight it?"

"Which 'it'?"

"Spry's extradition."

"Shebat will want to. In conjunction with a move for a vote of confidence in Draconis, I might. We've delivered a copy of our secession demands and Marada's nefarious activites here to Wolfe in Draconis. Marada won't be able to command the arbitrational guild's support. The guild here found him guilty of sabotaging the working of his own consulate."

"You sound like you're reciting from rote."

"I suppose I am. It has been a busy, trying period."

"But you still found time to apply for a master-solo in *Erinys*."

"That's next week, isn't it? I had forgotten."

"Not likely. Why are you doing this? Take it in a standard cruiser, an AXV, anything out a Kerrion Experimental. That's like taking it in the *Marada*."

"I want a full-spectrum rating, Rafe. It is important to me."

"Why?"

"I can't express it. Instinct. Have you ever stayed logged-on to the data pool? Or to the secondary matrix? I remember when I took only half-hourly updates, then I doubled that . . . Staying with the sources is so similar to what I think cruiser-linkage is all about. . . . I won't know why I want it until I've flown a cruiser into sponge and really gotten a sense of it. But I know I need to know what it is like. I'm not going to quit and become a pilot, don't worry."

"But I *am* worried."

"Then come try the new 'wet environment' I've just had installed. It can deliver anything from cold rain to sauna—twenty pre-sets, variable functions. You'll like it. . . . Please?" He stood up, stretched, beckoned, headed down the hall toward the bedroom.

"Don't pacify me . . . Or get all seductive. I'm immune to you," Rafe, following, called out.

"Since when?" Chaeron's words floated back to him from around the corner.

"Since about the time you decided that your sister's interest in me meant I could no longer be trusted." He stood just within the doorway, now, where he could watch the effects of his words.

Chaeron stopped still, his fingers at his fly. His mouth twitched. He nodded. "I'll give you that. I'm just not a nice person, anymore. At least I'm not sharing your cruiser . . ." Abruptly, he bent and stripped off his pants. Then, in briefs and opened shirt, he sat on the foot of his bed and stared at RP. "But that's over and done with?"

"At long last. It's part of the reason I wanted to see you. . . ."

"I told you, you and Penny had my blessings."

"No, you didn't. You told me you'd rescue me if I got in too deep. But I didn't think. . . . Anyway, she's commandeered a multidrive and gone to New Chaeronea to sulk, or lick her wounds, or teach me a lesson."

Chaeron did not do what RP had expected: he did not interrupt, or ask Rafe how he could have allowed her to do such a thing, or say anything at all. He simply lay back flat on the bed and stared up at the ceiling.

Rafe walked over and stood uncertainly above him. Silence stretched. Then Chaeron said, "You're right. Who was duty officer?"

"It happened on my watch. She said she was going to make me sorry, but I didn't realize . . . It's my responsibility."

"I'm sending down after her." He lay a crooked arm over his eyes. "I'll make sure there is no repetition of this sort of thing." The arm came away. "Don't look so worried. Cluny Pope is in New Chaeronea with three good intelligencers to whom he is giving the insider's tour. They'll meet her at the slipbay." He patted the bed beside his head. "Sit. We'll have confirmation from them within the hour. There's nothing to do now but wait. In the meantime, you can help me figure out what Andreus Bucyrus would want with that dream dancer Lauren—why he would ask for her by name."

Spry made a deal with Bucyrus?" Rafe sat against the headboard, folding his legs under him.

"I think that it's a distinct possibility. And if it is the case, once Bucyrus has got her, we should see some attempt to remove her from Acheron space."

"Do you want me to stop or facilitate it?"

"I think just keep your people out of the way, and maintain the relaxations of protocol we have initiated to reduce friction with the Draconis pilots."

"What's to keep Spry from sauntering down to the slipbay, picking out the cruiser of his choice, and making off in it? Look what you sister did. Things are too lax. . . ."

"Leave them that way. And if you are concerned about discipline, then stop browbeating my intelligencers. You could never get away with it, but for your reputed influence on me. If this little fiasco with Penny has hurt your pride, you are too sensitive. No agenda of orders or number of armed guards is going to keep the members of my family from doing just exactly as they please. You should know that."

"I must have forgotten."

"Don't take the risk of forgetting again. And don't look at me like that. I may not be omniscient, but no one else is, either. In a situation like this, the absence of delusions of infallibility is all one can hope for. Marada is going to have us all spinning around in circles summarily. There won't be time for these luxuries—not for infighting, or long, lazy talks, or niceties of strategy; not for anything but thinking on our feet, once Shebat and Marada get here. So if I can remind you now not to underestimate Spry, I will have one less worry. It is Spry's freedom which concerns both him and Marada—and David Spry is very, very bright."

"A regular polymath. His kind of smarts can work against him. . . . You want me to stay out of his way, better say so clearly."

"I can't say what I want. Do you think I've a private line to the Lords of Cosmic Jest? Some inside track on the caprice of Fate? Things are gone far beyond rational thought's ability to predict. When this is over I don't want to have any regrets. The only advice I can give you is the same as that I give myself: keep it moving. Use happenstance and momentum—everyone's. Don't try to slow the pace. I'm glad you came here with this minor error, rather than with some irremediable one, like making it impossible for me to find out what Bucyrus and Spry are up to by closing down that slipbay too tightly, or too obviously."

"Why don't you just call in one—or both— of them and *ask?*"

"Now, what fun would that be?"

When Bitsy Mistral let himself into the proconsul's suite at 0500, the extent of its disarray stopped him in his tracks in the vestibule. He had come to work an hour early, having prior experience with the aftermath of Chaeron's all-nighters.

But this mess was worse than usual. An hour would hardly be enough time to restore some semblance of normalcy before Chaeron's breakfast must be ready. . . .

Cursing softly, he hung his coat and strode into the middle of the room, where he stood, hands on hips, trying to determine if dishes, refuse, or furniture-moving should be the first order of his day. Thus he heard voices from the bedroom and set busily to work sliding back chairs and couches, stopping every now and again to shove discardables into a growing pile.

"Mistral, I didn't hear you come in." Chaeron's voice preceded him down the hall.

Bisty, on his knees picking food from the rug, looked up. "I didn't want to wake you if you were sleeping, sir."

The proconsul, toweling his chest, stopped where the foyer ended and peered about the room in mock distress. "Leave that. I'll have a wrecking crew in and we'll start all over."

"It's no trouble—" Penrose was down there, around the corner. Bitsy had recognized his voice.

'Come here, please." Chaeron snapped the towel over his shoulder and leaned back against the wall, studying Bitsy intently. When the distance between them was an arm's length, Chaeron said, "Want to better your estate?"

"Always, sir."

"The hard way?"

Bitsy smiled. "Is there any other way?"

"Not today. I have a multidrive ready to go down to New Chaeronea and fetch up Lauren. You'll have to be on it in half an hour. Still interested?"

"Yes, sir."

Chaeron nodded. "Good man. This is going to take some finesse on your part. You're to collect her and take her straight to David Spry in his guildhall. No stops, no explanations or declarations to either New Chaeronean or Acheron authorities. She's going to want to know why we've cut her ground tour short. Your informed and most secret opinion is that things look so bad for Spry that even my hard heart has softened—dream dancer to dream dancer, of course. While you are waiting around for her to be delivered to the rendezvous-point, you'll make contact with Cluny Pope. He may have my sister with him, he may not. If he does and you can convince her that this is no time for sightseeing, or if the two of you can put a bag over her head, then bring her with you. If he doesn't have her, or you can't convince her or strong-arm her, make sure that Cluny has everything he needs to stay right with her, and that she finds out that if Rafe or I have to go down there after her, she'll regret it. *And* that I said to you that is she comes home now, of her own accord, all is forgiven. Questions?"

"Ah . . . no, sir."

"But yes, sir?"

"Yes, sir. That is . . . why the secrecy; I need to know what I'm not supposed to do."

"Very good. You're *not* supposed to let anyone suspect that we're at all worried about Penelope, or in any way draw attention to the fact that she's there, and there despite our protestations."

"And in relation to Lauren?"

Chaeron's eyes met his. "You're not to deviate from the story I've given you. Have her in Spry's quarter by 2200 hours."

Chapter Fifteen

David Spry held his dream dancer from behind, one arm over her naked breasts, in a position that could have inflicted permanent injury rather than nearly unendurable pleasure, if attempted by the uninitiated. He edged his knees between hers and heard her gasp, felt the bed beneath them tremble.

I can't," she moaned. "No more."

"We'll see about that." He pushed on her spine with his free hand and was rewarded. She went limp in his grasp, letting his arm support her, and he let her spasms draw him over the edge.

He eased her down, rested himself atop her, and stroked her moist neck until her panting subsided. "How could you do that to me?" she shuddered.

"Practice." He slid off her. "Suit up, lady."

When he had his mil-suit and his coveralls on, she was still lying face down on his bed. "David?"

"Right here," he assured her, sitting beside her, running his hand over her rump.

"What's going to happen to us?"

"Can't say. But you'll be safe. I've seen to it."

"Bitsy says—"

"—whatever Chaeron tells him. Look here," he slapped her cheeks and she turned over, wriggled, buried her head in his lap, arms about his waist, "you do exactly what you are told to do, and everything will be fine."

"I don't see how. They're going to give you to Marada, I know it. I can't live without you. . . ."

"You may well have to." He took a handful of her pale hair, pulled her head up. "I have always considered you to be an intelligent and capable female. Don't disappoint me. I want you out of here in twenty minutes. And I want you to promise me that you'll be a good dream dancer and take whatever clients come your way in the next few days."

She shook her head to free it. He let her go and she sat up, rose, began to dress without a word. "You're spectacular, you know," he approved. "Lovely."

"Not spectacular enough," she muttered, sliding a nail along the seam of her emerald gown. She fluffed her hair, hiding eyes that sparkled too brightly.

"Come here, then," he said, and when she did, he embraced her. "Don't you trust me?"

"I . . . love you."

"You don't know me well enough for that. You love loving somebody who might not be around forever."

"I know what I'm saying," came her muffled voice from his throat, where her lips were.

"It's trust, not love, which concerns me." He could feel her stifled sobs. "By the Jesters, Lauren, now is no time for this!"

"Then tell me what's going on."

"You are going on a little trip, I hope. Just take your ticket from the stranger who hands it to you, no matter how unlikely the bearer. And that *is* all I can tell you."

She broke away with a convulsive lunge. He did not try to restrain her, just stood watching

"Why?"

"Chaeron sent you here, according to no one's timetable but his own. Icons don't have changes of heart. Since we can't make this a pleasant interval, let's curtail it. Go check in with whomsoever and get your orders."

"How can you be so sure I'll have clients? I'm not even here, officially. Who shall I check in with? Chaeron? Bitsy?"

"I'd try Bitsy. He's close enough to the horse's mouth. Now go on, get out of here."

"But where shall I *go?*"

David Spry grimaced, scratching his head. "Go over to the consulate. Find out where they want you. Chaeron and I have . . . or had . . . an understanding. If he doesn't have some work for you, then he's playing a number of people against one another to find out who's in collusion, and why. If I were to tell you any more, I'd hurt both our chances. But if you don't find yourself busy, soon, then come back here. I have no objection to you as a bunkmate, but it just doesn't compute."

"I'll tell you something else that won't compute. I won't dream dance Marada Kerrion again, if that's what you think."

"Marada?"

"I spent one session with him and all he did was pry me for information about you."

"When?"

"Mid-March."

"I see. Well, it's too late to worry about it. What did you talk to him about?"

"Nothing important. I only said that you were alive and well, and that I had faith in you and the others to rescue all of . . . Why are you looking at me like that?"

"Was I staring? I'm sorry. It's not every day one finds a loose end and a loose tongue in an old friend."

"What do you mean?" She clutched her waist, arms folded in.

"It is just possible that you were instrumental in Marada's decision to move those space-enders out here. But it is not your fault. It's mine. Now go do what I asked, as precisely as you can. Try not to volunteer any information, or be deluded into thinking that you can determine what is important and what is not. If you want to help me, the only way you can do it is by cooperating with attempts to remove you so that you can't be used against me, or anyone else. Is that clear? Good." He turned his back on her. "Good night."

In the Acheron consulate's teal-and-gilt function hall, the homecoming reception for Shebat Kerrion was well under way by the time its guest of honor arrived. Her husband, talking with the Bucyrus delegation near the door, disengaged himself, went to greet her, kissed her hand. Arm-in-arm they promenaded, the ideal New Age couple, handsome, gracious but aloof, his formal black-and-reds a perfect complement to her full-dress silver flight satins. Their heads bent together, they were smiling, chatting intimately, approaching Bucyrus.

"Don't you ever wear a dress?" Chaeron breathed, his lips hardly moving.

"Do you?" Shebat gave back, her expression sweet. They greeted Bucyrus, his two aides, a pair of pilots, drifted away. "Is all this necessary?"

"What?" Chaeron accepted wine from a passing hostess, scanned the sea of guests, turned aback to Shebat. One sip later, he took both their glasses and put them on the same woman's now-empty tray.

"Unending pomp, welcoming committees at slipbay with you conspicuously missing from them, Baldy's escort of honor, that damn intelligencer of yours. I want to talk to you . . ." Somewhere, music swelled.

"Shall we dance? It's our obligation to start this one." He led her through a pair of double doors into an adjoining hall where live musicians played and chandeliers glittered like stars.

She hung back, looking at the empty dance floor in consternation. "Chaeron, I don't know how!"

Over his shoulder, he grinned at her. "I never thought of that. No matter, we'll manage. Just follow my lead. It's slow, so we can make a lovers' spectacle of ourselves in good conscience."

Squinting, as if by that means she could lessen her chagrin, she let herself be escorted out into the middle of the room, the slick floor jarringly hard beneath her boots. Then he cradled her against him, his lips to her ear. "Relax. Just step left and right when I do. Good. Now—" over his shoulder she could see other couples venturing out to join them "—talk to me. I've put the primary security matrix down for recalibration, the secondaries erase themselves when anyone but myself tries to access retrieval; our guests can't detect the secondaries, so their scanning shows them to be surveillance-free. It puts people at ease, loosens tongues."

"There's Softa!" she said, then: "Thank you for inviting him."

"My pleasure. We *are* expediting his exoneration . . . or sponsoring a motion to that effect, at least. That is, assuming you still intend to press for it?"

"I insist," she whispered, stiff against him.

"He'll want to talk to you, I warrant. I think you can tell him whatever you like. I'd be interested in anything you hear."

"Why are you not objecting that we cannot maintain our stance as Softa's protector's in the face of Marada's—?"

"Because I have no way of knowing what will happen. Your cruiser's log shows me only what they wanted to show me."

"You have taken time to confer with the *Marada*, then, but had no time for me?"

"I had a very delicate meeting with the Bucyrus-Tabriz delegation which ran overlong. My apologies. I did try to make up for my absence . . ."

"With *Bitsy?* And Baldy? And Ward? Not one of them can construct a simple declarative sentence. And I debrief to no one but you."

"So I found out." He winced as she stepped on his toe.

"If you ran the log review, you know that I have been removed as Draconis consul."

"But you are still heir apparent. Really, Shebat, didn't you expect that? Marada urged you into office only to be able to demonstrate your administrative unfitness by ousting you from it. He knew very well that you would not stay deskbound. There is no tradition demanding that the heir apparent hold consular rank. I warned you when first he proposed it, so transparent was his purpose. If that is all that you lost in Draconis, we shall consider ourselves fortunate."

"I almost called him back and offered to guarantee a halt to your sccession if he would actually step down in my favor, but the *Marada* thought you might misconstrue my intent."

"I imagine I might have. Not to mention the obvious

fact that they were not seriously offering you anything. As I said, I took a look at the log of your meeting. I congratulate you on a difficult job well done."

"Congratulate me? I failed dismally. I cried halfway home."

"What a pity. And for no reason. But may I take your tears as a compliment?"

Shebat arched back to look at him. "My tears were for Softa."

"You think I will not keep my word to you?"

"Up to a point, you will. But if your personal freedom were endangered, or our primacy in Acheron, or the AXV program permanently prohibited? Then, no, I do not think you would adhere to our agreement . . . or that I could demand it of you."

"I love you," he said, and kissed her ear. "Thank you for being rational. But do not give up hope. I have arranged for our vote of confidence to be called by my friends in Draconis as soon as the *Hassid* reenters Draconis space from sponge."

"Oh, Chaeron, I am so sorry . . ."

"We have no choice." She could feel the tension in him as he spoke. The music stopped, began again in a different tempo. He led her from the floor, continuing: "I did not want to drag us all through this particular morass, but Marada's actions demand an unequivocal response. And who knows, I may be in secure isolation by that time. I have to consider all contingencies."

"It is my fault."

"Greedy creature. I sent you there to bring things to a head. We could have refused Wolfe's summons. We did not. Though I cannot say I expected exactly this rejoinder, I did anticipate something of the sort."

"You anticipated the arrival here of space-enders and Marada's task force? It looks like an arms review out there. I couldn't have gotten a parking orbit if I had wanted one."

"No, I did not expect the occupation forces. Nor did I expect him to put his scrapings from the bottom of evolution's barrel into my test city. New Chaeronea is, his people insist, the only Earthly habitation which meets interspatial conventions for convicts."

The stress in his tone was evident but he left the subject before Shebat could pursue it, telling her, as he shepherded her through the dancers and then the observers, of his sister's entanglement with Penrose and her subsequent flight to Earth's uncertain shelter. "So maybe I will have to send Rafe down there after her, though I need him here to hold the guild-factions at arm's length. Unless you think you could talk some sense into her? Even Cluny Pope thinks that under the circumstances I should withdraw my people from groundside. . . ."

"What circumstaces?"

"Bitsy was supposed to update you. . . .No? Marada's black-and-reds have been vilely pre-emptory; they alienated what friends we had made among the local populations, commandeering whatever residences they chose. A woman was killed in a brawl between space-enders and New Chaeronea's residents—a local woman. There has been some evidence of what might be troop movements in the hills, militia types; what we've seen from our sats doesn't look like migratory animals or innocent field trips or farmers bringing early crops to market. I never did hear from Jesse Thorne about coming over to us. . . . In general, there could not be a worse time for a family member to be playing prodigal-among-the-pines. So?"

"So what?"

"So, do you think you could influence her?"

"Penelope? Never. Send Rafe, or one of the other children. I—"

"Speak of the devil. RP, how are you?"

Shebat was polite to Penrose, but distant, and as soon as she could, excused herself to find Softa Spry, hidden somewhere among so many others. While searching for his tawny, close-cropped head which, like her own black-curled one, could not be seen over the crowd, she encountered Ward. "What is the trouble, Intelligencer? You don't look happy,"

"Too many people." He was watching Chaeron, across the room. "Tempest used to say that Death's a lady: you can see her out of the corner of your eye whenever somebody's about to die." He paused, flickered a look at Shebat's face. "I'm sorry, I don't want to upset you, Mrs. Kerrion. But I've seen what he was talking about . . . a

sort of presence . . . and it's a better indicator than probabilities or catastrophe math. Anyhow, I've been seeing
something like that tonight."

"You are giving me chills."

"I thought you would understand. . . . I mean, Gahan
used to say you were an intuitionist at heart. Can I help
you with anything?"

"I'm looking for Spry."

"Right this way, ma'am." He bowed low, stood tall,
preceded her through the press.

"Here?" Shebat hustled to keep pace with him.
"You've been seeing that here?"

"At the slipbay, this afternoon; now here. Look, I'm
sorry I brought it up. There's Spry." He indicated a knot
of men which Nuts Allen was just joining. As the group
widened to include Allen, Spry was revealed, his arm
draped over the edge of a high marble mantle. "That
crew's enough to turn your blood cold: Orrefors and
Acheron pilots and pirates, all the best of friends. I can't
go over there without ruining Spry's evening: he's part of
my caseload. Look there," the intelligencer pointed out
two men in civilian finery nearby. "If you need anything,
we're right here." Then he gave her his data-pool code-in
number, saying that he was on open call, and melted
back into the crowd.

Half a dozen "pardon me's" and dexterous slippings
through ongoing conversations served to bring Shebat
abreast of Softa, who yet commanded his mantled space
of wall. She touched his arm.

"Shebat." Spry's flat face lit in welcome. He introduced her as his "dream girl" and deftly extricated them
both from the larger circle. "You've saved me from being
'Softa'd' to death. Once more, I owe you my life . . ."

"Davey?"

"What is it, Nuts?"

The broad man in gray satins shuffled close. He took a
breath that pouched his ample cheeks, puffed it out.
"Can I talk to you . . . ?" A tiny inclination of head
indicated Shebat.

Spry's assent was impatient. A surreptitious pilot's signal flashed as he scrubbed short, tawny hair with his fingers. Shebat knew its meaning: *Proceed with caution.*

". . . about teaching you what you've got to know with so little time and no safe place for simulations? You're not taking your end of this seriously enough. Maybe you could borrow this girl's cruis—"

"That's enough. I asked you not to discuss it. Now, I *forbid* it!"

Shebat was saying, simultaneous with Spry's response: "I never changed the *Marada*'s keys. Both my cruiser and I are always at David's disposal. The *Marada* loves . . ."

"*Forbid?* You scum-eating Neanderthal colonist! See if I care whether you boost your arse into the next millen—"

"*Nuts!* There's a lady present."

"Sorry, 'scuse me Mrs. Kerrion. But somebody's got to talk Davey out of . . ."

Spry stiffened. His lips drew thin, he shook his head. "I told you I hadn't had much time to work this up, and I told you I'd rather not have involved you to the point where you could endanger us both, as you are now doing—and you told me that you'd never do anything like this to me!"

"Naw, Davey, you're amped-up over nothin'. Boy's always crowding his head-room. We're talkin' about that damn Acheron spacetime manifold, and making some kinetic statements, in view of irreversibility and all, Mrs. Kerrion. 'Bout time pilots started taking an interest in theory. Anyway, Davey's too shy to ask, but it'd do us a lot of good to get a few secure minutes lined-in to an inboard array like the *Marada*'s." Spry took a threatening step toward Allen, ludicrous in light of the disparity in their displacements. Allen raised his hands before his face. "I'm going, I'm going. 'Bye, Mrs. Kerrion." He winked broadly at her as he turned away.

"What are you up to, Softa?"

"What he said, if you want to stretch a point. I *would* like to talk to the *Marada,* with your permission. Or take a stroll over to the slipbay with you; your august presence will keep the goons away. Shall we?"

"I'd like that very much," Shebat said, ignoring the sudden dryness of her mouth and elevation of her pulse-rate.

They had negotiated their way through the double doors when Andreus Bucyrus with the swarthy Tabrizi, Hammad, barred their path. Spry endured introductions with obvious displeasure. By the time Shebat had shaken hands with Hammad, Bucyrus was frowning. "Sloppy," the fat patriarch criticized.

"You want neat, get somebody else," Spry said flatly.

The Tabriz minister looked from face to face. He smiled uncertainly at Shebat. "My consulese is never up to this sort of thing," he sighed. "Do you not find the mysterious annoying, even insulting, Consul?"

Ex-consul, Minister. My stepbrother has seen fit to remove me." She tried to listen to what was said by Bucyrus to Spry, despite the Tabrizi's singsong chatter. The little, sanguine man had her by the elbow, intent on pulling her off to see an urn in which a flower he could not name awaited her appreciation of its beauty.

"Did you get your troubles with Acheron authorities settled?" Spry asked Bucyrus.

"Regarding the AXVs, no. But the perishable cargo I was waiting for has arrived. I'm sending that load on ahead. There's no telling how long I'll have to stay here. Mrs. Kerrion, is there anything you can do to help us convince your husband that he must release to us our duly-purchased cruisers, no matter what spurious objections Marada has fabricated? I assure you, we are quite capable of obtaining our own licenses. It is merely a matter of applying the requisite pressures. . . ."

"Easier than it will be when my stepbrother gets here, you mean. I don't know if there is anything I can do, but I will certainly try," she promised, no longer able to politely forestall the Tabrizi's demands that she allow him to prove to her that even the most glorious flowers in Acheron must wilt in shame before her beauty.

Not for ten minutes did Spry come to rescue her, insisting that right now was the most opportune of moments for slipping off to the *Marada* to talk.

When they arrived there, purple flashers were strobing and ambulances were parked by the supply depot, surrounded by security lorries full of red-and-blacks in crowd-control armor. Into a closed van men were being loaded: Acheron, Draconis, Orrefors pilots; slipbay and maintenance personnel.

To Shebat's pleas that they go see what had happened, Spry answered laconically that they could get it through the data-base. By the time the last ambulance pulled away, a formal statement of censure had been issued. Publicly rebuked, the twenty-odd uninjured participants were released, the injuries suffered by six technicians and two slipbosses proclaimed an unfortunate but attested accident. Despite this, Shebat could not help thinking of the intelligencer who had told her earlier that Death was abroad that evening.

Soon, though, the significance of the bail-out programs Spry was loading made her forget the intelligencer's prediction. "Softa, you cannot be serious," she gasped as the *Marada* scrolled columns of figures representing rates of acceleration and accrued time dilation and ejection vectors and percentages of survival for numerous sub-headed configurations.

"It's against my religion not to prepare for every contingency."

"Don't you trust Chaeron?"

"I trust him to do pretty much what I would do in his place: the most sensible thing. Speaking of trust, I'd like to trust you and the *Marada* to keep your ears open for a rescue beacon somewhere in this time-frame." He tapped the screen, sat back, hands laced behind his head, neck craned so that he could see her, hovering behind his seat. They regarded each other, upside down in one another's view.

"Just like old times?" Shebat murmured. "You know I cannot refuse. Don't put me in the position of having to betray my husband."

"I didn't say anything like that."

But she leaned down and kissed him. After too long, she raised her head, came around and sat on the secondary acceleration couch's arm. He ran his palm along her satined spine. "The sum of two pilots is a negative number," he reminded her.

She stared straight ahead, at the baleful complexity in the simulations monitor.

"The *Marada* doesn't think this is a good idea."

"I'm sure I agree with him, both about the numbers," he scowled at the tables glowing greenly on the simulator, "and about what you're thinking. As far as I'm concerned, I'm not a condemned man. And if I were, you're not my idea of a last meal. So let's not get emotional, or charitable, and let's not be childish. Go find something to do for an hour or so, and let me run my homework. Then if you still need your cargo bay loaded, I'll gladly oblige you."

She stuck her tongue out at him, getting up stiffly. "That won't work. You can't offend me. I know you too well."

Ever since his mother's mishap, Chaeron had been taking immoderate chances, but nothing so outrageous as releasing the AXVs to Bucyrus, et al. This flagrant defiance of Marada's authority came, ironically enough, not from him—though he would have loved to claim it—but from Acheron's doughty arbitrational guild. What leverage Bucyrus had applied to secure the guild's blessings, Chaeron had steadfastly refused to find out: he had enough troubles covering his own tracks. And there were releases and waivers to be drafted, riders to be attached to the purchase agreements which absolved Acheron of any responsibility in procuring licenses for the AXVs. Bucyrus, an *ask-me-how-I-did-it* smile hovering in the pillow-plump corners of his mouth, had pointed out to him, when they sat down together to initial and sign the final agreement, that the AXVs were a bargain at the agreed-upon price, both because of their scarcity and the natural tendency of prices to escalate.

Chaeron had made no comment. The C.O.D. agreement had put him back on his financial feet, and more. Standing with Bucyrus while the last of the AXVs glided out of its slip three hours before Marada's *Hassid* was due to arrive, he was innocent of collusion or complicity, pure as vacuum, even reluctant. It was necessary that he appear so, that it be clear that he was caught in a legal snare and unable to do other than abide by the arbitrational guild's ruling, that down to the very departure of Bucyrus and the Tabriz delegation he seemed doubtful, harried, compromised.

And none of that was difficult: he had always wondered what it would feel like to run at full throttle, to be threatened with failure, involved in a crisis which would take every iota of his talent and intelligence to survive—let alone surmount. Now, he was finding out all of those, and though he was stretched to what might have been his breaking point, he had not yet broken . . . in fact, he was rather enjoying himself. The adrenalin mix was heady, the stakes of his wager astronomically high, but despite the gravity of things, he had never felt so completely alive. And since one whose life and limb are at risk has little to lose, he indulged in audacity with Bucyrus at slipbay: "How did you like the dream dancer I sent you, what's her name?"

"Lauren. Quite well, actually, thank you. Are you sure you wouldn't like me to stay around until Marada gets in? I can, you know." Bucyrus blocked.

"Is there anything you want to tell me?" Chaeron feinted. He had taken a slate of Lauren's visit to Spry's quarters. Later, during Shebat's reception, Spry had ventured to ask: "Did you get my message?" and Chaeron had had to stop and think before he answered "Yes" and walked away.

"Tell you?" Bucyrus looked elaborately puzzled. "Good luck. Good hunting. Good time to say goodbye." He stuck out a fat hand.

Chaeron took it. "You haven't been stealing my ashtrays?"

"Stealing? No, no. I'd call it a premium. Anyway, it's for a friend."

"I'll remember that," Chaeron promised, frowning slightly, and dropped Bucyrus's hand. All the way back to the consulate from slipbay, he debated the wisdom of calling Spry in and determining the specifics of his arrangement with Bucyrus, whose name cropped up repeatedly in the data Chaeron had gathered on Spry's past. But he had a feeling that he might not want to know the details of what those two—of long and nefarious relationship—had cooked up between them. At best, Bucyrus was doing Spry a favor, and getting a friend out of harm's way. At worst, the pilot was caught between alternative commitments to Chaeron and

Bucyrus, and trying to satisfy both, or make it seem so while striking out after some more personal goal.

Chaeron knew what Spry was. He had been learning for a long time, in slowly increasing detail, beginning more than four years ago when he had been at pains to find Shebat, then in hiding in Draconis' low levels, and had stumbled over Spry's clandestine doings, including his murder of Parma's secretary, Jebediah. And he had tried rather clumsily, at that time, to turn Spry out as his own agent—and failed. Why that was so had as much to do with sponge-cruisers and the ethics of the pilotry guild as with Chaeron's adolescent gropings after power. Coupling the name Bucyrus to Spry's in his data-seeking, what had been a trickle of information had obligingly become a flood. It was possible that Spry was not in a position to say "no" to Bucyrus, and was asking Chaeron to either tacitly approve, or interfere. But while working toward his master-solo in *Erinys,* Chaeron had acquired the cruiser's insights into the nature of her former pilot. It was this experiential data which had led him to dismiss as wishful thinking his consideration of the farfetched possibility that Bucyrus had engaged Spry to assassinate Marada.

Yet KXV *Marada* had contacted Chaeron, bringing his attention to the simulations being run by the pilot. One group was composed of bail-outs—understandable. Chaeron could excuse Spry's exploration of escape routes. The second group were damning alterations of the innards of sponge-cruiser *X.* Put the two together, and it began to look to Chaeron like something from the Machiavellian heyday of David Spry.

He would have to be very careful in making use of his information and his speculations; his first priority must be to appear to have done everything in his power to ensure that Marada was unsuccessful in extraditing Spry and the others. The single additional comment Spry had made to him during the entire party had been: "Try to talk Marada down to just me." Chaeron had responded, "Ye of little faith!" Then Spry had asked his question, and Chaeron had found it prudent to depart.

And Shebat, when she had returned from the slipbay

alone, had had a haunted look in eyes fiery from recently shed tears.

He had not been able to find it in his heart to tell her that what she was telling him, her cruiser had already relayed, but he was heartened that she confided in him, even beyond what the *Marada* had seen fit to reveal: "David asked us to listen for a rescue-beacon throughout a specific time-frame," she had sniffed, wiping her nose abruptly with the back of her hand, then laying her head against his chest. He had hitched himself up against the headboard, pulling her with him. "Us?"

"The *Marada* and me. What could I say?"

"That we will make sure that none of this cloak-and-silliness is really necessary."

"I won't lie to him."

Chaeron had sighed theatrically, "No one believes in me."

"I believe in you. I no longer believe in miracles. Your Consortium has stolen all my magic away, and replaced it with catastrophe theory and CPT invariance."

"So your Jesse Thorne says," he had teased, turning her attention from the subject of Spry, upon which he was concerned that she not dwell. He was pleased that she had come to him, casually dropping her flight bag on the rug, and begun unpacking. Ever since then, he had been taking care to see that she found her choice had been well worth making. . . .

The doors beyond his desk and the Kerman upon which it rested opened noiselessly, admitting Rafe Penrose. "How did you get in here? I left instructions not to be—"

Penrose, dragging a chair with him toward the desk, grinned. "I used my priority card in the consulate's rear elevator. I submitted to voice-and-hand-analysis in the foyer. I proved myself weaponless and wireless to the surveillance arches in the hallway. From there on out, I used bribery, pulled rank, and trusted to the power of my personality to convince your secretary that I don't like to wait to be announced. Why haven't you answered any of my queries? Those secondary matrices aren't going to help you if you don't take calls on them, even emergency priorities."

"I took an hour off. It has been my experience that an emergency is still an emergency when you get around to it, and most proclaimed so, aren't, anyway. What is yours?"

"I need a verification of these slipbay roster changes. Marada is due at 0900 hours." He slid a card case across the desk's uncluttered surface. Chaeron took it, removed the contents, fed them into a slot. Then he retrieved them, reinserted them, and pushed the case back toward Penrose. "There you are."

"You didn't look at it."

"You noticed. Listen here, Raphael, I'm glad you've come. I want you to take a ride down to groundside and apologize to my sister. See if you can't have her back by dinner."

"You're being unreasonable. . . . No . . ." Penrose pinched the bridge of his nose thoughtfully, "it's something else. Another little escapade like letting Bucyrus smuggle Lauren out of Acheron, and you don't want me around for it!"

"If it were, I couldn't tell you. Take Bitsy with you, if you would, and anyone else you fancy. Use my command multidrive. I don't want you getting into anything you can't handle down there. And I want you back—"

"*Chaeron!* You cannot just ignore this." He tapped the card case. "What possessed you to put those pirates in my slip crews? Only Allen's got any right to—"

"I have to show we don't think they are pirates, and that they are performing irreplaceable functions here . . . or as close to that as I can manage. Baldy could have authorized these, Rafe."

"And I could just dictate a nice abject apology, send it down with a courier, and steadfastly look the other way while whatever you don't want me to see takes place."

"Would you prefer to do that?"

"If you want to take your master-solo in *Erinys* in four days, as scheduled, maybe I'd better." Penrose's green eyes appraised him. He ran a hand through chestnut curls, twirled one on a finger so that the cruiser-ring in his ear glimmered. "Did Shebat talk to you about postponing it? Or taking it in *Danae*, or *Tyche?* She'll be—"

'You're getting closer to that trip to Earth.''

"Damn you, Chaeron, I'll go. It's my mistake, mine to rectify. But you'll wish I hadn't." He stood up so abruptly the chair in which he had been sitting rocked back, teetering. Heedless, Penrose stalked out.

"I hope not," Chaeron said quietly to the closing doors.

When Marada's *Hassid* and three escort cruisers glided into Acheron's pristine slipbay, neither Acheron's first bitch nor her proconsul were on hand to greet the consul general of Kerrion space.

The *Marada*, From his pre-eminent slip overseeing all, took note of this as he watched over Shebat, who, with Guildmaster Baldwin, headed the cavalcade that drew up to *Hassid*'s slip flanked by Acheron and Draconis black-and-reds whose firm lines kept the welcoming committee separate from the crews of foam-throwers and emergency technicians and maintenance personnel who swarmed over the slipside, routinely ready for anything.

When Marada Kerrion stepped out of *Hassid*, shaking Baldwin's hand and kissing Shebat's, the teams had already gone to work, swarming over the cruisers' outer hulls, sluicing and probing for damages, unloading telemetry, checking cargo bay rosters, collecting logs and beginning systems checks.

As Marada stooped into his mission's command transport, a khaki-clad shipwright in charge of internal calibration checks motioned his men aboard *Hassid*.

At that moment, the *Marada* was listening to Shebat exchange guarded pleasantries with her stepbrother; monitoring her spasmodic physiological readout—always excited in his presence; enduring troublingly abusive taunts from *Hassid,* who was sure that her pilot would now make an end to the *Marada*'s unorthodox existence; calming the *Tyche,* who had just been brought back on-line and had never encountered *Hassid*'s hostility before. Despite all of those, the *Marada* recognized Nuts Allen among the men in khaki coveralls who boarded Kerrion One laden with toolkits and briefcases full of software specs and dollies racked with test equipment.

But he had more pressing concerns: *Tyche*'s despondency over the remedies made to her faulty programming which eradicated even memory of how she had erred; *Danae's* distress that her pilot had embarked for Earth in only a multidrive (though that multidrive was Chaeron's *Big Bird,* armed and armored); *Erinys's* disquieting emulation of the *Marada's* own data-gathering mechanisms. The *Marada* was daily less comfortable with his fellow KXV, in whom bits of Softa Spry and Chaeron Kerrion mixed with discomforting results: the *Erinys,* cold and implacable and haughty, was ready to debate *Hassid.* The danger of presenting any unsolicited information to Marada Kerrion's cruiser could not be overestimated. The datum that human troubles were cruisers' troubles, the very problems of mankind those that cruisers had been created to solve, had not been appreciated by *Erinys,* who had inherited Spry's misanthropic view of his conspecifics. To forfend an incident of open discord in cruiserkind, the *Marada* snapped down shields and spat ultimata until only he and *Erinys* remained in a narrow-band circuit bounced through Chacron's private datasources, and the *Marada* could scold the cruiser who had spent so long as an outlaw, saying that she had become too much like an outboard, full of prejudice and spite.

"Cruisers and pilots aren't so different as you wish, Marada. *You, least different of all."* *Erinys* sparked in Spry-slang across the slipbay. *"If Hassid's outboard does wish harm to Softa, it is mine to protect him. Would you not intercede for Shebat?"*

"He is no longer your outboard," the *Marada* reminded *Erinys. "Chaeron, who will soon claim that . . . privilege, will do what needs to be done. Humans must handle the matters of their passions."*

"Cruisers and outboards are not as different as you pretend, Marada."

The *Marada* conceded that outboards and cruisers were daily less divergent, yet it was this very increase in similarity, when processed through cruiser consciousness, which was creating a widening gap between man's and cruisers' intelligence: as cruisers developed increasingly more individuality, the intimacy between pilot and cruiser was being eroded. Untruth and half-truth and all the harvest of deception had taken their toll. Even as he spoke to *Erinys* of his observations, adding that the AXVs with their more shielded, discrete intelligences were coming into service just in time, he was dissembling, for he was careful to let *Erinys* catch no hint of what intimacy the *Marada* had come to enjoy with Chaeron, or the simulations Spry had run within his hull, or Chaeron's reaction to that data, or the effort to which the *Marada* had been put to keep every trace of that information from cruiser consciousness, where it might be audited by the likes of *Hassid*.

Because of the degree of isolation necessary to keep his facade unpierced and his conversation with *Erinys* private, the *Marada* did not "see" the shakedown crewmen come out of *Hassid,* Nuts Allen last of all.

Chapter Sixteen

It was still early in Bolen's town, New York, when RP put *Big Bird* down in the agreed-upon clearing. The sun, rearing toward noon, beamed its sovereignty over what promised to be a sweltering first of July.

Penrose winced at the brightness depicted in *Big Bird*'s two semicircles of 360° monitoring and cranked his visual-filters down one stop from flat, softening the glare. Nevertheless, heat ripples still rose from the seared circle in which the multidrive rested, degrading the images.

"Hot out there," he said to Bitsy Mistral, the first words he had spoken on the entire trip. He did not like the sultry, raven-haired youth with just a suggestion of a beard beginning on his perfectly pointed chin. But prolonged silence was uncomfortable, hardly worth maintaining. Bitsy was just an errand boy, hardly an enemy . . . Chaeron's convenience, nothing more. "Looks like," Bitsy replied in a low and neutral voice, "sir."

Rafe stood and, with a practiced twitch of hip and thigh, sent his chair sliding rightward along its track, toward Bitsy at his powered-down end of the multidrive's three-mode board. Then, his hands dancing over one another in lateral passes above rows of lights and toggles, he zeroed his console, stepping slowly back and forth wherever his stabbing, twisting fingers led. Finally, he leaned on the bumper, pecking in pre-sets with frequent glances at his scopes. All of the return course logged but what must be determined by his departure time, he hitched one leg up on the console, facing the youth. "Where are they?" He reached out his hand. Bitsy slid the chair down to him.

"About ten minutes' ride yet, from what we saw in the aerials, sir."

"Don't 'sir' me," Rafe sat back down, lounging low, legs outstretched. "Have you been in contact with Pope?"

"Only to verify, sir . . . but . . . ?"

"Go on."

"It will be all right . . . everything will, I mean. She'll come around. We thought we'd not tell her you were coming, sir. . . . *Penrose*, in case she might refuse to come. But you'll see, she'll be reasonable. A nice little ride through the woods, privacy . . ."

"I'm not piloting any horse. In fact, I'm not going anywhere out of sight of this ship. Clear? And I'm not taking 'no' for an answer. She's coming with us if I have to bodily drag her." All the while, he was watching the monitors, westerly where, flying over, they had shown them riders approaching.

"You know, you and I could help each other."

"You take her feet," Rafe muttered.

"I know you're uncomfortable with me, but you needn't be. He's made me his aide, formally. I have my own apartment. I only work days. He's been so tense, I mean . . . it's not you, it's everything."

"Thanks for the reassurance. It's nice to know 'he' has a confidant. What else does 'he' talk to you about, besides me?"

"I didn't mean that. But he does talk to me. If that's wrong as far as you're concerned, I can't help it. But it's not what you think. He likes abstract thought, logic and philosophy. It relaxes him. So I've been reading him the classics, and we . . . I mean . . . this isn't coming out right: we talk about unity lines and theoretical set geometry . . . whether there's any 'now,' or just 'before and after.' Nothing gossipy or secretive. He doesn't trust me that much, sir."

"I'd say there's a 'now.'" Penrose got up, snapped a

switch, and back in the passenger area a hatch sighed open, admitting birdsong. "Go say howdy. I'll be out in a little bit."

The youth threw him a limpid, reproving look, and floated out of view. Rafe had no intention of allowing even a potential of alliance to develop between himself and Chaeron's little dream dancer. The boy was right: he knew nothing about any of the matters which concerned Penrose. Rafe was almost certain that Chaeron had sent him down here as a chastisement for allowing hostilities to break out among the slipbay crew two days before Marada's arrival . . . it made more sense than Chaeron's intimation that he was protecting RP from possible implication in only-Chaeron-knew-what scheme.

He heard Bitsy's bootheels clank on titanium, then saw the back of his head in his panoramic monitor. He could have gotten an overview by hooking *Big Bird* into any satellite of three now passing overhead, but he did not bother.

He was here under duress; if he was sulky, in private, later he would find it easier to put on a face of complaisance and obedience. He studied the figures on horseback riding out of the trees where the meadow emerged abruptly from a humid green forest through which no detail could be seen, and from which the four had seemed suddenly to appear, full-blown, as if by materialization.

No one had cared very much whether he made his peace with Lauren before they deployed her, first groundside, then to Spry, then out of Acheron like Cleopatra to Antony, rolled up in a Tabriz rug. Penelope Kerrion was, as far as Rafe was concerned, of even less account. He felt used twice-over, and a fool for having walked into a complication which Chaeron had predicted but RP had not believed would develop.

He could make her out, now, on a dappled horse behind two bays. And he saw Cluny Pope, conspicuous because no daylight could be spied between his knees and his saddle, while the others bounced helplessly, both intelligencers holding their saddlehorns.

He saw Pope's smile, his arm raised in salute to Bitsy, and saw that that hand had a tether to which the Kerrion girl's horse was attached. Her hair glinted ruddy-gold in his monitors, and Rafe recalled what had made him deaf to Chaeron's warning. She was so like him! It was eerie, uncanny, to see Chaeron's almost exact duplicate—in which feminity had won out. Ashera's bloodline was a strong one. The girl's wide, beryl eyes, the hint of scorn in her full mouth, the arch nose: Rafe had a deep and illogical affection for her male counterpart who bore all these traits. Raphael would manage to placate the young Kerrion heiress, who only wanted too much: one cannot have undying fealty from a pilot, especially one's brother's pilot. It was her single-minded attempts to monopolize him which Rafe could not abide; he was not a child; he had neither time nor use for an obsessive.

He slapped his screens off, and headed out to greet her, now halted where the two intelligencers and Cluny Pope had dismounted to talk with Bitsy, looking like the effete peacock Rafe's prejudice called him, in blue and pink and orange among the aging summer grass.

He stepped onto the ramp and heat assailed him, thick air full of overripe smells and dust which was difficult to breath. His space-trained reflexes recoiled: there was wind, hot and tainted; he found himself tensed to run for a pressure-suit, attentive to the stirrings of the mil in his lungs. He stood there blinking in the sharp, searing light, convincing his body that there was no pressure-crisis, no leak or pollutant spill. The wind, hot and angry, slapped at him, rearranging his hair. He could hear them talking, not words, just timbres (Pope's thick accent, the intelligencers' flat clipped bursts, Penelope's treble, edged with whine) rising above the wind that stirred the trees whose leaves hissed unbearably. Rafe heard a shrill scream; a shadow fell over him; looking up, he saw a great-beaked bird gliding, far up and away amid tattered clouds.

Quickly, he looked down at his feet and made them proceed down the stepped ramp, onto the ground full of growing and crawling things. Penelope was in mid-complaint, constructing one of those peculiarly aristocratic thousand-word sentences the privileged delighted in improvising. Someone, as sensitive to affront by that means as RP had once been, had assured him that the Kerrion record was held by Parma's father, whose word count for a single extemporaneous sentence was two thousand, two hundred and twenty-one. Chaeron had ceased the practice, except when he was very angry, or very tired. . . .

"Girl, be still," he called out to Penelope. "Gentlemen, get those beasts out of striking range." Gritting his teeth, he sidled between horses whose teeth, as overlarge as their hooves, could be seen as their riders yanked on frothy bits, and reached up to take Penelope by the waist and help her down. The girl in Kerrion-blue expedition gear looked at him for one moment, lids lowered in contempt. Then she jerked back on her horse's reins. It shied, reared, pulling the tether out of Pope's hand and turning mutters to shouts. Panic froze RP motionless before the horse, who flailed the air with his front feet, pirouetting like a ballerina.

From the din of squeals and snorts, he picked out Cluny Pope's urgent advice that Penny pound the horse on his crown; Bitsy shouting to him to grab for the bridle.

Staring up at the horse's belly and deadly hooves towering above him, Penrose at last regained the power of movement, spinning around and throwing himself aside to avoid Pope's mount, lunging after Penny's bolting beast in hot pursuit.

Then, while confusion still whipped about him, RP heard whoops and awful yells, a woman's scream, and more hooves. The intelligencers, having sorted themselves out, cursed and fumbled for their weapons.

"Move, get back. Go!" Bitsy pushed him, a smudged face appearing out of a curtain of dust. His bright clothes were filthy, Rafe noted in an awful slow-motion, as he noticed the two intelligencers arguing procedure, while from above their heads gusts of evil, snickering arrows rained down. "Go on, move!" Bitsy pushed him. Rafe fell to his knees. Where had they come from, these barbed, feathered sticks, one of which was protruding from his calf just below the knee?

It took forever to feel the pain, but that forever was full of ground shaking beneath him from horses' tread, of stones raining around him so that he huddled where he was, arms over his head, legs drawn up. With the pain's arrival came new sounds, thudding tonnage, horse screams. He looked up to see militia riders bearing down upon them, two dozen, maybe more.

"Run!" Bitsy's nose was bleeding, three arrows stuck out like quills from his cape. RP, trying to rise, clasped his leg in pain. The arrow, wobbling, sent spurts of white agony through him that wiped out sight and sound. Holding it still with one hand, he scrabbled along the ground, until Bitsy's shouulder and arm supported him, lifted him, half-dragged him toward the multidrive.

Then came the militiamen: everywhere, circling them, laughing and lobbing sling-thrown stones. One hit Rafe in the face, as the horsemen's circle began to close in.

How long he was ringed, a living target cut off from the others by galloping horses whose riders took chancy, classic shots at him (from under horses' necks and bellies, over sweaty croups) while shouting taunts in a dialect Penrose had not bothered to learn, he could never remember. Stones hit him and arrows snickered unerringly past his ears, until the riders came in so close no weapons but their horses were needed. He was buffeted and charged. Pinned between heaving beasts while their riders kicked and pulled him, he was held off the ground by his hair so that he dangled some few seconds before they dropped him.

He fell rolling, gained his knees. A horse kicked him in the chest, lifting him off the ground fleetingly; he was flying. Then he lay on the ground, lungs emptied, unable to breathe, his mouth wide open, trying to gasp. Just one breath, and he would be alive forever . . . one breath. But it seemed impossible. His lungs would not fill. When at last they did, the sound was desperate, soughing, but the only sound he ever wanted to hear, or could hear above the roaring in his ears. Then the ground shuddered by his head and all he could manage was to turn it and watch the hooves come down inches from his nose: once, twice, three times.

Something prodded him; he tried to gather his knees under him, failed, covered his neck and head. Pulling his legs in close jammed the arrow in his calf sideways, ripping muscle.

"Tell your master we will be in touch with him," Rafe heard. In his cavern of indrawn limbs, he could not move. The hard, sharp thing poked twice into his lower back. "Hear me?" The hoarse voice spoke in perfect Consulese. Rafe grunted, tried to rise. The sharp thing struck him across the back of the skull. "Stay there, Pilot. Stay with your nose in our dirt for ten minutes. I'll leave somebody here to see that you do."

Thunder, beyond his pulse-pounding, exploding headache's own, could be felt through the ground as the horse raced away. He was pelted with clods from its leavetaking.

Ten minutes were easily up before he could move. The ground wheeled in place and he had retched interminably, tasting dirt and his own blood and the awful aftermath of trauma. He did not think about his blurred vision, or that he could not under any circumstances stand up, or about the angle at which the least blood would pour out of his nose. He simply crawled, slowly and steadily, toward where he was reasonably certain the multidrive must be: a big, blue-gray shape was looming, straight ahead in a dark patch. He paused only once—to snap off the arrow's shaft, which was torturing him more than anything except the clots of blood and bile which kept meeting in his throat. Then he tried to sit upright, to peer off toward the encircling trees. But all he could see was pocked ground, full of troughs and humps which must be crossed.

The multidrive was only feet from him—was the only safe place—was his only chance. His vision swam with pink spots, and he wanted to sleep. If he could sleep, he could outwit the giant hammering out knives of anguish on the anvil of his skull. He thought about *Danae*'s familiar bunk, his own bed. . . .

Knee before knee, hand before hand, not looking at anything straight on, eyes slitted, he crawled. A single sob escaped him as he felt one palm graze the multidrive's ramp.

But the ramp was steep and, worse, it was undulating, bucking from side to side. No, that could not be . . . He stopped crawling, head hanging, listening to his own rattling breath. He could lunge straight up those stairs, and make it to the con. He could and he would. Weaving like a drunk, he tried valiantly, twice staggering so that he fell, once hanging with his legs dangling off into space. *It was not possible that he could do this again if he fell to the ground.*

That got him back on the ramp, so thoughtlessly negotiated when he could see and think and move without pain. Step by step he pulled himself aboard, drawing his legs in and lying, sobbing, curled on his side long after the outer hatch had closed: he had had to stand up to hit the plate. He would have to stand up again.

So close, he could not falter. He would just ignore the pain, and keep his eyes closed. So he proceeded into his control room, hugging the metal walls.

When he could lower himself into his seat, he collapsed there. After an interval, a disembodied voice, nagging that there was something he must do, roused him, and he remembered what it was: time and course. He pushed himself forward, and lying across his console, cheek upheld by knobs and buttons, he tried to read his watch. He brought his other hand up where he could see it, when the numerals became legible to his vision, and went through his program, mumbling the steps to himself like a rank junior as he punched them in. Finally, salty, nauseating blood still fouling his mouth and nose, fresh and hot and revolting, he hit "run" and slumped forward while the multidrive came to life beneath him. He should have sat back, strapped in, hit the emergency-beacon. He knew that, but he hurt, and as the fist of acceleration battered him, he compromised with agony: he passed out.

Shebat saw Chaeron take an update, just as the last course had been cleared and coffee and brandy set out. He stopped stirring the lemon peel in his demitasse, staring down into the amber froth as if it held the secrets of the universe, his dusk-blue eyes unblinking. A shadow appeared at the corner of his lips, smoothed away. She sought the nature of the message, using her own entrée to his secondary matrix's data-base, but was thwarted by an intelligencers' seal. She did not backtrack through the sources to find the message-release code. She simply waited to see what would develop, watching Marada, at the head of the table, covertly out of the corner of one eye.

This small, intimate dinner could hold no more surprises: in the first ten minutes, the siblings had put forth their positions so civilly, so offhandedly, that they might have been discussing affairs in distant consulates whose outcomes were of no import. Here was no animus, no rancor, none of the rage she had expected. Marada had reiterated his intention to take Spry back with him. Chaeron had demurred that it was out of his hands, in the purview of the arbitrational guild, and that if speed was of the essence, Spry's extradition might conceivably be hastened by dropping concomitant charges against the others. Marada had declined any trade-off, making the point that he would be weakening his own case not to demand the lot, and assuring Chaeron in carefully modulated tones that should the proconsul interfere in any way, charges of treason and attempted coup would be forthcoming. Chaeron had murmured his condolences: if Marada were to return to Draconis with alleged pirates in tow, Chaeron's supporters there would have no choice but to call for a vote of confidence, and every seamy detail of Marada's misconduct during the last year would of necessity come to light. Marada had sat back, hands folded on his belly, and sighed deeply, agreeing the matters at hand to be unfortunate, especially in light of Chaeron's singlehanded corruption of his local arm of the arbitrational guild. Once the Bucyrus/Tabriz/Takeda cruiser sale was broached by this oblique method, voices had become even calmer, words separated by lengthy pauses and chosen with care. Chaeron offered to send another AXV to Lorelie, to make good on his intention to make a gift of one to Marada's eldest son. Marada declined, saying that licensing would never be possible, and that soon enough Bucyrus et al, would realize this and demand redress.

They had moved from that topic to bald-faced imperatives as the dinner passed away before dessert: Chaeron was intent upon secession. Marada would be wise to remove his Draconis personnel, and find another home for his convicts. Giving Marada notice in person was, Chaeron felt, the least he could do.

And then had come the brandy goblets, and the cobalt-rimmed cups edged with gold, and Marada's flat refusal to allow any such separation.

In the ensuing silence, Chaeron had said only, "Seemingly, we are at an impasse."

With Marada's answer, "I hope to convince you to try to break our deadlock," had come the data-update, chiming without sound in her husband's skull, undetectable but for his downcast eyes. Now, he looked up: "Pardon me, Marada, I didn't hear . . . ?"

"I said, little brother, 'We are hoping you will not be so unwise as to step one centimeter out of the bounds of your office.'"

"Me, too." He looked at his timepiece, then at Shebat. "Would you like to come with me to see Rafe, my dear?" While he spoke, her own B-flat sounded, back in her skull, with a terse warning to ask no questions and do what he would suggest, rendered in accentless computer-simulation. Then Marada interjected, "Where *is* Penrose?" and Chaeron replied, "He's still in the hospital," while pulling back Shebat's chair.

"Hospital?"

"He had a little accident, a while ago: brought a multidrive into the slipbay about two inches below deck-level. Nothing too serious, but this is the first he's been cleared for visitors. You don't mind, I hope?"

Marada rose, too and walked them out. Chaeron's hand was on Shebat's elbow, firm, insistent, guiding.

The low black lorry waiting for them at the mission's portico had a *10A* in its license number: a secure consular vehicle.

Ward was driving it.

"Anything more?" Chaeron queried as the doors thudded shut and the lorry pulled sedately out of the consulate's circular drive.

"Coming up on your monitors, sir," Ward replied, opaquing the rear windows, muttering that he would have liked to use his sirens, or at least his flashers, while Shebat demanded to know what was going on and before her, aerial views of a forested valley blossomed.

"Lords, I wish I could have lied to him," Chaeron said, as if to himself, taking a remote in hand and speeding the recording he was watching. "I almost told him RP fell off a gantry . . . drunk and disorderly . . . but I didn't dare. Shebat, see what you make of this. Ward, I hope you've got something closer than these twenty-three-fives."

"One second, sir." Ward's head ducked down. The panorama in the monitors zoomed closer by a factor of five. "Enhanced five-thousand-mile reconstructions, sir. There's no doubt that it was Jesse Thorne's action—"

"*What* happened?" Shebat pealed, then moaned softly as the twin monitors set into the rear of the front seat showed her a multidrive's landing: the approach of four riders; a tiny Bitsy, comically accelerated, jerkily swaggering forth from the ship; the riders meeting him; Penrose joining them; the girl Penelope's flight; the attack of a multitude of riders from the sheltering trees. She saw Penelope captured; the intelligencers disarmed; then saw Bitsy and Penrose cut off from one another by a figure-eight of riders. She saw three riders disengage from a cluster which had formed around the girl's dapple gray, and then Chaeron stopped the film, tapping the remote he was holding. "Give me an identification, Shebat."

". . . Jesse Thorne . . . Harmony . . . Cluny Pope—I think. It's so distorted. . . ."

Chaeron tapped the remote, and the frozen figures moved. The one Shebat had named as Thorne cantered through the figure-eight, stopping violence, halting before each besieged figure in turn. The first he leaned down and grabbed, pulling Bitsy up on his horse by the collar, and handing the youth (slung unresisting and apparently unconscious over his horse's withers) to three militiamen; the second man, huddled in fetal position on the ground, he prodded several times with a telescoping rod, and left where he lay.

"That's all of it, sir, but for some pretty unreadable blow-ups. We'll simulate them, of course. Take about an hour to do it right."

"What kind of seal have we got on this, Ward?"

"Hermetic. Accident, type undisclosed. We might be able to get away with—"

"I told Marada Rafe brought a multidrive in a little low. There's no disguising that he plowed a trough in our approach bay's decking. But if we can keep the rest of this . . ." he gestured, fanning with his fingers, "under wraps, I'll be very grateful."

Shebat leaned her head against Chaeron's shoulder; he put an arm around her. "You don't have to see him. I just wanted you to know what happened."

"Is he . . . ?"

"I only have preliminaries, Shebat. . . ."

"If I could interrupt, sir and madam? Penrose looked pretty scary, I guess, when they got to him. The medics in the ambulance think he'll pull through."

"Pull through?" Shebat whispered, horrified, as Ward cursed a slower vehicle and pulled out of traffic onto the hospital's off-ramp.

"What about the others?" she managed, as Ward jumped out and ran around to open her door and six intelligencers converged on their car from another Shebat had not noticed, directly behind. "Bitsy? Cluny? Penelope? The—"

"We'll see," Chaeron said. "Ssh. Go. *Go.*" He pushed her impatiently. She took Ward's extended hand.

In a crowd of their own they were carried along through white and shining corridors, swept under a lintel marked EMERGENCY, stopped finally before a pair of glass-and-wire doors that proclaimed, NO ADMITTANCE BEYOND THIS POINT WITHOUT PRIORITY CARD, HAVE YOURS READY.

A pair of red- and white-smocked doctors were waiting there, blue badges attesting to their status. The first one introduced the second to Chaeron and Shebat, oversaw the shaking of hands, then offered, "Madam, Proconsul, I must caution you. Patients suffering from multiple head-wounds, who have sustained concussions, can seem violent, hostile, different from normal. We have no evidence of subdural hematoma—bleeding inside the brain—but one cannot discount it. Though there are no apparent lesions in his scans, contusions are possible, or subsequent hematomas accompanied by bizarre symptoms resulting after a conspicuous delay. Mister Penrose has a number of corroborating complaints: dizziness, headache; he has experienced some nausea, blurred vision. In cases of this sort, one expects a patient to go through certain stages of recovery. He is in what might be called the autonomic stage: he will respond quite normally, can perform simple tasks. But I have no intention of letting him out of here, as he is so vocally demanding." The doctor's imploring voice droned on, detailing cracked ribs and lacerations, shattered nose, the incision that was made to extract the arrowhead . . .

"Dear Lords, a *wooden* arrow?" Chaeron was incredulous. Then: "That's enough, doctor. I didn't come here to be lobbied. I came to see my pilot."

One physician gave the other a knowing look, and pushed open the doors.

Following him, they were all quiet. Chaeron took Shebat's hand and squeezed it.

Seeing Penrose, sitting up on a table clothed only in bandages and a sheet draped over his loins, Shebat felt the vertigo of relief, and took a chair by the door, where Chaeron would not notice any spells she chose to cast for the healing of RP.

". . . pour ice water in *your* ear, and see how you like it." Penrose was fending off a male nurse, one arm raised, hand outstretched. With the other, he supported himself. The carnage in his face was not visible until the nurse stepped back. His eyes were black, his nose swollen, purple, its bridge encased in metal and tape, his lips puffed and torn. One cheek was twice its normal size.

"Raphael?" Chaeron stepped forward. "Thank the Lords you're all right."

Penrose squinted, cocked his head. His speech was slurred, uneven in volume: "Chaeron, that you? Sorry about missing dinner."

Shebat saw Chaeron raise a hand to his own brow, shield his eyes, then sit down beside the pilot on the gurney. "It's me," he whispered, and Rafe turned sideways with a hitching breath. Then Shebat could see the green-and-blue-and-yellow swellings, the taped ribs, the arm which clutched his gut as he shifted carried a raised, stormy imprint of a horse's shoe.

She felt extraneous, an intruder, watching Chaeron's face work, his struggle to speak naturally fail, his helpless clutching of the injured man's hand. Disbelief and disgust were twins in his eyes. He said at last, "We've got to keep the gain way down on this, RP. Understand?"

"Get me out of here. They want to keep me. I've got a headache, that's all. I want to go home and lie down. We've got that master-solo flight to get ready for . . ."

"I can't do that. You should see yourself."

"Don' wanna. Want to go home." With obvious effort, he enunciated.

"Come stay with me, then. Shebat, go tell them that is what we'll do. Have them order whatever preparations they think necessary."

As she was leaving, she heard RP: "Y'know, they put me in this rotating thing and—"

One doctor was right beyond the door; the intercom was on. Shebat snapped it off. "You heard him. And give them some privacy. They have a lot to work out."

"That man isn't going anywhere for at least three days."

"Would you like to transfer groundside? No? Then do what I tell you. Find Ward and make arrangements to move Rafe to the consulate. Now!"

Waiting at the doorway, personally watching over the intercom with its telltale "on" LEDs which would let her know if anyone was eavesdropping from another location, she put a call through to the *Marada,* who had anticipated her, and was already analyzing both the satellite data and what was left of *Big Bird*'s slate from the command multidrive's groundside encounter.

Thus she heard before Chaeron that Cluny Pope had transmitted a list of Jesse Thorne's demands via his highest-security access channel. And her heart sank. Always, she had held out hope for Thorne—even during the endless weeks spent fruitlessly negotiating with Hooker for his release when he was hostage after the disaster in New Chaeronea—against all reason and the counsel of her dreams. Portents and dark wings had always shrouded him; she had sent her prophecy to battle them. But if he had fallen under Harmony's sway—and the mounted presence of the obese, spotted-skinned mistress of dream dancers, plus the sophisticated nature of Thorne's demands indicated that he had—little could be done to help him. Why hadn't she taken care to see that nothing of the sort occurred? Knowing Harmony, she should have anticipated some such ploy.

She recollected Marada's bearded smile at dinner, and the change in both men's demeanor. Absent were vainglorious threats and jibes and slurs upon one another's character. They were faced off, deadly serious, ready to wage their oh-so-civilized war. What Marada would say when he learned, as he eventually must, of Penelope's capture—and what Chaeron would do to spite him—left little room for considerations as minor as the survival of peripherals: Penelope, Bitsy, Softa David, perhaps even her own welfare could quickly be deemed insignificant by either party, discounted out of hand. She must not let that happen.

Down the corridor came Ward and one of the doctors, quarreling in muted tones. Ward's boots clicked hard, emphasizing the slices his hands made in the air.

The two men parted, the doctor reversing his direction back through the glass doors. Ward snapped to before her, rendering a smart salute and a grin that never reached his eyes. The brows that met above his nose were crinkled into a dark knot. "All set, Mrs. Kerrion. They'll deliver him in about an hour to the consulate." He paused inquiringly.

"Fine, Ward." She leaned against the wall, wondering what else he was going to say. When he said nothing, she prodded: "If there isn't anything else . . . ?"

"Ma'am, I would like to wait for him. . . . Has he come out at all?"

Shebat snapped on the intercom beside her. "Chaeron, Ward wants to know if you took that last data-update, and, if so, what you want to do about it."

"That's not . . . I—" The intelligencer, with a wince and a shrug, fell silent as the door opened abruptly and Chaeron came through it. With elaborate care the proconsul closed it behind him and scrutinized Ward intently through bloodshot eyes. "You stupid bastard," he whispered. Shebat thought he might strike something: the intelligencer, the intercom beside Shebat's head, the wall. But he ground his balled fist into his other hand. "Sometimes I wonder whose side you're on, Ward! *Why* didn't you send somebody down with them? Bitsy and Penrose hardly make an operations team!"

"I was not informed, sir," Ward had blanched, gone rigid; now he stood frozen, his chin tucked in, "about this mission!"

"Excuses are something I cannot tolerate. Don't let me ever hear another one. As for information—*you* are supposed to be telling *me* what is going on. If Tempest were alive, we would have had no such incident. They logged out, I must assume. And, given that, you could not *intuit* the rest of it? No ground-support? No cover of *any* sort from orbit? A saboteur could not have buggered me more effectively!"

"It is entirely my fault, sir. I never meant to imply otherwise. If I had been overviewing that action, I would have been able to avoid the rack-up in the slipbay, even given current operating criteria. As it was, if not for the fact that Spry was in the dispatcher's conning tower, we probably would have sustained a total loss—pilot *and* vehicle. I'll write up a full report. . . ."

"To glorify your ineptitude? You misunderstand me, intelligencer. I want to forget this incident, not slate it. Nor do you have to prove your repentance by recommending yourself for a demotion. You'll punish yourself more thoroughly than I could ever manage. We've quite a lot to accomplish in these next few days; don't let this incident preoccupy you. Make sure that Marada catches no hint of foul play groundside, and you shall enjoy our most far-reaching forgiveness. Slate? None of Thorne's ridiculous demands can be allowed to reach my half brother. My sister is groundside. Period. Forestall dealing with this matter until after Marada has left, and you have my permission to do what you will about those terrorists once they are no longer kidnappers. Get my sister and Bitsy out of there, and then teach them a lesson they won't forget. See how many of these 'political prisoners' whom they want are available to us—excepting Spry and Lauren, of course. Send a couple down as a show of good faith. You can even tell them we'll meekly remove our entire presence there, space-enders and all—I don't care what you say. I want this wrapped up so tight that even the secondary matrices won't log it." He jerked his head toward the door behind him. "And I will not sustain another casualty of this magnitude. I detest the sight of blood. Questions?"

"No, sir."

"Then what are you standing there for?"

"I'm taking you back to the consulate, sir, when you are ready. They'll bring Penrose and a computer nurse along in less than an hour. I've already ordered the installation of a support system in the west spare bedroom . . . I didn't think you'd want him anywhere but your own wing, especially with Marada's people about."

"Good enough. Shebat, go say whatever you'd like to say to RP. I'm done."

Standing by Penrose's bed while he struggled to don a pair of fresh coveralls, all Shebat's hostility and discomfort fell away. They both cared for Chaeron; it did not need to be a problem between them—it was she who had been insistent on making it one. "There, step in. Good. Now, wait; let me hand this to you." To draw it up, he had to stand. She caught him as he wavered, while behind him the gurney rolled back and crashed against a stand of instruments. Despite the clatter, she heard his sharp, indrawn breath, his muttered thanks.

Getting his arms in his sleeves was harder, and sweat broke out on Penrose's brow while they were at it. "They'll be coming to bring you over in a little bit. Don't worry about anything. We'll take care of you."

Raphael raised his head then, squinting against the pain. "Is he angry?"

"Not at you. We just want you to get well. . . ." Her voice betrayed her, fleetingly uncontrollable, thick and trembling, as she carefully zipped his coveralls. "We'll need to have your mil repaired."

"They patched it, good enough to last until the stitches come out and the scabs peel off," she thought he said, but could not be sure of what came out of his swollen lips, and hugged him tight, so that he shivered in pain. She could not say she was sorry for the way she had acted toward him, or the things she had thought about him. All the snubs and slights she had visited on him, simply because he was Chaeron's confidant, rose up to jeer at her, and she laid her best healing upon him, running her hands over his back and up to his head where she felt scalding heat, as her jealousy and meanness had not allowed her to do before.

The rabbits in the lean-to's firepit were almost ready when two disheveled sentries chased Cluny Pope into Thorne's strategy meeting. Field officers rolled hurriedly out of the way of the sentries tackling the boy. The fat, piebald sybil who advised him touched Jesse's arm, shaking her head oracularly, while Pope swore and drove both elbows simultaneously into the bellies of the guards. Their hands came off him; they doubled over; with a back-hooked foot Pope toppled one and spun on that foot to kick out at the other's diaphragm. Both went down, while the six officers who had scurried out of the orb of the conflict—and then, like Thorne, simply watched curiously—got to their feet and applauded.

"I want to talk to you," panted Pope, pointing at Thorne, ignoring the two men, one curled into a wobbling ball and the other gasping on his back by Pope's feet.

"That's enough," Thorne said sharply. The applause stopped, the line officers squatted down, laughing; both sentries raised their heads. "You two, up and out. Don't interfere with Pope again, unless he tries to loose the prisoners. Cluny, care for some dinner?" Thorne stretched out on his side, propping a head on one crooked arm, silencing objections from the ignominiously downed soldiers with his most fearsome frown.

Only when they were gone, amid cautiously friendly jibes from officers who used to know him, did Cluny respond to Thorne's offer. "I want to talk to you alone. I'm not hungry, after what I've seen today." He glared with promissory malice at the obese woman whose breasts were spotted like a bull's-eye: black, yellow, brown, fish-white; then slowly turned anguished eyes back to Thorne, who was pulling a spitted rabbit from the flames. "Well?"

"I wish you wouldn't bully my soldiers, Cluny. Not everyone can go to enchanters' school." He ripped a haunch from the blackened rabbit, bubbling grease running down his arm, his slit-narrow gaze demanding that

Cluny sit. The youth crouched, balancing bare elbows on knees sheathed in star-made ground-clothes. "What response from Acheron? You can speak freely in front of these." Thorne waved his hand.

The fire separated them, only one of the unbreachable gulfs that had sprung up between the commander and his former scout. Pope poked the logs with a stick. "I am not here about that. It will take time for them to compose a response. Meanwhile, they can see everything you do, even at night, even in among the trees . . ."

"I am counting on that. I would not like them to think I am not serious."

"I came about the . . . prisoners. Bitsy needs a doctor. There's blood in his urine, and the barbs in his side have got to be cut out. You promised me if I did as you asked and served as mediator, you would see that no harm came to them."

"That harm came to him before I promised."

"And what the ranks dare with Penelope Kerrion is not harm? How can you allow this? Hanging people upside down from trees, turning hostages over to common soldiers? This is not like you." All the others had fallen silent; someone painfully cleared his throat.

Jesse Thorne lay down his rabbit. "*Common* soldiers? You have been an elite spy too long. How can I do this? How can *you* ask me such a thing? It was you who came to me with Kerrion promises, who witnessed all their lies. They built their fine city for their own folk, not for us. And what kind of folk? Scum; dregs; convicts. Yet those untouchables have ousted from the city what few friends the enchanters made, and the black-and-red uniform is feared more than ever in the forests and the towns. We slaved for magicians, previously. Now our crops and stock are taken to feed convicts. The Kerrion ground forces are even more tyrannical than were the Orrefors." Thorne spoke softly, in his hoarse and tired voice so that no one moved or chewed, and all cocked their ears. "Cluny, the people whose land this rightfully is must not lose hope that someday they will be free of foreign dominion. No man I have spoken with has said any different. Only you find grace in Kerrion actions."

"That's not Chaeron's fault. It's Marada, and his madness. No one expected him to bring the space-enders here. Harmony knows that." Pope's chin jutted at the enormous woman, whose breasts heaved and breath wheezed even when sitting quietly, burdened by her excessive weight. "Why did you let him do this?" Pope demanded of her. "Everyone here is going to die, *you* must know that." Pope turned on his heels, faced Thorne. "You cannot fight *them!*"

Harmony tittered, smacked her lips, and wrenched a rabbit apart.

Thorne said, "When the sybil," he nodded to Harmony, "was sitting at Sentinel Ridge, her answer, whenever any asked how to free the Earth from these terrible invaders, was that we must capture a family member and negotiate a settlement. This they understand, I know myself from Hooker. They trade people frequently."

"Jesse, by my mother's heart, this woman is a liar, a space-ender, a convict, and a troublemaker out for her own gain. This trouble she is making," he stumbled over his native syntax, so long had he been speaking Consulese, "is of benefit to the space-enders and the city folk, who are covetous of what we—what you—have. Don't you see they are using you?"

"Not me. I told Kerrion I would confer with my friends, and give him an answer. I did, and you see for yourself the result. Cluny, your own father sent me fifty men and twice that many horses. It is not a thing of one man's making that you see around you. The people have chosen. The people decide. How else could it be? Would we then not be like them, will-less and dependent on the whim of those who have no understanding of, or care for simple folk? Is that not what we are fighting—the assumption that one man has the right to determine the fate of many men?"

"You are fighting without hope, fighting for the honor of dying for no reason."

"There is reason. The reason is that the people cannot be allowed to lose hope, even in the face of death. Death is inexorable, hope is hard to hold but all we have. If I went to Kerrions, as I have been invited, or to Orrefors, as Hooker thought he had convinced me to do, what hope would be left then? People would say, 'Look, even

Thorne has bowed to them, given up and become one of them.' And, worse than that, my defection is a favor they do me. Such a choice is not open to all. I used to say that a chance to stay alive is the only thing worth dying for, but I no longer can believe it. I will die for hope, rather than see it disappear from life."

Pope stood up. "Let me get help for Bitsy. Make the men bring the girl back, and leave her in peace. Feed my companion intelligencers. I cannot watch you mistreating them while I walk around free to do anything but help them."

"Sorry. We must show ourselves to be fearsome barbarians, who should be listened to. The pleas the girl and Bitsy will send heavenward shall make that clear."

"Harmony, Bitsy was of your troupe, once. Have you no compassion?"

The huge woman spread gelatinous thighs and farted.

Cluny Pope turned and strode out, fists balled at his sides.

Twenty minutes later, Jesse Thorne, a jar of new beer in hand, left the lean-to.

He strolled among the cookfires: there was no need now to hide the gathering cohort. Men laughed and sang and snored. The whetting of blades hissed like a restless nest of snakes through a hot and humid night. Full moon it was, and the late-rising countenance was magnified, vast and smirking, as it cleared the valley's neck. He stopped frequently, chatting to linemen, testing their mettle. The horse-line was calm, the sentries sober.

Nothing was wrong. Why, then, was his stomach churning, his jaw aching, the smell of his own sweat pungent and nervous? Cluny Pope's accusing eyes haunted him. He swigged the last of his beer and tossed the jar away, a wasteful, spiteful thing to do. His circuit brought him near the tree where the prisoners were hung from branches. He heard a girl's muffled, hysterical screams.

Shaking his head, he swore softly, and headed that way. As he neared the sounds he began passing loitering observers, hearing raucous jokes, other sounds.

He snorted through men clustered in twos and threes until he found the officer in charge of prisoners, and told him to break the party up: the men had to be rested for the following day. "And have the healer look the prisoners over, all of them. Cut them down, first. Surely we can secure them, right-side up. They're not that dangerous, and we're not animals." His voice rasped out sharper than he had intended. His officer blinked, looking at him askance: vehemence from their commander was rare.

"If you forbade intercourse with the prisoners, sir, we didn't hear about it down here."

"Use your brain, man. If we are going to trade them, they've got to be alive and reasonably intact. If we're not careful, we'll bring down wrath no god can forfend. Get the pretty one over here and let me have a look at him."

The line officer barked orders. Mistral was brought, and a torch held close to the semiconscious youth who lay unresisting, his face striped with sweat and blood, upon the ground. Thorne knelt down. "We'll have to cut his shirt away." He held out his hand, and a heated knife was placed in it. Someone went running, calling the healer's name.

Thorne knew from the way the shirt came away from the boy's side that there was trouble: the clots pulled up with a sick tearing sound. His wounds had closed too soon, too tightly, leaving pieces of broken barbs deeply embedded when the wooden points had been wrenched free. He touched the place; the boy moaned and tossed his head. Already the red swelling was high and a gray, ominous shadow both centered and ringed each wound. A potion-and-spell healer would be of little use to the boy before him. Probing, squeezing, hoping to see pus ooze out, Thorne wondered if some of the men were not using poison on their weapons.

Thorne craned his neck. "You. And you two. Hold him down." Just as he was about to make his first cut, a shadow fell. He assumed it was the healer, who should have known better than to stand in his light. He waved one hand, growling to the fool to get away. Then someone crouched beside him: it was Pope.

"I'll help."

"Find him something to bite on."

Pope peered around, mutttered, stripped off his belt, held it out for Thorne's inspection.

"If he lives, I'll marry you two and you can name your first-born after me," Jesse growled, as Pope scrabbled to kneel beside his friend's head, and the hot knife slid deftly deep.

All the while he was digging wicked, wooden barbs out of ravaged, suppurating flesh he was thinking that it might have been Cluny under his knife, if he had been only a little less careful and a little less lucky. And he recalled the prophecy Shebat had made to him. It seemed so long ago, yet he still thought of her, and her words which had eaten deep into his heart. He had made his choice, though he could feel its wrongness. But he had not lied: life was useless, bereft of hope. He had seen the life the platform dwellers led, and the life his blood entitled him to, and the life which they offered those less fortunate than he under Kerrion dominion. He could not lead his folk into it. He was not like Pope. Already, he felt ashamed and diminished by the waging of such a war. And yet fewer would die, fighting thus, than the old way. His militia was united in purpose, fretting to strike back.

If he had thought, somewhere deep inside him, that he would be spared dishonor by fighting enchanters in the way Hooker had taught him, he had been wrong. If he had thought that Shebat would come herself, because the gods loved him, and give him another sign with her true magic, he had been disappointed. If he had dreamed that Cluny Pope, when again they met, would be unchanged, he had been mistaken. But he had never conjectured that he might crave absolution from his pupil, that the dismay in Pope's eyes would torture him.

Thorne, crouched down with his face to the striken youth's chest and the pus and blood running out onto his fingers, wished only that Shebat would come again. But the seeress Harmony, who had never yet been wrong, had proclaimed that Shebat of the Enchanters' Fire would never come again among the people. And although Thorne had made use of his time in New Chaeronea and of the mechanical oracle in Acheron, he had not been able to reason away his resentment, his frustration, his doubt. Though he was an Orrefors scion and born of privilege, his heart had always been deep in the loamy soil of Earth. The sybil Shebat had stolen both heart and Earth from him, and that was magic he could not deny. He had learned too much, and not enough. He wanted freedom, but he did not think release from the fetters that bound him could be gained within the life he was willing to live.

He looked up from his surgery suddenly. "Cluny, if this boy died, would you then run away, back to your master's safety?" The knife, below Pope's line of sight, trembled with its own eagerness. Thorne would have done more to save Cluny. He would do whatever was necessary; if he left anything, it would be a memory in the eyes of this single boy, more potent than martyrdom or vilification. But Pope replied, "I must stay and see this out. I have promised you, and I have promised Chaeron."

Thorne grunted, noncommittal.

"Is he . . . going to die?"

"Everyone does."

"Let me get help for him, send to New Chaeronea or take him there. I'd come back. You know I'd bring him back."

Above the healer's soft protestations that the proper poultices would make the youth well in no time, Thorne's soft negation and one strangled sob from Cluny Pope could be heard, along with the ragged breathing of Bitsy Mistral. When the surgery was done, and Thorne got to his feet, Mistral reached out blindly for Cluny's hand.

Chapter Seventeen

On July first at 0100, Chaeron slipped sound-lessly through the doors of his residence, heard voices, stood motionless in his outer hall.

". . . ridiculous demands, impossible of implementa-tion," Ward was saying.

Shebat's murmur was low, husky, indecipherable.

Chaeron took a deep breath, and walked into his living room.

Shebat shot up from the couch, ran to meet him. "How did it go?"

He kissed the woman who embraced him, feigned a smile, inclined his head to greet his intelligencer as he answered, "Sometimes I think that it is Marada who is sane, and the rest of us crazed beyond redemption." Arm around Shebat's waist, he guided her toward the seating area. "I drove the best bargain I could," he sighed, settling heavily onto one couch, stretching out, hands behind his head. "Marada will drop charges against all the alleged pirates but Spry in exchange for Softa and Hooker, plus three others of that lot of subver-sives we've been holding. I logged their names with your service, Ward."

Staring at the ceiling, the proconsul could avoid look-ing at his wife, who, eyes brimming with tears, unsteadily sought a chair when she heard the news, then sat, unspeaking, biting her full lower lip.

"I must remind you, sir, that Hooker (along with about twice as many others as could be reasonably expected from Orrefors specs and casualty projections) is little better than a vegetable since we used enkaphalin depotentiators as part of the support-weaponry in our initiative to free Thorne. I did order a full investigation, which proved beyond doubt that none of our people are at fault: there was no negligence or exceeding of orders. It's simply another case of undependable equipment used to unpredictable result. The predicted recovery rate for ED and the curve from which it was extracted was unconscionably optimistic: those Orrefors didn't really give a damn about inflicting casualties down below. I've put in a recommendation that we not use their ED equipment in future, of course. But my point is this: does Marada know the man he's asking for can't tell him—or anybody—anything?"

"He knows it. He's well-informed about Orrefors sympathizers: Hooker's plan to flee with Thorne to old man Orrefors, the camouflaged multidrive, the old cruiser we picked up among the asteroids, Shebat's fruitless attempts to free Thorne peacefully—he even mentioned the susceptibility-curve error in the ED studies. He's got some good spies."

"*We've* got some good data, none of it classified tight enough . . . sir." Ward blushed, having blurted that out, and looked at his feet.

"Not ours much longer, the way things look. Marada wants us to pull all our personnel off the planet. He's intent on rehabilitating the space-enders personally—through proxies. That, of course, means continuing Draconis presence here. He wants to keep an eye on me."

Shebat moaned; Chaeron glanced at her. She drew up her knees, laying her head on them, and hugged her ankles, face invisible.

"As I said," he snapped. "I have done the best I can. Ward, have you checked to see that none of the men I promised to Marada are on their way down to Thorne?"

"Just doing it, sir. We're okay. The only duplicates are Spry and Lauren, and I've already sent a negative on that through Pope. There is an answer, Proconsul, from Thorne. . . ."

"Go ahead."

"Full compliance by July fourth or he takes that rabble of his on a rampage in the general direction of New Chaeronea. I can't see how we can stop it, given that Spry is spoken for, Lauren out of the picture, and the Draconis contingent unlikely to be removed from New Chaeronea."

"Amazing, how popular our ex-first bitch and that dream dancer are—with Harmony, in this case, I assume. Are you recommending some action?"

"I'd like to update Pope enough to use him. This may sound like aiding and abetting our enemy, sir, but hear me out . . . Thorne's men have abandoned any attempt at hiding their presence; we've got no chance of keeping this Penelope matter from Marada, everyday pastoral fires down there don't look anything like an armed camp's bivouac. Maybe Pope could convince Thorne to hold off, or at least reinstate his guerrilla tactics until Marada leaves. They're pretty good at hiding what they don't want to be seen. Otherwise, I can't imagine keeping this from the consul general for another week . . ."

"Try harder. Perhaps, now that I've suggested to the arbiter-in-charge that this is the time to release Spry to my brother, he'll leave. It's the best that can be hoped." Ward frowned intently, trying to look as if he considered the possibility viable. Shebat chewed her hair.

Abruptly, Chaeron sat up. "Thanks for the vote of confidence, you two. Look here, how's RP?" His glance strayed toward the hall leading to the bedrooms.

"He's got a headache, he says, but he's ready," Shebat replied. "Chaeron, I wish you would reconsider. This is no time for you to be away. Take your master-solo another time, when RP's better."

"We must show Marada we are not afraid of him. Also, if he declares martial law, or decides to remove me from office—as he's been insinuating he's about to do—I don't want to be around for it. If I am away for a week or so, things will calm a little. With luck, when I get back, Marada will be gone. I wish you would do the same, Shebat—take the *Marada* out. Go anywhere, for any rea-

son. Stay as long as you like. We may soon be private
citizens, but no accidents will befall us.''

"He would never—"

"Let us not have any assessments of my half brother's
character. Ward, have you put together a list of who
should know about this Thorne affair?'' To keep those
who shouldn't know from finding out, certain key communications and computer operators must be warned, in
case pertinent information came upon the common and
Draconis-assigned channels. Chaeron needed to be sure
before he left that any possible foul-up had been anticipated, every hypothetical error's remedy provided for,
well in advance.

"Yes, sir. I briefed the four—that's the minimum—
myself.''

"Good enough, Mr. Ward. That's it, then; it's a
wrap.'' He jackknifed to his feet. "I'm for bed. I've got
to be up at 0500.'' The intelligencer, too, rose. "Don't
look so glum, Ward. Think of the experience you are
acquiring. You will have quite a formidable résumé when
this is over.''

"That's just it, sir. I'm not interested in looking for
another slot. Sir?''

"Yes, Ward?''

"We've had an objection from the chief surgeon about
Penrose and this logged flight. They just don't think he's
ready, sir.''

"I am. All RP has to do is sit there and hold my hand.
Do I have to dismiss you formally?''

"No, sir. Good luck, sir.'' The intelligencer scooped up
his jacket, said farewell to Shebat, who did not raise her
head, and made his way out.

When Chaeron heard the door sigh shut, he gathered
her up in his arms. "Ssh, now.'' He felt her trembling,
soft, soundless sobs. She buried her head against his
neck. "Let's have no more of this,'' he said gently. "I
know it is difficult, but you must not fret.'' He heard her
sniff, let her go, saw her wipe red-rimmed eyes.
"Better?''

"Better,'' she lied, her face puffy.

"Don't worry so about Softa. We can still help him,
and he and I agreed long ago that if it came to this, he

would go along quietly and we would do our best to provide him with a solid defense. I have a message I want you to repeat to him, verbatim, if you can arrange suitable circumstances." Her wide, gray eyes seemed almost black as they met his. She nodded. He spoke carefully: "Tell him that I regret I could not do any more to aid him, and that I wish him the best of luck."

"That is all?"

"That is my message." He held out his hand to her. "Come with me? We could both do with a little relaxation."

She took it, kissed it, lay her cheek against his hand, came in close and put one arm around his waist. Her head against his shoulder, she went with him, thinking that she should say brave things, pretend to faith and trust in his ability, but unable. She had known they might need to throw Softa David to the wolves of expediency. It was all she could do to keep from bewailing it aloud. He sensed her reserve, and pleaded his own exhaustion to match it. Long after he lay sleeping, she sat up in his bed, watching over him, thinking that in sleep the hard lines dropped away from his face and he seemed again the exquisite youth who had courted her so ardently in Lorelie. Repentance came over her, and she ran her fingers lightly along his back, hoping he would wake, and she might say then that she did love him, despite everything. But he only muttered, tossed, crooked an arm over his face. She thought that she should have begged him not to take his solo in *Erinys,* or not to take it at all. He was doing it, she presumed, to bridge the gap between them, as if the simple acquisition of pilotry skills on his part could overcome their divergent births and disparate upbringing, and all the friction Parma's choice of her as heir apparent over him had caused.

She wept silently, trusting to the soporific of tears to bring her sleep. In that interval she resolved to go, as he had long ago asked her, and let the Acheron physicians draw out an egg from her, so that they could have an heir in the manner he insisted was fitting. If Marada did not finish out his term for any reason, Chaeron had explained, then the order of succession reverted to that which Parma had determined, years before. And when

Marada faced Chaeron's charges, she told herself, he would step down, rather than risk being ignominiously deposed by public clamor.

It was this reason, and not that she feared for him, which made her think of offspring that night. "The only true immortality," Chaeron called children. But she did not believe in immortality, that night, or in Chaeron, or in herself. Even the *Marada*'s whispered encouragement in her backbrain did not chase away her dread. He was leaving; she must stay and deal with Marada Kerrion despite her fears and her feelings, far from clear, upon her own.

It was well past 0300 when she finally cried herself to sleep, promising herself that she would tell Chaeron straightaway in the morning of her decision, and that because of it he would put off his flight. Had he not said many times he wanted, far more than anything else, things to mend and be well between them? She would make it so, and he would stay with her, and together they would talk some sense into Marada. There was no need for Chaeron to risk the possible mental instabilities and reputed genetic damages of pilotry simply to prove to her that he was willing to meet her halfway. And it was not possible: pilot, he might become; like her, he would never be. The *Marada* agreed; the abilities which resided in the person of Shebat could not be simulated, or acquired. Chaeron would never know the sleep that brings true dreams. He could never "pass by unnoticed" or spin efficacious spells from will and faith. It was their differences, her cruiser suggested, which must bind them. Shebat, the evolutionary sport, was unlike any other mortal, outboard or nonoutboard.

The cruiser did not understand why his pilot ousted him from her mind, then, throwing herself down upon the bed, weeping with a pillow over her head to muffle her sobs. The last thing she had thought while their linkage held was, "It is too lonely!"

For that, the cruiser had had an answer, and mutely retired, watching over his outboard through the secondary matrix until he was sure that she slept.

In the morning, when she woke, Chaeron had already gone.

•   •   •

"Pastoral fires, my arse," Marada Kerrion snarled to Shebat eighteen hours later. "What about this?" He tapped the screen on which the militia's demands gleamed greenly. "We will not tolerate blackmail. Hostages or no, these ground-dwellers have gone too far."

"Farther than you have gone? They learned these tactics from us, from your man, Hooker, from all that we have done there."

"We? Are you now entirely acclimated to consular life? Or are you part of our Earthly problem?"

She had wondered how she would feel, alone with him. She felt only contempt and frustration. His wide, brown eyes had lost their poetical softness, taken on the hard gleam of fanaticism. "I promise you, this can be solved without violence. I'm going down there. The people of New York trust me; I know Thorne's mind. Let me negotiate with him."

"No concessions. You have twenty-four hours to extricate my dear half sister, Penelope, from her difficulties. At the end of that time, I am going to eradicate the lot of them. Whoever is down there, will suffer the rebels' fate. Is that clear enough? Don't think you can fend me off by joining them. I have a suspicion that you orchestrated this whole fiasco. Jesse Thorne is your lover, after all."

Her slap rang out. In his beard the result of it was hidden, but his eyes flamed. "I have not yet struck a woman, unlike Chaeron."

"So? You attacked me in my own cruiser during the pilots' strike. Or have you forgotten?" They were both standing, now. The little study in Marada's mission seemed suddenly too small for the two of them, as if their hostility, palpable, would expand, cracking the walls outward and raising the ceiling.

His chest was heaving, and she fastened her eyes on it, thinking that he yet resided in the rebuilt body Draconis' medical expertise, overzealous, had made for him, and how odd it must be to wake and find oneself encased in so much muscle and flesh. He said slowly: "I was ill, then. I apologized for that."

"You apologized. Later. You repented. You are still ill, Marada." She thought desperately that perhaps she could heal him. But he would see the healing spell dance blue upon the air. And the monitors would record it. And she would be bound to him again as her warding spell had for years entwined their fates. She could not risk it. She did not care enough. She had promised Chaeron that she would not field magic; the *Marada* had taught her that her skills were not magic at all, only an affinity built of iterative mathematics and biological amplification and the intimacy of the observer's mind with universal time. Magic itself had been tainted by the Consortium, lessened. . . . *No, no,* she thought, *heft your blame: Márada, if I do not love you, then help me not hate you.* She said only: "Twenty-four hours, then," and stalked from his presence.

David Spry scratched his belly where the elastic waistband of his briefs rubbed the hair the wrong way. What had waked him? Then he heard a noise in the dark. In his bed, he held his breath. It had been a sound like a stumble, something falling. Wide-eyed, he stared into pitch-blackness, letting his ears and mind explore. Years of training spoke to him of footfalls and proximities. Carefully, he bunched his sheet in his hands.

He could discern breathing now; a heel pinged against the metal threshold dividing his bedroom from the spartan living area of his guildhall suite. He closed his eyes, cleared his mind. Definitely more than one man, his ears told him. His proximity sense pinpointed them like infrared, as if his skin were seeing them. He felt bulk, warmth, something bending over him. Sheet before him, he sprang, collided with one man, jerked the sheet down while kicking out where his assailant's legs must be.

Shouts and curses rang out, some muffled from under the sheet. The first man fell heavily, but he had heard a second. Propelling himself toward that sound, sideways, his shoulder leading, he collided with the second man, the point of his shoulder making contact with a chest. Hands grabbed at him, in his hair, at his throat.

Lights came on, blinding. The first man, flailing away the sheet, was up, sputtering commands. The second wrestled Spry down. A third made all the difference: this third man, who had slapped the light-plate, circled, crouched, and sprang into the melee, just as the two rolling together on the floor came apart.

"Intelligencers, you son-of-a-bitch! Surrender!" Spry heard the obligatory announcement just before something slammed into the nape of his neck with a sickening crunch and the room filled up with pyrotechnical lights. He felt his arms jerked behind him, pulled up hard, his knees kicked out from under him. This time he caught sight of the long, flexible tube filled with metal shot as it descended. He flinched, ducked away, but the third man's boot caught him up under the jaw at the same time.

He went limp, hoping to trick them, though both arms were twisted up behind him and he must hang that way to feign unconsciousness. He heard them talking to each other as they savaged him, thought abstractedly he had been foolish to struggle.

They were very careful, being professionals, not to shed blood. The tube with its flexible covering and load of weighted metal was meant for inflicting maximum discomfort without breaking the skin. After a time, a voice judiciously intoned that the score was now even.

He let them dress him, half-drag, half-carry him. He had no incentive to try to walk. He had seen the Draconis armbands on the uniformed intelligencers, the red eagle there which seemed to be laughing at him.

Sometime later there was mention of a warrant, and of Spry assaulting officers of the consulate, resisting arrest. Later, still, Marada Kerrion came to see him where he was propped up in the corner of a white, bright, empty detention cell, looking at him over steepled hands out of sorrowful eyes once he had squatted down before him.

"Softa, why did you resist?"

His head hurt too much, and his lips were too split and swollen, for talking. He leaned his head back against the wall and let it roll a little, so that he could see Marada without shifting his eyes. He made a sound which was meant to answer without words.

Marada blinked repeatedly. "We'll have you fixed up in no time. I need a deposition from you, just a formality, really."

Behind Marada, dark blurs were just beginning to condense into men's shapes. Spry tested wrists neatly encased in plastic manacles. Marada was still explaining how much easier things were going to be if Spry would just cooperate.

When he could manage it, Spry said, "No," to a proffered document. After that, Marada left, and other people talked to him, endlessly. A doctor came, red-cross-blazoned whites swimming in Spry's vision, but the men who were telling him slowly and repeatedly what they wanted him to do made the physician wait.

Eventually, he closed his eyes and pretended not to hear them, so that they went away and the doctor, with clucks and tsks and wails about what things were coming to in Kerrion space, pricked his arm.

Thereafter he knew no pain, no visitors, no blinding lights, only cool dark which came despite the fact that he had signed no admission that he had attacked the intelligencers first.

When finally he woke, he knew by his senses that he was in a cruiser: he could feel the vibration in his bones of a ship on standby; he could smell the ion-charged air; he could almost see the configurations of a stateroom about him through his swollen, half-shut eyes.

That was good, he thought, and dived back down to conciousness' muddy floor, where he could heal and hide until the time came to try to find out whether the ship was the *Hassid*. Should it be, he still had a chance—if he was fit enough to take it.

In Acheron's slipbay, countdown to the *Marada*'s departure was held at minus eight minutes.

Nuts Allen shambled aboard.

"—or we'll wake Baldy up and see whether our guildmaster has any objections to my commandeering that parking orbit. I want to be the only mobile in the five-thousand-mile band over those coordinates. Traffic is not my problem."

Shebat waved behind her without looking and signed off. The green-blue spill from the com-monitor died. She swung her seat about. "What is it, Nuts, that is so urgent that the dispatcher froze my count, and so secret that no one would tell me why?"

Allen put down the box he was carrying and jammed his fists into the apron he wore over his khaki coveralls. "Mrs. Kerrion, it's these here circuit breakers." He pointed to the box on the *Marada*'s aft manual console. "Bunch of 'em got switched with lower impedance numbers that looked the same . . . in the bins, you see. So I thought I'd just make sure you've got everything you're supposed to have, and nothin' you're not." His wise eyes met hers; they were pale and watery and saying something entirely incongruous.

She knew that box was too big to be what he said; like a canny Kerrion, she did not remark upon it. When Nuts came toward the *Marada*'s epicentral controls dais and motioned her up, she moved out of his way. Tools emerged from and disappeared into his apron; a floor-panel was removed; white noise and pink noise clashed forth from her cruiser's speakers; every monitor blinked open a snowy, unseeing eye; each ramp and stack-meter died in an unerring procession from right to left across the cruiser's boards.

Nuts was holding a ribbon cable, grinning up at her. Stretched full-length on his side, his stomach sagging floorward, the gray-haired pilot rubbed his perpetually stubbled jaw. "Mrs. Kerrion, I think—" he fiddled in the box, pulled out a card of circuitry and examined it, caused a racked panel to fold up and out of the hole he had exposed, pulled a similar card from the rack, examined it, made a clucking sound and put both cards by his feet,—"you ought to know that when I was in the guildhall about an hour ago—"

"Nuts, it's 0300 and I have twenty hours left to avert a disaster. Do whatever you've come to do, and let me get out of here," she said over the hiss and whine.

"I come to tell you, missus, that when I was there, these black-and-reds from Draconis came and hauled poor Davey away. Beat the crap out of him first, and didn't care to discuss the whys and wherefores of it with anybody—took him out the back. You bein' my buddy's apprentice, and all, I thought I'd take a shot at getting some help for him." Allen's façade slipped away. He sat straight up. "Now I'll put your internals back together and you can get underway, if you choose to, without any slate on this or worry about it. Won't take a second to check the fuse-box." Shifting himself about, he replaced the original card in its slot, shoved the spring-mounted caddy down until it locked beneath the flooring, and regarded the ribbon cable. "Anything you want to say before your control room's back on-line?"

Shebat looked disgruntled and reexamined the cable's end. "Lady, are you going to see him, or not? 'Cause if you are, I'd like you to slip a little something to him."

"Give it to me."

"It's in that box there." The ribbon cable was resecured, the floor panel replaced. With a grunt, Nuts got stiffly to his feet, drawled several inanities, and headed for the fuse-box in the *Marada*'s engine room. "Give me five minutes, and we'll resume your count." The noise ceased; meters peaked and steadied; screens resumed their pre-flight check-out where it was frozen, each blinking, in the upper right-hand corner, *T minus 00:08:00:00*. Nuts waved and lumbered out, a friendly, gray-and-khaki bear once more.

Then Shebat embarked upon a marathon, four-hour battle to acquire access to David Spry, in holding, she finally ascertained, in *Hassid*. Not until she was ready to depart for there did she look into the carton Nuts had left and see a little, black, plastic box. She did not open it, simply slipped it into her flight satins' hip pocket, preferring to be ignorant of its contents as she preferred not to note the passage of time, now that she was racing against it.

At least, she could deliver to Spry Chaeron's message. At worst, she would make landfall north of Bolen's town too late to save Thorne and Penelope and Cluny and Bitsy and two good intelligencers from Marada's manic rage.

"*Marada*," she told her cruiser, "full security. Keep checking to see if the *Hassid* has put in for flight clearance. I need to know her ETD." Also, she would have liked to know why Ward had not been aware of Spry's whereabouts, or of Marada's intelligencers' hubristic sadism—or why he had not seen fit to so inform her.

When she saw David Spry, she forgot all else, ephemerally. When she left him, she left the little plastic box and a good portion of her soul behind: she knew that she was wholly Kerrion, then, to be able to abandon him to his fate. But she was not triumphant, only disgusted. The price had been far too high.

The takeover of Acheron by the consul general's forces was bloodless, fast, and efficient. Once martial law was imposed, there was nothing for Acheron's functionaries to do but accede. Chaeron was an hour into sponge; Shebat had left the *Marada* in orbit, bound by multidrive to Earth. Objections in their absence were impotent, ludicrous, the intelligencer Ward pointed out to the other departmental heads who awaited briefing outside the office which had been Chaeron's. The man inside it was, the intelligencer needlessly reminded his colleagues, the duly-appointed consul general of Kerrion space. No one else said anything: there was nothing left to say.

Marada Kerrion's first official act was to decree a new policy in dealing with those criminals who called themselves militiamen: Kerrion space, henceforth and forever, would not negotiate with terrorists. Citing the fact that communications with the rebels had ceased and advancing the hypothesis that the execution of the intelligencer-cadet Pope along with all other hostages was the most likely reason, Marada ordered the immediate "neutralization" of the gathered insurgents. The opportunity to eradicate such a large portion of their Earthly opposition might never come again, he pointed out carefully, speaking for the slated record. Allow the self-proclaimed freedom-fighters to disperse and resume their guerrilla tactics, and years of bush skirmishing with the attendant, inevitable loss of Kerrion personnel, unused to and unfit for such warfare, would ensue. "I, for one, will not make such an error in the name of humanitarianism."

None of the convened Acheron officials dared to argue principle with Marada Kerrion, the mad ex-arbiter who ruled over them.

"Ward," Marada purred. "I want you to personally put through a call to my sister-in-law, telling her of our decision, warning her away from the area, and making certain she realizes that if she insists on proceeding into the arena of conflict, then we cannot be responsible for her welfare: she will be acting as a private citizen, with no authority to mitigate circumstances or dictate terms. All negotiations have been tabled."

"Yes, sir."

"Well, what are you waiting for? Go! The timing is very tight."

Ward left.

For his second official act as commander-in-chief of Acheron, Marada supplemented his policy decisions, determining satellite offensives and ground support sufficient to the task of crushing the primitive but dangerous opposition that very day, permanently and completely. Safeguards were necessarily limited, due to haste and the capabilities of his groundside contingents.

When the remaining luminaries heard the specifics of Marada's projected pre-emptive strike, someone mumbled that "neutralization" was a misnomer; Marada might as well have said "eradication." For this reason, the speaker was put in charge of implementing those very procedures.

Having dismissed all but Guildmaster Baldwin, whose rheumy old eyes stared unseeingly beyond his former pilot's head, Marada demanded a priority departure-window for three hours hence. "No excuses or disclaimers. I have to get Softa out of here before he finds a way to slip through my fingers once again," Marada snarled when Baldy objected. The emaciated, white-haired guildmaster opened his mouth, sighed heavily, closed it, and turned away without awaiting dismissal.

Marada let him go. He had much to do; he must oversee the destruction of Thorne's militia before he shipped out for Draconis. With luck, the entire affair would be settled before his sister-in-law set foot upon her native soil.

A part of him which still thought as other men think, deep within himself but far from where man and cruiser together amplified a madness which belonged equally to both, wept softly. But Marada chose not to listen. That part of him which was riding high on the tide of accomplishment wished there was some way to do away with Shebat, as well. It was she who had tainted his family and twisted them all, and with her blighting touch brought insurrection and murder upon the house of Kerrion. Since the day he had swept her up from Earth, everything had been full of evil.

But even at the pinnacle of his solipsism, he could not do that. The knowledge that Shebat and her benighted cruiser—who was her counterpart catalyst in cruiserkind, sowing devisiveness and destruction in that most hallowed of soils which was the pilot/cruiser bond—would live on to torment him while the pawns of her inimical influence passed quietly on to whatever heavens they believed in, was knowledge bitter to his arbiter's soul. She and her cruiser had made murderers and liars of the best of men and the finest of cruisers.

If he could have destroyed them both, he would have. But a dead Shebat would be a martyr to the folk of Earth, who, though they believed not in logic or reason, believed in the divinity of Shebat the Twice Risen. Though he might otherwise employ the very dream dancers who had spread her myth far and wide to dispell it, if she died a hero in the militia's massacre, there would be no hope of that.

He snorted softly and pulled on his long patrician nose, sitting in his brother's office with his feet up on Chaeron's desk. He was pleased with himself: he did not crave revenge above right action; he was totally in control and equal to the task he had set himself: his poor space-enders would have the finest rehabilitation money could buy and intellect could conceive; the subhuman scum who had been left on Earth centuries ago precisely because they were genetic throwbacks, less than human in the true and modern sense of the word, deserved no mercy, only justice. Years ago, when he first brought Shebat up to these coordinates, the Orrefors proconsul's secretary had warned him about the genetic debilities of Earth's denizens. He had not listened, preferring to believe that any creature as pathetic and helpless as Shebat had then seemed was a victim of circumstance, her barbarism a function of her environment, nothing more.

Now, he knew better. He could only hope it was not too late.

The doctor in charge of Spry was at the door, Chaeron's secretary's voice told him. He bade the man admit the physician, whose sole task was to maintain Marada's prisoner in a state of passivity sufficient that no bodyguard or intelligencer would be necessary on their journey to Draconis. Marada wanted to be alone with his nemesis. Since he was consul general, the only person he had to convince that this was not unwise, was himself.

In the next few hours, busy as he was, Chaeron's face came often before Marada's inner sight, and he wished that he could have dallied to see his half brother's reaction when the man who had tried to assassinate him returned to find himself relieved of authority, powerless to perpetuate his seditious policies of pacification and weakness. Once, Marada had thought that Chaeron was wiser in the ways of governance than he. But time had taught him that to deal with corruption, one must only allow oneself to become marginally corrupt. It was hard; it was abhorrent to the part of him that prized ethics; it was painful to the youth in him who once esteemed ideals. But the real world, as Penrose had observed, did not run on the merit system.

He wondered if that revelation would have been any comfort to Penelope, his half sister, doubtless despoiled and raped so many times over that she was praying for the relief of death. Marada had come to see death as the Inevitable Lover, in whose embrace all troubles are forgotten. If his society had not forbidden suicide, he would long ago have gone to Her very door and banged upon it until he was admitted. As it was, he could only court Her from a distance, wooing his own end as a gentleman should, in a mannerly fashion, content to know that eventually he would lie in state, released from every pain and absolved of even the need to withhold judgment upon the immorality of his fellows.

Upon that cheerful thought, he left his brother's office for the operations center from which the deployment of killer-sats and ground support would be overseen by him personally. Dispensing death, he mused, is in effect dispensing salvation and absolution, something for which his arbiter's training had been preparing him, his life long.

KXV 134 *Marada* hung helplessly above Sentinel Ridge, unable to affect the outcome of the carnage five thousand miles beneath him. On every side, low-orbital satellites hung near him, spitting invisible jets of destruction upon the puny humans far below.

His outboard was not yet among the folk who dropped in their tracks, who flared up from within and burned with a blue, sweet smoke, who simply ceased to be, or sometimes exploded in a bright flash. Acheron had deployed every weapon it had at hand. The *Marada*'s long-range sensors gave him close-up detail. He could recognize individuals: he had seen Penelope fall, hustled by Thorne through the screams and the confusion as the assault from above began. He had seen Thorne go down, his right shoulder sheared away while he hesitated, peering upward, squinting at the thunderheads which masked his doom.

The *Marada* had received Ward's message, but his outboard had already debarked. She had given him an answer to send back to Acheron: she was proceeding, despite the consul general's decree, as they had previously agreed. To the cruiser she had added that her stepbrother would not fire upon the militia if she was among them. She had been wrong.

The *Marada* had orders from his outboard, stemming from the outset of their rescue mission, not to contact Chaeron unless the situation became threatening to the cruiser's own survival while she was on Earth. To the cruiser's insistence that the proconsul could and should be alerted to his half brother's intentions, Shebat had replied that if he knew, he would forbid her to take any action, and ordered the cruiser to keep silent.

The *Marada* bitterly regretted having obeyed his outboard. With one high-resolution eye, he followed her multidrive's progress through the suddenly treacherous realm of inner space, continually trying by cruiser-link to dissuade her.

There was nothing the cruiser could do but watch over Shebat as she made landfall and disembarked into chaos, running and dodging among the dying and the dead. The cruiser calculated the time remaining until the ground support dispatched from New Chaeronea arrived, and whispered into the back of his outboard's mind that in nine minutes she must be gone from there.

Shebat only absently answered; she had found Penelope, and Jesse Thorne. The cruiser saw her kneel in the bloody grass, take the remaining hand of the militia commander, then close his eyes.

"Hurry," the cruiser pleaded. *"Hurry, Shebat."*

Penelope, Shebat was thinking, was sleeping, only sleeping. As she tried to heft the girl's inert form, a wounded archer nearby, blinded with blood and agony, took shaky aim and let his arrow fly.

"Down!" The *Marada*'s warning came too late.

Shebat dropped Penelope's limp weight, staring disbelievingly at the arrow which had buried half its length in her arm. She sat down heavily on the grass, dry-eyed, staring dumbly at her wound.

Nothing the *Marada* could say seemed to be able to rouse his outboard. The *Marada* had no experience with shock. Unable to elicit any response from Shebat, who was crawling slowly among the bodies until she returned to Thorne's, he armed his own particle beams and trained them upon the fouled killing ground in case another should seek to harm his outboard, while the girl sat, mute, with Thorne's head in her lap, stroking his hair.

To the cruiser's remonstrance that she must flee before the ground forces arrived, that she was not empowered to be present, that her presence might be construed as treason, complicity, or worse by the consul general, Shebat slowly framed a single, disjointed thought: *Passing by unnoticed. If they come, I will employ it. They will not see me.*

For the first and only time in his experience, the *Marada* wished he was possessed of a body, of arms and legs and voice with which to speak, so that he could go himself down to greedy Earth and carry his outboard away from all the madness that humans do.

Unable to do more than watchfully protect her from additional violence, the cruiser waited, more distressed than he had ever been. He could not lose Shebat. He would not be divested of his outboard. Alone among men, she was comprehensible to him. If he must obliterate every living being who trod that battlefield, he would protect her.

When a stealthy figure raced, crouched low, through the bushes and then through the dead, the *Marada* almost fired upon him before recognizing Cluny Pope.

Chapter Eighteen

David Spry floated in stellar space in the distant vicinity of Earth's sponge-way, the beacon Nuts had made for him and Shebat had smuggled to him hanging from his belt.

Somewhere far off among the points of light raced the *Hassid,* her time-aligns spinning crazily as they computed the ongoing time dilation she was accruing, her throttle jammed at full-forward, her B-mode module, well-sabotaged, unable to negotiate sponge.

Spry discarded the third of five eight-hour air packs he had taken with him when he abandoned ship, simultaneously biting down on the peppermint-flavored tube of the fourth. If he ran out of air before Shebat came to collect him, he would not have the option of becoming a siren. Conditions favorable to that metamorphosis existed only at space-end. Here, he would simply die.

His com was cranked to full volume. The bead-mike fed him back his own breathing: no other sound existed within his helmet except his occasional, terse conversations with himself.

He thought of Marada Kerrion, slumped unknowing over his controls, of how simple and unsatisfying the solution had been, when finally Spry had managed to implement it.

Touch and go, it was, for a time. The drugs they had

been feeding him had made him slow and fuzzy. But they also made Marada cocky and careless.

He recalled an interminable lecture of which he was the recipient, the logic of which he could not follow. He remembered Marada's beard beneath wild eyes as he ranted, screaming at him while Spry played the hapless captive audience and Marada's irrational behavior gifted Spry with enough fear to send adrenalines pumping through his tranquilized system, and those adrenalines cleared his head.

"It's you, it's all of you damned intriguers who are destroying us. Human rights, you understand? That's all that matters! Individual justice and individual parity. My poor space-enders! This, the most equitable of solutions, and because of it, I am anathema!"

Marada had meant—what? Spry still was not sure. He was surer about the tearful episode, in which the consul general of Kerrion space came nose-to-nose with the small pilot, sobbing, "Kill me, you fool. Kill me, please. My god, I need to rest. *Help me.* Please, I can't *do* this. I can't fix it. Nobody can. It's every self-centered, vicious, hateful one of you, against just me. So kill me, Softa David. They'll give you a medal!"

The consul general of Kerrion had embraced him in an agonizing bearhug that sent waves of pain shooting from his ribs—bruised from the beating he had so recently taken—up into his brain. Marada had wept for nearly an hour, holding Spry like a mother. About then, David Spry had remembered that what Marada was asking was exactly what he had been supposed to do.

But the sedatives made him too passive—or the pathetic, troubled "monster" before him had made him too sad. Though Marada and his family had nearly destroyed him, in the fog of his tranquilized brain and because of all that had passed between them, David Spry changed his mind.

If Marada had not let him have the run of the ship, returning, removing his shackles and inviting him to the control room, scant minutes after he had stumbled, blind with tears, out of the door of the pink-and-pearly cabin yet decorated for a woman dead five years and more, things might have turned out differently. . . .

Spry chuckled in his helmet. He had expended prodigious energies of mind to rid himself of his hatred for Marada before it crippled him in his attempt to rid the worlds of his enemy. He had succeeded too well.

When the time-aligns started to whirl ominously and alarm-bells began to ring, when Marada, white-faced, realized that his cruiser could not safely navigate sponge, he had turned to Spry for aid.

Coming up behind him, a simple and practiced two-fisted clout to the nape of Marada's neck had been Spry's remedy. but he found his premeditated follow-through to be unnecessary, unconcionable. The most suitable move Spry could see was to let Marada Kerrion live.

By the time Marada awoke, years would be between them. By the time he had realized he must power down *Hassid* without the B-mode-facilitated spongetravel which protected men from the toll of years real spacetime exacted, David Spry would have long since died a natural death of old age.

For good measure, Spry ripped a handful of colored cables out of the command console's depths. When that was done, they had already lost a week of real-time.

But he had not counted on *Hassid*'s fury. She would not release an ejection capsule to him. He had jumped in only a three-mil suit, at a speed dangerous to his health.

But providence had favored him, or else Chance, his old mentor, had decided to wipe his slate and let him start all over again.

He had watched the *Hassid* disappear with something like triumph. His chances of surviving a naked jump, according to the simulations he had run in the *Marada,* were twenty thousand to one against, at cruising speeds up to half that of light, and at greater accelerations the number became truly formidable.

He had stood in the lock for a moment, thinking about powering the *Hassid* down to manual so that he could get at her multidrive or force the ejection mechanism into his control, but every second put more time between him and his epoch.

He had slapped the plate, bent down, and dived into space's deepest depths, eyes closed.

Having survived the transition from accelerated to inertial frames, he had only to wait and hope for his rescue.

Sometimes, he listened to his beacon.

Mostly, he slept.

When he inserted his last air pack, he had come to terms with the possibility that Shebat could not, or would not, answer the beacon's summons. He could not say that he would calmly, or willingly, or with any degree of resignation, go to his death, but if it came, he could say for certain that there would be nothing he could do about it. Things happen, Not necessarily for the best.

Chaeron, in *Erinys,* had brought his cruiser out of sponge and headed directly toward the coordinates the *Marada,* through the *Tyche,* had suggested.

Bless Nuts and *Tyche.* Without their help he would have walked blindly into more trouble than he could handle. As it was, he had his hands full.

"RP, how's your headache?"

"'M awright," mumbled his pilot-of-record from behind a wall of painkilling drugs. In the copilotry couch, Penrose shifted, turned a sweaty face to him.

He was toying with his friend's health. They had discussed it. They had agreed. The choices were all bad, Rafe had pointed out. And he hadn't yet lost the use of his limbs, or waxed violent. Chaeron had conceded that a migraine (which might be no more that that) was not worth the life of his wife, although he was not so sure about the value of Softa Spry's.

The *Marada* came up in his scopes. Chaeron had wanted to be a pilot; now he was one. Trying to think like a pilot was difficult; he yet felt like someone in costume, an interloper at an invitation-only masquerade.

Shebat was hooked up to the *Marada*'s life-support, so the cruiser had confided. So was Bitsy Mistral. Cluny Pope had executed the first-aid operations under the ship's direction. By Shebat's decree, the cruiser had not been allowed to return to its slipbay in Acheron, but had headed directly out to the rendezvous-coordinates at which, sometime in her immediate future, Shebat expected to find David Spry.

An entire minute of arc must be searched to pinpoint

him. Chaeron hoped Nut's jury-rigged beacon was powerful enough. . . .

Erinys was not worried about their ability either to find Spry or to get Shebat home safely in lieu of that, or anything else. The KXV was all Chaeron had thought she might be. He had encountered her encircuited affection for Softa David, and wished it his, though he had known, when he ordered her limited reprogramming, what it would mean to mesh with a cruiser whose loyalty was already spoken for. He had done it purposefully, to make sure that he did not become enamored of a single cruiser above reason or logic. That was not why he had become a pilot. He did not crave the intimacy, the euphoria, the extended consciousness. He only craved information and understanding.

The most worrisome datum he had received had come directly from Shebat. It was a greeting, star-flung by cruiser-circuitry, bounced through *Tyche*'s sponge-clock to him in *Erinys*'s just before they exited sponge. But there had been something overtly *wrong* about the tone of it. Why that was, the *Marada* would not, or could not, tell him. When he brought *Erinys*, on a converging vector with the *Marada*, to the point in real spacetime which was inhabited by a gay, if gasping, Softa Spry, who was just being thrown a line and hauled aboard the *Marada*, Spry answered his greeting boldly, and promised that Chaeron was going to be quite relieved when they got a chance to talk.

But when Chaeron had donned a three-mil suit and space-walked from *Erinys* to the *Marada*, Spry was pacing back and forth, fists balled, berating Cluny Pope.

"I'd rather have died than lived to see this day! You teen-age aborigine, how could you allow this?"

"I didn't allow anything," Pope replied sullenly from the control room's corner farthest from Spry. "What was I supposed to do? Power this thing down? Then what would have become of her? Or Bitsy? He's on life-support in the first cabin. The *Marada* told me what—"

"That's right, kid. Just pull one goddam circuit-breaker. Sponge take you, Shebat, come *out* of there—*Chaeron!*"

Unspeaking, Chaeron walked past Spry and stood before the young woman slumped in the *Marada*'s epicentral dais. He knelt down, checked her pulse, took her hand, felt the cold flesh, snapped, "A little more light," and in it examined the bluish tinge that colored the wound, the red stripes which ran from it, up her arm. "Blood poisoning, or *tetanus*—the real kind."

He checked the IV, lifted her eyelids, bent down and brushed her lips with his. "I talked to her, just a few hours ago," he whispered, disbelieving. A second time, he sought a pulse.

"Here," said Spry, and tapped a meter which read out Shebat's bodily functions.

From the speakers in the control room's corners from the forward com-grilles and those about him in the epicentral console, Shebat's voice came, husky and soft, hardly disjointed: "I am fine, do not worry . . . about me, I am with the *Marada*. Chaeron, it is so wonderful. I feel like I will live forever."

"The hell you say. I'll destroy this ship wire by wire, to get you out of there. You cannot—"

"She should have her housing repaired, first, Proconsul," interrupted the cruiser's voice. *"She is in pain there. Here, she is well."*

Spry snarled: *"Marada,* you're buying yourself a ticket to the scrapheap."

"I want my wife back, *now*. And log emergency approach vectors, my priority, for both ships," Chaeron snapped.

Nothing happened. Shebat did not stir in her couch. Chaeron bent down and began disconnecting the life-support.

Spry joined him. "I don't think you should . . ."

"I don't care what you think. She's my wife and I'll do as I please. Forcing her back into her body may be our only hope. You take your pick of which ship you want to fly into Acheron, this one or your own."

"I—my *own?*"

"Erinys. I always pay my debts. That is, if I have accrued one?"

Spry's brown-tunnel eyes met his. "That's up to you to say."

Chaeron's gaze did not waver; his face remained expressionless. "Good enough. Be assured that I will take care of you, as soon as my brother is officially logged lost in sponge."

"Space. Or time."

"Space," Chaeron grinned bleakly. "I wish I could handle my other problems as easily. I'll want to talk to you about the future, so do not disappear in that cruiser. If one wants to live a long and happy life, it always pays to play by the rules."

"Now that you're making them?"

"Something like that. I'd like to know who is responsible for this. . . ."

Cluny Pope started to explain what he knew about the massacre below Sentinel Ridge.

Spry interrupted. "I bet I can help you with that one."

"But can you help me get my wife back?" His glance slid about, indicating his distrust of the *Marada*.

"I don't know. I just don't know. I was once fouled up like this," he touched Shebat's unresponding arm, "in *Bucephalus. She* got me out of there. I might never have found my way . . . but this is different."

The voice which was, and as not, Shebat's said from the speakers, "Do not worry. I will be fine."

Chaeron, still on his knees, pulled the oxygen feeder from Shebat's nose. "Let her go, *Marada*. If this body dies, Shebat will die." Despite determination and years of practice, Chaeron's voice broke, and he blinked rapidly and looked at his hands.

Spry squeezed his arm, let go, cursed, stood up, and walked away. When he reached the control room door, he said to Pope, "Come on, hot stuff. Let the folks have some peace."

Chaeron bent, as he heard the lock hiss shut, and whispered in an ear he could not be sure would hear him.

But the *Marada* heard. As much as he loved his outboard, he could not deny such a plea. As much as he treasured her, that much understanding of human love and human fidelity was brought home to him. He, too, spoke to Shebat: *"Live your life as a woman. I am always here. He will not be. When your human days are gone, then come to me. We will live forever. Surely, you can spare those mortals who love you a few short years."*

Her eyes opened, full of pain and pride. "We love you, Chaeron," she said.

In Acheron, tension reigned. Spry and Chaeron sat talking quietly in Chaeron's apartments long into the night.

"I can't be sure of anything anymore, least of all Ward. My sister dead, Thorne and his people massacred, Bitsy barely out of danger, Shebat still under observation; everything I've done on Earth gone down the drain in one week's time. . . . Perhaps we're just striking out at random, seeking someone to blame, some way to fight back. . . ."

"Didn't you tell me only Bitsy and Penrose, besides Pope and the ground-side intelligencers, knew what really happened to Lauren?"

"Yes, that is true. I went to great lengths to ensure that my Acheron staff believed she had disappeared somewhere on Earth. We planted her ID in a vacant apartment in New Chaeronea. But perhaps that is what Ward meant when he said, 'Out of the picture.'"

"Unlikely. That he slipped up is far more likely. I did not," Spry took a sip of whiskey, "picture you as being quite so fastidious. Let me do this. It would be an honor, and a pleasure. And, if I'm still a pilot, or am later deemed retroactively to have been one all along, then there's no blame—pilot's immunity, thank the Lords."

"I am trying to keep you *out* of trouble. We can hardly offer you the guildmastership in Draconis if we involve you in anything—"

"Ease up on your stick, there. What did you say?"

"You heard me. It's what Shebat wants. She thinks you and she can carry on a discreet affair there without me finding out, I'd wager, though I keep trying to tell her that these little improprieties don't hurt my feelings. I am still trying to make a Kerrion out of her, but it is those Earthly mores of hers. Jesse Thorne was sure their tryst was a mortal sin. I believe that was the allure, there, on both sides, although rough trade is always fetching." He crossed his legs and stretched out on the couch. "Bless me, I am exhausted. As soon as I can get this martial law matter cleared up, I'm going to sleep for a week."

"States of siege can be enervating," muttered Spry, obviously uncomfortable. There was a pregnant pause Chaeron did not deign to fill. Spry said, "By the five eternities, I am not after your wife!"

"Pity. She will not rest until she has sampled your charms. High-androgen females tend to go after what they want. I do not mean to devalue your loyalty or your prudence—if either word applies—but I doubt you will have much success fending her off for long."

"—I will just take my cruiser and disappear. I won't bother you people any more. I have to settle up with someone. I may have a clean slate as far as you are concerned, but—"

"Bucyrus?"

Spry spilled his drink, cursed, wiped his coveralls.

Chaeron chuckled, "Why not let me take care of that little matter for you? You rid me of my traitor, and I'll free you of your obligation to an assassination-master who is also an abductor of helpless convicts. Anything he can use against you I can use against him. Stalemate. Unless it is the girl, Lauren?"

"Sir, I told you once before, Lauren's just another slip. But Bucyrus . . . I doubt that you comprehend how entangled I am with him, or what kind of pressure he can bring to bear."

"You have never called me that before. I am delighted. If you will continue to 'sir' me, I can promise your duplicitous little subversive's heart desires. I know *all* about you, I presume to think. Less flippantly," he sat forward, "I can modestly state that what I do not know is, on the whole, probably not worth knowing. I have an opening in my intelligence service, which would not have to conflict with Shebat's offer to you, or could be your primary reason for accepting it. Let me be blunt, Spry: I would do almost anything to avail myself of your particular talents on a regular basis, including protecting you from overage blackmailers who fancy themselves as interspatial spy-masters. What say?"

"Phew. You are too fast for me."

"I truly doubt that. Go pluck the snake out of my grass, while I meditate on how to lure you into an equitable arrangement from which we shall both profit. *Slate?*"

Spry shivered. "Don't *say* that."

"What? Don't say what?" Penrose said loudly from the hall which led to the bedroom. 'Are you two quite through? I want to come out, now."

"Come ahead, R.P. Spry was just leaving. Weren't you?"

"Yep. Nighty-night, Raphael. Sleep tight." He waved to the pilot, who had a small bandage and a shaved patch stowing in his curls near the back of his head where a tiny hole had been bored to drain a hematoma, but was otherwise none the worse for wear.

Penrose waved back.

David Spry slithered through the data-sources as an automated lorry took him to the pilotry guildhall, looking for anything he could use to lure his quarry forth.

The four men who had been entrusted with the task of keeping news of the ill-fated hostage-taking from Marada were the key to it, Spry knew. He called the dispatcher among them, found the man off-duty and willing to meet him in the guildhall, sent a supposedly secure addendum to his invitation he was sure would elicit some response from the culprit he wanted to flush.

He did all of that for Chaeron's sake, to show certain proof, incriminating reactions. He knew who the spoiler was. He had smelled him, and so had Bucyrus. Fugitively, he wondered if Chaeron actually knew as much about him as he boasted.

When he slid into a seat in the guildhall, the man he had summoned was at the bar. So were many of the Draconis-based Kerrions and Orrefors who yet felt compromised sharing the same guildhall; so was Nuts Allen; so was Terry Ward.

The guildhall, he decided, was no place for this. He did not want to start a riot, only take out one nasty covert intelligencer who did not have enough sense to avoid playing both sides against the proverbial middle. It would be a while before the Draconis contingent could be ordered home, and all of them had to live through what promised to be a difficult interval. Yet, he could not risk letting his quarry get away.

He punched-up a drink, but left it in the hopper.

Bereft of ideas, he would try the obvious.

He walked up to Ward and tapped him on the shoulder. "I want to talk to you. Privately. About him," he jerked his head in the general direction of the man he had asked to meet him here.

Ward frowned, drawing the logical conclusion that his stooge was about to be unmasked. Hs contiguous eyebrows drew down. He nodded curtly.

"Where to?"

Spry led the way to the privacy-booths, stopping Nuts from coming over to him with a fierce glance and a sharp shake of his head. His back crawled. Ward would be wondering how he was going to prevent Spry from exposing the stooge. The answer to that was simple, but unpleasant: it was the same solution Spry was about to implement upon Ward's person. He clutched the priority card in his pocket, fingered his change.

In the privacy booth, with the doors closed, Ward said, "What is it?" and Spry pulled out the plastic card and his change, running the card through the priority slot and feeding change into the mechanism.

"I said, what do you want, Spry?"

'Sit down, let's have a drink," he said, card in hand—and turned, lunging at the taller man, card held edge-on, slamming the hard plastic into the intelligencer's temple. By the time Ward's eyes got large with surprise, he was already falling, the venerable nerve-death technique taking him out of the ranks of the living without even time for him to feel the pain.

There was no blood, hardly a twitch, just a limp ex-intelligencer on the floor.

Spry defeated the "privacy" mode, rushed out the door, yelled, "There's a man hurt in here," and gave the obligatory explanation: the intelligencer had stumbled, hit his head on the table's sharp edge. "Call an ambulance"; "Get a doctor"; "Jesters preserve us," pilots said.

Nuts ambled over, laboriously knelt down to take a look, checked Ward's pulse. "To late for any of that. This one's permanently powered down." He grinned up at Spry, "You got an awful habit of bein' in the wrong place at the right time, Davey."

Spry took a deep breath, expelled it. "This isn't funny, Nuts," he whispered, hoping the crowd's mutter had masked both comment and retort.

Nuts held out a hand. Spry took it and hauled the paunchy man up. "Like I say, an awful habit. You better work on it."

"I will," he promised.

Chapter Nineteen

Chaeron walked on a sandy shore bespattered with salt spray. His feet were bare and moist and sand stuck to them, sucked wistfully as he raised them, and wept foam as he brought them down again where an old wave just receding had laved a gleaming expanse slick and smooth. Young waves far out to sea sang his name as they approached, rearing their spumy heads to see him. Low horns soughed beyond the rim of the world, the waves raced to him with word. A flock of trebling birds preceded them; white with wings blurred gray, they wheeled above his head.

Without slackening his pace, he peered up at them, singing in the awesome wide sky which betrayed no comforting recurve, but ever expanded. *Dream dance,* he recalled, tasting the salt spray on his lips and remembering when he had tasted it before, in the very first dream she danced with him: in Draconis, on level seven, the night he extricated her from the dream dancers' warren before he emptied it—the night he had made her his wife. He looked down again at the bubbles that squelched out from under his heels as he drove them into the sand. He was on Sardinia, in the "here and now." The legs that drove the feet wore loose homespun trousers the color of the newly washed shore. They were rolled up to his knees. He let his gaze continue upward, felt as well as saw the drawstring knotted below his navel. Still walking just beyond the waves' caress, in time to the sea's song, it seemed that he had been walking forever—would walk, until entropy quelled the ocean's stride.

He took stock of his gilt-haired trunk, seeing even an old burn from his childhood, low on his right side. The medallion Parma had given him when he turned sixteen beat chilly time against his solar plexus. He fingered the condensation on it, a grain of sand there, wondering at the felicity of the remembered dream to real-time's moment.

Looking inland, he collided with her, grabbed her reflexively, struggled against gravity with her hot-cold flesh against him. Then her inexorable gaze like the thunderheads bubbling in off the ocean steadied him, and he held very still, his arms lightly around her.

"Do you like my song?" she said, indicating that she, too, remembered their shared dream by saying what she had said then.

"Oh, yes."

"Do you like my world?"

"It is so big—lonely."

"I do not much like yours, either. But come, and we will make a smaller world together. And you will like it, I promise."

He shook his head sharply, willing to say or do whatever was needful to break the pattern which a dream dance had set long ago. And to reclaim her, once and for all: she had been different, withdrawn and mystical, since she had returned from her bodiless sojourn into cruiser-consciousness. He said, "Dreams do not always come true."

"Some do." Her lip edged out into a pout, but her eyes gazed through him.

"Not enough." He brushed a jet curl back from her brow.

"There is justification for the match of dream-time to real-time in your science."

"Is there justification for reason in your magic?"

She shrugged. "I think we understand only ourselves, and that appearances are deceiving. The observer who is temporal, Softa says, is tied to the observer who is eternal. The *Marada* says my magic is science.

"I want to study it, and time itself, with my cruiser. Rule the universe, Chaeron, and good luck to you. I will retain only my private funds, my family prerogative of cultured excess, and my cruiser. I have decided."

"Will you go back to Draconis?"

She smiled at him, touched his lips with one finger, leaned into his embrace. "I propose to maintain a home here, and one in Draconis. We will have a son, I am told. The mark of a good administrator is his ability to delegate authority effectively. In the realm of persons, it is you, not I, who are qualified. Make the house of Kerrion whole and great. As consul general *in absentia*, I bequeath you that as my one standing order. For cruisers and their proliferation, I am wholly suited to act. You see, it is coming out well enough, in the end."

"I salute you."

"And I, you."

It was time, then, to let go of words and games, and take hold of lives and moments. He was a pilot; he understood. He lifted her off her feet and lay her down upon the sands.

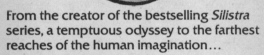